WOMEN

Other titles by Charles Bukowski published by Virgin Books:

Novels:
Post Office
Factotum
Pulp

Anthologies:
The Most Beautiful Woman in Town
Notes of a Dirty Old Man
Tales of Ordinary Madness

Poems:
New Poems One
New Poems Two
New Poems Three
New Poems Four

Letters:
Selected Letters Volume 1: 1958–1965
Selected Letters Volume 2: 1965–1970
Selected Letters Volume 3: 1971–1986
Selected Letters Volume 4: 1987–1994

WOMEN

Charles Bukowski

Introduction by Barry Miles

Published by Virgin Books 2009

2 4 6 8 10 9 7 5 3 1

First published in Great Britain in 1981 by W.H. Allen & Co. Ltd.
First published by Virgin Books Ltd in 1993

This edition first published in Great Britain in 2009 by
Virgin Books
Random House, 20 Vauxhall Bridge Road
London SW1V 2SA

www.virginbooks.com
www.rbooks.co.uk

Addresses for companies within The Random House Group Limited can be
found at: www.randomhouse.co.uk/offices.htm

The Random House Group Limited Reg. No. 954009

A CIP catalogue record for this book is available from the British Library

ISBN 9780753518144

The Random House Group Limited supports The Forest Stewardship
Council [FSC], the leading international forest certification organisation.
All our titles that are printed on Greenpeace approved FSC certified paper
carry the FSC logo.
Our paper procurement policy can be found at
www.rbooks.co.uk/environment

Mixed Sources
Product group from well-managed
forests and other controlled sources
www.fsc.org Cert no. TT-COC-2139
© 1996 Forest Stewardship Council

Typeset by TW Typesetting, Plymouth, Devon
Printed and bound in Great Britain by CPI Bookmarque Ltd, Croydon CR0 4TD

Introduction

By Barry Miles

Charles Bukowski was the poet of Los Angeles. Not the LA of ranch homes in the Hollywood Hills with the breathtaking views of the glittering chequerboard of lights, the swimming pools, palm trees and sports cars lined up in the drive, but the LA of tarnished dreams, of dead-end jobs, of hookers and workers in the sex industry, of beaten down, damaged, dysfunctional people. His people. He loved old Hollywood: the cheaply built bungalows shaken by the freeways, dead palm trees and cracked sidewalks, overflowing garbage cans, cars up on blocks, the neighbours' TVs blaring through open windows, screams in the night and police helicopters circling overhead. He loved the corner bars, the tawdry fast-food outlets, the sex shops and brothels, the graffiti on walls and thick steel security bars on the shop fronts and liquor stores. It was his city.

He was born in Andernach, Germany, in 1920 to a German mother and a German-American father stationed with the American army of occupation in Germany after the First World War. At the age of four, his father relocated the family to his home town of Los Angeles. Bukowski was an only child, raised in a very strict, cold, authoritarian family where he was beaten regularly. In adolescence he developed such a bad case of acne that he had to be withdrawn from school. The boils spread across his face and back, even on his eyelids. Each day he went to the outpatients clinic at the LA County Hospital to have them lanced. Self-conscious about his looks, friendless and insecure at school, he withdrew to an interior world of his own.

He became an alcoholic and a bum, wandering around America on what he described as a 'ten-year-drunk'. His experiences as a down-and-out became the subject matter of his stories, but it would be a mistake to regard them as strictly autobiographical. He was a fiction writer and he was always one to sacrifice the truth for a good story. Also, it must be remembered that some of them were stories told to him by other people then rendered in the first person. They are told in the manner of a bar raconteur: easy-flowing, humorous and self-effacing, designed to amuse and entertain; tales of fights, of days at the racetrack, of hangovers and evictions, tough stories of the hard life.

It was his love life that produced the best stories. He had been a very slow starter. His first sexual encounter was with 'a 300 pound whore' in Philadelphia that got him so excited that they broke the bedstead. His second was at the age of 27 when he met Jane Cooney Baker. She was ten years older than him, an alcoholic ex-showgirl living off a sugar daddy. They moved from rooming-house to rooming-house together, usually in the Westlake area of the old downtown Los Angeles near MacArthur Park, constantly getting evicted for fighting, for drunkenness and, most often, for non-payment of rent. Bukowski took a series of dead-end jobs, mostly working in warehouses, but he was often so hungover that he was unable to get in to work so they rarely lasted long. Jane sometimes worked as a typist with similar results. It was his relationship with Jane and this period of cheap hotel living that he used as the basis for *Barfly*, which was subsequently made into a film starring Mickey Rourke and Faye Dunaway.

It all came to an end in the spring of 1955 when he awoke with blood pouring from his mouth and ass. He was taken to the Charity Ward of Los Angeles General Hospital where he almost died because he didn't have any 'blood credits' (medical insurance) so they did not give him the much-needed blood transfusion. He was lucky to survive. On his second night there he threw up blood and passed out on the floor while trying to get to the bathroom. When he regained consciousness he was surrounded by nurses and heard a doctor angrily demanding that he be given a transfusion. He needed nine pints of blood and eight of glucose to stabilise him. In Bukowski's own view, he suffered permanent harm including some brain damage because of the hospital's neglect which left him with large gaps in his memory and a pronounced slowing of his speech.

By 1958, Bukowski had published enough poems in minor literary magazines to bring out a small chapbook. *Flower, Fist and Bestial Wail* was not published until 1960, but it was the first step. Throughout the sixties he inundated little literary magazines with his work and when the underground press started up, he began a regular column, called 'Notes From a Dirty Old Man', for the LA paper *Open City*. These columns were prose, short stories drawing on his experiences during his ten-year bender, his arrests, fights and his stormy relationships with women. The columns were published in book form under the same name and helped to build his reputation.

From the late fifties and throughout the sixties Bukowski worked the night shift at the LA Central Post Office. It was backbreaking work but it enabled him to lie around during the day and to visit the racetrack. All this time, small chapbooks, broadsides and magazine pieces were appearing. In 1969, encouraged by his publisher at Black Sparrow Press, John Martin, he quit his job and became a full-time writer. The lack of security scared him so much that he wrote his first novel, *Post Office*, in 21 days.

Bukowski's life ran parallel to the Beat Generation: he was of the same age group but came from a very different background and though there were a few Beats in Los Angeles, notably Stewart Z. Perkoff and the Venice scene, he knew nothing about it. Nonetheless, he is often grouped with the Beats because of his tough, uncompromising attitudes: no subject matter is taboo, no matter how embarrassing, indelicate, or personal. His love life appears to be forever plagued with temporary impotence caused by alcohol but when he managed to have sex, he tells us every detail. He loses most of his bar fights and just about breaks even at the racetrack. He writes about ordinary labouring people, fellow workers at the warehouses or at the post office; he writes about his neighbours, his postman, and most of all he writes about his women.

Women is Bukowski's punk novel. Written in 1977, it is fast, conversational, uses few long words, and just zips along. It was written quickly, aided by three bottles of white wine each night.

Bukowski was in his late fifties when he wrote it and it reveals a thirties mentality towards women; it's Hollywood *noir* films of the forties, it's James Thurber's 'Battle of the Sexes'; a pre-hippie, certainly pre-PC view of women. Bukowski was of a different time, but while he tries hard to understand what is going on, he is not helped by the fact that many of the women of his acquaintance are manipulative, crazy, drugged-up or borderline psychotic. Others are literary groupies, lonely women struck by his writing who wrote to contact him, or young German or Dutch tourists who dropped by to fuck Bukowski as part of their vacation in America. For someone who found it very difficult to get a woman at all for the first thirty years of his life it was all very confusing.

Bukowski knows how to bring out the humour in this and uses it well. When his neighbours, Brad and Tiny Darby, the manager of a sex shop and a stripper, invite him over to watch her try on some revealing new outfits from Frederick's of Hollywood, Bukowski sweats and mops his brow, exclaiming all the time in wonder at her breasts or legs, hollering 'Jesus, look at that!'. Of course his girlfriend sees the photographs of Tina sitting naked on his lap. In fact, he liked the rocky road: he needed the screaming rows, the broken glass, his books and clothes strewn all over the yard. His strict emotionless childhood had turned him into what he called 'the frozen man'. It took a lot to get through to him. All the bar fights and drinking were an attempt to actually feel something. His relations with women had to be tempestuous in order to be real. But when he fell in love, he fell deeply.

Bukowski shared Burroughs and Ginsberg's love of Louis-Ferdinand Céline, but his two biggest influences were Knut Hamsun, the Nobel Prize winner, whose novel *Hunger* (1890) mirrored Bukowski's own experiences during his decade as a bum, and John Fante, whose *Ask the Dust* (1939), about the harsh reality of working-class existence in Los Angeles in the thirties, had a profound impact on him. Bukowski wrote: 'He had a great influence on me. I liked his writing style. It was open and easy, and it was clear and it was emotional, and it was just damned good writing.' Bukowski's style is modelled very much on that of Fante. Years later, when Bukowski was rich and famous, he befriended Fante who was then blind and sick, and helped him to write and publish one final novel.

Women is episodic and so he structured it like *The Decameron*. Both books are divided into short, independent sections. Boccaccio had 103 sections, Bukowski naturally had one more. He treats the traditional American male view of women and sex with considerable irony, but it wasn't enough to prevent the book from being criticised by feminists and also by many of the women who are portrayed within it, particularly Linda King who was astonished by his portrait of her. When he finished it, Bukowski wrote to his friend A.D. Winans saying: 'I may get killed on this one. It's written as some type of high-low comedy and I look worse than anybody but they're only going to think about how I painted them.' However, he said, 'It's a jolly roaring blast.'

"Many a good man has been put under the bridge
by a woman."

— HENRY CHINASKI

1

I was 50 years old and hadn't been to bed with a woman for four years. I had no women friends. I looked at them as I passed them on the streets or wherever I saw them, but I looked at them without yearning and with a sense of futility. I masturbated regularly, but the idea of having a relationship with a woman— even on non-sexual terms—was beyond my imagination. I had a 6 year old daughter born out of wedlock. She lived with her mother and I paid child support. I had been married years before at the age of 35. That marriage lasted two and one half years. My wife divorced me. I had been in love only once. She had died of acute alcoholism. She died at 48 when I was 38. My wife had been 12 years younger than I. I believe that she too is dead now, although I'm not sure. She wrote me a long letter each Christmas for 6 years after the divorce. I never responded. . . .

I'm not sure when I first saw Lydia Vance. It was about 6 years ago and I had just quit a twelve year job as a postal clerk and was trying to be a writer. I was terrified and drank more than ever. I was attempting my first novel. I drank a pint of whiskey and.two six packs of beer each night while writing. I smoked cheap cigars and typed and drank and listened to classical music on the radio until dawn. I set a goal of ten pages a night but I never knew until the next day how many pages I had written. I'd get up in the morning, vomit, then walk to the front room and look on the couch to see how many pages were there. I always exceeded my ten. Sometimes there were 17, 18, 23, 25 pages. Of course, the work of each night had to be cleaned up or thrown away. It took me twenty-one nights to write my first novel.

The owners of the court where I then lived, who lived in the back, thought I was crazy. Each morning when I awakened there would be a large brown paper bag on the porch. The contents varied but mostly the bags contained tomatoes, radishes, oranges, green onions, cans of soup, red onions. I drank beer with them every other night until 4 or 5 AM. The old man would pass out and the old lady and I would hold hands and I'd kiss her now and then. I always gave her a big one at the door. She was terribly wrinkled but she couldn't help that. She was Catholic and looked cute when she put on her pink hat and went to church on Sunday morning.

I THINK I met Lydia Vance at my first poetry reading. It was at a bookstore on Kenmore Ave., The Drawbridge. Again, I was terrified. Superior yet terrified. When I walked in there was standing room only. Peter, who ran the store and was living with a black girl, had a pile of cash in front of him. "Shit," he said to me, "if I could always pack them in like this I'd have enough money to take another trip to India!" I walked in and they began applauding. As far as poetry readings were concerned, I was about to bust my cherry.

I read 30 minutes then called a break. I was still sober and I could feel the eyes staring at me from out of the dark. A few people came up and talked to me. Then during a lull Lydia Vance walked up. I was sitting at a table drinking beer. She put both hands on the edge of the table, bent over and looked at me. She had long brown hair, quite long, a prominent nose, and one eye didn't quite match the other. But she projected vitality—you knew that she was there. I could feel vibrations running between us. Some of the vibrations were confused and were not good but they were there. She looked at me and I looked back. Lydia Vance had on a suede cowgirl jacket with a fringe around the neck. Her breasts were good. I told her, "I'd like to rip that fringe off your jacket—we could begin there!" Lydia walked off. It hadn't worked. I never knew what to say to the ladies. But she had a behind. I watched that beautiful behind as she walked away. The seat of her blue-jeans cradled it and I watched it as she walked away.

I finished the second half of the reading and forgot about Lydia just as I forgot about the women I passed on the sidewalks. I took my money, signed some napkins, some pieces of paper, then left, and drove back home.

I WAS still working each night on the first novel. I never started writing until 6:18 PM. That was when I used to punch in at the Terminal Annex Post Office. It was 6 PM when they arrived: Peter and Lydia Vance. I opened the door. Peter said, "Look, Henry, look what I brought you!"

Lydia jumped up on the coffee table. Her bluejeans fit tighter than ever. She flung her long brown hair from side to side. She was insane; she was miraculous. For the first time I considered the possibility of actually making love to her. She began reciting poetry. Her own. It was very bad. Peter tried to stop her, "*No! No! No rhyming poetry in Henry Chinaski's house!*"

"Let her go, Peter!"

I wanted to watch her buttocks. She strode up and down that old coffeetable. Then she danced. She waved her arms. The poetry was terrible, the body and the madness weren't.

Lydia jumped down.

"How'd you like it, Henry?"

"What?"

"The poetry."

"Hardly."

Lydia stood there with her sheets of poetry in her hand. Peter grabbed her. "Let's fuck!" he said to her. "Come on, let's fuck!" She pushed him off.

"All right," Peter said. "Then I'm leaving!"

"So leave. I've got my car," Lydia said. "I can get back to my place."

Peter ran to the door. He stopped and turned. "All right, Chinaski! Don't forget what I brought you!"

He slammed the door and was gone. Lydia sat down on the couch, near the door. I sat about a foot away from her. I looked at her. She looked marvelous. I was afraid. I reached out and touched her long hair. The hair was magic. I pulled my hand

3

away. "Is all that hair really yours?" I asked. I knew it was. "Yes," she said, "it is." I put my hand under her chin and very awkwardly I tried to turn her head toward mine. I was not confident in these situations. I kissed her lightly.

Lydia jumped up. "I've got to go. I'm paying a baby sitter." "Look," I said, "stay. I'll pay. Just stay a while."

"No, I can't," she said, "I've got to go."

She walked to the door. I followed her. She opened the door. Then she turned. I reached for her one last time. She lifted up her face and gave me the tiniest kiss. Then she pulled away and put some typed papers in my hand. The door closed. I sat on the couch with the papers in my hand and listened to her car start.

THE POEMS were stapled together, mimeographed and called *HERRRR*. I read some of them. They were interesting, full of humor and sexuality, but badly written. They were by Lydia and her three sisters—all so jolly and brave and sexy together. I threw the sheets away and I opened my pint of whiskey. It was dark outside. The radio played mostly Mozart and Brahms and the Bee.

2

A DAY OR so later I got a poem in the mail from Lydia. It was a long poem and it began:

> Come out, old troll,
> Come out of your dark hole, old troll,
> Come out into the sunlight with us and
> Let us put daisies in your hair . . .

The poem went on to tell me how good it would feel to dance in the fields with female fawn creatures who would bring me joy and true knowledge. I put the letter in a dresser drawer.

* * *

I WAS awakened the next morning by a knocking on the glass panes of my front door. It was 10:30 AM.

"Go away," I said.

"It's Lydia."

"All right. Wait a minute."

I put on a shirt and some pants and opened the door. Then I ran to the bathroom and vomited. I tried to brush my teeth but only vomited again—the sweetness of the toothpaste turned my stomach. I came out.

"You're sick," Lydia said. "Do you want me to leave?"

"Oh no, I'm all right. I always wake up like this."

Lydia looked good. The light came through the curtains and shone on her. She had an orange in her hand and was tossing it into the air. The orange spun through the sunlit morning.

"I can't stay," she said, "but I want to ask you something."

"Sure."

"I'm a sculptress. I want to sculpt your head."

"All right."

"You'll have to come to my place. I don't have a studio. We'll have to do it at my place. That won't make you nervous, will it?"

"No."

I wrote down her address, and instructions how to get there.

"Try to show up by eleven in the morning. The kids come home from school in mid-afternoon and it's distracting."

"I'll be there at eleven," I told her.

I SAT across from Lydia in her breakfast nook. Between us was a large mound of clay. She began asking questions.

"Are your parents still alive?"

"No."

"You like L.A.?"

"It's my favorite city."

"Why do you write about women the way you do?"

"Like what?"

"You know."

"No, I don't."

"Well, I think it's a damned shame that a man who writes as well as you do just doesn't know anything about women."

I didn't answer.

"Damn it! What did Lisa do with . . . ?" She began searching the room. "Oh, little girls who run off with their mother's tools!"

Lydia found another one. "I'll make this one do. Hold still now, relax but hold still."

I was facing her. She worked at the mound of clay with a wooden tool tipped with a loop of wire. She waved the tool at me over the mound of clay. I watched her. Her eyes looked at me. They were large, dark brown. Even her bad eye, the one that didn't quite match the other, looked good. I looked back. Lydia worked. Time passed. I was in a trance. Then she said, "How about a break? Care for a beer?"

"Fine. Yes."

When she got up to go to the refrigerator I followed her. She got the bottle out and closed the door. As she turned I grabbed her around the waist and pulled her to me. I put my mouth and body against hers. She held the beer bottle out at arm's length with one hand. I kissed her. I kissed her again. Lydia pushed me away.

"All right," she said, "enough. We have work to do."

WE SAT back down and I drank my beer while Lydia smoked a cigarette, the clay between us. Then the doorbell rang. Lydia got up. A fat woman stood there with frantic, pleading eyes.

"This is my sister, Glendoline."

"Hi."

Glendoline pulled up a chair and started talking. She *could* talk. If she was a sphinx she could have talked, if she was a stone she could have talked. I wondered when she'd get tired and leave. Even after I stopped listening it was like being battered with tiny pingpong balls. Glendoline had no concept of time or any idea that she might be intruding. She talked on and on.

"Listen," I said finally, "when are you going to leave?"

Then a sister act began. They began talking to each other. They were both standing up, waving their arms at each other. The voices pitched higher. They threatened each other with physical harm. At last—near the world's end—Glendoline did a gigantic twist of torso and flung herself out of the doorway through the large flapbang of the screen door and was gone— but still heard, ignited and bemoaning—down to her apartment in the back of the court.

Lydia and I walked back to the breakfast nook and sat down. She picked up her sculptor's tool. Her eyes looked into mine.

3

ONE MORNING a few days later I entered Lydia's courtyard as she was walking in from the alley. She had been over to see her friend Tina who lived in an apartment house on the corner. She looked electric that morning, much like the first time she had come over, with the orange.

"Ooooh," she said, "you've got on a new shirt!"

It was true. I had bought the shirt because I was thinking about her, about seeing her. I knew that she knew that, and was making fun of me, yet I didn't mind.

Lydia unlocked the door and we went inside. The clay sat in the center of the breakfast nook table under a wet cloth. She pulled the cloth off. "What do you think?"

Lydia hadn't spared me. The scars were there, the alcoholic nose, the monkey mouth, the eyes narrowed to slits, and there was the dumb, pleased grin of a happy man, ridiculous, feeling his luck and wondering why. She was 30 and I was over 50. I didn't care.

"Yes," I said, "you've got me down. I like it. But it looks almost finished. I'm going to be depressed when it's done. There have been some great mornings and afternoons."

"Has it interfered with your writing?"

"No, I only write after it gets dark. I can never write in the day."

Lydia picked up her modeling tool and looked at me. "Don't worry. I have a lot more work to do. I want to get this one right."

AT HER first break she got a pint of whiskey out of the refrigerator.

"Ah," I said.

"How much?" she asked holding up a tall water glass.

"Half and half."

She fixed the drink and I drank it right down.

"I've heard about you," she said.

"Like what?"

"About how you throw guys off your front porch. That you beat your women."

"Beat my women?"

"Yes, somebody told me."

I grabbed Lydia and we went into our longest kiss ever. I held her against the edge of the sink and began rubbing my cock against her. She pushed me away but I caught her again in the center of the kitchen.

Lydia's hand reached for mine and pushed it down the front of her jeans and into her panties. One fingertip felt the top of her cunt. She was wet. As I continued to kiss her I worked my finger down into her cunt. Then I pulled my hand out, broke away, got the pint and poured myself another drink. I sat back down at the breakfast nook table and Lydia went around to the other side, sat down and looked at me. Then she began working on the clay again. I drank my whiskey slowly.

"Look," I said, "I know your tragedy."

"What?"

"I know your tragedy."

"What do you mean?"

"Listen," I said, "just forget it."

"I want to know."

"I don't want to hurt your feelings."

"I want to know what the hell you're talking about."

"O.K., if you give me another drink I'll tell you."

"All right." Lydia took my empty glass and gave me half-whiskey, half-water. I drank it down again.

"Well?" she asked.

"Hell, you know."

"Know what?"

"You've got a big pussy."

"*What?*"

"It's not uncommon. You've had two children."

Lydia sat silently working on the clay. Then she laid down her tool. She walked over to the corner of the kitchen near the back door. I watched her bend down and pull her boots off. Then she pushed down her jeans and her panties. Her cunt was right there looking at me.

"All right, you bastard," she said. "I'm going to show you you're wrong."

I took off my shoes, pants and shorts. I got down on my knees on the linoleum floor, and then eased down on top of her, stretching out. I began to kiss her. I hardened quickly and felt myself penetrate her.

I began to stroke . . . one, two, three. . . .

There was a knock on the front door. It was a child's knock—tiny fists, frantic, persistent. Lydia quickly pushed me off. "It's *Lisa!* She didn't go to school today! She's been over at. . . ." Lydia jumped up and began pulling her clothes on.

"Get dressed!" she said to me.

I got dressed as quickly as I could. Lydia went to the door and there was her five year old daughter: "MOMMY! MOMMY! I cut my finger!"

I wandered into the front room. Lydia had Lisa on her lap. "Oooo, let *Mommy* see. Oooo, let *Mommy* kiss your finger. *Mommy* will make it better!"

"MOMMY, it hurts!"

I looked at the cut. It was almost invisible.

"Look," I told Lydia finally, "I'll see you tomorrow."

"I'm sorry," she said.

"I know."

Lisa looked up at me, the tears were coming and coming.

"Lisa won't let anything *bad* happen to her Momma," Lydia said.

I opened the door, closed the door and walked to my 1962 Mercury Comet.

4

I WAS EDITING a little magazine at the time, *The Laxative Approach*. I had two co-editors and we felt that we were printing the best poets of our time. Also some of the other kind. One of the editors was a 6-foot-2 subnormal high school drop-out, Kenneth Mulloch (black), who was supported partly by his mother and partly by his sister. The other editor was Sammy Levinson (Jewish), 27, who lived with his parents and was supported by them.

The sheets were printed. Now we had to collate them and staple them into the covers.

"What you do," said Sammy, "is throw a collating party. You serve drinks and a little bullshit and let *them* do the work."

"I hate parties," I said.

"I'll do the inviting," said Sammy.

"All right," I said, and I invited Lydia.

THE NIGHT of the party Sammy arrived with the sheets already collated. He was a nervous sort with a head-tic and he hadn't been able to wait to see his own poems in print. He had collated *The Laxative Approach* all by himself, and then stapled the covers on. Kenneth Mulloch was not to be found—he probably was either in jail or had been committed.

People arrived. I knew very few of them. I walked to my landlady's in the back court. She came to the door.

"I'm having a big party, Mrs. O'Keefe. I want you and your husband to come. Plenty of beer, pretzels and chips."

"Oh, my God, no!"

"What's the matter?"

"I've seen the people going in there! Those beards and all that hair and those raggedy-ass clothes! Bracelets and beads . . . they

look like a bunch of communists! How can you *stand* people like
that?"

"I can't stand those people either, Mrs. O'Keefe. We just
drink beer and talk. It doesn't mean anything."

"You watch them. That kind will steal the plumbing."

She closed the door.

LYDIA ARRIVED late. She came through the door like an actress.
The first thing I noticed was her large cowboy hat with a
lavender feather pinned to the side. She didn't speak to me but
immediately sat down next to a young bookstore clerk and
began an intense conversation with him. I began drinking more
heavily and some of the drive and humor left my conversation.
The bookstore clerk was a good enough sort, trying to be a
writer. His name was Randy Evans but he was too far into
Kafka to accomplish any kind of literary clarity. We had
published him in *The Laxative Approach* rather than hurt his
feelings and also to get distribution for the magazine through
his bookstore.

I drank my beer and wandered around. I walked out on the
back porch, sat on the stoop in the alley and watched a large
black cat trying to get into a garbage can. I walked down towards
him. He leaped off the garbage can as I approached. He stood
3 or 4 feet away watching me. I took the lid off the garbage can.
The stench was horrible. I puked into the can. I dropped the lid
on the pavement. The cat leaped up, stood, all four feet together
upon the rim of the can. He hesitated, then brilliant under a
half-moon, he leaped into it all.

Lydia was still talking to Randy, and I noticed that under the
table one of her feet was touching one of Randy's. I opened
another beer.

Sammy had the crowd laughing. I was a little better at it than
he was when I wanted to get the crowd laughing but I wasn't
very good that night. There were 15 or 16 men and two
women—Lydia and April. April was on ATD and fat. She was
stretched out on the floor. After an hour or so she got up and
left with Carl, a burned-out speed freak. That left 15 or 16 men

and Lydia. I found a pint of scotch in the kitchen, took it out on the back porch, and had a bite now and then.

The men began leaving gradually as the night went on. Even Randy Evans left. Finally there was only Sammy, Lydia and myself. Lydia was talking to Sammy. Sammy said some funny things. I was able to laugh. Then he said he had to go.

"Please don't go, Sammy," said Lydia.

"Let the kid go," I said.

"Yeah, I gotta go," said Sammy.

After Sammy left Lydia said, "You didn't have to drive him away. Sammy's funny, Sammy's really funny. You hurt his feelings."

"But I want to talk to you alone, Lydia."

"I enjoy your friends. I don't get to meet all kinds of people the way you do. I *like* people!"

"I don't."

"I know you don't. But I *do*. People come to see you. Maybe if they didn't come to see you you'd like them better."

"No, the less I see them the better I like them."

"You hurt Sammy's feelings."

"Oh shit, he's gone home to his mother."

"You're jealous, you're insecure. You think I want to go to bed with every man I talk to."

"No I don't. Listen, how about a little drink?"

I got up and mixed her one. Lydia lit a long cigarette and sipped at her drink. "You sure look good in that hat," I said. "That purple feather is something."

"It's my father's hat."

"Won't he miss it?"

"He's dead."

I pulled Lydia over to the couch and gave her a long kiss. She told me about her father. He had died and left all 4 sisters a bit of money. That had enabled them to be independent and had enabled Lydia to divorce her husband. She also told me she'd had some kind of breakdown and spent time in a madhouse. I kissed her again. "Look," I said, "let's lay down on the bed. I'm tired."

To my surprise she followed me into the bedroom. I stretched out on the bed and felt her sit down. I closed my eyes and could tell she was pulling her boots off. I heard one boot hit the floor, then the other. I began to undress on the bed. I reached up and shut off the overhead light. I continued undressing. We kissed some more.

"How long has it been since you've had a woman?"

"Four years."

"Four years?"

"Yes."

"I think you deserve some love," she said. "I had a dream about you. I opened your chest like a cabinet, it had doors, and when I opened the doors I saw all kinds of soft things inside you—teddy bears, tiny fuzzy animals, all these soft, cuddly things. Then I had a dream about this other man. He walked up to me and handed me some pieces of paper. He was a writer. I took the pieces of paper and looked at them. And the pieces of paper had cancer. His writing had cancer. I go by my dreams. You deserve some love."

We kissed again.

"Listen," she said, "after you stick that thing inside me, pull it out just before you come. O.K.?"

"I understand."

I climbed on top of her. It was good. It was something happening, something real, and with a girl 20 years younger than I was and really, after all, beautiful. I did about 10 strokes—and came inside of her.

She leaped up.

"You son-of-a-bitch! You came inside of me!"

"Lydia, it's been so *long* . . . it felt so good . . . I couldn't help it. It sneaked up on me! Honest to Christ, I couldn't help it."

She ran into the bathroom and let the water run into the tub. She stood in front of the mirror running a comb through her long brown hair. She was truly beautiful.

"You son-of-a-bitch! God, what a dumb high school trick. That's high school shit! And it couldn't have happened at a worse time! Well, we're shackjobs now! We're shackjobs now!"

13

I moved toward her in the bathroom. "Lydia, I love you."

"Get the hell away from me!"

She pushed me out, closed the door, and I stood out in the hall, listening to the bath water run.

5

I DIDN'T SEE Lydia for a couple of days, although I did manage to phone her 6 or 7 times during that period. Then the weekend arrived. Her ex-husband, Gerald, always took the children over the weekend.

I drove up to her court about 11 AM that Saturday morning and knocked. She was in tight bluejeans, boots, orange blouse. Her eyes seemed a darker brown than ever and in the sunlight, as she opened the door, I noticed a natural red in her dark hair. It was startling. She allowed me to kiss her, then she locked the door behind us and we went to my car. We had, decided on the beach—not for bathing—it was mid-winter—but for something to do.

We drove along. It felt good having Lydia in the car with me.

"That was *some* party," she said. "You call that a collating party? That was a copulating party, that's what that was. A copulating party!"

I drove with one hand and rested the other on her inner thigh. I couldn't help myself. Lydia didn't seem to notice. As I drove along the hand slid down between her legs. She went on talking. Suddenly she said, "Take you hand off. That's my pussy!"

"Sorry," I said.

Neither of us said anything until we reached the parking lot at Venice beach. "You want a sandwich and a Coke or something?" I asked. "All right," she said.

We went into the small Jewish delicatessen to get the things and we took them to a knoll of grass that overlooked the sea. We had sandwiches, pickles, chips and soft drinks. The beach was almost deserted and the food tasted fine. Lydia was not talking. I was amazed at how quickly she ate. She ripped into her sandwich with a savagery, took large swallows of Coke, ate half a pickle in one bite and reached for a handful of potato chips. I am, on the contrary, a very slow eater.

Passion, I thought, she has passion.

"How's that sandwich?" I asked.

"Pretty good. I was hungry."

"They make good sandwiches. Do you want anything else?"

"Yes, I'd like a candy bar."

"What kind?"

"Oh, any kind. Something good."

I took a bite of my sandwich, a swallow of Coke, put them down and walked over to the store. I bought two candy bars so that she might have a choice. As I walked back a tall black man was moving toward the knoll. It was a chilly day but he had his shirt off and he had a very muscular body. He appeared to be in his early twenties. He walked very slowly and erect. He had a long slim neck and a gold earring hung from the left ear. He passed in front of Lydia, along the sand on the ocean side of the knoll. I came up and sat down beside Lydia.

"Did you see that guy?" she asked.

"Yes."

"Jesus Christ, here I am with you, you're twenty years older than I am. I could have something like that. What the hell's wrong with me?"

"Look. Here are a couple of candy bars. Take one."

She took one, ripped the paper off, took a bite and watched the young black man as he walked away along the shore.

"I'm tired of the beach," she said, "let's go back to my place."

WE REMAINED apart a week. Then one afternoon I was over at Lydia's place and we were on her bed, kissing. Lydia pulled away.

"You don't know anything about women, do you?"

"What do you mean?"

"I mean, I can tell by reading your poems and stories that you just don't know anything about women."

"Tell me more."

"Well, I mean for a man to interest me he's got to eat my pussy. Have you ever eaten pussy?"

"No."

"You're over 50 years old and you've never eaten pussy?"

"No."

"It's too late."

"Why?"

"You can't teach an old dog new tricks."

"Sure you can."

"No, it's too late for you."

"I've always been a slow starter."

Lydia got up and walked into the other room. She came back with a pencil and a piece of paper. "Now, look, I want to show you something." She began to draw on the paper. "Now, this is a cunt, and here is something you probably don't know about—the clit. That's where the feeling is. The clit hides, you see, it comes out now and then, it's pink and very *sensitive*. Sometimes it will hide from you and you have to find it, you just *touch* it with the tip of your tongue. . . ."

"O.K.," I said, "I've got it."

"I don't think you can do it. I tell you, you can't teach an old dog new tricks."

"Let's take our clothes off and lay down."

We undressed and stretched out. I began kissing Lydia. I dropped from the lips to the neck, then down to the breasts. Then I was down at the bellybutton. I moved lower.

"No you *can't*," she said. "Blood and pee come out of there, think of it, blood and pee. . . ."

I got down there and began licking. She had drawn an accurate picture for me. Everything was where it was supposed to be. I heard her breathing heavily, then moaning. It excited me. I got a hard-on. The clit came out but it wasn't exactly pink, it was purplish-pink. I teased the clit. Juices appeared and mixed with the cunt hairs. Lydia moaned and moaned. Then I heard the front door open and close. I heard footsteps. I looked up. A small black boy about 5 years old stood beside the bed.

"What the hell do you want?" I asked him.

"You got any empty bottles?" he asked me.

"No, I don't have any empty bottles," I told him.

He walked out of the bedroom, into the front room, out the front door and was gone.

"God," said Lydia, "I thought the front door was locked. That was Bonnie's little boy."

Lydia got up and locked the front door. She came back and stretched out. It was about 4 PM on a Saturday afternoon.

I ducked back down.

6

LYDIA LIKED PARTIES. And Harry was a party-giver. So we were on our way to Harry Ascot's. Harry was the editor of *Retort*, a little magazine. His wife wore long see-through dresses, showed her panties to the men, and went barefoot.

"The first thing I liked about you," said Lydia, "was that you didn't have a t.v. in your place. My ex-husband looked at t.v. every night and all through the weekend. We even had to arrange our lovemaking to fit the t.v. schedule."

"Umm. . . ."

"Another thing I liked about your place was that it was filthy. Beer bottles all over the floor. Lots of trash everywhere. Dirty dishes, and a shit-ring in your toilet, and the crud in your bathtub. All those rusty razorblades laying around the bathroom sink. I knew that you would eat pussy."

"You judge a man according to his surroundings, right?"

"Right. When I see a man with a tidy place I know there's something wrong with him. And if it's too tidy, he's a fag."

We drove up and got out. The apartment was upstairs. The music was loud. I rang the bell. Harry Ascot answered the door. He had a gentle and generous smile. "Come in," he said.

The literary crowd was in there drinking wine and beer, talking, gathered in clusters. Lydia was excited. I looked around and sat down. Dinner was about to be served. Harry was a good fisherman, he was a better fisherman than he was a writer, and

17

a much better fisherman than he was an editor. The Ascots lived on fish while waiting for Harry's talents to start bringing in some money.

Diana, his wife, came out with the plates of fish and passed them around. Lydia sat next to me.

"Now," she said, "this is how you eat a fish. I'm a country girl. Watch me."

She opened that fish, she did something with her knife to the backbone. The fish was in two neat pieces.

"Oh, I really *liked* that," said Diana. "Where did you say you were from?"

"Utah. Muleshead, Utah. Population 100. I grew up on a ranch. My father was a drunk. He's dead now. Maybe that's why I'm with him. . . ." She jerked a thumb at me.

We ate.

After the fish was consumed Diana carried the bones away. Then there was chocolate cake and strong (cheap) red wine.

"Oh, this cake is good," said Lydia, "can I have another piece?"

"Sure, darling," said Diana.

"Mr. Chinaski," said a dark-haired girl from across the room, "I've read translations of your books in Germany. You're very popular in Germany."

"That's nice," I said. "I wish they'd send me some royalties. . . ."

"Look," said Lydia, "let's not talk about literary crap. Let's *do* something!" She leaped up and did a bump and a grind. "LET'S DANCE!"

Harry Ascot put on his gentle and generous smile and walked over and turned up the stereo. He turned it up as loud as it would go.

Lydia danced around the room and a young blond boy with ringlets glued to his forehead joined her. They began dancing together. Others got up and danced. I sat there.

Randy Evans was sitting next to me. I could see he was watching Lydia too. He began talking. He talked and he talked. Thankfully I couldn't hear him, the stereo was too loud.

I watched Lydia dance with the boy with the ringlets. Lydia could move it. Her movements lurked upon the sexual. I looked at the other girls and they didn't seem to be dancing that way; but, I thought, that's only because I know Lydia and I don't know them.

Randy kept on talking even though I didn't answer. The dance ended and Lydia came back and sat down next to me.

"Ooooh, I'm pooped! I think I'm out of shape."

Another record dropped into place and Lydia got up and joined the boy with the golden ringlets. I kept drinking beer and wine.

There were many records. Lydia and the boy danced and danced—center stage as the others moved around them, each dance more intimate than the last.

I kept drinking the beer and the wine.

A wild loud dance was in progress. . . . The boy with the golden ringlets raised both hands above his head. Lydia pressed against him. It was dramatic, erotic. They held their hands high over their heads and pressed their bodies together. Body against body. He kicked his feet back, one at a time. Lydia imitated him. They stared into each other's eyes. I had to admit they were good. The record went on and on. Finally, it ended.

Lydia came back and sat down next to me. "I'm really pooped," she said.

"Look, I said, "I think I've had too much to drink. Maybe we ought to get out of here."

"I've watched you pouring it down."

"Let's go. There'll be other parties."

We got up to leave. Lydia said something to Harry and Diana. When she came back we walked toward the door. As I opened it the boy with the golden ringlets came up to me. "Hey, man, what do you think of me and your girl?"

"You're O.K."

When we got outside I began vomiting, all the beer and the wine came up. It poured and splattered into the brush—across the sidewalk—a gusher in the moonlight. Finally I straightened up and wiped my mouth with my hand.

"That guy worried you, didn't he?" she asked.

"Yes."

"Why?"

"It almost seemed like a fuck, maybe better."

"It didn't mean anything, it was just *dancing*."

"Suppose that I grabbed a woman on the street like that? Would music make it all right?"

"You don't understand. Each time I finished dancing I came back and sat down next to *you*."

"O.K., O.K.," I said, "wait a minute."

I puked up another gusher on somebody's dying brush. We walked down the hill out of the Echo Park district toward Hollywood Boulevard.

We got into the car. It started and we drove west down Hollywood toward Vermont.

"You know what we call guys like you?" asked Lydia.

"No."

"We call them," she said, "party-poopers."

7

WE CAME IN low over Kansas City, the pilot said the temperature was 20 degrees, and there I was in my thin California sports coat and shirt, lightweight pants, summer stockings, and holes in my shoes. As we landed and taxied toward the ramp everybody was reaching for overcoats, gloves, hats, mufflers. I let them all get off and then climbed down the portable stairway. There was Frenchy leaning against a building and waiting. Frenchy taught drama and collected books, mostly mine. "Welcome to Kansas Shitty, Chinaski!" he said and handed me a bottle of tequila. I took a good gulp and followed him into the parking lot. I had no baggage, just a portfolio full of poems. The car was warm and pleasant and we passed the bottle.

The roadways were frozen over with ice.

"Not everybody can drive on this fucking kind of ice," said Frenchy. "You got to know what you're doing."

I opened the portfolio and began reading Frenchy a love poem Lydia had handed me at the airport:

"... *your purple cock curved like a* ...

"... *when I squeeze your pimples, bullets of puss like sperm* ..."

"Oh SHIT!" hollered Frenchy. The car went into a spin. Frenchy worked at the steering wheel.

"Frenchy," I said, lifting the tequila bottle and taking a hit, "we're not going to make it."

We spun off the road and into a three foot ditch which divided the highway. I handed him the bottle.

We got out of the car and climbed out of the ditch. We thumbed passing cars; sharing what was left of the bottle. Finally a car stopped. A man in his mid-twenties, drunk, was at the wheel. "Where you fellows going?"

"A poetry reading," said Frenchy.

"A poetry reading?"

"Yeah, at the University."

"All right, get in."

He was a liquor salesman. The back seat of his car was packed with cases of beer.

"Have a beer," he said, "and get me one too."

He got us there. We drove right up into the campus center and parked on the lawn in front of the auditorium. We were only 15 minutes late. I got out, vomited, then we all walked in together. We had stopped for a pint of vodka to get me through the reading.

I read about 20 minutes, then put the poems down. "This shit bores me," I said, "let's talk to each other."

I ended up screaming things at the audience and they screamed back at me. That audience wasn't bad. They were doing it for free. After about another 30 minutes a couple of professors got me out of there. "We've got a room for you, Chinaski," one of them said, "in the women's dormitory."

"In the women's dorm?"

"That's right, a nice room."

... It was true. Up on the third floor. One of the profs had brought a fifth of whiskey. Another gave me a check for the reading, plus air fare, and we sat around and drank the whiskey and talked. I blacked out. When I came to everybody was gone and there was half a fifth left. I sat there drinking and thinking, hey, you're Chinaski, Chinaski the legend. You've got an image. Now you're in the women's dorm. Hundreds of women in this place, *hundreds* of them.

All I had on were my shorts and stockings. I walked out into the hall up to the nearest door. I knocked.

"Hey, I'm Henry Chinaski, the immortal writer! Open up! I wanna show you something!"

I heard the girls giggling.

"O.K. now," I said, "how many of you are in there? 2? 3? It doesn't matter. I can handle 3! No problem! Hear me? Open up! I have this HUGE purple thing! Listen, I'll beat on the door with it!"

I took my fist and beat on the door. They kept giggling.

"So. You're not going to let Chinaski in, eh? Well, FUCK YOU!"

I tried the next door. "Hey, girls! This is the best poet of the last 18 hundred years! Open the door! I'm gonna show you something! Sweet meat for your vaginal lips!"

I tried the next door.

I tried all the doors on that floor and then I walked down the stairway and worked all the doors on the second floor and then all the doors on the first. I had the whiskey with me and I got tired. It seemed like hours since I had left my room. I drank as I walked along. No luck.

I had forgotten where my room was, which floor it was on. All I wanted, finally, was to get back to my room. I tried all the doors again, this time silently, very conscious of my shorts and stockings. No luck. "The greatest men are the most alone."

BACK ON the third floor I twisted a doorknob and the door opened. There was my portfolio of poems ... the empty drinking glasses, ashtrays full of cigarette stubs ... my pants, my shirt, my shoes, my coat. It was a wonderful sight. I closed the door, sat down on the bed and finished the bottle of whiskey that I had been carrying with me.

I AWAKENED. It was daylight. I was in a strange clean place with two beds, drapes, t.v., bath. It appeared to be a motel room. I got up and opened the door. There was snow and ice out there. I closed the door and looked around. There was no explanation. I had no idea where I was. I was terribly hung over and depressed. I reached for the telephone and placed a long distance call to Lydia in Los Angeles.

"Baby, I don't know where I am!"

"I thought you went to Kansas City?"

"I did. But now I don't know where I am, you understand? I opened the door and looked and there's nothing but frozen roads, ice, snow!"

"Where were you staying?"

"Last thing I remember I had a room in the women's dorm."

"Well, you probably made an ass out of yourself and they moved you to a motel. Don't worry. Somebody will show up to take care of you."

"Christ, don't you have any sympathy for my situation?"

"You made an ass out of yourself. You generally always make an ass out of yourself."

"What do you mean 'generally always'?"

"You're just a lousy drunk," Lydia said. "Take a warm shower."

She hung up.

I walked over to the bed and stretched out. It was a nice motel room but it lacked character. I'd be damned if I'd take a shower. I thought of turning on the t.v.

I slept finally. . . .

THERE WAS a knock on the door. Two bright young college boys stood there, ready to take me to the airport. I sat on the edge of the bed putting on my shoes. "We got time for a couple at the airport bar before take-off?" I asked.

"Sure, Mr. Chinaski," one of them said, "anything you want."
"O.K." I said. "Then let's get the fuck out of here."

8

I GOT BACK, made love to Lydia several times, got in a fight with her, and left L.A. International late one morning to give a reading in Arkansas. I was lucky enough to have a seat by myself. The flight captain announced himself, if I heard correctly, as Captain Winehead. When the stewardess came by I ordered a drink.

I was certain I knew one of the stewardesses. She lived in Long Beach, had read some of my books, had written me a letter enclosing her photo and phone number. I recognized her from the photo. I had never gotten around to meeting her but I called her a number of times and one drunken night we had screamed at each other over the phone.

She stood up front trying not to notice me as I stared at her behind and her calves and her breasts.

We had lunch, saw the Game of the Week, the after-lunch wine burned my throat, and I ordered two Bloody Marys.

When we got to Arkansas I transferred to a small two engine job. When the propellers started up the wings began to vibrate and shake. They looked like they might fall off. We lifted off and the stewardess asked if anybody wanted a drink. By then we all needed one. She staggered and wobbled up and down the aisle selling drinks. Then she said, loudly, "DRINK UP! WE'RE GOING TO LAND!" We drank up and landed. Fifteen minutes later we were up again. The stewardess asked if anybody wanted a drink. By then we all needed one. Then she said, loudly, "DRINK UP! WE'RE GOING TO LAND!"

Professor Peter James and his wife, Selma, were there to meet me. Selma looked like a movie starlet but with much more class. "You're looking great," said Pete.

"Your wife's looking great."

"You've got two hours before the reading."

Pete drove to their place. It was a split-level house with the guestroom on the lower level. I was shown my bedroom, downstairs. "You want to eat?" Pete asked. "No, I feel like I'm going to vomit." We went upstairs.

BACKSTAGE, JUST before the reading, Pete filled a water pitcher with vodka and orange juice. "An old woman runs the readings. She'd cream in her panties if she knew you were drinking. She's a nice old girl but she still thinks poetry is about sunsets and doves in flight."

I went out and read. S.R.O. The luck was holding. They were like any other audience: they didn't know how to handle some of the good poems, and during others they laughed at the wrong times. I kept reading and pouring from the water pitcher.

"What's that you're drinking?"

"This," I said, "is orange juice mixed with life."

"Do you have a girlfriend?"

"I'm a virgin."

"Why did you seek to become a writer?"

"Next question, please."

I read some more. I told them I had flown in with Captain Winehead and had seen the Game of the Week. I told them that when I was in good spiritual shape I ate off one dish and then washed it immediately. I read some more poems. I read poems until the water pitcher was empty. Then I told them the reading was over. There was a bit of autographing and we went to a party at Pete's house. . . .

I DID MY Indian dance, my Belly dance and my Broken-Ass-in-the-Wind dance. It's hard to drink when you dance. And it's hard to dance when you drink. Peter knew what he was doing. He had couches and chairs lined up to separate the dancers from the drinkers. Each could go their own way without bothering the other.

Pete walked up. He looked around the room at the women. "Which one do you want?" he asked.

CHARLES BUKOWSKI

"Is it that easy?"
"It's just southern hospitality."

THERE WAS one I had noticed, older than the others, with protruding teeth. But her teeth protruded perfectly—pushing the lips out like an open passionate flower. I wanted my mouth on that mouth. She wore a short skirt and her pantyhose revealed good legs that kept crossing and uncrossing as she laughed and drank and tugged at her skirt which would just not stay down. I sat next to her. "I'm—" I started to say. . . .
"I know who you are. I was at your reading."
"Thanks. I'd like to eat your pussy. I've gotten pretty good at it. I'll drive you crazy."
"What do you think of Allen Ginsberg?"
"Look, don't get me off the track. I want your mouth, your legs, your ass."
"All right," she said.
"See you soon. I'm in the bedroom downstairs."
I got up, left her, had another drink. A young guy—at least 6 feet 6 inches tall—walked up to me. "Look, Chinaski, I don't believe all that shit about you living on skidrow and knowing all the dope dealers, pimps, whores, junkies, horse players, fighters and drunks. . . ."
"It's partly true."
"Bullshit," he said and walked off. A literary critic.
Then this blonde, about 19, with rimless glasses and a smile walked up. The smile never left. "I want to fuck you," she said. "It's your face."
"What about my face?"
"It's magnificent. I want to destroy your face with my cunt."
"It might be the other way around."
"Don't bet on it."
"You're right. Cunts are indestructible."
I went back to the couch and started playing with the legs of the one with the short skirt and moist flower lips whose name was Lillian.

26

The party ended and I went downstairs with Lilly. We undressed and sat propped against the pillows drinking vodka and vodka mix. There was a radio and the radio played. Lilly told me that she had worked for years to put her husband through college and then when he had gotten his professorship he had divorced her.

"That's shaggy," I said.

"You been married?"

"Yes."

"What happened?"

" 'Mental cruelty,' according to the divorce papers."

"Was it true?" she asked.

"Of course: both ways."

I kissed Lilly. It was as good as I had imagined it would be. The flower mouth was open. We clasped, I sucked on her teeth. We broke.

"I think you," she said, looking at me with wide and beautiful eyes, "are one of the two or three best writers of today."

I switched off the bed lamp fast. I kissed her some more, played with her breasts and body, then went down on her. I was drunk, but I think I did O.K. But after that I couldn't do it the other way. I rode and rode and rode. I was hard but I couldn't come. Finally I rolled off and went to sleep. . . .

In the morning Lilly was flat on her back, snoring. I went to the bathroom, pissed, brushed my teeth and washed my face. Then I crawled back into bed. I turned her toward me and started playing with her parts. I am always very horny when hungover—not horny to eat but horny to blast. Fucking was the best cure for hangovers. It got all the parts ticking again. Her breath was so bad that I didn't want the flower mouth. I mounted. She gave a small groan. For me, it was very good. I don't think I gave her more than twenty strokes before I came.

After a while I heard her get up and walk to the bathroom. Lillian. By the time she came back I had turned my back to her and was nearly asleep.

After 15 minutes she got out of bed and began to dress.

27

"What's wrong?" I asked.

"I've got to get out of here. I've got to take my kids to school."

Lillian closed the door and ran up the stairway.

I got up, walked to the bathroom, and stared for a while at my face in the mirror.

AT TEN AM I went upstairs for breakfast. I found Pete and Selma. Selma looked great. How did one get a Selma? The dogs of this world never ended up with a Selma. Dogs ended up with dogs. Selma served us breakfast. She was beautiful and one man owned her, a college professor. That was not quite right, somehow. Educated hotshot smoothies. Education was the new god, and educated men the new plantation masters.

"It was a damned good breakfast," I told them. "Thanks much."

"How was Lilly?" Pete asked.

"Lilly was very good."

"You've got to read again tonight, you know. It'll be at a smaller college, more conservative.

"All right. I'll be careful."

"What are you going to read?"

"Old stuff, I guess."

We finished our coffee and walked into the front room and sat down. The phone rang, Pete answered, talked, then turned to me. "Guy from the local paper wants to interview you. What'll I tell him?"

"Tell him all right."

Pete relayed the answer, then walked over and picked up my latest book and a pen. "I thought you might want to write something in this for Lilly."

I opened the book to the title page. "Dear Lilly," I wrote. "You will always be part of my life. . . .

Henry Chinaski."

9

LYDIA AND I were always fighting. She was a flirt and it irritated me. When we ate out I was sure she was eyeballing some man across the room. When my male friends came by to visit and Lydia was there I could hear her conversation become intimate and sexual. She always sat very close to my friends, positioning herself as near them as possible. It was my drinking that irritated Lydia. She loved sex and my drinking got in the way of our lovemaking. "Either you're too drunk to do it at night or too sick to do it in the morning," she'd say. Lydia would go into a rage if I even drank a bottle of beer in front of her. We split up at least once a week—"Forever"—but always managed to make up, somehow. She had finished sculpting my head and had given it to me. When we'd split I'd put the head in my car next to me on the front seat, drive it over to her place and leave it outside her door on the porch. Then I'd go to a phone booth, ring her up and say, "Your goddamned head is outside the door!" That head went back and forth. . . .

WE HAD just split again and I had dropped off the head. I was drinking, a free man again. I had a young friend, Bobby, a rather bland kid who worked in a porno bookstore and was a photographer on the side. He lived a couple of blocks away. Bobby was having trouble with himself and with his wife, Valerie. He phoned one evening and said he was bringing Valerie over to stay the night with me. It sounded fine. Valerie was 22, absolutely lovely, with long blond hair, mad blue eyes and a beautiful body. Like Lydia, she had also spent some time in a madhouse. After a while I heard them drive up on the lawn in front of my court. Valerie got out. I remembered Bobby telling me that when he first introduced Valerie to his parents they had commented on her dress—that they liked it very much—and she had said, "Yeah, well how about the rest of me?" She had pulled her dress up over her hips. And didn't have any panties on.

Valerie knocked. I heard Bobby drive off. I let her in. She looked fine. I poured two scotch and waters. Neither of us spoke. We drank those and I poured two more. After that I said, "Come on, let's make a bar." We got into my car. The Glue Machine was right around the corner. I had been 86'd earlier that week but nothing was said when we walked in. We got a table and ordered drinks. We still didn't talk. I just looked into those mad blue eyes. We were sitting side by side and I kissed her. Her mouth was cool and open. I kissed her again and our legs pressed together. Bobby had a nice wife. Bobby was crazy to pass her around.

We decided on dinner. We each ordered a steak and we drank and we kissed while we waited. The barmaid said, "Oh, you're in love!" and we both laughed. When the steaks came Valerie said, "I don't want to eat mine." "I don't want to eat mine either," I said.

We drank for another hour and then decided to go back to my place. As I drove the car up on the front lawn I saw a woman in the driveway. It was Lydia. She had an envelope in her hand. I got out of the car with Valerie and Lydia looked at us. "Who's that?" asked Valerie. "The woman I love," I told her.

"Who's the bitch?" screamed Lydia.

Valerie turned and ran down the sidewalk. I could hear her high heels on the pavement. "Come on in," I told Lydia. She followed me in.

"I came here to give this letter to you and it looks like I came at the right time. Who was she?"

"Bobby's wife. We're just friends."

"You were going to fuck her, weren't you?"

"Now look, I told her I love *you*."

"You were going to fuck her, weren't you?"

"Now look, baby . . ."

Suddenly she shoved me. I was standing in front of the coffee table which was in front of the couch. I fell backward over the coffee table and into the space between the table and the couch. I heard the door slam. And as I got up I heard the engine of Lydia's car start. Then she drove off.

Son-of-a-bitch, I thought, one minute I've got two women and the next I've got none.

10

I WAS SURPRISED the next morning when April knocked on the door. April was the one on ATD who had been at Harry Ascot's party and who had left with the speed freak. It was 11 AM. April came in and sat down.

"I've always admired your work," she said.

I got her a beer and got myself a beer.

"God is a hook in the sky," she said.

"*All right*," I said.

April was on the heavy side but not too fat. She had big hips and a large ass and her hair fell straight down. There was something about the size of her—rugged, like she could handle an ape. Her mental deficiency was attractive to me because she didn't play games. She crossed her legs, showing me enormous white flanks.

"I planted tomato seeds down in the basement of the apartment house I live in," she said.

"I'll take some when they come up," I said.

"I've never had a driver's license," April said. "My mother lives in New Jersey."

"My mother's dead," I said. I walked over and sat next to her on the couch. I grabbed her and kissed her. While I was kissing her she looked right into my eyes. I broke off. "Let's fuck," I said.

"I have an infection," said April.

"What?"

"It's sort of a fungus. Nothing serious."

"Could I catch it?"

"It's kind of a milky discharge."

"Could I catch it?"

"I don't think so."

"Let's fuck."

"I don't know if I want to fuck."

"It'll feel good. Let's go into the bedroom."

April walked into the bedroom and started taking off her clothes. I took mine off. We got under the sheets. I began

31

playing with her parts and kissing her. I mounted her. It was very strange. As if her cunt ran from side to side. I knew I was in there, it felt like I was in there, but I kept slipping sideways, to the left. I kept humping. It was exciting like that. I finished and rolled off.

Later I drove her to her apartment and we went up. We talked for a long while and I left only after making note of the apartment number and the address. As I walked through the lobby I recognized the apartment house lock boxes. I had delivered mail there many times as a mailman. I went out to my car and drove off.

11

LYDIA HAD TWO children: Tonto, a boy of 8, and Lisa, the little girl of 5 who had interrupted our first fuck. We were together at the table one night eating dinner. Things were going well between Lydia and me and I stayed for dinner almost every night, then slept with Lydia and left about 11 AM the next morning to go back to my place to check the mail and write. The children slept in the next room on a waterbed. It was an old, small house which Lydia rented from an ex Japanese wrestler now into real estate. He was obviously interested in Lydia. That was all right. It was a nice old house.

"Tonto," I said as we were eating, "you know that when your mother screams at night I'm not beating her. You know who's *really* in trouble."

"Yes, I know."

"Then why don't you come in and help me?"

"Uh-uh. I know her."

"Listen, Hank," said Lydia, "don't turn my kids against me."

"He's the ugliest man in the *world*," said Lisa.

I liked Lisa. She was going to be a sexpot some day, a sexpot with personality.

After dinner Lydia and I went to our bedroom and stretched out. Lydia was into blackheads and pimples. I had a bad complexion. She moved the lamp down near my face and began. I liked it. It made me tingle and sometimes I got a hard-on. Very intimate. Sometimes between squeezes Lydia would give me a kiss. She always worked on my face first and then moved on to my back and chest.

"You love me?"

"Yeh."

"Oooh, look at this one!"

It was a blackhead with a long yellow tail.

"It's nice," I said.

She was laying flat on top of me. She stopped squeezing and looked at me. "I'll put you in your grave, you fat fuck!"

I laughed. Then Lydia kissed me.

"I'll put you back in the madhouse," I told her.

"Turn over. Let me get your back."

I turned over. She squeezed at the back of my neck. "Oooh, there's a good one! It shot out! It hit me in the eye!"

"You ought to wear goggles."

"Let's have a little *Henry!* Think of it, a little Henry Chinaski!"

"Let's wait a while."

"I want a baby *now!*"

"Let's wait."

"All we do is sleep and eat and lay around and make love. We're like slugs. Slug-love, I call it."

"I like it."

"You used to write over here. You were busy. You'd bring ink and make your drawings. Now you go home and do all the interesting things there. You just eat and sleep here and then leave first thing in the morning. It's dull."

"I like it."

"We haven't been to a party in months! I like to see people! I'm *bored!* I'm so bored I'm about to go crazy! I want to do things! I want to DANCE! I want to *live!*"

"Oh, shit."

"You're too old. You just want to sit around and criticize everything and everybody. You don't want to do anything. Nothing's good enough for you!"

I rolled out of bed and stood up. I began putting my shirt on.

"What are you doing?" she asked.

"I'm getting out of here."

"There you go! The minute things don't go your way you jump up and run out of the door. You never want to talk about things. You go home and get drunk and then you're so sick the next day you think you're going to die. *Then* you phone me!"

"I'm getting the hell out of here!"

"But why?"

"I don't want to stay where I'm not wanted. I don't want to stay where I'm disliked."

Lydia waited. Then she said, "All right. Come on, lay down. We'll turn off the light and just be still together."

I waited. Then I said, "Well, all right."

I undressed entirely and got under the blanket and sheet. I pressed my flank against Lydia's flank. We were both on our backs. I could hear the crickets. It was a nice neighborhood. A few minutes passed. Then Lydia said, "I'm going to be great."

I didn't answer. A few more minutes passed. Then Lydia leaped out of bed. She threw both of her hands up in the air toward the ceiling and said in a loud voice: "I'M GOING TO BE GREAT! I'M GOING TO BE TRULY GREAT! NO-BODY KNOWS HOW GREAT I'M GOING TO BE!"

"All right," I said.

Then she said in a lower voice, "You don't understand. I'm going to be great. I have more *potential* than you have!"

"Potential," I said, "doesn't mean a thing. You've got to do it. Almost every baby in a crib has more potential than I have."

"But I'm GOING to do it! I'M GOING TO BE TRULY GREAT!"

"All right," I said. "But meanwhile come on back to bed."

Lydia came back to bed. We didn't kiss each other. We weren't going to have sex. I felt weary. I listened to the crickets. I don't know how much time went by. I was almost asleep, not quite, when Lydia suddenly sat straight up in bed. And she screamed. It was a loud scream.

"What is it?" I asked.

"Be quiet."

I waited. Lydia sat there, without moving, for what seemed to be about ten minutes. Then she fell back on her pillow.

"I saw God," she said, "I just saw God."

"Listen, you bitch, you are going to drive me crazy!"

I got up and began dressing. I was mad. I couldn't find my shorts. The hell with them, I thought. I left them wherever they were. I had all my clothes on and was sitting on the chair pulling my shoes on my bare feet.

"What are you doing?" Lydia asked.

I couldn't answer. I went into the front room. My coat was flung over a chair and I picked it up, put it on. Lydia ran into the front room. She had put on her blue negligee and a pair of panties. She was barefooted. Lydia had thick ankles. She usually wore boots to hide them.

"YOU'RE NOT GOING!" she screamed at me.

"Shit," I said, "I'm getting out of here."

She leaped at me. She usually attacked me while I was drunk. Now I was sober. I sidestepped and she fell to the floor, rolled over and was on her back. I stepped over her on my way to the front door. She was in a spitting rage, snarling, her lips pulled back. She was like a leopardess. I looked down at her. I felt safe with her on the floor. She let out a snarl and as I started to leave she reached up and dug her nails into the sleeve of my coat, pulled and ripped the sleeve off my arm. It was ripped from the coat at the shoulder.

"Jesus Christ," I said, "look what you've done to my new coat! I just bought it!"

I opened the door and jumped outside with one bare arm.

I had just unlocked the door to my car when I heard her bare feet on the asphalt behind me. I leaped in and locked the door. I punched the starter.

"*I'll kill this car!*" she screamed. "*I'll kill this car!*"

Her fists beat on the hood, on the roof, against the windshield. I moved the car ahead very slowly so as not to injure her. My '62 Mercury Comet had fallen apart, and I'd recently purchased a '67 Volks. I kept it shined and waxed. I even had a whisk broom in the glove compartment. As I pulled away Lydia kept beating on the car with her fists. When I was clear of her I shoved it into second. I looked in the rear view mirror and saw her standing all alone in the moonlight, motionless in her blue negligee and panties. My gut began to twitch and roll. I felt ill, useless, sad. I was in love with her.

12

I WENT TO my place, started drinking. I snapped on the radio and found some classical music. I got my Coleman lantern out of the closet. I turned out the lights and sat playing with the Coleman lantern. There were tricks you could play with a Coleman lantern. Like turning it off and then on again and watching the heat of the wick relight it. I also liked to pump the lantern and bring up the pressure. And then there was simply the pleasure of looking at it. I drank and watched the lantern and listened to the music and smoked a cigar.

The phone rang. It was Lydia. "What are you doing?" she asked.

"Just sitting around."

"You're sitting around and drinking and listening to symphony music and playing with that goddamned Coleman lantern!"

"Yes."

"Are you coming back?"

"No."

"All right, drink! Drink and get sick! You know that stuff almost killed you once. Do you remember the hospital?"

"I'll never forget it."

"All right, drink, DRINK! KILL YOURSELF! SEE IF I GIVE A SHIT!"

Lydia hung up and so did I. Something told me she wasn't as worried about my possible death as she was about her next fuck. But I needed a vacation. I needed a rest. Lydia liked to fuck at least five times a week. I preferred three. I got up and went into the breakfast nook where my typewriter stood on the table. I turned on the light, sat down and typed Lydia a 4-page letter. Then I went into the bathroom, got a razorblade, came out, sat down and had a good drink. I took the razorblade and sliced the middle finger of my right hand. The blood ran. I signed my name to the letter in blood.

I went down to the corner mailbox and dropped the letter in.

The phone rang several times. It was Lydia. She screamed things at me.

"I'm going out DANCING! I'm not going to sit around alone while you drink!"

I told her, "You act like drinking is like my going with another woman."

"It's worse!"

She hung up.

I kept drinking. I didn't feel like sleeping. Soon it was midnight, then 1 AM, 2 AM. The Coleman lantern burned on. . . .

AT 3:30 AM the phone rang. Lydia again. "Are you still drinking?"

"Sure!"

"You rotten son of a bitch!"

"In fact just as you called I was peeling the cellophane off this pint of Cutty Sark. It's beautiful. You ought to see it!"

She slammed down the phone. I mixed another drink. There was good music on the radio. I leaned back. I felt very good.

The door banged open and Lydia ran into the room. She stood there panting. The pint was on the coffee table. She saw it and grabbed it. I jumped up and grabbed her. When I was drunk and Lydia was insane we were nearly an equal match. She held the bottle high in the air, away from me, and tried to get out of the door with it. I grabbed the arm that held the bottle, and tried to get it away from her.

"YOU WHORE! YOU HAVE NO RIGHT! GIVE ME THAT FUCKING BOTTLE!"

Then we were out on the porch, wrestling. We tripped on the stairs and fell to the pavement. The bottle smashed and broke on the cement. She got up and ran off. I heard her car start. I lay there and looked at the broken bottle. It was a foot away. Lydia drove off. The moon was still up. In the bottom of what was left of the bottle I could see a swallow of scotch. Stretched out there on the pavement I reached for it and lifted it to my mouth. A long shard of glass almost poked into one of my eyes as I drank what remained. Then I got up and went inside. The thirst in me was terrible. I walked around picking up beer bottles and drinking the bit that remained in each one. Once I got a mouthful of ashes as I often used beer bottles for ashtrays. It was 4:14 AM. I sat and watched the clock. It was like working in the post office again. Time was motionless while existence was a throbbing unbearable thing. I waited. I waited. I waited. I waited. Finally it was 6 AM. I walked to the corner to the liquor store. A clerk was opening up. He let me in. I purchased another pint of Cutty Sark. I walked back home, locked the door and phoned Lydia.

"I have here one pint of Cutty Sark from which I am peeling the cellophane. I am going to have a drink. And the liquor store will now be open for 20 hours."

She hung up. I had one drink and then walked into the bedroom, stretched out on the bed, and went to sleep without taking off my clothes.

13

A WEEK LATER I was driving down Hollywood Boulevard with Lydia. A weekly entertainment newspaper published in California at that time had asked me to write an article on the life of the writer in Los Angeles. I had written it and was driving over to the editorial offices to submit it. We parked in the lot at Mosley Square. Mosley Square was a section of expensive bungalows used as offices by music publishers, agents, promoters and the like. The rents were very high.

We went into one of the bungalows. There was a handsome girl behind the desk, educated and cool.

"I'm Chinaski," I said, "and here's my copy."

I threw it on the desk.

"Oh, Mr. Chinaski, I've always admired your work very much!"

"Do you have anything to drink around here?"

"Just a moment. . . ."

She went up to a carpeted stairway and came back down with a bottle of expensive red wine. She opened it and pulled some glasses from a hidden bar. How I'd like to get in bed with her, I thought. But there was no way. Yet, somebody was going to bed with her regularly.

We sat and sipped our wine.

"We'll let you know very soon about the article. I'm sure we'll take it. . . . But you're not at all the way I expected you to be. . . ."

"What do you mean?"

"Your voice is so soft. You seem so nice."

Lydia laughed. We finished our wine and left. As we were walking toward my car I heard a voice. "Hank!"

I looked around and there sitting in a new Mercedes was Dee Dee Bronson. I walked over.

"How's it going, Dee Dee?"

"Pretty good. I quit Capitol Records. Now I'm running that place over there." She pointed. It was another music company, quite famous, with its home office in London. Dee Dee used to drop by my place with her boyfriend when he and I both had columns in a Los Angeles underground newspaper.

"Jesus, you're doing good," I said.

"Yes, except . . ."

"Except what?"

"Except I need a man. A good man."

"Well, give me your phone number and I'll see if I can find one for you."

"All right."

Dee Dee wrote her phone number on a slip of paper and I put it in my wallet. Lydia and I walked over to my old Volks and got in. "You're going to phone her," Lydia said. "You're going to use that number."

I started the car and got back on Hollywood Boulevard.

"You're going to use that number," she said. "I just know you're going to use that number!"

"Cut the shit!" I said.

It looked like another bad night.

14

WE HAD ANOTHER fight. Later I was back at my place but I didn't feel like sitting there alone and drinking. The night harness racing meet was on. I took a pint and went out to the track. I arrived early and got all my figures together. By the time the first race was over the pint was surprisingly more than half gone. I was mixing it with hot coffee and it went down easily.

I won three of the first four races. Later I won an exacta and was nearly $200 ahead by the end of the 5th race. I went to the bar and played off the toteboard. That night they gave me what I called "a good toteboard." Lydia would have shit if she could have seen me pulling in all that cash. She hated it when I won at the track, especially when she was losing.

I kept drinking and hitting. By the time the 9th race was over I was $950 ahead and very drunk. I put my wallet in one of my side pockets and walked slowly to my car.

I sat in my car and watched the losers leave the parking lot. I sat there until the traffic thinned out then I started the engine. Just outside the track was a supermarket. I saw a lighted phone booth at one end of the parking lot, drove in and got out. I walked to the phone and dialed Lydia's number.

"Listen," I said, "listen, you bitch. I went to the harness races tonight and won $950. I'm a winner! I'll always be a winner! You don't deserve me, bitch! You've been playing with me! Well, it's over! I want out! This is it! I don't need you and your goddamned games! Do you understand me? Do you get the message? Or is your head thicker than your ankles?"

"Hank . . ."

"Yes?"

"This isn't Lydia. This is Bonnie. I'm baby sitting for Lydia. She went out tonight."

I hung up and walked back to my car.

15

LYDIA PHONED ME in the morning. "Whenever you get drunk," she said, "I'm going out dancing. I went to the Red Umbrella last night and I asked men to dance with me. A woman has a right to do that."

"You're a whore."

"Yeah? Well, if there's anything worse than a whore it's a bore."

"If there's anything worse than a bore it's a boring whore."

"If you don't want my pussy," she said, "I'll give it to somebody else."

"That's your privilege."

"After I finished dancing, I went to see Marvin. I wanted to get his girlfriend's address and go see her. Francine. You went to see his girl Francine one night yourself," Lydia said.

"Look, I never fucked her. I was just too drunk to drive home after a party. We didn't even kiss. She let me sleep on her couch and I went home in the morning."

"Anyhow, after I got to Marvin's, I decided not to ask for Francine's address."

Marvin's parents had money. He had a house down by the seashore. Marvin wrote poetry, better poetry than most. I liked Marvin.

"Well, I hope you had a good time," I said and hung up.

I had no sooner hung up when the phone rang again. It was Marvin. "Hey, guess who came by real late last night? Lydia. She knocked on the window and I let her in. She gave me a hard-on."

"O.K., Marvin. I understand. I'm not blaming you."

"You're not pissed?"

"Not at you."

"All right then . . ."

I TOOK the sculpted head and loaded it into my car. I drove over to Lydia's and put the head on her doorstep. I didn't ring the bell. I started to walk away. Lydia came out.

"Why are you such an ass?" she asked.

I turned. "You are not selective. One man's the same as another to you. I'm not going to eat your shit."

"I'm not going to eat your shit either!" she screamed and slammed the door.

I walked to my car, got in and started it. I put it in first. It didn't move. I tried second. Nothing. Then I went back to first. I checked to be sure the brake was off. It wouldn't move. I tried reverse. The car moved backwards. I braked and tried first again. The car wouldn't move. I was still very angry with Lydia. I thought, well, I'll drive the fucking thing home backwards. Then I thought about the cops stopping me and asking me what the hell I was doing. Well, officers, I had a fight with my girl and this was the only way I could get home.

I didn't feel so angry with Lydia anymore. I climbed out and went to her door. She had taken my head inside. I knocked. Lydia opened the door. "Look," I asked, "are you some kind of witch?"

"No, I'm a whore, remember?"

"You've got to drive me home. My car will only run backwards. The goddamned thing is hexed."

"Are you serious?"

"Come on, I'll show you."

Lydia followed me out to the car. "The gears have been working fine. Then all of a sudden the car will only run backwards. I was going to drive it home that way."

I got in. "Now watch."

I started the car and put it in first, let out the clutch. It jumped forward. I put it in second. It went into second and moved faster. I put it into third. It moved nicely forward. I made a U-turn and parked on the other side of the street. Lydia walked over.

"Listen," I said, "you've got to believe me. A minute ago the car would only run backwards. Now it's all right. Please believe me."

"I believe you," she said. "God did it. I believe in that sort of thing."

"It must mean something."

"It does."

I got out of the car. We walked into her house.

"Take off your shirt and shoes," she said, "and lay down on the bed. First I want to squeeze your blackheads."

16

THE EX-JAPANESE wrestler who was into real estate sold Lydia's house. She had to move out. There was Lydia, Tonto, Lisa and the dog, Bugbutt. In Los Angeles most landlords hang out the same sign: ADULTS ONLY. With two children and a dog it was very difficult. Only Lydia's good looks could help her. A male landlord was needed.

I drove them all around town. It was useless. Then I stayed out of sight in the car. It still didn't work. As we drove along Lydia screamed out the window, "Isn't there *anybody* in this town who will rent to a woman with two kids and a dog?"

Unexpectedly a vacancy occurred in my court. I saw the people moving out and I went right down and talked to Mrs. O'Keefe.

"Listen," I said, "my girlfriend needs a place to live. She has two kids and a dog but they're all well-behaved. Will you let them move in?"

"I've seen that woman," said Mrs. O'Keefe. "Haven't you noticed her eyes? She's crazy."

"I know she's crazy. But I care for her. She has some good qualities, really."

"She's too young for you! What are you going to do with a young woman like that?"

I laughed.

43

Mr. O'Keefe walked up behind his wife. He looked at me through the screen door. "He's pussy-whipped, that's all. It's quite simple, he's pussy-whipped."

"How about it?" I asked.

"All right," said Mrs. O'Keefe. "Move her in. . . ."

So Lydia rented a U-Haul and I moved her in. It was mostly clothes, all the heads she had sculpted, and a large washing machine.

"I don't like Mrs. O'Keefe," she told me. "Her husband looks all right, but I don't like her."

"She's a good Catholic sort. And you need a place to live."

"I don't want you drinking with those people. They're out to destroy you."

"I'm only paying 85 bucks a month rent. They treat me like a son. I have to have a beer with them now and then."

"Son, *shit!* You're almost as old as they are."

ABOUT THREE weeks passed. It was late one Saturday morning. I had not slept at Lydia's the night before. I bathed and had a beer, got dressed. I disliked weekends. Everybody was out on the streets. Everybody was playing Ping-Pong or mowing their lawn or polishing their car or going to the supermarket or the beach or to the park. Crowds everywhere. Monday was my favorite day. Everybody was back on the job and out of sight. I decided to go to the racetrack despite the crowd. That would help kill Saturday. I ate a hard-boiled egg, had another beer and stepping out on my porch, locked the door. Lydia was outside playing with Bugbutt, the dog.

"Hi," she said.

"Hi," I said. "I'm going to the track."

Lydia walked over to me. "Listen, you know what the racetrack does to you."

She meant that I was always too tired to make love after going to the racetrack.

"You were drunk last night," she continued. "You were horrible. You frightened Lisa. I had to run you out."

"I'm going to the racetrack."

"All right, you go ahead and go to the racetrack. But if you do I won't be here when you get back."

I got into my car which was parked on the front lawn. I rolled down the windows and started the motor. Lydia was standing in the driveway. I waved goodbye to her and pulled out into the street. It was a nice summer day. I drove down to Hollywood Park. I had a new system. Each new system brought me closer and closer to wealth. It was simply a matter of time.

I LOST $40 and drove home. I parked my car on the lawn and got out. As I walked around the porch to my door Mr. O'Keefe walked up the driveway. "She's gone!"

"What?"

"Your girl. She moved out."

I didn't answer.

"She rented a U-Haul and loaded her stuff in it. She was mad. You know that big washing machine?"

"Yes."

"Well, that thing's heavy. I couldn't lift it. She wouldn't let the boy help her. She just lifted the thing and put it in the U-Haul. Then she got the kids, the dog, and drove off. She had a week's rent left."

"All right, Mr. O'Keefe. Thanks."

"You coming down to drink tonight?"

"I don't know."

"Try to make it."

I unlocked the door and went inside. I had lent her an air-conditioner. It was sitting in a chair outside of the closet. There was a note on it and a pair of blue panties. The note was in a wild scrawl:

> "Bastard, here is your air-conditioner. I am gone. I am gone for good, you son-of-a-bitch! When you get lonely you can use these panties to jack-off into. Lydia."

I went to the refrigerator and got a beer. I drank the beer and then walked over to the air-conditioner. I picked up the panties and stood there wondering if it would work. Then I said, "Shit!" and threw them on the floor.

I went to the phone and dialed Dee Dee Bronson. She was in. "Hello?" she said.

"Dee Dee," I said, "this is Hank. . . ."

17

DEE DEE HAD a place in the Hollywood Hills. Dee Dee shared the place with a friend, another lady executive, Bianca. Bianca took the top floor and Dee Dee the bottom. I rang the bell. It was 8:30 PM when Dee Dee opened the door. Dee Dee was about 40, had black, cropped hair, was Jewish, hip, freaky. She was New York City oriented, knew all the names: the right publishers, the best poets, the most talented cartoonists, the right revolutionaries, anybody, everybody. She smoked grass continually and acted like it was the early 1960's and Love-In Time, when she had been mildly famous and much more beautiful.

A long series of bad love affairs had finally done her in. Now I was standing at her door. There was a good deal left of her body. She was small but buxom and many a young girl would have loved to have her figure.

I followed her in. "So Lydia split?" Dee Dee asked.

"I think she went to Utah. The 4th of July dance in Muleshead is coming up. She never misses it."

I sat down in the breakfast nook while Dee Dee uncorked a red wine. "Do you miss her?"

"Christ, yes. I feel like crying. My whole gut is chewed up. I might not make it."

"You'll make it. We'll get you over Lydia. We'll pull you through."

"Then you know how I feel?"

"It has happened to most of us a few times."

"That bitch never cared to begin with."

"Yes, she did. She still does."

I decided it was better to be there in Dee Dee's large home in the Hollywood Hills than to be sitting all alone back in my apartment and brooding.

"It must be that I'm just not good with the ladies," I said.

"You're good enough with the ladies," Dee Dee said. "And you're a helluva writer."

"I'd rather be good with the ladies."

Dee Dee was lighting a cigarette. I waited until she was finished, then I leaned across the table and gave her a kiss. "You make me feel good. Lydia was always on the attack."

"That doesn't mean what you think it means."

"But it can get to be unpleasant."

"It sure as hell can."

"Have you found a boyfriend yet?"

"Not yet."

"I like this place. But how do you keep it so neat and clean?"

"We have a maid."

"Oh?"

"You'll like her. She's big and black and she finishes her work as fast as she can after I leave. Then she goes to bed and eats cookies and watches t.v. I find cookie crumbs in my bed every night. I'll have her fix you breakfast after I leave tomorrow morning."

"All right."

"No, wait. Tomorrow's Sunday. I don't work Sundays. We'll eat out. I know a place. You'll like it."

"All right."

"You know, I think I've always been in love with you."

"What?"

"For years. You know, when I used to come and see you, first with Bernie and later with Jack, I would want you. But you never noticed me. You were always sucking on a can of beer or you were obsessed with something."

"Crazy, I guess, near crazy. Postal Service madness. I'm sorry I didn't notice you."

"You can notice me now."

Dee Dee poured another glass of wine. It was good wine. I

liked her. It was good to have a place to go when things went bad. I remembered the early days when things would go bad and there wasn't anywhere to go. Maybe that had been good for me. Then. But now I wasn't interested in what was good for me. I was interested in how I felt and how to stop feeling bad when things went wrong. How to start feeling good again.

"I don't want to fuck you over, Dee Dee," I said. "I'm not always good to women."

"I told you I love you."

"Don't do it. Don't love me."

"All right," she said, "I won't love you, I'll *almost* love you. Will that be all right?"

"It's much better than the other."

We finished our wine and went to bed. . . .

18

IN THE MORNING Dee Dee drove me to the Sunset Strip for breakfast. The Mercedes was black and shone in the sun. We drove past the billboards and the nightclubs and the fancy restaurants. I slouched low in my seat, coughing over my cigarette. I thought, well, things have been worse. A scene or two flashed through my head. One winter in Atlanta I was freezing, it was midnight, I had no money, no place to sleep, and I walked up the steps of a church hoping to get inside and get warm. The church door was locked. Another time in El Paso, sleeping on a park bench, I was awakened in the morning by some cop smacking the soles of my shoes with his club. Still, I kept thinking about Lydia. The good parts of our relationship felt like a rat walking around and gnawing at the inside of my stomach.

Dee Dee parked outside a fancy eating place. There was a sun patio with chairs and tables where people sat eating, talking, and drinking coffee. We passed a black man in boots, jeans, and with a heavy silver chain coiled around his neck. His motorcycle helmet, goggles and gloves were on the table. He was with a thin blond girl in a peppermint jumpsuit who sat sucking on her little finger. The place was crowded. Everybody looked young, scrubbed, bland. Nobody stared at us. Everybody was talking quietly.

We went inside and a pale slim boy with tiny buttocks, tight silver pants, an 8-inch studded belt and shiny gold blouse seated us. His ears were pierced and he wore tiny blue earrings. His pencil-thin mustache looked purple.

"Dee Dee," he said, "what is happening?"

"Breakfast, Donny."

"A drink, Donny," I said.

"I know what he needs, Donny. Give him a Golden Flower, double."

We ordered breakfast and Dee Dee said, "It will take a while to prepare. They cook everything to order here."

"Don't spend too much, Dee Dee."

"It all goes on the expense account."

She took out a little black book. "Now, let's see. Who am I taking to breakfast? Elton John?"

"Isn't he in Africa . . ."

"Oh, that's right. Well, how about Cat Stevens?"

"Who's that?"

"You don't know?"

"No."

"Well, I *discovered* him. You can be Cat Stevens."

DONNY BROUGHT the drink and he and Dee Dee talked. They seemed to know the same people. I didn't know any of them. It took a lot to excite me. I didn't care. I didn't like New York. I didn't like Hollywood. I didn't like rock music. I didn't like anything. Maybe I was afraid. That was it—I was afraid. I wanted to sit alone in a room with the shades down. I feasted upon that. I was a crank. I was a lunatic. And Lydia was gone.

I finished my drink and Dee Dee ordered another. I began to feel like a kept man and it felt great. It helped my blues. There is nothing worse than being broke and having your woman leave you. Nothing to drink, no job, just the walls, sitting there staring at the walls and thinking. That's how women got back at you, but it hurt and weakened them too. Or so I like to believe.

The breakfast was good. Eggs garnished with various fruits . . . pineapple, peaches, pears . . . some grated nuts, seasoning. It was a good breakfast. We finished and Dee Dee ordered me another drink. The thought of Lydia still remained inside of me, but Dee Dee was nice. Her conversation was decisive and entertaining. She was able to make me laugh, which I needed. My laughter was all there inside of me waiting to roar out: HAHAHAHAHA, o my god o my HAHAHAHA. It felt so good when it happened. Dee Dee knew something about life. Dee Dee knew that what happened to one happened to most of us. Our lives were not so different—even though we liked to think so.

Pain is strange. A cat killing a bird, a car accident, a fire. . . . Pain arrives, BANG, and there it is, it sits on you. It's real. And to anybody watching, you look foolish. Like you've suddenly become an idiot. There's no cure for it unless you know somebody who understands how you feel, and knows how to help.

We went back to the car. "I know just where to take you to cheer you up," said Dee Dee. I didn't answer. I was being catered to as if I was an invalid. Which I was.

I asked Dee Dee to stop at a bar. One of hers. The bartender knew her.

"This," she told me as we entered, "is where a lot of the script writers hang out. And some of the little-theatre people."

I disliked them all immediately, sitting around acting clever and superior. They nullified each other. The worst thing for a writer is to know another writer, and worse than that, to know a number of other writers. Like flies on the same turd.

"Let's get a table," I said. So there I was, a $65 a week writer sitting in a room with other writers, $1000 a week writers. Lydia, I thought, I am getting there. You'll be sorry. Some day I'll go into fancy restaurants and I'll be recognized. They'll have a special table for me in the back near the kitchen.

We got our drinks and Dee Dee looked at me. "You give good head. You give the best head I ever had."

"Lydia taught me. Then I added a few touches of my own."

A dark young boy jumped up and came over to our table. Dee Dee introduced us. The boy was from New York, wrote for the *Village Voice* and other New York newspapers. He and Dee Dee name-dropped a while and then he asked her, "What's your husband do?"

"I got a stable," I said. "Fighters. Four good Mexican boys. Plus one black boy, a real dancer. What do you weigh?"

"158. Were you a fighter? Your face looks like you caught a few."

"I've caught a few. We can put you in at 135. I need a southpaw lightweight."

"How'd you know I was a southpaw?"

"You're holding your cigarette in your left hand. Come on down to the Main Street gym. Monday AM. We'll start your training. Cigarettes are out. Put that son of a bitch out!"

"Listen, man, I'm a writer. I use a typewriter. You never read my stuff?"

"All I read is the metropolitan dailies—murders, rapes, fight results, swindles, jetliner crashes and Ann Landers."

"Dee Dee," he said, "I've got an interview with Rod Stewart in 30 minutes. I gotta go." He left.

Dee Dee ordered another round of drinks. "Why can't you be decent to people?" she asked.

"Fear," I said.

"HERE WE are," she said and drove her car into the Hollywood cemetery.

"Nice," I said, "real nice. I had forgotten all about death."

We drove around. Most of the tombs were above ground. They were like little houses, with pillars and front steps. And each had a locked iron door. Dee Dee parked and we got out. She tried one of the doors. I watched her behind wiggle as she worked at the door. I thought about Nietzsche. There we were: a German stallion and a Jewish mare. The Fatherland would adore me.

We got back into the M. Benz and Dee Dee parked outside of one of the bigger units. They were all stuck into the walls in there. Rows and rows of them. Some had flowers, in little vases, but most of the blooms were withered. The majority of the niches didn't have flowers. Some of them had husband and wife neatly side by side. In some cases one niche was empty and waiting. In all cases the husband was the one already dead.

Dee Dee took my hand and led me around the corner. There he was, down near the bottom, Rudolph Valentino. Dead 1926. Didn't live long. I decided to live to be 80. Think of being 80 and fucking an 18 year old girl. If there was any way to cheat the game of death, that was it.

Dee Dee lifted one of the flower vases and dropped it into her purse. The standard trip. Rip off whatever wasn't tied down. Everything belonged to everybody. We went outside and Dee Dee said, "I want to sit on Tyrone Power's bench. He was my favorite. I loved him!"

We went and sat on Tyrone's bench next to his grave. Then we got up and walked over to Douglas Fairbanks Sr.'s tomb. He had a good one. His own private reflector pool in front of the tomb. The pool was filled with water lillies and pollywogs. We walked up some stairs and there at the back of the tomb was a place to sit. Dee Dee and I sat. I noticed a crack in the wall of the tomb with small red ants running in and out. I watched the small red ants for a while, then put my arms around Dee Dee and kissed her, a good long long kiss. We were going to be good friends.

19

DEE DEE HAD to pick up her son at the airport. He was coming home from England for his vacation. He was 17, she told me, and his father was an ex-concert pianist. But he'd fallen for speed and coke, and later on burned his fingers in an accident. He could no longer play the piano. They'd been divorced for some time.

The son's name was Renny. Dee Dee had told him about me during several trans-Atlantic telephone conversations. We got to the airport as Renny's flight was disembarking. Dee Dee and Renny embraced. He was tall and thin, quite pale. A lock of hair hung over one eye. We shook hands.

I went to get the baggage while Renny and Dee Dee chatted. He addressed her as "Mommy." When we got back to the car he climbed into the back seat and said, "Mommy, did you get my bike?"

"I've ordered it. We'll pick it up tomorrow."

"Is it a good bike, Mommy? I want a ten-speed with a hand brake and pedal grips."

"It's a good bike, Renny."

"Are you sure it will be ready?"

We drove back. I stayed overnight. Renny had his own bedroom.

In the morning we all sat in the breakfast nook together waiting for the maid to arrive. Dee Dee finally got up to fix breakfast for us. Renny said, "Mommy, how do you break an egg?"

Dee Dee looked at me. She knew what I was thinking. I remained silent.

"All right, Renny, come here and I'll show you."

Renny walked over to the stove. Dee Dee picked up an egg. "You see, you just break the shell against the side of the pan . . . like this . . . and let the egg fall out of the shell into the pan . . . like this. . . ."

"Oh . . ."

"It's simple."

"And how do you cook it?"

"We fry it. In butter."

"Mommy, I can't eat that egg."

"Why?"

"Because the yoke is broken!"

Dee Dee turned around and looked at me. Her eyes said, "Hank, don't say a goddamned word."

A few mornings later found us all in the breakfast nook again. We were eating while the maid worked in the kitchen. Dee Dee said to Renny, "You've got your bike now. I want you to pick up a 6-pack sometime today. When I get home I want a Coke or two to drink."

"But, Mommy, those Cokes are heavy! Can't you get them?"

"Renny, I work all day and I'm tired. You get the Cokes."

"But, Mommy, there's a hill. I'll have to pedal over the hill."

"There's no hill. What hill?"

"Well, you can't see it with your *eyes*, but it's there. . . ."

"Renny, you get those Cokes, understand?"

Renny got up, walked to his bedroom and slammed the door. Dee Dee looked away. "He's testing me. He wants to see if I love him."

"I'll get the Cokes," I said.

"That's all right," said Dee Dee, "I'll get them."

Finally, none of us got them. . . .

DEE DEE and I were at my place a few days later picking up the mail and looking around when the phone rang. It was Lydia. "Hi," she said, "I'm in Utah."

"I got your note," I said.

"How are you doing?" she asked.

"Everything's all right."

"Utah's nice in the summer. You ought to come up here. We'll go camping. All my sisters are here."

"I can't get away right now."

"Why?"

"Well, I'm with Dee Dee."

"Dee Dee?"

"Well, yes . . ."

"I knew you'd use that phone number," she said. "I told you you'd use that number!"

Dee Dee was standing next to me. "Please tell her," she said, "to give me until September."

"Forget her," Lydia said. "To hell with her. You come up here and see me."

"I can't drop everything just because you phone. Besides," I said, "I'm giving Dee Dee until September."

"September?"
"Yes."

Lydia screamed. It was a long loud scream. Then she hung up.

AFTER THAT Dee Dee kept me away from my place. Once, while we were at my place going over the mail, I noticed the phone off the hook. "Never do that again," I told her.

Dee Dee took me for long rides up and down the coast. She took me on trips to the mountains. We went to garage sales, to movies, to rock concerts, to churches, to friends, to dinners and lunches, to magic shows, picnics and circuses. Her friends photographed us together.

The trip to Catalina was horrible. I waited with Dee Dee on the dock. I was really hungover. Dee Dee got me an Alka-Seltzer and a glass of water. The only thing that helped was a young girl sitting across from us. She had a beautiful body, long good legs, and she wore a mini-skirt. With the mini-skirt she wore long stockings, a garter belt, and she had on pink panties under the red skirt. She even wore high heeled shoes.

"You're looking at her, aren't you?" asked Dee Dee.
"I can't stop."
"She's a slut."
"Sure."

The slut got up and played pinball, wiggling her behind to help the balls fall in. Then she sat back down, showing more than ever.

THE SEAPLANE came in, unloaded, and then we stood out on the dock and waited to board. The seaplane was red, of 1936 vintage, had two propellers, one pilot and 8 or 10 seats.

If I don't puke in that thing, I thought, I will have fooled the world.

The girl in the mini-skirt wasn't getting on.

Why was it that every time you saw a woman like that you were always with another woman?

We got on, strapped ourselves in.

"Oh," said Dee Dee, "I'm so excited! I'm going up and sit with the pilot!"

"O.K."

So we took off and Dee Dee was up there sitting with the pilot. I could see her talking away. She did enjoy life or she appeared to. Lately it didn't mean much to me—I mean her excited and happy reaction to life—it irritated me somewhat, but mostly it left me without feeling. It didn't even bore me.

We flew and we landed, the landing was rough, we swung low along some cliffs and bounced and the spray went up. It was something like being in a speed boat. Then we taxied to another dock and Dee Dee came back and told me all about the seaplane and the pilot, and the conversation. There was a big piece cut out of the floor up there, and she'd asked the pilot, "Is this thing safe?" and he had answered, "Damned if I know."

Dee Dee had gotten us a hotel room right on the shore, on the top floor. There was no refrigeration so she got a plastic tub and packed ice in it for my beer. There was a black and white t.v. and a bathroom. Class.

We went for a walk along the shore. The tourists were of two types—either very young or very old. The old walked about in pairs, man and woman, in their sandals and dark shades and straw hats and walking shorts and wildly-colored shirts. They were fat and pale with blue veins in their legs and their faces were puffed and white in the sun. They sagged everywhere, folds and pouches of skin hung from their cheekbones and under their jowls.

The young were slim, and seemed made of smooth rubber. The girls had no breasts and tiny behinds and the boys had tender soft faces and grinned and blushed and laughed. But they all seemed contented, young high school people and old people. There was very little for them to do, but they lounged in the sun and seemed fulfilled.

Dee Dee went into the shops. She was delighted with the shops, buying beads, ashtrays, toy dogs, postcards, necklaces, figurines, and seemed happy with everything. "Oooh, *look!*" She talked to the shop owners. She seemed to like them. She promised one lady that she would write when she got back to the mainland. They had a mutual friend—a man who played percussion in a rock band.

Dee Dee bought a cage with two love birds and we went back to the hotel. I opened a beer and turned on the t.v. The selection was limited.

"Let's go for another walk," said Dee Dee. "It's so lovely outside."

"I'm going to sit here and rest," I said.

"You don't mind if I go without you?"

"It's all right."

She kissed me and left. I turned off the t.v. and opened another beer. Nothing to do on this island but get drunk. I walked to the window. On the beach below Dee Dee was sitting next to a young man, talking happily, smiling and gesturing with her hands. The young man grinned back. It felt good not to be part of that sort of thing. I was glad I wasn't in love, that I wasn't happy with the world. I like being at odds with everything. People in love often become edgy, dangerous. They lose their sense of perspective. They lose their sense of humor. They become nervous, psychotic bores. They even become killers.

Dee Dee was gone 2 or 3 hours. I looked at some t.v. and typed 2 or 3 poems on a portable typer. Love poems—about Lydia. I hid them in my suitcase. I drank some more beer.

Then Dee Dee knocked and entered. "Oh, I had the most *wonderful* time! First I went on the glass-bottom boat. We could see all the different fish in the sea, everything! Then I found another boat that takes people out to where their boats are moored. This young man let me ride for hours for a dollar! His back was sunburned and I rubbed it with lotion. He was *terribly* burned. We took people out to their boats. And you should have seen the people on those boats! Mostly old men, craggy old men, with young girls. The young girls all wore boots and were drunk and on dope, strung-out, moaning. Some of the old guys had young boys, but most of them had young girls, sometimes two or three or four young girls. Every boat stank of dope and booze and lechery. It was wonderful!"

"That does sound good. I wish I had your knack of turning up interesting people."

"You can go tomorrow. You can ride all day for a dollar."

"I'll pass."

"Did you write today?"

"A little."

"Was it good?"

"You never know until 18 days later."

Dee Dee went over and looked at the love birds, talked to them. She was a good woman. I liked her. She was really concerned about me, she wanted me to do well, she wanted me to write well, she wanted me to fuck well, look well. I could feel it. It was fine. Maybe we could fly to Hawaii together some day. I walked up behind her and kissed her on the right ear, down by the lobe.

"Oh, *Hank*," she said.

BACK IN L.A., after our week in Catalina, we were sitting around my place one evening, which was unusual. It was late at night. We were lying on my bed, naked, when the phone rang in the next room.

It was Lydia.

"Hank?"

"Yes?"

"Where've you been?"

"Catalina."

"With her?"

"Yes."

"Listen, after you told me about her I got mad. I had an affair. It was with a homosexual. It was awful."

"I've missed you, Lydia."

"I want to come back to L.A."

"That'd be good."

"If I come back will you give her up?"

"She's a good woman, but if you come back I'll give her up."

"I'm coming back. I love you, old man."

"I love you too."

We went on talking. I don't know how long we talked. When it was over I walked back into the bedroom. Dee Dee seemed asleep. "Dee Dee?" I asked. I lifted one of her arms. It felt very limp. The flesh felt like rubber. "Stop joking, Dee Dee, I know you're not asleep." She didn't move. I looked around and noticed her bottle of sleeping pills was empty. It had been full. I had tried those pills. Just one of them put you to sleep, only it was more like being knocked out and buried underground.

"You took the pills. . . ."

"I . . . don't . . . care . . . you're going back to her . . . I don't . . . care. . . .

I ran into the kitchen and got the dishpan, came back and placed it on the floor by the bed. Then I pulled Dee Dee's head and shoulders over the edge and stuck my fingers down her throat. She vomited. I lifted her up and let her breathe a moment, then repeated the process. I did it again and again. Dee Dee kept vomiting. Once, as I lifted her up, her teeth popped out. They lay there on the sheet, uppers and lowers.

"Oooh . . . my teeth," she said. Or tried to say.

"Don't worry about your teeth."

I stuck my fingers down her throat again. Then I pulled her back.

"I don'," she said, "wans ya to seee my teethhhs. . . ."

"They're all right, Dee Dee. They're really not bad."

"Ooooh . . ."

She revived long enough to put her teeth back in. "Take me home," she said, "I want to go home."

"I'll stay with you. I won't leave you alone tonight."

"But you will leave me, finally?"

"Let's get dressed," I said.

VALENTINO WOULD have kept both Lydia and Dee Dee. That's why he died so young.

20

LYDIA RETURNED AND found a nice apartment in the Burbank area. She seemed to care a lot more for me than before we parted. "My husband had this big cock and that's all he had. He had no personality, no vibes. Just a big cock and he thought that was all he had to have. But Christ he was dull! With you, I keep getting vibes . . . this electric feedback, it never stops." We were on the bed together.

"And I didn't even know he had a big cock because his cock was the first one I had ever seen." She was examining me closely. "I thought they were all like that."

"Lydia . . ."

"What is it?"

"I've got to tell you something."

"What is it?"

"I've got to go see Dee Dee."

"*Go see Dee Dee?*"

"Don't be funny. There's a reason."

"You said it was all over."

"It is. I just don't want to let her down too hard. I want to explain to her what happened. People are too cold with each other. I don't want her back, I just want to try to explain what happened, so she'll understand."

"You want to fuck her."

"No, I don't want to fuck her. I hardly wanted to fuck her when I was with her. I just want to explain."

"I don't like it. It sounds . . . *icky* . . . to me."

"Let me do it. Please. I just want to clear things up. I'll be back soon."

"All right. But make it soon."

I GOT into the Volks, cut over to Fountain, went a few miles, then took a north at Bronson and cut up to where the rents were high. I parked outside, got out. I walked up the long flight of stairs and rang the bell. Bianca answered the door. I remembered one night she had answered the door naked and I had grabbed her and as we were kissing Dee Dee came down and said, "What the hell's going on here?"

This time it wasn't like that. Bianca said, "What do you want?"

"I want to see Dee Dee. I want to talk to her."

"She's sick. Really sick. I don't think you should get to see her after the way you've treated her. You're a real grade-A son of a bitch."

"I just want to talk to her a while, to explain things."

"All right. She's in her bedroom."

I walked down the hall and into the bedroom. Dee Dee was on the bed in just her panties. One arm was flung over her eyes. Her breasts looked good. There was an empty pint of whiskey by her bed and a pan on the floor. The pan smelled of vomit and booze.

"Dee Dee . . ."

She lifted her arm. "What? Hank, you've come back?"

"No, wait, I just want to talk to you. . . ."

"Oh Hank, I've missed you something awful. I've been nearly crazy, the pain has been awful. . . ."

"I want to make it easier. That's why I came by. I may be stupid, but I don't believe in outright cruelty. . . ."

"You don't know how I've felt. . . ."

"I know. I've been there."

"Want a drink?" she pointed.

I picked up the empty pint and sadly put it down again. "There's too much coldness in the world," I told her. "If people would only talk things out together it would help."

"Stay with me, Hank. Don't go back to her, please. Please. I've lived long enough to know how to be a good woman. You know that. I'd be good to you and for you."

"Lydia has a grip on me. I can't explain it."

"She's a flirt. She's impulsive. She'll leave you."

"Maybe that's some of the attraction."

"You want a whore. You're afraid of love."

"You might be right."

"Just kiss me. Would it be too much to ask you to kiss me?"

"No."

I stretched out next to her. We embraced. Dee Dee's mouth smelled of vomit. She kissed, we kissed and she held me. I broke away as gently as I could.

"Hank," she said, "Stay with me! Don't go back to her! Look, *I have nice legs!*"

Dee Dee lifted one of her legs and showed it to me. "And I have nice ankles too! Look!"

She showed me her ankles.

I was sitting on the edge of the bed. "I can't stay with you, Dee Dee—"

She sat up and began punching me. Her fists were as hard as rocks. She threw punches with both hands. I sat there as she landed blows. She hit me above the eye, in the eye, on the forehead and cheeks. I even caught one in the throat. "Oh, you bastard! Bastard, bastard, bastard! I HATE YOU!"

I grabbed her wrists. "All right, Dee Dee, that's enough." She fell back on the bed as I got up and walked out, down the hall and out the door.

WHEN I got back Lydia was sitting in an armchair. Her face looked dark. "You've been gone a long time. Look at me! You *fucked* her, didn't you?"

"No, I didn't."

"You were gone an awful long time. Look, she scratched your face!"

"I tell you, nothing happened."

"Take off your shirt. I want to look at your back!"

"Oh, shit, Lydia."

"Take off your shirt and undershirt."

I took them off. She walked around behind me.

"What's that scratch on your back?"

"What scratch?"

"There's a long one there . . . from a woman's fingernail."

"If it's there you put it there. . . ."

"All right. I know one way to find out."

"How?"

"Let's go to bed."
"All *right!*"

I PASSED the test, but afterwards I thought, how can a man test a woman's fidelity? It seemed unfair.

21

I KEPT GETTING letters from a lady who lived only a mile or so away. She signed them Nicole. She said she had read some of my books and liked them. I answered one of her letters and she responded with an invitation to visit. One afternoon, without saying anything to Lydia, I got into the Volks and drove on over. She had a flat over a dry cleaner's on Santa Monica Boulevard. Her door was on the street and I could see a stairway through the glass. I rang the bell. "Who is it?" came a woman's voice through a little tin speaker. "I'm Chinaski," I said. A buzzer sounded and I pushed the door open.

Nicole stood at the top of the stairs looking down at me. She had a cultured, almost tragic face and wore a long green housedress cut low in front. Her body seemed to be very good. She looked at me with large dark brown eyes. There were lots of tiny wrinkles around her eyes, perhaps from too much drinking or crying.

"Are you alone?" I asked.

"Yes," she smiled, "come on up."

I went up. It was spacious, two bedrooms, with very little furniture. I noticed a small bookcase and a rack of classical records. I sat on the couch. She sat next to me. "I just finished," she said, "reading *The Life of Picasso.*"

There were several copies of *The New Yorker* on the coffee table.

"Can I fix you some tea?" Nicole asked.

"I'll go out and get something to drink."

"That's not necessary. I have something."

"What?"

CHARLES BUKOWSKI

"Some good red wine?"

"I'd like some," I said.

Nicole got up and walked into the kitchen. I watched her move. I had always liked women in long dresses. She moved gracefully. She seemed to have a lot of class. She returned with two glasses and the bottle of wine and poured. She offered me a Benson and Hedges. I lit one.

"Do you read *The New Yorker*?" she asked. "They print some good stories."

"I don't agree."

"What's wrong with them?"

"They're too educated."

"I like them."

"Well, shit," I said.

We sat drinking and smoking.

"Do you like my apartment?"

"Yes, it's nice."

"It reminds me of some of the places I've had in Europe. I like the space, the light."

"Europe, huh?"

"Yes, Greece, Italy . . . Greece, mostly."

"Paris?"

"Oh yes, I liked Paris. London, no."

Then she told me about herself. Her family had lived in New York City. Her father was a communist, her mother a seamstress in a sweatshop. Her mother had worked the front machine, she was number one, the best of all of them. Tough and likeable. Nicole was self-educated, had grown up in New York, had somehow met a famous doctor, married, lived with him for ten years, then divorced him. She now received only $400 a month alimony, and it was difficult to manage. She couldn't afford her apartment, but she liked it too much to leave.

"Your writing," she said to me, "it's so raw. It's like a sledge hammer, and yet it has humor and tenderness. . . ."

"Yeah," I said.

I put my drink down and looked at her. I cupped her chin in my hand and drew her towards me. I gave her the tiniest kiss.

64

Nicole continued talking. She told me quite a few interesting stories, some of which I decided to use myself, either as stories or poems. I watched her breasts as she bent forward and poured drinks. It's like a movie, I thought, like a fucking movie. It seemed funny to me. It felt as if we were on camera. I liked it. It was better than the racetrack, it was better than the boxing matches. We kept drinking. Nicole opened a new bottle. She talked on. It was easy to listen to her. There was wisdom and some laughter in each of her tales. Nicole was impressing me more than she knew. That worried me, somewhat.

We walked out on the veranda with our drinks and watched the afternoon traffic. She was talking about Huxley and Lawrence in Italy. What shit. I told her that Knut Hamsun had been the world's greatest writer. She looked at me, astonished that I'd heard of him, then agreed. We kissed on the veranda, and I could smell the exhaust from the cars in the street below. Her body felt good against mine. I knew we weren't going to fuck right away, but I also knew that I would be coming back. Nicole knew it too.

22

LYDIA'S SISTER ANGELA came to town from Utah to see Lydia's new house. Lydia had made a down payment on a little place and the monthly payments were very low. It was a very good buy. The man who sold the house believed he was going to die and he had sold it much too cheap. There was an upstairs bedroom for the children, and an extremely large backyard filled with trees and clumps of bamboo.

Angela was the oldest of the sisters, the most sensible, with the best body, and was the most realistic. She sold real estate. But there was the problem of where to put Angela. We didn't have room. Lydia suggested Marvin.

"Marvin?" I asked.

"Yes, Marvin," said Lydia.

"All right, let's go," I said.

We all climbed into Lydia's orange Thing. The Thing. That's what we called her car. It looked like a tank, very old and ugly. It was late evening. We had already phoned Marvin. He had said he'd be home all evening.

We drove down to the beach and there was his little house by the shore. "Oh," said Angela, "what a nice house."

"He's rich, too," said Lydia.

"And he writes good poetry," I said.

We got out. Marvin was in there with his saltwater fish tanks and his paintings. He painted pretty well. For a rich kid he had survived nicely, he had come through. I made the introductions. Angela walked around looking at Marvin's paintings. "Oh, very nice." Angela painted too, but she wasn't very good.

I had brought some beer and had a pint of whiskey hidden in my coat pocket which I nipped on from time to time. Marvin brought out some more beer and a mild flirtation began between Marvin and Angela. Marvin seemed eager enough but Angela seemed inclined to laugh at him. She liked him, but not well enough to fuck him right away. We drank and talked. Marvin had bongo drums and a piano and some grass. He had a good, comfortable house. In a house like this I could write better, I thought, my luck would be better. You could hear the ocean and there were no neighbors to complain about the noise of a typewriter.

I continued to nip at the whiskey. We stayed 2 or 3 hours, then left. Lydia took the freeway back.

"Lydia," I said, "you fucked Marvin, didn't you?"

"What are you talking about?"

"The time you went over there late at night, alone."

"Goddamn you, I don't want to hear that!"

"Well, it's true, you fucked him!"

"Listen, if you keep it up I'm not going to stand for it!"

"You fucked him."

Angela looked frightened. Lydia drove over to the shoulder of the freeway, stopped the car and pushed the door open on my side. "Get out!" she said.

I got out. The car drove off. I walked along the shoulder of the freeway. I took the pint out and had a nip. I walked along about 5 minutes when the Thing pulled up alongside me. Lydia opened the door. "Get in." I got in.

"Don't say a word."

"You fucked him. I know you did."

"Oh Christ!"

Lydia drove back on to the shoulder of the freeway and pushed the door open again. "Get out!"

I got out. I walked along the shoulder. Then I came to an offramp that led to a deserted street. I walked down the offramp and along the street. It was very dark. I looked into the windows of some of the houses. Apparently I was in a black district. I saw some lights ahead at an intersection. There was a hot dog stand. I walked up to it. A black man was behind the counter. There was nobody else around. I ordered coffee. "Goddamned women," I said to him. "They are beyond all reason. My girl let me off on the freeway. Want a drink?"

"Sure," he said.

He took a good hit and handed it back.

"You got a phone?" I asked. "I'll pay you."

"Is it a local call?"

"Yes."

"No charge."

He pulled a phone from underneath the counter and handed it to me. I took a drink and handed him the bottle. He took one.

I called the Yellow Cab Co., gave them the location. My friend had a kind and intelligent face. Goodness could be found sometimes in the middle of hell. We passed the bottle back and forth as I waited for the cab. When the cab arrived I got into the back and gave the cabby Nicole's address.

23

I BLACKED OUT after that. I guess I had consumed more whiskey than I thought. I don't remember arriving at Nicole's. I awakened in the morning with my back to somebody in a strange bed. I looked at the wall facing me and there was a large decorative letter hanging there. It said "N." The "N" was for "Nicole." I felt sick. I went to the bathroom. I used Nicole's toothbrush, gagged. I washed my face, combed my hair, crapped and pissed, washed my hands and drank a great deal of water from the bathroom faucet. Then I went back to bed. Nicole got up, did her toilet, came back. She faced me. We began to kiss and fondle one another.

I am innocent in my fashion, Lydia, I thought. I am faithful to thee in my fashion.

No oral sex. My stomach was too upset. I mounted the famous doctor's ex-wife. The cultured world traveler. She had the Brontë sisters in her bookcase. We both liked Carson McCullers. *The Heart Is a Lonely Hunter.* I gave her 3 or 4 particularly mean rips and she gasped. Now she knew a writer firsthand. Not a very well-known writer, of course, but I managed to pay the rent and that was astonishing. One day she'd be in one of my books. I was fucking a culture-bitch. I felt myself nearing a climax. I pushed my tongue into her mouth, kissed her, and climaxed. I rolled off feeling foolish. I held her a while, then she went into the bathroom. She would have been a better fuck in Greece, maybe. America was a shitty place to fuck.

AFTER THAT I visited Nicole 2 or 3 times a week in the mid-afternoons. We drank wine, talked, and now and then made love. I found I wasn't particularly interested in her, it was just something to do. Lydia and I had made up the next day. She would question me about where I went in the afternoon. "I've been to the supermarket," I'd tell her, and it was true. I'd go to the supermarket first.

"I've never seen you spend so much time at the supermarket."

I got drunk one night and mentioned to Lydia that I knew a certain Nicole. I told her where Nicole lived, but that "not much was going on." Why I told her this was not quite clear to me, but when one drinks one sometimes thinks unclearly. . . .

ONE AFTERNOON I was coming from the liquor store and had just reached Nicole's. I was carrying two 6-packs of bottled beer and a pint of whiskey. Lydia and I had recently had another fight and I had decided to stay the night with Nicole. I was walking along, already a bit intoxicated, when I heard someone run up behind me. I turned. It was Lydia. "Ha!" she said. "Ha!"

She grabbed the bag of liquor out of my hand and began pulling out the beer bottles. She smashed them on the pavement one by one. They made large explosions. Santa Monica Boulevard is very busy. The afternoon traffic was just beginning to build up. All this action was taking place just outside Nicole's door. Then Lydia reached the pint of whiskey. She held it up and screamed up at me, "Ha! You were going to drink this and then you were going to FUCK her!" She smashed the pint on the cement.

Nicole's door was open and Lydia ran up the stairway. Nicole was standing at the top of the stairs. Lydia began hitting Nicole with her large purse. It had long straps and she swung it as hard as she could. "He's *my* man! He's *my* man! You stay away from my man!"

Then Lydia ran down past me, out the door and into the street.

"Good god," said Nicole, "who was that?"

"That was Lydia. Let me have a broom and a large paper bag."

I went down into the street and began sweeping up the broken glass and placing it in the brown paper bag. That bitch has gone too far this time, I thought. I'll go and buy more liquor. I'll stay the night with Nicole, maybe a couple of nights.

I was bent over picking up the glass when I heard a strange sound behind me. I looked around. It was Lydia in the Thing. She had it up on the sidewalk and was driving straight towards me at about 30 MPH. I leaped aside as the car went by, missing me by an inch. The car ran down to the end of the block, bumped down off the curb, continued up the street, then took a right at the next corner and was gone.

I went back to sweeping up the glass. I got it all swept up and put away. Then I reached down into the original paper bag and found one undamaged bottle of beer. It looked very good. I really needed it. I was about to unscrew the cap when someone grabbed it out of my hand. It was Lydia again. She ran up to Nicole's door with the bottle and hurled it at the glass. She hurled it with such velocity that it went straight through like a large bullet, not smashing the entire window but leaving just a round hole.

Lydia ran off and I walked up the stairway. Nicole was still standing there. "For god's sake, Chinaski, leave with her before she kills everybody!"

I turned and walked back down the stairway. Lydia was sitting in her car at the curbing with the engine running. I opened the door and got in. She drove off. Neither of us spoke a word.

24

I BEGAN RECEIVING letters from a girl in New York City. Her name was Mindy. She had run across a couple of my books, but the best thing about her letters was that she seldom mentioned writing except to say that she was not a writer. She wrote about things in general and men and sex in particular. Mindy was 25, wrote in longhand, and the handwriting was stable, sensible, yet humorous. I answered her letters and was always glad to find one of hers in my mailbox. Most people are much better at saying things in letters than in conversation, and some people can write artistic, inventive letters, but when they try a poem or story or novel they become pretentious.

Then Mindy sent some photographs. If they were faithful she was quite beautiful. We wrote for several more weeks and then she mentioned that she had a 2 week vacation coming up.

Why don't you fly out? I suggested.

All right, she replied.

We began to phone one another. Finally she gave me her arrival date at L.A. International.

I'll be there, I told her, nothing will stop me.

25

I KEPT THE date in mind. It was never any problem creating a split with Lydia. I was naturally a loner, content just to live with a woman, eat with her, sleep with her, walk down the street with her. I didn't want conversation, or to go anywhere except the racetrack or the boxing matches. I didn't understand t.v. I felt foolish paying money to go into a movie theatre and sit with other people to share their emotions. Parties sickened me. I hated the game-playing, the dirty play, the flirting, the amateur drunks, the bores. But parties, dancing, small talk energized Lydia. She considered herself a sexpot. But she was a little too obvious. So our arguments often grew out of my wish for no-people-at-all versus her wish for as-many-people-as-often-as-possible.

A couple of days before Mindy's arrival I started it. We were on the bed together.

"Lydia, for Christ's sake, why are you so stupid? Don't you realize I'm a loner? A recluse? I have to be that way to write."

"How can you learn anything about people if you don't meet them?"

"I already know all about them."

"Even when we go out to eat in a restaurant, you keep your head down, you don't *look* at anybody."

"Why make myself sick?"

"I *observe* people," she said. "I study them."

"Shit!"

"You're afraid of people!"

"I hate them."

"How can you be a writer? You don't *observe!*"

"O.K., I don't look at people, but I earn the rent with my writing. It beats tending sheep."

"You're not going to last. You'll never make it. You're doing it all wrong."

"That's *why* I'm making it."

"*Making* it? Who the hell knows who you are? Are you famous like *Mailer*? Like *Capote*?"

"They can't write."

"But *you* can! Only you, Chinaski, can write!"

"Yes, that's how I feel."

"Are you famous? If you went to New York City, would anybody know you?"

"Listen I don't care about that. I just want to go on writing. I don't need trumpets."

"You'd take all the trumpets you could get."

"Maybe."

"You like to pretend you're already famous."

"I have always acted the same way, even before I wrote."

"You're the most unknown famous man I ever met."

"I'm just not ambitious."

"You are but you're lazy. You want it for nothing. When do you write anyhow? When do you do it? You're always in bed or drunk or at the racetrack."

"I don't know. It's not important."

"What's important then?"

"You tell me," I said.

"Well, I'll tell you what's important!" Lydia said. "We haven't had a party for a long time. I haven't seen any people for a long time! I LIKE people! My sisters LOVE parties. They'll drive a thousand miles to go to a party! That's how we were raised in Utah! There's nothing wrong with parties. It's just people LETTING GO and having a good time! You've got this crazy idea in your head. You think having fun leads to *fucking!* Jesus Christ, people are *decent!* You just don't know how to have a good time!"

"I don't like people," I said.

Lydia leaped off of the bed. "Jesus, you make me *sick!*"

"All right, then, I'll give you some room."

I swung my legs off the bed and began putting my shoes on.

"Some room?" Lydia asked. "What do you mean by 'some room'?"

"I mean, I am getting the hell out of here!"

"O.K., but listen to *this*: if you walk out the door now you won't see me again!"

"Fair enough," I said.

I stood up, walked to the door, opened it, closed it and walked down to the Volks. I started the engine and drove off. I had made some room for Mindy.

26

I SAT IN the airport and waited. You never knew about photos. You could never tell. I was nervous. I felt like vomiting. I lit a cigarette and gagged. Why did I do these things? I didn't want her now. And Mindy was flying all the way from New York City. I knew plenty of women. Why always more women? What was I trying to do? New affairs were exciting but they were also hard work. The first kiss, the first fuck had some drama. People were interesting at first. Then later, slowly but surely, all the flaws and madness would manifest themselves. I would become less and less to them; they would mean less and less to me.

I was old and I was ugly. Maybe that's why it felt so good to stick it into young girls. I was King Kong and they were lithe and tender. Was I trying to screw my way past death? By being with young girls did I hope I wouldn't grow old, feel old? I just didn't want to age badly, simply quit, be dead before death itself arrived.

Mindy's plane landed and taxied in. I felt I was in danger. Women knew me beforehand because they had read my books. I had exposed myself. On the other hand, I knew nothing of them. I was the real gambler. I could get killed, I could get my balls cut off. Chinaski without balls. *Love Poems of a Eunuch.*

I stood waiting for Mindy. The passengers came out of the gate.

Oh, I hope *she's* not the one.

Or her.

Or especially her.

Now that one would be fine! Look at those legs, that behind, those eyes. . . .

One of them moved towards me. I hoped it was her. She was the best of the whole damned lot. I couldn't be that lucky. She walked up to me and smiled. "I'm Mindy."

"I'm glad you're Mindy."

"I'm glad you're Chinaski."

"Do you have to wait for your baggage?"

"Yes, I brought enough for a long stay!"

"Let's wait in the bar."

We walked in and found a table. Mindy ordered a vodka and tonic. I ordered a vodka-7. Ah, almost in tune. I lit her cigarette. She looked fine. Almost virginal. It was difficult to believe. She was small, blond and perfectly put together. She was more natural than sophisticated. I found it easy to look at her eyes—blue-green. She wore 2 tiny earrings. And she wore high heels. I had told Mindy that high heels excited me.

"Well," she said, "are you frightened?"

"Not so much anymore. I like you."

"You look much better than your photos," she said. "I don't think you're ugly at all."

"Thanks."

"Oh, I don't mean you're handsome, not the way people think of handsome. Your face seems kind. But your eyes—they're beautiful. They're wild, crazy, like some animal peering out of a forest on fire. God, something like that. I'm not very good with words."

"I think that you're beautiful," I said. "And very nice. I feel good around you. I think it's good that we're together. Drink up. We need another. You're like your letters."

We had the second drink and went down for the luggage. I was proud to be with Mindy. She walked with style. So many women with good bodies just slouched along like overloaded creatures. Mindy flowed.

I kept thinking, this is too good. This is simply not possible.

BACK AT my place Mindy took a bath and changed clothes. She came out in a light blue dress. She had changed her hair style, just a bit. We sat on the couch together with the vodka and the vodka mix. "Well," I said, "I'm still scared. I'm going to get a little drunk."

"Your place is just the way I thought it would be," she said.

She was looking at me, smiling. I reached out and touched her just behind the neck, moved her towards me, and gave her a light kiss.

The phone rang. It was Lydia.

"What are you doing?"

"I'm with a friend."

"It's a woman, isn't it?"

"Lydia, our relationship is over," I said. "You know that."

"IT'S A WOMAN, ISN'T IT?"

"Yes."

"Well, all right."

"All right. Goodbye."

"Goodbye," she said.

Lydia's tone had suddenly calmed down. I felt better. Her violence frightened me. She always claimed that I was the jealous one, and I was often jealous, but when I saw things working against me I simply became disgusted and withdrew. Lydia was different. She reacted. She was the Head Cheerleader at the Game of Violence.

But by her tone I knew that she had given up. That she was not enraged. I knew that voice.

"That was my ex," I told Mindy.

"Is it over?"

"Yes."

"Does she still love you?"

"I think so."

"Then it's not over."

"It's over."

"Should I stay?"

"Of course. Please."

"You're not just using me? I've read all those love poems . . . to Lydia."

"I *was* in love. And I'm not using you."

Mindy pressed her body against me and kissed me. It was a long kiss. My cock rose. I had recently been taking a lot of vitamin E. I had my own ideas about sex. I was constantly horny and masturbated continually. I'd make love to Lydia and then come back to my place and masturbate in the morning. The thought of sex as something forbidden excited me beyond all reason. It was like one animal knifing another into submission.

When I came I felt it was in the face of everything decent, white sperm dripping down over the heads and souls of my dead parents. If I had been born a woman I would certainly have been a prostitute. Since I had been born a man, I craved women constantly, the lower the better. And yet women—good women—frightened me because they eventually wanted your soul, and what was left of mine, I wanted to keep. Basically I craved prostitutes, base women, because they were deadly and hard and made no personal demands. Nothing was lost when they left. Yet at the same time I yearned for a gentle, good woman, despite the overwhelming price. Either way I was lost. A strong man would give up both. I wasn't strong. So I continued to struggle with women, with the idea of women.

MINDY AND I finished the bottle and then went to bed. I kissed her for a while, then apologized, and drew away. I was too drunk to perform. One hell of a great lover. I promised her many great experiences in the near future, then fell asleep with her body pressed against me.

In the morning I awakened, sickened. I looked at Mindy, naked next to me. Even then, after all the drinking, she was a miracle. Never had I known a young girl so beautiful and at the same time so gentle and intelligent. Where were her men? Where had they failed?

I went into the bathroom and tried to get cleaned up. I gagged on Lavoris. I shaved and put on some shaving lotion. I wet my hair and combed it. I went to the refrigerator, took a 7-UP, drank it down.

I went back to the bed and climbed in. Mindy was warm, her body was warm. She seemed to be asleep. I liked that. I rubbed my lips against hers, softly. My cock rose. I felt her breasts against me. I took one and sucked on it. I felt the nipple harden. Mindy stirred. I reached down and felt along her belly, down towards the cunt. I began rubbing her cunt, easily.

It's like making a rosebud open, I thought. This has meaning. This is good. It's like two insects in a garden moving slowly towards each other. The male works his slow magic. The female slowly opens. I like it, I like it. Two bugs. Mindy is opening, she is getting wet. She is beautiful. Then I mounted her. I slid it in, my mouth on hers.

27

WE DRANK ALL day and that night I tried again to make love to Mindy. I was astounded and dismayed to find she had a large pussy. An extra large pussy. I hadn't noticed it the night before. That was a tragedy. Woman's greatest sin. I worked and I worked. Mindy lay there as if she was enjoying it. I hoped to god she was. I began to sweat. My back ached. I was dizzy, sick. Her pussy seemed to get larger. I couldn't feel anything. It was like trying to fuck a large, loose paper bag. I was just barely touching the sides of her cunt. It was agony, it was relentless work without a reward. I felt damned. I didn't want to hurt her feelings. I desperately wanted to come. It wasn't just the drinking. I performed better than most when drinking. I heard my heart. I felt my heart. I felt it in my chest. I felt it in my throat. I felt it in my head. I couldn't bear it. I rolled off with a gasp.

"Sorry, Mindy, Jesus Christ, I'm sorry."

"It's all right, Hank," she said.

I rolled over on my stomach. I stank with sweat. I got up and poured two drinks. We sat upright in bed and drank the drinks, side by side. I couldn't understand how I had managed to come the first time. We had a problem. All that beauty, all that gentleness, all that goodness, and we had a problem. I was unable to tell Mindy what it was. I didn't know how to tell her she had a big cunt. Maybe nobody had ever told her.

"It will be better when I'm not drinking so much," I told her.

"Please don't worry, Hank."

"O.K."

We went to sleep or we pretended to go to sleep. Finally I did. . . .

28

MINDY STAYED ABOUT a week. I introduced her to my friends. We went places. But nothing was resolved. I couldn't climax. She didn't seem to mind. It was strange.

Around 10:45 PM one evening Mindy was drinking in the front room and reading a magazine. I was lying on the bed in just my shorts, drunk, smoking, a drink on the chair. I was staring at the blue ceiling, not feeling or thinking about anything.

There was a knock on the front door.

Mindy said, "Should I get it?"

"Sure," I said, "go ahead."

I heard Mindy open the door. Then I heard Lydia's voice. "I just came over to check out my competition."

Oh, I thought, this is *nice*. I'll get up and pour them both a drink, we'll all drink together and talk. I like my women to understand each other.

Then I heard Lydia say: "You're a *cute* little thing, aren't you?"

Then I heard Mindy scream. And Lydia screamed. I heard scuffling, grunts, bodies flying. Furniture was upset. Mindy screamed again—the scream of one being attacked. Lydia screamed—the tigress at the, kill. I leaped out of bed. I was going to separate them. I ran into the front room in my shorts. It was a hair-pulling, spitting, scratching, mad scene. I ran over to pull them apart. I stumbled over one of my shoes on the rug, fell heavily. Mindy ran out the door with Lydia right behind. They ran down the walk toward the street. I heard another scream.

Several minutes passed. I got up and closed the door. Evidently Mindy had gotten away because suddenly Lydia walked in. She sat down in a chair near the door. She looked at me.

"I'm sorry. I've pissed myself."

It was true. There was a dark stain in her crotch and one pant leg was soaked.

"It's all right," I said.

I poured Lydia a drink and she sat there holding it in her hand. I couldn't hold my drink in my hand. No one spoke. A short time later there was a knock on the door. I got up in my shorts and opened it. My huge, white, flabby belly hung out over the top of the shorts. Two policemen stood at the door.

"Hello," I said.

"We're answering a disturbance of the peace call."

"Just a little family argument," I said.

"We've got some details," said the cop standing closest to me. "There are two women."

"There usually are," I said.

"All right," said the first cop. "I just want to ask you one question."

"O.K."

"Which of the two women do you want?"

"I'll take that one." I pointed to Lydia sitting in the chair, all pissed over herself.

"All right, sir, are you sure?"

"I'm sure."

The cops walked off and there I was with Lydia again.

29

THE PHONE RANG the next morning. Lydia had gone back to her place. It was Bobby, the kid who lived in the next block and worked in the porno bookstore. "Mindy's down here. She wants you to come and talk to her."

"All right."

I walked over with 3 bottles of beer. Mindy was dressed in high heels and a black see-through outfit from Frederick's. It resembled a doll's dress and you could see her black panties. There was no brassiere. Valerie wasn't around. I sat down and twisted the beer caps off, passed the bottles.

CHARLES BUKOWSKI

"Are you going back to Lydia, Hank?" Mindy asked.

"Sorry, yes. I'm back."

"That was rotten, what happened. I thought you and Lydia were finished?"

"I thought we were. Those things are very strange."

"All my clothes are down at your place. I'll have to come get them."

"Of course."

"Are you sure she's gone?"

"Yes."

"She acts like a bull, that woman, she acts like a dyke."

"I don't think she is."

Mindy got up to go to the bathroom. Bobby looked at me. "I fucked her," he said. "Don't blame her. She had no other place to go."

"I don't blame her."

"Valerie took her to Frederick's to cheer her up. Got her a new outfit."

Mindy came out of the bathroom. She'd been crying.

"Mindy," I said, "I've got to go."

"I'll be down later for my clothes."

I got up and walked out the door. Mindy followed me out there. "Hold me," she said.

I held her. She was crying.

"You're *never* going to forget me . . . *never!*"

I walked back to my place thinking, I wonder if Bobby fucked Mindy? Bobby and Valerie were into lots of strange new things. I didn't care for their lack of common feeling. It was the *way* they did everything without any show of emotion. The same way another person might yawn or boil a potato.

30

To PACIFY LYDIA I agreed to go to Muleshead, Utah. Her sister was camping in the mountains. The sisters actually owned much of the land. It had been inherited from their father. Glendoline, one of the sisters, had a tent pitched in the woods. She was writing a novel, *The Wild Woman of the Mountains*. The other sisters were to arrive any day. Lydia and I arrived first. We had a pup tent. We squeezed in there the first night and the mosquitoes squeezed in with us. It was terrible.

The next morning we sat around the campfire. Glendoline and Lydia cooked breakfast. I had purchased $40 worth of groceries which included several 6-packs of beer. I had them cooling in a mountain spring. We finished breakfast. I helped with the dishes and then Glendoline brought out her novel and read to us. It wasn't really bad, but it was very unprofessional and needed a lot of polishing. Glendoline presumed that the reader was as fascinated by her life as she was—which was a deadly mistake. The other deadly mistakes she had made were too numerous to mention.

I WALKED to the spring and came back with 3 bottles of beer. The girls said no, they didn't want any. They were very anti-beer. We discussed Glendoline's novel. I figured that anybody who would read their novel aloud to others had to be suspect. If that wasn't the old kiss of death, nothing was.

The conversation shifted and the girls started chatting about men, parties, dancing, and sex. Glendoline had a high, excited voice, and laughed nervously, laughed constantly. She was in her mid-forties, quite fat and very sloppy. Besides that, just like me, she was simply ugly.

Glendoline must have talked non-stop for over an hour, entirely about sex. I began to get dizzy. She waved her arms over her head, "I'M THE WILD WOMAN OF THE MOUNTAINS! O WHERE O WHERE IS THE MAN, THE REAL MAN WITH THE COURAGE TO TAKE ME?"

Well, he's certainly not here, I thought.

I looked at Lydia. "Let's go for a walk."

"No," she said, "I want to read this book." It was called *Love and Orgasm: A Revolutionary Guide to Sexual Fulfillment*.

"All right," I said, "I'll take a walk then."

* * *

I WALKED up to the mountain spring. I reached in for another beer, opened it and sat there drinking. I was trapped in the mountains and woods with two crazy women. They took all the joy out of fucking by talking about it all the time. I liked to fuck too, but it wasn't my religion. There were too many ridiculous and tragic things about it. People didn't seem to know how to handle it. So they made a toy out of it. A toy that destroyed people.

The main thing, I decided, was to find the right woman. But how? I had a red notebook and a pen with me. I scribbled a meditative poem into it. Then I walked up to the lake. Vance Pastures, the place was called. The sisters owned most of it. I had to take a shit. I took off my pants and squatted in the brush with the flies and the mosquitoes. I'd take the conveniences of the city any time. I had to wipe with leaves. I walked over to the lake and stuck one foot in the water. It was ice cold.

Be a man, old man. Enter.

My skin was ivory white. I felt very old, very soft. I moved out into the ice water. I went in up to my waist, then I took a deep breath and leaped forward. I was all the way in! The mud swirled up from the bottom and got into my ears, my mouth, my hair. I stood there in the muddy water, my teeth chattering.

I waited a long time for the water to settle and clear. Then I walked back out. I got dressed and made my way along the edge of the lake. When I got to the end of the lake I heard a sound like that of a waterfall. I went into a forest, moving toward the sound. I had to climb around some rocks across a gully. The sound came closer and closer. The flies and mosquitoes swarmed all over me. The flies were large and angry and hungry, much larger than city flies, and they knew a meal when they saw one.

I pushed my way through some thick brush and there it was: my first real honest-to-Christ waterfall. The water just poured down the mountain and over a rocky ledge. It was beautiful. It kept coming and coming. That water was coming from somewhere. And it was running off somewhere. There were 3 or 4 streams that probably led to the lake.

WOMEN

Finally I got tired of watching it and decided to go back. I also decided to take a different route back, a shortcut. I worked my way down to the opposite side of the lake and cut off toward camp. I knew about where it was. I still had my red notebook. I stopped and wrote another poem, less meditative, then I went on. I kept walking. The camp didn't appear. I walked some more. I looked around for the lake. I couldn't find the lake, I didn't know where it was. Suddenly it hit me: I was LOST. Those horny sex bitches had driven me out of my mind and now I was LOST. I looked around. There was the backdrop of mountains and all around me were trees and brush. There was no center, no starting point, no connection between anything. I felt fear, real fear. Why had I let them take me out of my city, my Los Angeles? A man could call a cab there, he could telephone. There were reasonable solutions to reasonable problems.

Vance Pastures stretched out around me for miles and miles. I threw away my red notebook. What a way for a writer to die! I could see it in the newspaper:

HENRY CHINASKI, MINOR POET, FOUND DEAD IN UTAH WOODS

Henry Chinaski, former post office clerk turned writer, was found in a decomposed state yesterday afternoon by forest ranger W. K. Brooks Jr. Also found near the remains was a small red notebook which evidently contained Mr. Chinaski's last written work.

I walked on. Soon I was in a soggy area full of water. Every now and then one of my legs would sink to the knee in the bog and I'd have to haul myself out.

I came to a barbed wire fence. I knew immediately that I shouldn't climb the fence. I knew that it was the wrong thing to do, but there seemed no alternative. I climbed over the fence and stood there, cupped both hands around my mouth and screamed: "LYDIA!"

83

There was no answer.

I tried it again: "LYDIA!"

My voice sounded very mournful. The voice of a coward.

I moved on. It would be nice, I thought, to be back with the sisters, hearing them laugh about sex and men and dancing and parties. It would be so nice to hear Glendoline's voice. It would be nice to run my hand through Lydia's long hair. I'd faithfully take her to every party in town. I'd even dance with all the women and make brilliant jokes about everything. I'd endure all that subnormal driveling shit with a smile. I could almost hear myself. "Hey, that's a *great* dance tune! Who wants to really *go?* Who wants to *boogie* on out?"

I KEPT walking through the bog. Finally I reached dry land. I got to a road. It was just an old dirt road, but it looked good. I could see tire marks, hoof prints. There were even wires overhead that carried electricity somewhere. All I had to do was follow those wires. I walked along the road. The sun was high in the sky, it must have been noon. I walked along feeling foolish.

I came to a locked gate across the road. What did that mean? There was a small entry at one side of the gate. Evidently the gate was a cattle guard. But where were the cattle? Where was the owner of the cattle? Maybe he only came around every six months.

The top of my head began to ache. I reached up and felt where I had been blackjacked in a Philadelphia bar 30 years before. Some scar tissue remained. Now the scar tissue, baked by the sun, was swollen. It stood up like a small horn. I broke a piece off and threw it in the road.

I walked another hour, then decided to turn back. It meant having to walk all the way back yet I felt it was the thing to do. I took my shirt off and draped it over my head. I stopped once or twice and screamed, "LYDIA!" There was no reply.

Some time later I got back to the gate. All I had to do was walk around it but there was something in the way. It stood in front of the gate, about 15 feet from me. It was a small doe, a fawn, a something.

I moved slowly toward it. It didn't budge. Was it going to let me by? It didn't seem to fear me. I guessed it sensed my confusion, my cowardice. I approached closer and closer. It wouldn't get out of the way. It had large beautiful brown eyes, more beautiful than the eyes of any woman I had ever seen. I couldn't believe it. I was within 3 feet of it, ready to back off, when it bolted. It ran off the road and into the woods. It was in excellent shape; it could really run.

As I walked further along the road I heard the sound of running water. I needed water. You couldn't live very long without water. I left the road and moved toward the sound of rushing water. There was a little hill covered with grass and as I topped the hill there it was: water spilling out of several cement pipes in the face of a dam and into some kind of reservoir. I sat down at the edge of the reservoir and took off my shoes and stockings, pulled up my pants, and stuck my legs into the water. Then I poured water over my head. Then I drank—but not too much or too fast—just like I'd seen it done in the movies.

After recovering a bit I noticed a pier that went out over the reservoir. I walked out on the pier and came to a large metal box bolted to the side of the pier. It was locked with a padlock. There was probably a telephone in there! I could phone for help!

I went and found a large rock and started smashing it against the lock. It wouldn't give. What the hell would Jack London do? What would Hemingway do? Jean Genet?

I kept smashing the rock against the lock. Sometimes I missed and my hand hit the lock or the metal box itself. Skin ripped, blood flowed. I gathered myself and gave the lock one final blow. It opened. I took it off and opened the metal box. There was no telephone. There were a series of switches and some heavy cables. I reached in, touched a wire, and got a terrible shock. Then I pulled a switch. I heard the roar of water. Out of 3 or 4 of the holes in the concrete face of the dam shot giant white jets of water. I pulled another switch. Three or four other holes opened up, releasing tons of water. I pulled a third switch and the whole dam let loose. I stood and watched the water pouring forth. Maybe I could start a flood and cowboys would come on horses or in rugged little pickup trucks to rescue me. I could see the headline:

HENRY CHINASKI, MINOR POET, FLOODS UTAH COUNTRYSIDE IN ORDER TO SAVE HIS SOFT LOS ANGELES ASS

I decided against it. I threw all the switches back to normal, closed the metal box, and hung the broken lock back on it.

I left the reservoir, found another road up the way, and began following it. This road seemed more used than the other. I walked along. I had never been so tired. I could hardly see. Suddenly there was a little girl about 5 years old walking towards me. She wore a little blue dress and white shoes. She looked frightened when she saw me. I tried to look pleasant and friendly as I edged towards her.

"Little girl, don't go away. I won't hurt you. I'M LOST! Where are your *parents?* Little girl, take me to your *parents!*"

The little girl pointed. I saw a trailer and a car parked up ahead. "HEY, I'M LOST!" I shouted. "CHRIST, AM I GLAD TO SEE YOU."

Lydia stepped around the side of the trailer. Her hair was done up in red curlers. "Come on, city boy," she said. "Follow me home."

"I'm so glad to see you, baby, kiss me!"

"No. Follow me."

Lydia took off running about 20 feet in front of me. It was hard keeping up.

"I asked those people if they had seen a city boy around," she called back over her shoulder. "They said, No."

"Lydia, I *love* you!"

"Come on! You're slow!"

"Wait, Lydia, *wait!*"

She vaulted over a barbed wire fence. I couldn't make it. I got tangled in the wire. I couldn't move. I was like a trapped cow. "LYDIA!"

She came back with her red curlers and started helping me get loose from the barbs. "I tracked you. I found your red notebook. You got lost deliberately because you were pissed."

"No, I got lost out of ignorance and fear. I am not a complete person—I'm a stunted city person. I am more or less a failed drizzling shit with absolutely nothing to offer."

"Christ," she said, "don't you think *I* know that?"

She freed me from the last barb. I lurched after her. I was back with Lydia again.

31

IT WAS 3 or 4 days before I had to fly to Houston to give a reading. I went to the track, drank at the track, and afterwards I went to a bar on Hollywood Boulevard. I went home at 9 or 10 PM. As I moved through the bedroom towards the bathroom I tripped over the telephone cord. I fell against the corner of the bed frame—an edge of steel like a knife blade. When I got up I found I had a deep gash just above the ankle. The blood ran into the rug and I left a bloody trail as I went to the bathroom. The blood ran over the tiles and I left red footprints as I walked about.

There was a knock on the door and I let Bobby in. "Jesus Christ, man, what happened?"

"It's DEATH," I said. "I'm bleeding to death. . . ."

"Man," he said, "you better do something about that leg."

Valerie knocked. I let her in too. She screamed. I poured Bobby and Valerie and myself drinks. The phone rang. It was Lydia.

"Lydia, baby, I'm bleeding to death!"

"Is this one of your dramatic trips again?"

"No, I'm bleeding to death. Ask Valerie."

Valerie took the phone. "It's true, his ankle is cut open. There's blood everywhere and he won't do anything about it. You better come over. . . ."

When Lydia arrived I was sitting on the couch. "Look, Lydia: DEATH!" Tiny veins were hanging out of the wound like strings of spaghetti. I yanked at some of them. I took my cigarette and tapped ashes into the wound. "I'm a MAN! Hell, I'm a MAN!"

Lydia went and got some hydrogen peroxide and poured it into the wound. It was nice. White foam gushed out of the wound. It sizzled and bubbled. Lydia poured some more in.

"You better go to a hospital," Bobby said.

"I don't need a fucking hospital," I said. "It will cure itself. . . ."

THE NEXT morning the wound looked horrible. It was still open and seemed to be forming a nice crust. I went to the drugstore for some more hydrogen peroxide, some bandages, and some epsom salts. I filled the tub full of hot water and epsom salts and got in. I began thinking about myself with only one leg. There were advantages:

HENRY CHINASKI IS, WITHOUT A DOUBT, THE GREATEST ONE-LEGGED POET IN THE WORLD

Bobby came by that afternoon. "You know what it costs to get a leg amputated?"

"$12,000."

After Bobby left I phoned my doctor.

I WENT to Houston with a heavily bandaged leg. I was taking antibiotic pills in an attempt to cure the infection. My doctor mentioned that any drinking would nullify the good the antibiotic pills had.

At the reading, which was at the modern art museum, I went on sober. After I read a few poems somebody in the audience asked, "How come you're not drunk?"

"Henry Chinaski couldn't make it," I said. "I'm his brother Efram."

I read another poem and then confessed about the antibiotics. I also told them it was against museum rules to drink on the premises. Somebody from the audience came up with a beer. I drank it and read some more. Somebody else came up with another beer. Then the beers began to flow. The poems got better.

There was a party and a dinner afterwards at a cafe. Almost directly across the table from me was absolutely the most beautiful girl I had ever seen. She looked like a young Katherine Hepburn. She was about 22, and she just radiated beauty. I kept making wisecracks, calling her Katherine Hepburn. She seemed to like it. I didn't expect anything to come of it. She was with a girlfriend. When it came time to leave I said to the museum director, a woman named Nana, at whose house I was staying, "I'm going to miss her. She was too good to believe."

"She's coming home with us."

"I don't believe it."

. . . but later there she was, at Nana's place, in the bedroom with me. She had on a sheer nightgown, and she sat on the edge of the bed combing her very long hair and smiling at me. "What's your name?" I asked.

"Laura" she said.

"Well, look, Laura, I'm going to call you Katherine."

"All right," she said.

Her hair was reddish-brown and so very long. She was small but well proportioned. Her face was the most beautiful thing about her.

"Can I pour you a drink?" I asked.

"Oh no, I don't drink. I don't like it."

Actually; she frightened me. I couldn't understand what she was doing there with me. She didn't appear to be a groupie. I went to the bathroom, came back and turned out the light. I could feel her getting into bed next to me. I took her in my arms and we began kissing. I couldn't believe my luck. What right had I? How could a few books of poems call this forth? There was no way to understand it. I certainly was not about to reject it. I became very aroused. Suddenly she went down and took my cock in her mouth. I watched the slow movement of her head and body in the moonlight. She wasn't as good at it as some, but it was the very fact of *her* doing it that was amazing. Just as I was about to come I reached down and buried my hand in that mass of beautiful hair, pulling at it in the moonlight as I came in Katherine's mouth.

32

LYDIA MET ME at the airport. She was horny as usual.

"Jesus Christ," she said. "I'm *hot!* I play with myself but it doesn't do any good."

We were driving back to my place.

"Lydia, my leg is still in terrible shape. I just don't know if I can handle it with this leg."

"*What?*"

"It's true. I don't think I can fuck with my leg the way it is."

"What the hell good are you then?"

"Well, I can fry eggs and do magic tricks."

"Don't be funny. I'm asking you, what the hell *good* are you?"

"The leg will heal. If it doesn't they'll cut it off. Be patient."

"If you hadn't been drunk you wouldn't have fallen and cut your leg. It's *always* the bottle!"

"It's not always the bottle, Lydia. We fuck about 4 times a week. For my age that's pretty good."

"Sometimes I think you don't even enjoy it."

"Lydia, sex isn't *everything!* You are obsessed. For Christ's sake, give it a rest."

"A rest until your leg heals? How am I going to make it meanwhile?"

"I'll play Scrabble with you."

Lydia screamed. The car began to swerve all over the street. "YOU SON-OF-A-BITCH! I'LL KILL YOU!"

She crossed the double yellow line at high speed, directly into oncoming traffic. Horns sounded and cars scattered. We drove on against the flow of traffic, cars approaching us peeling off to the left and right. Then just as abruptly Lydia swerved back across the double line into the lane we had just vacated.

Where are the police? I thought. Why is it that when Lydia does something the police become nonexistent?

"All right," she said. "I'm taking you home and that's it. I've had it. I'm going to sell my house and move to Phoenix. Glendoline lives in Phoenix now. My sisters warned me about living with an old fuck like you."

We drove the remainder of the way without talking. When we reached my place I took out my suitcase, looked at Lydia, said, "Goodbye." She was crying without making a sound, her whole face was wet. Suddenly she drove off toward Western Avenue. I walked into the court. Back from another reading. . . .

I CHECKED the mail and then phoned Katherine who lived in Austin, Texas. She seemed truly glad to hear from me, and it was good to hear that Texas accent, that high laughter. I told her that I wanted her to come visit me, that I'd pay air fare both ways. We'd go to the racetrack, we'd go to Malibu, we'd . . . whatever she wanted. "But, Hank, don't you have a girlfriend?"

"No, none. I'm a recluse."

"But you're always writing about women in your poems."

"That's past. This is present."

"But what about Lydia?"

"Lydia?"

"Yes, you told me all about her."

"What did I tell you?"

"You told me how she beat up two other women. Would you let her beat me up? I'm not very big, you know."

"It can't happen. She's moved to Phoenix. I tell you, Katherine, you are *the* exceptional woman I've been looking for. Please, trust me."

"I'll have to make arrangements. I have to get somebody to take care of my cat."

"All right. But I want you to know that everything is clear here."

"But, Hank, don't forget what you told me about your women."

"Told you what?"

"You said, 'They always come back.' "

"That's just macho talk."

"I'll come," she said. "As soon as I get things straight here I'll make a reservation and let you know the details."

WHEN I was in Texas Katherine had told me about her life. I was only the third man she had slept with. There had been her husband, an alcoholic track star, and me. Her ex-husband, Arnold, was into show business and the arts in some way. Exactly how it worked I didn't know. He was continually signing contracts with rock stars, painters and so forth. The business was $60,000 in debt, but flourishing. One of those situations where the further you were in debt the better off you were.

I don't know what happened to the track star. He just ran off, I guess. And then Arnold got on coke. The coke changed him overnight. Katherine said she didn't know him anymore. It was terrifying. Ambulance trips to hospitals. And then he'd be back at the office the next morning as if nothing had happened. Then Joanna Dover entered the picture. A tall, stately semimillionairess. Educated and crazy. She and Arnold began to do business together. Joanna Dover dealt in the arts like some people deal in corn futures. She discovered unknown artists on the way up, bought their work cheap, and sold high after they became recognized. She had that kind of eye. And a magnificent 6-foot body. She began to see a lot of Arnold. One evening Joanna came to pick up Arnold dressed in an expensive tight-fitting gown. Then Katherine knew that Joanna really meant business. So, after that, she went along whenever Arnold and Joanna would go out. They were a trio. Arnold had a *very* low sex drive, so Katherine wasn't worried about that. She was worried about the business. Then Joanna dropped out of the picture, and Arnold got more and more into coke. More and more ambulance trips. Katherine finally divorced him. She still saw Arnold, however. She took coffee to the office at 10:30 every morning for the staff and Arnold put her on the payroll. Which enabled her to keep the house. She and Arnold had dinner there now and then, but no sex. Still, he needed her, she felt protective towards him. Katherine also believed in health foods and the only meat she ate was chicken and fish. She was a beautiful woman.

33

WITHIN A DAY or two, about 1 PM in the afternoon there was a knock at my door. It was a painter, Monty Riff, or so he informed me. He also told me that I used to get drunk with him when I lived on DeLongpre Avenue.

"I don't remember you," I said.

"Dee Dee used to bring me over."

"Oh yeah? Well, come on in." Monty had a 6-pack with him and a tall stately woman.

"This is Joanna Dover," he introduced me to her.

"I missed your reading in Houston," she said.

"Laura Stanley told me all about you," I said.

"You know her?"

"Yes. But I've renamed her Katherine, after Katherine Hepburn."

"You really *know* her?"

"Fairly well."

"How well?"

"She's flying out to visit me in a day or two."

"Really?"

"Yes."

We finished the 6-pack and I left to go get some more. When I got back Monty was gone. Joanna told me that he had an appointment. We got to talking about painting and I brought out some of mine. She looked at them and decided that she'd like to buy two of them. "How much?" she asked.

"Well, $40 for the small one and $60 for the large one."

Joanna wrote me out a check for $100. Then she said, "I want you to live with me."

"What? This is pretty sudden."

"It would pay off. I have some money. Just don't ask me how much. I've been thinking of some reasons why we should live together. Do you want to hear them?"

"No."

"One thing, if we lived together I'd take you to Paris."

"I hate to travel."

"I'd show you a Paris you'd really like."

"Let me think it over."

I leaned over and gave her a kiss. Then I kissed her again, this time a little longer.

"Shit," I said, "let's go to bed."

"All right," said Joanna Dover.

We undressed and climbed in. She was 6 feet tall. I'd always had small women. It was strange—every place I reached there seemed to be more woman. We warmed up. I gave her 3 or 4 minutes of oral sex, then mounted. She was good, she was really good. We cleaned up, got dressed and then she took me to dinner in Malibu. She told me she lived in Galveston, Texas. She gave me her phone number, the address and told me to come and see her. I told her that I would. She told me that she was serious about Paris and the rest. It had been a good fuck and the dinner was excellent too.

34

THE NEXT DAY Katherine phoned me. She said she had the tickets and would be landing at L.A. International Friday at 2:30 PM.

"Katherine," I said, "there's something I've got to tell you."

"Hank, don't you want to see me?"

"I want to see you more than anybody I know."

"Then what is it?"

"Well, you know Joanna Dover . . ."

"Joanna Dover?"

"The one . . . you know . . . your husband . . ."

"What about her, Hank?"

"Well, she came to see me."

"You mean she came to your place?"

"Yes."

"What happened?"

"We talked. She bought two of my paintings."

"Anything else happen?"

"Yeah."

Katherine was quiet. Then she said, "Hank, I don't know if I want to see you now."

"I understand. Look, why don't you think it over and call me back? I'm sorry, Katherine. I'm sorry it happened. That's all I can say."

She hung up. She won't phone back, I thought. The best woman I ever met and I blew it. I deserve defeat, I deserve to die alone in a madhouse.

I sat by the telephone. I read the newspaper, the sports section, the financial section, the funny papers. The phone rang. It was Katherine. "FUCK Joanna Dover!" she laughed. I'd never heard Katherine swear like that before.

"Then you're coming?"

"Yes. Do you have the arrival time?"

"I have it all. I'll be there."

We said goodbye. Katherine was coming, she was coming for at least a week with that face, that body, that hair, those eyes, that laugh. . . .

35

I CAME OUT of the bar and checked the message board. The plane was on time. Katherine was in the air and moving towards me. I sat down and waited. Across from me was a well-groomed woman reading a paperback. Her dress was up around her thighs, showing all that flank, that leg wrapped in nylon. Why did she insist on doing that? I had a newspaper, and I looked over the top, up her dress. She had great thighs. Who was getting those thighs? I felt foolish staring up her dress, but I couldn't help myself. She was built. Once she had been a little girl, someday she would be dead, but now she was showing me her upper legs. The goddamned strumpet, I'd give her a hundred strokes; I'd give her 7-and-one-half inches of throbbing purple! She crossed her legs and her dress inched higher. She looked up from her paperback. Her eyes looked into mine as I watched over the top of the newspaper. Her expression was indifferent. She reached into her purse and took out a stick of gum, took the wrapper off and put the gum in her mouth. Green gum. She chewed on the green gum and I watched her mouth. She didn't pull her skirt down. She knew that I was looking. There was nothing I could do. I opened my wallet and took out 2 fifty dollar bills. She looked up, saw the bills, looked back down. Then a fat man plopped down next to me. His face was very red and he had a massive nose. He was dressed in a jumpsuit, a light brown jumpsuit. He farted. The lady pulled her dress down and I put the bills back in my wallet. My cock softened and I got up and went to the drinking fountain.

Out in the landing area Katherine's plane was taxiing toward the ramp. I stood and waited. Katherine, I adore you.

Katherine walked off the ramp, perfect, with red-brown hair, slim body, a blue dress clinging as she walked, white shoes, slim, neat ankles, youth. She wore a white hat with a wide brim, the brim turned down just right. Her eyes looked out from under the brim, large and brown and laughing. She had class. She'd never show her ass in an airport waiting area.

And there I was, 225 pounds, perpetually lost and confused, short legs, ape-like upper body, all chest, no neck, head too large, blurred eyes, hair uncombed, 6 feet of geek, waiting for her.

Katherine moved toward me. That long clean red-brown hair. Texas women were so relaxed, so natural. I gave her a kiss and asked about her baggage. I suggested a stop at the bar. The waitresses had on short red dresses that showed their ruffled white panties. The necklines of their dresses were cut low to show their breasts; they earned their salaries, they earned their tips, every cent. They lived in the suburbs and they hated men.

They lived with their mothers and brothers and were in love with their psychiatrists.

We finished our drinks and went to get Katherine's baggage. A number of men tried to catch her eye, but she walked close by my side, holding my arm. Few beautiful women were willing to indicate in public that they belonged to someone. I had known enough women to realize this. I accepted them for what they were, and love came hard and very seldom. When it did it was usually for the wrong reasons. One simply became tired of holding love back and let it go because it *needed* some place to go. Then usually, there was trouble.

AT MY place Katherine opened her suitcase and took out a pair of rubber gloves. She laughed.

"What is this?" I asked.

"Darlene—my best friend—she saw me packing and she said, 'What the hell are you *doing?*' And I said, 'I've never seen Hank's place, but I *know* that before I can cook in it and live in it and sleep in it I've got to clean it up!'"

Then Katherine gave off that happy Texas laugh. She went into the bathroom and put on a pair of bluejeans and an orange blouse, came out barefooted and went into the kitchen with her rubber gloves.

I went into the bathroom and changed clothes also. I decided that if Lydia came by I'd never let her touch Katherine. Lydia? Where was she? What was she doing?

I sent up a little prayer to the gods who watched over me: please keep Lydia away. Let her suck on the horns of cowboys and dance until 3 AM—but please keep her away. . . .

When I came out Katherine was on her knees scrubbing at two years' worth of grease on my kitchen floor.

"Katherine," I said, "let's go out on the town. Let's go have dinner. This is no way to begin."

"All right, Hank, but I've got to finish this floor first. Then we'll go."

I sat and waited. Then she came out and I was sitting in a chair, waiting. She bent over and kissed me, laughing, "You *are* a dirty old man!" Then she walked into the bedroom. I was in love again, I was in trouble. . . .

36

AFTER DINNER WE came back and we talked. She was a health food addict and didn't eat meat except for chicken and fish. It certainly worked for her.

"Hank," she said, "tomorrow I'm going to clean your bath-room."

"All right," I said over my drink.

"And I must do my exercises every day. Will that bother you?"

"No, no."

"Will you be able to write while I'm fussing around here?"

"No problem."

"I can go for walks."

"No, not alone, not in this neighborhood."

"I don't want to interfere with your writing."

"There's no way I can stop writing, it's a form of insanity."

Katherine came over and sat by me on the couch. She seemed more a girl than a woman. I put down my drink and kissed her, a long, slow kiss. Her lips were cool and soft. I was very conscious of her long red-brown hair. I pulled away and had another drink. She confused me. I was used to vile drunken wenches.

We talked for another hour. "Let's go to sleep," I told her, "I'm tired."

"Fine. I'll get ready first," she said.

I sat drinking. I needed more to drink. She simply was too much.

"Hank," she said, "I'm in bed."

"All right."

I went into the bathroom and undressed, brushed my teeth, washed my face and hands. She came all the way from Texas, I thought, she came on a plane just to see me and now she's in my bed, waiting.

I didn't have any pyjamas. I walked toward the bed. She was in a nightie. "Hank," she said, "we have about 6 days when it's safe, then we'll have to think of something else."

I got into bed with her. The little girl-woman was ready. I pulled her towards me. Luck was mine again, the gods were smiling. The kisses became more intense. I placed her hand on my cock and then pulled up her nightie. I began to play with her cunt. Katherine with a cunt? The clit came out and I touched it gently, again and again. Finally, I mounted. My cock entered halfway. It was very tight. I moved it back and forth, then pushed. The remainder of my cock slid in. It was glorious. She gripped me. I moved and her grip held. I tried to control myself. I stopped stroking and waited to cool off. I kissed her, working her lips apart, sucking at the upper lip. I saw her hair spread wide across the pillow. Then I gave up trying to please her and simply fucked her, ripping viciously. It was like murder. I didn't care; my cock had gone crazy. All that hair, her young and beautiful face. It was like raping the Virgin Mary. I came. I came inside of her, agonizing, feeling my sperm enter her body, she was helpless, and I shot my come deep into her ultimate core—body and soul—again and again. . . .

LATER ON, we slept. Or Katherine slept. I held her from the back. For the first time I thought of marriage. I knew that there certainly were flaws in her that had not surfaced. The beginning of a relationship was always the easiest. After that the unveiling began, never to stop. Still, I thought of marriage. I thought of a house, a dog and a cat, of shopping in supermarkets. Henry Chinaski was losing his balls. And didn't care.

At last I slept. When I awakened in the morning Katherine was sitting on the edge of the bed brushing those yards of red-brown hair. Her large dark eyes looked at me as I awakened. "Hello, Katherine," I said, "will you marry me?"

"Please don't," she said, "I don't like it."

"I mean it."

"Oh, *shit*, Hank!"

"What?"

"I said, 'shit,' and if you talk that way I'm taking the first plane out."

"All right."

"Hank?"

"Yes?"

I looked at Katherine. She kept brushing. her long hair. Her large brown eyes looked at me, and she was smiling. She said, "It's just *sex*, Hank, it's *just sex!*" Then she laughed. It wasn't a sardonic laugh, it was really joyful. She brushed her hair and I put my arm around her waist and rested my head against her leg. I wasn't quite sure of anything.

37

I TOOK WOMEN either to the boxing matches or to the racetrack. That Thursday night I took Katherine to the boxing matches at the Olympic auditorium. She had never been to a live fight. We got there before the first bout and sat at ringside. I drank beer and smoked and waited.

"It's strange," I told her, "that people will sit here and wait for two men to climb up there into that ring and try to punch each other out."

"It does seem awful."

"This place was built a long time ago," I told her as she looked around the ancient arena. "There are only two restrooms, one for men, the other for women, and they are small. So try to go before or after intermission."

"All right."

The Olympic was attended mostly by Latinos and lower class working whites, with a few movie stars and celebrities. There were many good Mexican fighters and they fought with their hearts. The only bad fights were when whites or blacks fought, especially the heavyweights.

Being there with Katherine felt strange. Human relationships were strange. I mean, you were with one person a while, eating and sleeping and living with them, loving them, talking to them, going places together, and then it stopped. Then there was a short period when you weren't with anybody, then another woman arrived, and you ate with her and fucked her, and it all seemed so normal, as if you had been waiting just for her and she had been waiting for you. I never felt right being alone; sometimes it felt good but it never felt right.

The first fight was a good one, lots of blood and courage. There was something to be learned about writing from watching boxing matches or going to the racetrack. The message wasn't clear but it helped me. That was the important part: the message wasn't clear. It was wordless, like a house burning, or an earthquake or a flood, or a woman getting out of a car, showing her legs. I didn't know what other writers needed; I didn't care, I couldn't read them anyway. I was locked into my own habits, my own prejudices. It wasn't bad being dumb *if* the ignorance was all your own. I knew that some day I would write about Katherine and that it would be hard. It was easy to write about whores, but to write about a good woman was much more difficult.

The second fight was good, too. The crowd screamed and roared and swilled beer. They had temporarily escaped the factories, the warehouses, the slaughterhouses, the car washes—they'd be back in captivity the next day but *now* they were out—they were wild with freedom. They weren't thinking about the slavery of poverty. Or the slavery of welfare and food stamps. The rest of us would be all right until the poor learned how to make atom bombs in their basements.

All the fights were good. I got up and went to the restroom. When I got back Katherine was very still. She looked more like she should be attending a ballet or a concert. She looked so delicate and yet she was such a marvelous fuck.

I kept drinking and Katherine would grab one of my hands when a fight became exceptionally brutal. The crowd loved knockouts. They screamed when one of the fighters was on the way out. *They* were landing those punches. Maybe they were punching out their bosses or their wives. Who knew? Who cared? More beer.

I suggested to Katherine that we leave before the final bout. I'd had enough.

"All right," she said.

We walked up the narrow aisle, the air blue with smoke. There was no whistling, no obscene gestures. My scarred and battered face was sometimes an asset.

We walked back to the small parking lot under the freeway. The '67 blue Volks was not there. The '67 model was the last good Volks—and the young men knew it.

"Hepburn, they stole our fucking car."

"Oh Hank, surely not!"

"It's gone. It was sitting there." I pointed. "Now it's gone."

"Hank, what will we do?"

"We'll take a taxi. I really feel bad."

"Why do people do that?"

"They have to. It's their way out."

We went into a coffee shop and I phoned for a cab. We ordered coffee and doughnuts. While we had been watching the fights they had pulled the coathanger and hotwire trick. I had a saying, "Take my woman, but leave my car alone." I would never kill a man who took my woman; I might kill a man who took my car.

The cab came. At my place, luckily, there was beer and some vodka. I had given up all hope of staying sober enough to make love. Katherine knew it. I paced up and down talking about my '67 blue Volks. The last good model. I couldn't even call the police. I was too drunk. I'd have to wait until morning, until noon.

"Hepburn," I told her, "it's not *your* fault, *you* didn't steal it!"

"I wish I had, you'd have it now."

I thought of 2 or 3 young kids racing my blue baby down along the Coast Highway, smoking dope, laughing, opening it up. Then I thought of all the junkyards along Santa Fe Avenue. Mountains of bumpers, windshields, doorhandles, wiper motors, engine parts, tires, wheels, hoods, jacks, bucket seats, front wheel bearings, brake shoes, radios, pistons, valves, carburetors, cam shafts, transmissions, axles—my car soon would be just a pile of accessories.

That night I slept up against Katherine, but my heart was sad and cold.

38

LUCKILY I HAD auto insurance that paid for a rental car. I drove Katherine to the racetrack in it. We sat in the sundeck at Hollywood Park near the stretch turn. Katherine said she didn't want to bet but I took her inside and showed her the toteboard and the betting windows.

I put 5 win on a 7 to 2 shot with early lick, my favorite kind of horse. I always figured if you're going to lose you might as well lose in front; you had the race won until somebody beat you. The horse went wire to wire, pulling away at the end. It paid $9.40 and I was $17.50 ahead.

The next race she remained in her seat while I went to make my bet. When I came back she pointed to a man two rows below us. "See that man there?"

"Yes."

"He told me he won $2,000 yesterday and that he's $25,000 ahead for the meet."

"Don't you want to bet? Maybe we all can win."

"Oh no, I don't know anything about it."

"It's simple: you give them a dollar and they give you 84 cents back. It's called the 'take.' The state and the track split it about even. They don't care *who* wins the race, their take is out of the total mutual pool."

In the second race my horse, the 8 to 5 favorite, ran second. A longshot had nosed me at the wire. It paid $45.80.

The man two rows down turned and looked at Katherine. "I had it," he told her, "I had ten on the nose."

"Ooh," she told him, smiling, "that's good."

I turned to the third race, an affair for 2-year-old maiden colts and geldings. At 5 minutes to post I checked the tote and went to bet. As I walked away I saw the man two rows down turn and begin talking to Katherine. There were at least a dozen of them at the track every day, who told attractive women what big winners they were, hoping that somehow they would end up in bed with them. Maybe they didn't even think that far; maybe they only hoped vaguely for something without being quite sure what it was. They were addled and dizzied, taking the 10-count. Who could hate them? Big winners, but if you watched them bet, they were usually at the 2 dollar window, their shoes down at the heels and their clothing dirty. The lowest of the breed.

I took the even money shot and he won by 6 and paid $4.00. Not much, but I had him ten win. The man turned around and looked at Katherine. "I had it," he told her. "$100 to win."

Katherine didn't answer. She was beginning to understand. Winners didn't shoot off their mouths. They were afraid of getting murdered in the parking lot.

After the fourth race, a $22.80 winner, he turned again and told Katherine, "I had that one, ten across."

She turned away. "His face is yellow, Hank. Did you see his eyes? He's sick."

"He's sick on the dream. We're all sick on the dream, that's why we're out here."

"Hank, let's go."

"All right."

That night she drank half a bottle of red wine, good red wine, and she was sad and quiet. I knew she was connecting me with the racetrack people and the boxing crowd, and it was true, I was with them, I was one of them. Katherine knew that there was something about me that was not wholesome in the sense of wholesome is as wholesome does. I was drawn to all the wrong things: I liked to drink, I was lazy, I didn't have a god, politics, ideas, ideals. I was settled into nothingness; a kind of non-being, and I accepted it. It didn't make for an interesting person. I didn't want to be interesting, it was too hard. What I really wanted was only a soft, hazy space to live in, and to be left alone. On the other hand, when I got drunk I screamed, went crazy, got all out of hand. One kind of behavior didn't fit the other. I didn't care.

The fucking was very good that night, but it was the night I lost her. There was nothing I could do about it. I rolled off and wiped myself on the sheet as she went into the bathroom. Overhead a police helicopter circled over Hollywood.

39

THE NEXT NIGHT Bobby and Valerie came over. They had recently moved into my apartment building and now lived across the court. Bobby had on his tight knit shirt. Everything always fitted Bobby perfectly, his pants were snug and just the right length, he wore the right shoes and his hair was styled. Valerie also dressed mod but not quite as consciously. People called them the "Barbie Dolls." Valerie was all right when you got her alone, she was intelligent and very energetic and damned honest. Bobby, too, was more human when he and I were alone, but when a new woman was around he became very dull and obvious. He would direct all his attention and conversation to the woman, as if his very presence was an interesting and marvelous thing, but his conversation became predictable and dull. I wondered how Katherine would handle him.

They sat down. I was in a chair near the window and Valerie sat between Bobby and Katherine on the couch. Bobby began. He bent forward and, ignoring Valerie directed his attention to Katherine.

"Do you like Los Angeles?" he asked.

"It's all right," answered Katherine.

"Are you going to stay here much longer?"

"A while longer."

"You're from Texas?"

"Yes."

"Are your parents from Texas?"

"Yes."

"Anything good on t.v. out there?"

"It's about the same."

"I've got an uncle in Texas."

"Oh."

"Yes, he lives in Dallas."

Katherine didn't answer. Then she said, "Excuse me, I'm going to make a sandwich. Does anybody want anything?"

We said we didn't. Katherine got up and went into the kitchen. Bobby got up and followed her. You couldn't quite hear his words, but you could tell that he was asking more questions. Valerie stared at the floor. Katherine and Bobby were in the kitchen a long time. Suddenly Valerie raised her head and began talking to me. She spoke very rapidly and nervously.

"Valerie," I stopped her, "we needn't talk, we don't have to talk."

She put her head down again.

Then I said, "Hey, you guys have been in there a long time. Are you waxing the floor?"

Bobby laughed and began tapping his foot in rhythm on the floor.

Finally Katherine came out followed by Bobby. She walked over to me and showed me her sandwich: peanut butter on cracked wheat with sliced bananas and sesame seeds.

"It looks good," I told her.

She sat down and began eating her sandwich. It became quiet. It remained quiet. Then Bobby said, "Well, I think we'd better go. . . ."

They left. After the door closed Katherine looked at me and said, "Don't think anything, Hank. He was just trying to impress me."

"He's done that with every woman I've known since I've known him."

The phone rang. It was Bobby. "Hey, man, what have you done to my wife?"

"What's the matter?"

"She just *sits* here, she's completely depressed, she won't talk!"

"I haven't done anything to your wife."

"I don't understand it!"

"Goodnight, Bobby."

I hung up.

"It was Bobby," I told Katherine. "His wife is depressed."

"Really?"

"It seems so."

"Are you sure you don't want a sandwich?"

"Can you make me one just like yours?"

"Oh, yes."

"I'll take it."

40

KATHERINE STAYED 4 or 5 more days. We had reached the time of the month when it was risky for Katherine to fuck. I couldn't stand rubbers. Katherine got some contraceptive foam. Meanwhile, the police had recovered my Volks. We went down to where it was impounded. It was intact and in good shape except for a dead battery. I had it hauled to a Hollywood garage where they put it in order. After a last goodbye in bed I drove Katherine to the airport in the blue Volks, TRV 469.

It wasn't a happy day for me. We sat not saying much. Then they called her flight and we kissed.

"Hey, they all saw this young girl kissing this old man."

"I don't give a damn. . . ."

Katherine kissed me again.

"You're going to miss your flight," I said.

"Come see me, Hank. I have a nice house. I live alone. Come see me."

"I will."

"Write!"

"I will. . . ."

Katherine walked into the boarding tunnel and was gone.

I walked back to the parking lot, got in the Volks, thinking, I've still got this. What the hell, I haven't lost everything.

It started.

41

THAT EVENING I started drinking. It wasn't going to be easy without Katherine. I found some things she had left behind—earrings, a bracelet.

I've got to get back to the typewriter, I thought. Art takes discipline. Any asshole can chase a skirt. I drank, thinking about it.

At 2:10 AM the phone rang. I was drinking my last beer.

"Hello?"

"Hello." It was a woman's voice, a young woman.

"Yes?"

"Are you Henry Chinaski?"

"Yes."

"My girlfriend admires your writing. It's her birthday and I told her I'd phone you. We were surprised to find you in the phonebook."

"I'm listed."

"Well, it's her birthday and I thought it might be nice if we could come to see you."

"All right."

"I told Arlene that you probably had women all over the place."

"I'm a recluse."

"Then it's all right if we come over?"

I gave them the address and directions.

"Only one thing, I'm out of beer."

"We'll get you some beer. My name's Tammie."

"It's after 2 AM."

"We'll get some beer. Cleavage can work wonders."

THEY ARRIVED in 20 minutes with the cleavage but without the beer.

"That son-of-a-bitch," said Arlene. "He always gave it to us before. This time he seemed scared."

"Fuck him," said Tammie.

They both sat down and announced their ages.

"I'm 32," said Arlene.

"I'm 23," said Tammie.

"Add your ages together," I said, "and you've got me."

Arlene's hair was long and black. She sat in the chair by the window combing her hair, making up her face, looking into a large silver mirror, and talking. She was obviously high on pills. Tammie had a near-perfect body and long natural red hair. She was on pills too, but wasn't as high.

"It will cost you $100 for a piece of ass," Tammie told me.

"I'll pass."

Tammie was hard like so many women in their early twenties. Her face was shark-like. I disliked her, right off.

They left around 3:30 AM and I went to bed alone.

42

TWO MORNINGS LATER, at 4 AM, somebody beat on the door.

"Who is it?"

"It's a redheaded floozie."

I let Tammie in. She sat down and I opened a couple of beers.

"I've got bad breath, I have these two bad teeth. You can't kiss me."

"All right."

We talked. Well, I listened. Tammie was on speed. I listened and looked at her long red hair and when she was preoccupied I looked and looked at that body. It was bursting out of her clothing, begging to get out. She talked on and on. I didn't touch her.

At 6 AM Tammie gave me her address and phone number.

"I've got to go," she said.

"I'll walk you to your car."

It was a bright red Camaro, completely wrecked. The front was smashed in, one side was ripped open and the windows were gone. Inside were rags and shirts and Kleenex boxes and news-papers and milk cartons and Coke bottles and wire and rope and paper napkins and magazines and paper cups and shoes and bent colored drinking straws. This mass of stuff was piled above seat level and covered the seats. Only the driver's area had a little clear space.

Tammie stuck her head out the window and we kissed.

Then she tore away from the curb and by the time she reached the corner she was doing 45. She did hit the brakes and the Camaro bobbed up and down, up and down. I walked back inside.

I went to bed and thought about her hair. I'd never known a real redhead. It was fire.

Like lightning from heaven, I thought.

Somehow her face didn't seem to be as hard anymore. . . .

43

I PHONED HER. It was 1 AM. I went over.

Tammie lived in a small bungalow behind a house.

She let me in.

"Be quiet. Don't wake Dancy. She's my daughter. She's 6 years old and she's asleep in the bedroom."

I had a 6-pack of beer. Tammie put it in the refrigerator and came out with two bottles.

"My daughter mustn't see anything. I still have the two bad teeth which makes my breath bad. We can't kiss."

"All right."

The bedroom door was closed.

"Look," she said, "I've got to take some vitamin B. And I'm going to have to pull my pants down and stab myself in the ass. Look the other way."

"All right."

I watched her draw liquid into the syringe. I looked the other way.

"I've got to get it all," she said.

When it was done she turned on a small red radio.

"Nice place you got here."

"I'm a month behind on the rent."

"Oh . . ."

"It's all right. The landlord—he lives in the place up front—I can hold him off."

"Good."

"He's married, the old fuck. And guess what?"

"I can't."

"The other day his wife was gone somewhere and the old fuck asked me to come over. I went over and sat down and guess what?"

"He pulled it out."

"No, he put on dirty movies. He thought that shit would turn me on."

"It didn't?"

"I said, 'Mr. Miller, I have to leave now. I have to pick Dancy up at school.'"

Tammie gave me an upper. We talked and talked. And drank beer.

At 6 AM Tammie opened the couch we had been sitting on. There was a blanket. We took off our shoes and climbed under the blanket with our clothes on. I held her from the back, my face in all that red hair. I got hard. I dug it into her from behind, through her clothing. I heard her fingers clawing and digging into the edge of the couch.

"I've got to go," I told Tammie.

"Listen, all I've got to do is to make Dancy some breakfast and drive her to school. It's O.K. if she sees you. Just wait here until I get back."

"I'm going," I said.

I drove home, drunk. The sun was really up, painful and yellow. . . .

44

I HAD BEEN sleeping on a terrible mattress with the springs sticking into me for several years. That afternoon when I awakened I pulled the mattress off the bed, dragged it outside, and leaned it against the trashbin.

I walked back in and left the door open.

It was 2 PM and hot.

Tammie walked in and sat on the couch.

"I've got to go," I told her. "I've got to go buy a mattress."

"A mattress? Well, I'll leave."

"No, Tammie, wait. Please. The whole thing will take about 15 minutes. Wait here and have a beer."

"All right," she said. . . .

THERE WAS a rebuilt mattress shop about three blocks down on Western. I parked in front and ran through the door. "Fellows! I need a mattress . . . FAST!"

"What kind of bed?"

"Double."

"We've got this one for $35."

"I'll take it."

"Can you take it in your car?"

"I've got a Volks."

"All right, we'll deliver it. Address?"

TAMMIE WAS still there when I got back.

"Where's the mattress?"

"It'll be along. Have another beer. You got a pill?"

She gave me a pill. The light shot through her red hair.

Tammie had been voted Miss Sunny Bunny at the Orange County Fair in 1973. It was four years later now, but she still had it. She was big and ripe in all the right places.

The delivery man was at the door with the mattress.

"Let me help you."

The delivery man was a good soul. He helped me put it on the bed. Then he saw Tammie sitting on the couch. He grinned. "Hi," he said to her.

"Thanks very much," I told him. I gave him 3 dollars and he left.

I went into the bedroom and looked at the mattress. Tammie followed. The mattress was wrapped in cellophane. I began ripping it off. Tammie helped.

"Look at it. It's pretty," she said.

"Yes, it is."

It was bright and colorful. Roses, stems, leaves, curling vines. It looked like the Garden of Eden, and for $35.

Tammie looked at it. "That mattress turns me on. I want to break it in. I want to be the first woman to fuck you on that mattress."

"I wonder who will be the second?"

Tammie walked into the bathroom. There was a silence. Then I heard the shower. I put on fresh sheets and pillow cases, undressed and climbed in. Tammie came out, young and wet, she sparkled. Her pubic hair was the same color as the hair on her head: red, like fire.

She paused before the mirror and pulled in her stomach. Those huge breasts rose toward the glass. I could see her, back and front, simultaneously.

She walked over and climbed under the sheet.

We slowly worked into it.

We got into it, all that red hair on the pillow, as outside the sirens howled and the dogs barked.

45

TAMMIE CAME BY that night. She appeared to be high on uppers. "I want some champagne," she said.

"All right," I said.

I handed her a twenty.

"Be right back," she said, walking out the door.

Then the phone rang. It was Lydia. "I just wondered how you were doing. . . ."

"Things are all right."

"Not here. I'm pregnant."

"What?"

"And I don't know who the father is."

"Oh?"

"You know Dutch, the guy who hangs around the bar where I'm working now?"

"Yes, old Baldy."

"Well, he's really a nice guy. He's in love with me. He brings me flowers and candy. He wants to marry me. He's been real nice. And one night I went home with him. We did it."

"All right."

"Then there's Barney, he's married but I like him. Of all the guys in the bar he's the only one who never tried to put the make on me. It fascinated me. Well, you know, I'm trying to sell my house. So he came over one afternoon. He just came by. He said he wanted to look the house over for a friend of his. I let him in. Well, he came at just the right time. The kids were in school so I let him go ahead. . . . Then one night this stranger came into the bar late. He asked me to go home with him. I told him no. Then he said he just wanted to sit in my car with me, talk to me. I said all right. We sat in the car and talked. Then we shared a joint. Then he kissed me. That kiss did it. If he hadn't kissed me I wouldn't have done it. Now I'm pregnant and I don't know who. I'll have to wait and see who the child looks like."

"All right, Lydia, lots of luck."

"Thanks."

I hung up. A minute passed and then the phone rang again. It was Lydia. "Oh," she said, "I wondered how *you* were doing?"

"About the same, horses and booze."

"Then everything's all right with you?"

"Not quite."

"What is it?"

"Well, I sent this woman out for champagne. . . ."

"Woman?"

"Well, girl, really . . ."

"A girl?"

"I sent her out with $20 for champagne and she hasn't come back. I think I've been taken."

"Chinaski, I don't want to *hear* about your women. Do you understand that?"

"All right."

114

Lydia hung up. There was a knock on the door. It was Tammie. She'd come back with the champagne and the change.

46

IT WAS NOON the next day when the phone rang. It was Lydia again.

"Well, did she come back with the champagne?"

"Who?"

"Your whore."

"Yes, she came back. . . ."

"Then what happened?"

"We drank the champagne. It was good stuff."

"Then what happened?"

"Well, you know, shit . . ."

I heard a long insane wail like a wolverine shot in the arctic snow and left to bleed and die alone. . . .

She hung up.

I SLEPT most of the afternoon and that night I drove out to the harness races.

I lost $32, got into the Volks and drove back. I parked, walked up on the porch and put the key into the door. All the lights were on. I looked around. Drawers were ripped out and overturned on the floor, the bed covers were on the floor. All my books were missing from the bookcase, including the books I had written, 20 or so. And my typewriter was gone and my toaster was gone and my radio was gone and my paintings were gone.

Lydia, I thought.

All she'd left me was my t.v. because she knew I never looked at it.

I walked outside and there was Lydia's car, but she wasn't in it. "Lydia," I said. "Hey, baby!"

I walked up and down the street and then I saw her feet, both of them, sticking out from behind a small tree up against an apartment house wall. I walked up to the tree and said, "Look, what the hell's the matter with you?"

Lydia just stood there. She had two shopping bags full of my books and a portfolio of my paintings.

"Look, I've got to have my books and paintings back. They belong to me."

Lydia came out from behind the tree—screaming. She took the paintings out and started tearing them. She threw the pieces in the air and when they fell to the ground she stomped on them. She was wearing her cowgirl boots.

Then she took my books out of the shopping bags and started throwing them around, out into the street, out on the lawn, everywhere.

"Here are your paintings! Here are your books! AND DON'T TELL ME ABOUT YOUR WOMEN! DON'T TELL ME ABOUT YOUR WOMEN!"

Then Lydia ran down to my court with a book in her hand, my latest, *The Selected Works of Henry Chinaski*. She screamed, "So you want your books back? So you want your books back? Here are your goddamned books! AND DON'T TELL ME ABOUT YOUR WOMEN!"

She started smashing the glass panes in my front door. She took *The Selected Works of Henry Chinaski* and smashed pane after pane, screaming, "You want your books back? Here are your goddamned books! AND DON'T TELL ME ABOUT YOUR WOMEN! I DON'T WANT TO HEAR ABOUT YOUR WOMEN!"

I stood there as she screamed and broke glass.

Where are the police? I thought. Where?

Then Lydia ran down the court walk, took a quick left at the trash bin and ran down the driveway of the apartment house next door. Behind a small bush was my typewriter, my radio and my toaster.

Lydia picked up the typewriter and ran out into the center of the street with it. It was a heavy old-fashioned standard machine. Lydia lifted the typer high over her head with both hands and smashed it in the street. The platen and several other parts flew off. She picked the typer up again, raised it over her head and screamed, "DON'T TELL ME ABOUT YOUR WOMEN!" and smashed it into the street again.

Then Lydia jumped into her car and drove off.

Fifteen seconds later the police cruiser drove up.

"It's an orange Volks. It's called the Thing, looks like a tank. I don't remember the license number, but the letters are HZY, like HAZY, got it?"

"Address?"

I gave them her address. . . .

Sure enough, they brought her back. I heard her in the back seat, wailing, as they drove up.

"STAND BACK!" said one cop as he jumped out. He followed me up to my place. He walked inside and stepped on some broken glass. For some reason he shone his flashlight on the ceiling and the ceiling mouldings.

"You want to press charges?" the cop asked me.

"No. She has children. I don't want her to lose her kids. Her ex-husband is trying to get them from her. But *please* tell her that people aren't supposed to go around doing this sort of thing."

"O.K.," he said, "now sign this."

He wrote it down in hand in a little notebook with lined paper. It said that I, Henry Chinaski, would not press charges against one Lydia Vance.

I signed it and he left.

I locked what was left of the door and went to bed and tried to sleep.

In an hour or so the phone rang. It was Lydia. She was back home.

"YOU-SON-OF-A-BITCH, YOU EVER TELL ME ABOUT YOUR WOMEN AGAIN AND I'LL DO THE SAME THING ALL OVER AGAIN!"

She hung up.

47

Two NIGHTS LATER I went over to Tammie's place on Rustic Court. I knocked. The lights weren't on. It seemed empty. I looked in her mailbox. There were letters in there. I wrote a note, "Tammie, I have been trying to phone you. I came over and you weren't in. Are you all right? Phone me. . . . Hank."

I drove over at 11 AM the next morning. Her car wasn't out front. My note was still stuck in the door. I rang anyhow. The letters were still in the mailbox. I left a note in the mailbox: "Tammie, where the hell are you? Contact me. . . . Hank."

I drove all over the neighborhood looking for that smashed red Camaro.

I returned that night. It was raining. My notes were wet. There was more mail in the box. I left her a book of my poems, inscribed. Then I went back to my Volks. I had a Maltese cross hanging from my rearview mirror. I cut the cross down, took it back to her place and tied it around her doorknob.

I didn't know where any of her friends lived, where her mother lived, where her lovers lived.

I went back to my court and wrote some love poems.

48

I WAS SITTING with an anarchist from Beverly Hills, Ben Solvnag, who was writing my biography when I heard her footsteps on the court walk. I knew the sound—they were always fast and frantic and sexy—those tiny feet. I lived near the rear of the court. My door was open. Tammie ran in.

We were both into each other's arms, hugging and kissing. Ben Solvnag said goodbye and was gone.

"Those sons of bitches confiscated my stuff, all my stuff! I couldn't make the rent! That dirty son-of-a-bitch!"

"I'll go over there and kick his ass. We'll get your stuff back."

"No, he has guns! All kinds of guns!"

"Oh."

"My daughter is at my mother's."

"How about something to drink?"

"Sure."

"What?"

"Extra dry champagne."

"O.K."

The door was still open and the afternoon sunlight came in through her hair—it was so long and so red it burned.

"Can I take a bath?" she asked.

"Of course."

"Wait for me," she said.

IN THE morning we talked about her finances. She had money coming in: child support plus a couple of unemployment checks with more to come.

"There's a vacancy in the place in back, right above me."

"How much is it?"

"$105 with half of the utilities paid."

"Oh hell, I can make that. Do they take children? A child?"

"They will. I've got pull. I know the managers."

By Sunday she was moved in. She was right above me. She could look into my kitchen where I typed my things on the breakfast nook table.

49

THAT TUESDAY NIGHT we were sitting at my place drinking; Tammie, me and her brother, Jay. The phone rang. It was Bobby.

"Louie and his wife are down here and she'd like to meet you."

Louie was the one who had just vacated Tammie's place. He played in jazz groups at small clubs and wasn't having much luck. But he was an interesting sort.

"I'd rather just forget it, Bobby."

CHARLES BUKOWSKI

"Louie will be hurt if you don't come down here."
"O.K., Bobby, but I'm bringing a couple of friends."

WE WENT down and the introductions went around. Then Bobby brought out some of his bargain beer. There was stereo music going, and it was loud.

"I read your story in *Knight*," said Louie. "It was a strange one. You've never fucked a dead woman, have you?"

"It just seemed like some of them were dead."

"I know what you mean."

"I hate that music," said Tammie.

"How is the music going, Louie?"

"Well, I've got a new group now. If we can hang together long enough we might make it."

"I think I'll suck somebody off," said Tammie, "I think I'll suck off Bobby, I think I'll suck off Louie, I think I'll suck off my brother!"

Tammie was dressed in a long outfit that looked something like an evening dress and something like a nightgown.

Valerie, Bobby's wife, was at work. She worked two nights a week as a barmaid. Louie and his wife, Paula, and Bobby had been drinking for some time.

Louie took a gulp of the bargain beer, started to get sick, jumped up and ran out the front door. Tammie jumped up and ran out the door after him. After a bit they both walked in together.

"Let's get the hell out of here," Louie said to Paula.

"All right," she said.

They got up and left together.

Bobby got out some more beer. Jay and I talked about something. Then I heard Bobby:

"Don't blame me! Hey, man, don't blame me!"

I looked. Tammie had her head in Bobby's lap and she had her hand on his balls and then she moved it up and grabbed his cock and held his cock, and all the time her eyes looked directly at me.

I took a hit of my beer, put it down, got up and walked out.

50

I saw bobby out front the next day when I went to buy a newspaper. "Louie phoned," he said, "he told me what happened to him."

"Yeah?"

"He ran outside to vomit and Tammie grabbed his cock while he was vomiting and she said, 'Come on upstairs and I'll suck you off. Then we'll stick your dick in an Easter egg.' He told her 'No' and she said, 'What's the matter? Aren't you a man? Can't you hold your liquor? Come upstairs and I'll suck you off!'"

I went down to the corner and bought the newspaper. I came back and checked the race results, read about the knifings, the rapes, the murders.

There was a knock. I opened the door. It was Tammie. She came in and sat down.

"Look," she said, "I'm sorry if I hurt you acting like I did, but that's all I'm sorry for. The rest of it is just me."

"That's all right," I said, "but you hurt Paula too when you ran out the door after Louie. They're together, you know."

"SHIT!" she screamed at me, "I DON'T KNOW PAULA FROM ADAM!"

51

That night i took Tammie to the harness races. We went upstairs to the second deck and sat down. I brought her a program and she stared at it a while. (At the harness races, past performance charts are printed in the program.)

"Look," she said, "I'm on pills. And when I'm on pills I sometimes get spaced and I get lost. Keep your eye on me."

"All right. I've got to bet. You want a few bucks to bet with?"

"No."

"All right, I'll be right back."

I walked to the windows and bet 5 win on the 7 horse.

When I got back Tammie wasn't there. She's just gone to the ladies' room, I thought.

I sat and watched the race. The 7 horse came in at 5 to one. I was 25 bucks up.

Tammie still wasn't back. The horses came out for the next race. I decided not to bet. I decided to look for Tammie.

First I walked to the upper deck and checked the grandstand, all the aisles, the concession stands, the bar. I couldn't find her.

The second race started and they went around. I heard the players screaming during the stretch run as I walked down to the ground floor. I looked all round for that marvelous body and that red hair. I couldn't find her.

I walked down to Emergency First Aid. A man was sitting in there smoking a cigar. I asked him, "Do you have a young redhead in there? Maybe she fainted . . . she's been sick."

"I don't have any redheads in here, sir."

My feet were tired. I went back to the second deck and began thinking about the next race.

By the end of the eighth race I was $132 ahead. I was going to bet 50 win on the 4 horse in the last race. I got up to bet and then I saw Tammie standing in the doorway of a maintenance room. She was standing between a black janitor with a broom and another black man who was very well dressed. He looked like a movie pimp. Tammie grinned and waved at me.

I walked over. "I was looking for you. I thought maybe you'd o.d.'d."

"No, I'm all right, I'm fine."

"Well, that's good. Goodnight, Red. . . ."

I walked off toward the betting window. I heard her running behind me. "Hey, where the hell you going?"

"I want to get it down on the 4 horse."

I got it down. The 4 lost by a nose. The races were over. Tammie and I walked out to the parking lot together. Her hip bounced against me as we walked.

"You had me worried," I said.

We found the car and got in. Tammie smoked 6 or 7 cigarettes on the way back, smoking them part way, then bending them out in the ashtray. She turned on the radio. She turned the sound up and down, changed stations and snapped her fingers to the music.

When we got to the court she ran to her place and locked the door.

52

BOBBY'S WIFE WORKED two nights a week and when she was gone he got on the telephone. I knew that on Tuesday and Thursday nights he would be lonely.

It was Tuesday night when the phone rang. It was Bobby. "Hey, man, mind if I come down and have a few beers?"

"All right, Bobby."

I was sitting in a chair across from Tammie who was on the couch. Bobby came in and sat on the couch. I opened him a beer. Bobby sat and talked to Tammie. The conversation was so inane that I tuned out. But some of it seeped through.

"In the morning," Bobby said, "I take a cold shower. It really wakes me up."

"I take a cold shower in the morning too," said Tammie.

"I take a cold shower and then I towel myself off," Bobby continued, "then I read a magazine or something. Then I'm ready for the day."

"I just take a cold shower, but I don't wipe myself off," said Tammie, "I just let the little drops stay there."

Bobby said, "Sometimes I take a real *hot* bath. The water's so hot that I've got to slip in real slow."

Then Bobby got up and demonstrated how he slipped into his real hot bath.

The conversation moved on to movies and television programs. They both seemed to love movies and television programs.

They talked for 2 or 3 hours, nonstop.

Then Bobby got up. "Well," he said, "I've got to go."

"Oh, *please* don't go, Bobby," said Tammie.

"No, I've got to go."

Valerie was due home from work.

53

ON THURSDAY NIGHT Bobby phoned again. "Hey, man, what are you doing?"

"Not much."

"Mind if I come down and have a few beers?"

"I'd rather not have any visitors tonight."

"Oh, come on, man, I'll just stay for a few beers. . . ."

"No, I'd rather not."

"WELL, FUCK YOU THEN!" he screamed.

I hung up and went into the other room.

"Who was that?" Tammie asked.

"Just somebody who wanted to come by."

"That was Bobby, wasn't it?"

"Yes."

"You treat him mean. He gets lonely when his wife is at work. What the hell's the matter with you?"

Tammie jumped up and ran into the bedroom and started dialing. I had just bought her a fifth of champagne. She hadn't opened it. I took it and hid it in the broom closet.

"Bobby," she said over the phone, "this is Tammie. Did you just phone? Where's your wife? Listen, I'll be right down."

She hung up and came out of the bedroom. "Where's the champagne?"

"Fuck off," I said, "you're not taking it down there and drinking it with him."

"I want that champagne. Where is it?"

"Let him furnish his own."

Tammie picked up a pack of cigarettes from the coffee table and ran out the door.

I GOT out the champagne, uncorked it and poured myself a glass. I was no longer writing love poems. In fact, I wasn't writing at all. I didn't feel like writing.

The champagne went down easy. I drank glass after glass.

Then I took my shoes off and walked down to Bobby's place. I looked through the blinds. They were sitting very close together on the couch, talking.

I walked back. I finished the last of the champagne and started in on the beer.

The phone rang. It was Bobby. "Look," he said, "Why don't you come down and have a beer with Tammie and me?"

I hung up.

I drank some more beer and smoked a couple of cheap cigars. I got drunker and drunker. I walked down to Bobby's apartment. I knocked. He opened the door.

Tammie was down at the end of the couch snorting coke, using a McDonald's spoon. Bobby put a beer in my hand.

"The trouble," he told me, "is that you're insecure, you lack confidence in yourself."

I sucked at the beer.

"That's right, Bobby's right," said Tammy.

"Something hurts inside of me."

"You're just insecure," said Bobby, "it's quite simple."

I HAD two phone numbers for Joanna Dover. I tried the one in Galveston. She answered.

"It's me, Henry."

"You sound drunk."

"I am. I want to come see you."

"When?"

"Tomorrow."

"All right."

"Will you meet me at the airport?"

"Sure, baby."

"I'll get a flight and call you back."

I GOT flight 707, leaving L.A. International the next day at 12:15 PM. I relayed the information to Joanna Dover. She said she'd be there.

* * *

THE PHONE rang. It was Lydia.

"I thought I'd tell you," she said, "that I sold the house. I'm moving to Phoenix. I'll be gone in the morning."

"All right, Lydia. Good luck."

"I had a miscarriage. I almost died, it was awful. I lost so much blood. I didn't want to bother you about it."

"Are you all right now?"

"I'm all right. I just want to get out of this town, I'm sick of this town."

We said goodbye.

I OPENED another beer. The front door opened and Tammie walked in. She walked in wild circles, looking at me.

"Did Valerie get home?" I asked. "Did you cure Bobby's loneliness?"

Tammie just kept circling around. She looked very good in her long gown, whether she had been fucked or not.

"Get out of here," I said.

She made one more circle, ran out the door and up to her place.

I couldn't sleep. Luckily, I had some more beer. I kept drinking beer and finished the last bottle about 4:30 AM. I sat and waited until 6 AM, then went out and got some more.

Time went slowly. I walked around. I didn't feel good but I started singing songs. I sang songs and walked around—from bathroom to bedroom to the front room to the kitchen and back, singing songs.

I looked at the clock. 11:15 AM. The airport was an hour away. I was dressed. I had on shoes but no stockings. All I took was a pair of reading glasses which I stuffed into my shirt pocket. I ran out the door without baggage.

The Volks was in front. I got in. The sunlight was very bright. I put my head down on the steering wheel a moment. I heard a voice from the court, "Where the hell does he think he's going like that?"

I started the car, turned the radio on and drove off. I had trouble steering. My car kept pulling across the double yellow line and into the oncoming traffic. They honked and I pulled back.

I got to the airport. I had 15 minutes left. I had run red lights, stop signs, had exceeded the speed limit, grossly, all the way. I had 14 minutes. The parking lot was full. I couldn't find a space. Then I saw a place in front of an elevator, just large enough for a Volks. A sign read, NO PARKING. I parked. As I locked the car my reading glasses fell out of my pocket and broke on the pavement.

I ran down the stairway and across the street to the airline reservations desk. It was hot. The sweat rolled off me. "Reservation for Henry Chinaski. . . ." The clerk wrote out the ticket and I paid cash. "By the way," said the clerk, "I've read your books."

I ran up to security. The buzzer went off. Too much change, 7 keys and my pocketknife. I put them on the plate and walked through again.

Five minutes. Gate 42.

Everyone had boarded. I walked on. Three minutes. I found my seat, strapped in. The flight captain was talking over the intercom.

We taxied down the runway, we were in the air. We swung out over the ocean and made the big turn.

54

I WAS THE last one off the plane and there was Joanna Dover.

"My god!" she laughed. "You look *awful!*"

"Joanna, let's have a Bloody Mary while we wait for my baggage. Oh hell, I don't *have* any baggage. But let's have a Bloody Mary anyhow."

We walked into the bar and sat down.

"You'll never make Paris this way."

"I'm not crazy about the French. Born in Germany, you know."

"I hope you'll like my place. It's simple. Two floors and plenty of space."

"As long as we're in the same bed."

"I've got paints."

"Paints?"

"I mean, you can paint if you want."

"Shit, but thanks, anyhow. Did I interrupt anything?"

"No. There was a garage mechanic. But he petered out. He couldn't stand the pace."

"Be kind to me, Joanna, sucking and fucking aren't everything."

"That's why I got the paints. For when you're resting."

"You are a lot of woman, even forgetting the 6 feet."

"Christ, don't I know it."

I LIKED her place. There were screens on every window and door. The windows swung open, large windows. There were no rugs on the floors, two bathrooms, old furniture, and lots of tables everywhere, large and small. It was simple and convenient.

"Take a shower," said Joanna.

I laughed. "These are all the clothes I have, what I'm wearing."

"We'll get you some more tomorrow. After you have your shower we'll go out and get a nice seafood meal. I know a good place."

"They serve drinks?"

"You asshole."

I didn't take a shower. I took a bath.

We drove quite a distance. I had never realized that Galveston was an island.

"The dope runners are hijacking the shrimp boats these days. They kill everybody on board and then run the stuff in. That's one reason the price of shrimp is going up—it's become a hazardous occupation. How's your occupation going?"

"I haven't been writing. I think it's over for me."

"How long has it been?"

"Six or seven days."

"This is the place. . . ."

Joanna pulled into a parking lot. She drove very fast, but she didn't drive fast as if she meant to break the law. She drove fast as if it were her given right. There was a difference and I appreciated it.

We got a table away from the crowd. It was cool and quiet and dark in there. I liked it. I went for the lobster. Joanna went for something strange. She ordered it in French. She was sophisticated, traveled. In a sense, as much as I disliked it, education helped when you were looking at a menu or for a job, especially when you were looking at a menu. I always felt inferior to waiters. I had arrived too late and with too little. The waiters all read Truman Capote. I read the race results.

The dinner was good and out on the gulf were the shrimp boats, the patrol boats and the pirates. The lobster tasted good in my mouth, and I drank him down with fine wine. Good fellow. I always liked you in your pink-red shell, dangerous and slow.

BACK AT Joanna Dover's place we had a delicious bottle of red wine. We sat in the dark watching the few cars pass in the street below. We were quiet. Then Joanna spoke.

"Hank?"

"Yes?"

"Was it some woman who drove you here?"

"Yes."

"Is it over with her?"

"I'd like to think so. But if I said 'no' . . ."

"Then you don't know?"

"Not really."

"Does anybody ever know?"

"I don't think so."

"That's what makes it all stink so."

"It does stink."

"Let's fuck."

"I've drunk too much."

"Let's go to bed."

"I want to drink some more."

"You won't be able to . . ."

"I know. I hope you'll let me stay four or five days."

"It will depend on your performance," she said.

"That's fair enough."

By the time we finished the wine I could barely make it to bed. I was asleep by the time Joanna came out of the bathroom. . . .

55

UPON AWAKENING I got up and used Joanna's toothbrush, drank a couple of glasses of water, washed my hands and face and got back into bed. Joanna turned around and my mouth found hers. My cock began to rise. I put her hand on my cock. I grabbed her hair, pulling her head back, kissing her, savagely. I played with her cunt. I teased her clit for a long time. She was very wet. I mounted and buried it. I held it in. I could feel her responding. I was able to work a long time. Finally I was unable to hold back any longer. I was wet with sweat and my heart beat so loudly that I could hear it.

"I'm not in very good shape," I told her.

"I liked it. Let's have a joint."

She produced a joint, already rolled. We passed it back and forth. "Joanna," I told her, "I'm still sleepy. I could use another hour."

"Sure. As soon as we finish this joint."

We finished the joint and stretched out in bed again. I slept.

56

THAT EVENING AFTER dinner Joanna produced some mescaline.

"You ever tried this stuff?"

"No."

"Want to try some?"

"All right."

Joanna had some paints and brushes and paper spread on the table. Then I remembered she was an art collector. And that she had bought some of my paintings. We had been drinking Heinekens most of the evening, but were still sober.

"This is very powerful stuff."

"What does it do?"

"It gives you a strange kind of high. You might get sick. When you vomit you get higher but I prefer not to vomit so we take a little baking soda along with it. I guess the main thing about mescaline is that it makes you feel terror."

"I've felt that without any help at all."

I BEGAN painting. Joanna turned the stereo on. It was very strange music, but I liked it. I looked around and Joanna was gone. I didn't care. I painted a man who had just committed suicide, he had hung himself from the rafters with a rope. I used many yellows, the dead man was so bright and pretty. Then something said, "Hank . . .

It was right behind me. I leaped out of my chair, "JESUS CHRIST! OH, JESUS SHIT CHRIST!"

Tiny icy bubbles ran from my wrists to my shoulders and down my back. I shivered and trembled. I looked around. Joanna was standing there.

"Never do that to me again," I told her. "Never sneak up on me like that or I'll kill you!"

"Hank, I just went to get some cigarettes."

"Look at this painting."

"Oh, it's great," she said, "I really love it!"

"It's the mescaline, I guess."

"Yes, it is."

"All right, give me a smoke, lady."

Joanna laughed and lit us up two.

I began painting again. This time I really did it: A huge, green wolf fucking a redhead, her red hair flowing back while the green wolf slammed it to her through lifted legs. She was helpless and submissive. The wolf sawed away and overhead the night burned, it was outdoors, and long-armed stars and the moon watched them. It was hot, hot, and full of color.

"Hank . . ."

I leaped up. And turned. It was Joanna behind me. I got her by the throat. "I told you, goddamn you, *not to sneak up* . . ."

CHARLES BUKOWSKI

57

I STAYED FIVE days and nights. Then I couldn't get it up any more. Joanna drove me to the airport. She had bought me a new piece of luggage and some new clothing. I hated that Dallas-Fort Worth airport. It was the most inhuman airport in the U.S.

Joanna waved me off and I was in the air. . . .

THE TRIP to Los Angeles was without incident. I disembarked, wondering about the Volks. I took the elevator up in the parking area and didn't see it. I figured it must have been towed away. Then I walked around to the other side—and there it was. All I had was a parking ticket.

I drove home. The apartment looked the way it always had—bottles and trash everywhere. I'd have to clean it up a bit. If anybody saw it that way they'd have me committed.

There was a knock. I opened the door. It was Tammie. "Hi!" she said.

"Hello."

"You must have been in an awful hurry when you left. All the doors were unlocked. The back door was wide open. Listen, promise you won't tell if I tell you something?"

"All right."

"Arlene went in and used your phone, long distance."

"All right."

"I tried to stop her but I couldn't. She was on pills."

"All right."

"Where've you been?"

"Galveston."

"Why did you go flying off like that? You're crazy."

"I've got to leave again Saturday."

"Saturday? What's today?"

"Thursday."

"Where are you going?"

"New York City."

"Why?"

132

"A reading. They sent the tickets two weeks ago. And I get a percentage of the gate."

"Oh, take me *with* you! I'll leave Dancy with Mother. I want to go!"

"I can't afford to take you. It'll eat up my profits. I've had some heavy expenses lately."

"I'll be *good*! I'll be *so* good! I'll never leave your side! I really missed you."

"I can't do it, Tammie."

She went to the refrigerator and got a beer. "You just don't give a fuck. All those love poems, you didn't mean it."

"I meant it when I wrote them."

The phone rang. It was my editor. "Where've you been?"

"Galveston. Research."

"I hear you're reading in New York City this Saturday."

"Yes, Tammie wants to go, my girl."

"Are you taking her?"

"No, I can't afford it."

"How much is it?"

"$316 round trip."

"Do you really want to take her?"

"Yes, I think so."

"All right, go ahead. I'll mail you a check."

"Do you mean it?"

"Yes."

"I don't know what to say. . . ."

"Forget it. Just remember Dylan Thomas."

"They won't kill *me*."

We said goodbye. Tammie was sucking on her beer.

"All right," I told her, "you've got two or three days to pack."

"You mean, I'm *going?*"

"Yes, my editor is paying your way."

Tammie leaped up and grabbed me. She kissed me, grabbed my balls, pulled at my cock. "You're the sweetest old fuck!"

New York City. Outside of Dallas, Houston, Charleston, and Atlanta, it was the worst place I had ever been. Tammie pushed up against me and my cock rose. Joanna Dover hadn't gotten it all. . . .

58

WE HAD A 3:30 PM flight out of Los Angeles that Saturday. At 2 PM I went up and knocked on Tammie's door. She wasn't there. I want back to my place and sat down. The phone rang. It was Tammie. "Look," I said, "we have to think about leaving. I have people meeting me at Kennedy airport. Where are you?"

"I'm $6 short on a prescription. I'm getting some Quaaludes."

"Where are you?"

"I'm just below Santa Monica Boulevard and Western, about a block. It's an Owl drugstore. You can't miss it."

I hung up, got into the Volks and drove over. I parked a block below Santa Monica and Western, got out and looked around. There was no pharmacy.

I got back in the Volks and drove along looking for her red Camaro. Then I saw it, five blocks further down. I parked and walked in. Tammie was sitting in a chair. Dancy ran up and made a face at me.

"We can't take the kid."

"I know. We'll drop her off over at my mother's."

"Your mother's? That's 3 miles the other way."

"It's on the way to the airport."

"No, it's in the other direction."

"Do you have the 6 bucks?"

I gave Tammie the six.

"I'll see you back at your place. You packed?"

"Yes, I'm ready."

I drove back and waited. Then I heard them.

"Mommy!" Dancy said, "I want a Ding-Dong!"

They went up the stairs. I waited for them to come down. They didn't come down. I went up. Tammie was packed, but she was down on her knees zipping and unzipping her baggage.

"Look," I said, "I'll carry your other stuff down to the car."

She had two large paper shopping bags, stuffed, and three dresses on hangers. All this besides her luggage.

I took the shopping bags and the dresses down to the Volks. When I came back she was still zipping and unzipping her luggage.

"Tammie, let's go."

"Wait a minute."

She knelt there running the zipper back and forth, up and down. She didn't look into the baggage. She just ran the zipper up and down.

"Mommy," said Dancy, "I want a Ding-Dong."

"Come on, Tammie, let's go."

"Oh, all right."

I picked up the zipper bag and they followed me out.

I FOLLOWED her battered red Camaro to her mother's place. We went in. Tammie stood at her mother's dresser and started pulling drawers out, in and out. Each time she pulled a drawer out she reached in and mixed everything up. Then she'd slam the drawer and go to the next. Same thing.

"Tammie, the plane is ready to take off."

"Oh no, we've got plenty of time. I *hate* hanging around airports."

"What are you going to do about Dancy?"

"I'm going to leave her here until Mother gets home from work."

Dancy let out a wail. Finally she knew, and she wailed, and the tears ran, and then she stopped, balled her fists and screamed, "I WANT A DING-DONG!"

"Listen, Tammie, I'll be waiting in the car."

I went out and waited. I waited five minutes then went back in. Tammie was still sliding the drawers in and out.

"Please, Tammie, let's leave!"

"All right."

She turned to Dancy. "Look, you stay here until Grandma gets home. Keep the door locked and don't let *anybody* in but Grandma!"

Dancy wailed again. Then she screamed, "I HATE YOU!"

* * *

Tammie followed me and we got into the Volks. I started the engine. She opened the door and was gone. "I HAVE TO GET SOMETHING OUT OF MY CAR!"

Tammie ran over to the Camaro. "Oh shit, I locked it and I don't have the key for the door! Do you have a coat hanger?"

"No," I screamed, "I *don't* have a coat hanger!"

"Be *right* back!"

Tammie ran back to her mother's apartment. I heard the door open. Dancy wailed and shouted. Then I heard the door slam and Tammie returned with a coat hanger. She went to the Camaro and jimmied the door.

I walked over to her car. Tammie had climbed into the back seat and was going through that incredible mess—clothing, paper bags, paper cups, newspapers, beer bottles, empty cartons—piled in there. Then she found it: her camera, the Polaroid I had given her for her birthday.

As I drove along, racing the Volks like I was out to win the 500, Tammie leaned over.

"You really love me, don't you?"

"Yes."

"When we get to New York I'm going to fuck you like you've *never* been fucked before!"

"You mean it?"

"Yes."

She grabbed my cock and leaned against me.

My first and only redhead. I was lucky. . . .

59

We ran up the long ramp. I was carrying her dresses and the shopping bags.

At the escalator Tammie saw the flight insurance machine.

"Please," I said, "we only have five minutes until take-off."

"I want Dancy to have the money."

"All right."

"Do you have two quarters?"

I gave her two quarters. She inserted them and a card jumped out of the machine.

"You got a pen?"

Tammie filled out the card and then there was an envelope. She put the card in the envelope. Then she tried to insert it in the slot in the machine.

"This thing won't go in!"

"We're going to miss the plane."

She kept trying to jam the envelope in the slot. She couldn't get it in.

She stood there and kept jamming the envelope at the slot. Now the envelope was completely bent in half and all the edges were bent.

"I'm going mad," I told her. "I can't *stand* it."

She jammed a few more times. It wouldn't go. She looked at me. "O.K., let's go."

We went up the escalator with her dresses and shopping bags.

We found the boarding gate. We got two seats near the back. We strapped in. "You see," she said, "I told you we had plenty of time."

I looked at my watch. The plane started to roll. . . .

60

WE WERE IN the air twenty minutes when she took a mirror out of her purse and began to make up her face, mostly the eyes. She worked at her eyes with a small brush, concentrating on the eyelashes. While she was doing this she opened her eyes very wide and she held her mouth open. I watched her and began to get a hard-on.

Her mouth was so very full and round and open and she kept working on her eyelashes. I ordered two drinks.

Tammie stopped to drink, then she continued.

A young fellow in the seat to the right of us began playing with himself. Tammie kept looking at her face in the mirror, holding her mouth open. It looked like she could really suck with that mouth.

She continued for an hour. Then she put the mirror and the brush away, leaned against me and went to sleep.

There was a woman in the seat to our left. She was in her mid-forties. Tammie was sleeping next to me.

The woman looked at me.

"How old is she?" she asked me.

It was suddenly very quiet on that jet. Everyone nearby was listening.

"23."

"She looks 17."

"She's 23."

"She spends two hours making up her face and then goes to sleep."

"It was about an hour."

"Are you going to New York?" the lady asked me.

"Yes."

"Is she your daughter?"

"No, I'm not her father *or* her grandfather. I'm not related to her in any way. She's my girlfriend and we're going to New York." I could see the headline in her eyes:

MONSTER FROM EAST HOLLYWOOD DRUGS 17 YEAR OLD GIRL, TAKES HER TO NEW YORK CITY WHERE HE SEXUALLY ABUSES HER, THEN SELLS HER BODY TO NUMEROUS BUMS

The lady questioner gave up. She stretched back in her seat and closed her eyes. Her head slipped down toward me. It was almost in my lap, it seemed. Holding Tammie, I watched that head. I wondered if she would mind if I crushed her lips with a crazy kiss. I got another hard-on.

* * *

WE WERE ready to land. Tammie seemed very limp. It worried me. I strapped her in.

"Tammie, it's *New York City!* We're getting ready to *land!* Tammie, *wake up!*"

No response.

An o.d.?

I felt her pulse. I couldn't feel anything.

I looked at her enormous breasts. I watched for some sign of breathing. They didn't move. I got up and found a stewardess.

"Please take your seat, sir. We are preparing to land."

"Look, I'm worried. My girlfriend won't wake up."

"Do you think she's dead?" she whispered.

"I don't know," I whispered back.

"All right, sir. As soon as we land I'll come back there."

The plane was starting to drop. I went into the crapper and wet some paper towels. I came back, sat next to Tammie and rubbed them over her face. All that makeup, wasted. Tammie didn't respond.

"You whore, wake up!"

I ran the towels down between her breasts. Nothing. No movement. I gave up.

I'd have to ship her body back somehow. I'd have to explain to her mother. Her mother would hate me.

We landed. The people got up and stood in line, waiting to get out. I sat there. I shook Tammie and pinched her. "It's New York City, Red. The rotten apple. Come around. Cut out the shit."

The stewardess came back and shook Tammie.

"Honey, what's the matter?"

Tammie started responding. She moved. Then her eyes opened. It was only the matter of a *new* voice. Nobody listened to an old voice anymore. Old voices became a part of one's self, like a fingernail.

Tammie got out her mirror and started combing her hair. The stewardess was patting her shoulder. I got up and got the dresses out of the overhead compartment. The shopping bags were up there too. Tammie continued to look into the mirror and comb her hair.

"Tammie, we're in New York. Let's get off."

She moved quickly. I had the two shopping bags and the dresses. She went through the exit wiggling the cheeks of her ass. I followed her.

61

OUR MAN WAS there to meet us, Gary Benson. He also wrote poetry and drove a cab. He was very fat but at least he didn't look like a poet, he didn't look North Beach or East Village or like an English teacher, and that helped because it was very hot in New York that day, nearly 110 degrees. We got the baggage and got into his car, not his cab, and he explained to us why it was almost useless to own a car in New York City. That's why there were so many cabs. He got us out of the airport and he started driving and talking, and the drivers of New York City were just like New York City—nobody gave an inch or a damn. There was no compassion or courtesy: fender jammed against fender, they drove on. I understood it: anybody who gave an inch would cause a traffic jam, a disturbance, a murder. Traffic flowed endlessly like turds in a sewer. It was marvelous to see, and none of the drivers were angry, they were simply resigned to the facts.

But Gary *did* like to talk shop. "If it's O.K. with you I'd like to tape you for a radio show, I'd like to do an interview."

"All right, Gary, let's say tomorrow after the reading."

"I'm going to take you to see the poetry coordinator now. He has everything organized. He'll show you where you're staying and so forth. His name is Marshall Benchly and don't tell him I told you but I hate his guts."

We drove along and then we saw Marshall Benchly standing in front of a brownstone. There was no parking. He leaped in the car and Gary drove off. Benchly looked like a poet, a private-income poet who had never worked for a living; it showed. He was affected and bland, a pebble.

"We'll take you to your place," he said.

He proudly recited a long list of people who had stayed at my hotel. Some of the names I recognized, others I didn't.

Gary drove into the unloading zone in front of the Chelsea Hotel. We got out. Gary said, "See you at the reading. And see you tomorrow."

Marshall took us inside and we went up to the desk clerk. The Chelsea certainly wasn't much, maybe that's where it got its charm.

Marshall turned and handed me the key. "It's Room 1010, Janis Joplin's old room."

"Thanks."

"Many great artists have stayed in 1010."

He walked us over to the tiny elevator.

"The reading's at 8. I'll pick you up at 7:30. We've been sold out for two weeks. We're selling some standing-room tickets but we've got to be careful because of the fire department."

"Marshall, where's the nearest liquor store?"

"Downstairs and take a right."

We said goodbye to Marshall and took the elevator up.

62

IT WAS HOT that night at the reading, which was to be held at St. Mark's Church. Tammie and I sat in what was used as the dressing room. Tammie found a full-length mirror leaning against the wall and began combing her hair. Marshall took me out in back of the church. They had a burial ground back there. Little cement tombstones sat on the earth and carved on the tombstones were inscriptions. Marshall walked me around and showed me the inscriptions. I always got nervous before a reading, very tense and unhappy. I almost always vomited. Then I did. I vomited on one of the graves.

"You just vomited on Peter Stuyvesant," Marshall said.

I WALKED back into the dressing room. Tammie was still looking at herself in the mirror. She looked at her face and her body, but mostly she was worried about her hair. She piled it on top of her head, looked at it that way and then let it fall back down.

Marshall put his head into the room. "Come on, they're waiting!"

"Tammie's not ready," I told him.

Then she piled her hair up on top of her head again and looked at herself. Then she let it fall. Then she stood close to the mirror and looked at her eyes.

Marshall knocked, then came in. "Come on, Chinaski!"

"Come on, Tammie, let's go."

"All right."

I walked out with Tammie at my elbow. They started applauding. The old Chinaski bullshit was working. Tammie went down into the crowd and I started to read. I had many beers in an ice bucket. I had old poems and new poems. I couldn't miss. I had St. Mark's by the cross.

63

WE GOT BACK to 1010. I had my check. I'd left word that we didn't want to be disturbed. Tammie and I sat drinking. I'd read 5 or 6 love poems about her.

"They knew who I was," she said. "Sometimes I giggled. It was embarassing."

They had known who she was all right. She glistened with sex. Even the roaches and the ants and the flies wanted to fuck her.

There was a knock on the door. Two people had slipped through, a poet and his woman. The poet was Morse Jenkins from Vermont. His woman was Sadie Everet. He had four bottles of beer.

He wore sandals and old torn bluejeans; turquoise bracelets; a chain around his throat; he had a beard, long hair; orange blouse. He talked, and he talked. And walked around the room.

There is a problem with writers. If what a writer wrote was published and sold many, many copies, the writer thought he was great. If what a writer wrote was published and sold a medium number of copies, the writer thought he was great. If what a writer wrote was published and sold very few copies, the writer thought he was great. If what the writer wrote never was published and he didn't have the money to publish it himself, then he thought he was truly great. The truth, however, was that there was very little greatness. It was almost nonexistent, invisible. But you could be sure that the worst writers had the most confidence, the least self-doubt. Anyway, writers were to be avoided, and I tried to avoid them, but it was almost impossible. They hoped for some sort of brotherhood, some kind of togetherness. None of it had anything to do with writing, none of it helped at the typewriter.

"I sparred with Clay before he became Ali," said Morse. Morse jabbed and shuffled, danced. "He was pretty good, but I gave him a workout."

Morse shadow-boxed about the room.

"Look at my legs!" he said. "I've got great legs!"

"Hank's got better legs than you have," said Tammie.

Being a leg-man, I nodded.

Morse sat down. He pointed a beer bottle at Sadie. "She works as a nurse. She supports me. But I'm going to make it someday. They'll hear from me!"

Morse would never need a mike at his readings.

He looked at me. "Chinaski, you're one of the two or three best living poets. You're really making it. You write a tough line. But I'm coming on too! Let me read you my shit. Sadie, hand me my poems."

"No," I said, "wait! I don't want to hear them."

"Why not, man? Why not?"

"There's been too much poetry tonight, Morse. I just want to lay back and forget it."

"Well, all right. . . . Listen, you never answer my letters."

"I'm not a snob, Morse. But I get 75 letters a month. If I answered them that's all I would ever do."

"I'll bet you answer the women!"

"That depends. . . ."

143

"All right, man, I'm not bitter. I still like your stuff. Maybe I'll never be famous but I think I will and I think you'll be glad you met me. Come on, Sadie, let's go. . . ."

I walked them to the door. Morse grabbed my hand. He didn't pump it, and neither of us quite looked at the other. "You're a good old guy," he said.

"Thanks, Morse. . . ."

And then they were gone.

64

THE NEXT MORNING Tammie found a prescription in her purse. "I've got to get this filled," she said. "Look at it."

It was wrinkled and the ink had run.

"What happened here?"

"Well, you know my brother, he's a pill head."

"I know your brother. He owes me twenty bucks."

"Well, he tried to get this prescription away from me. He tried to strangle me. I put the prescription in my mouth and swallowed it. Or I *pretended* to swallow it. He wasn't sure. That was the time I phoned you and asked you to come over and kick the shit out of him. He split. But I still had the prescription in my mouth. I haven't used it yet. But I can get it filled here. It's worth a try."

"All right."

We took the elevator down to the street. It was over 100 degrees. I could hardly move. Tammie started walking and I followed along behind her as she weaved from one edge of the sidewalk to the other.

"Come on!" she said. "Keep up!"

She was on something, it appeared to be downers. She was woozy. Tammie walked up to a newsstand and began staring at a periodical. I think it was *Variety*. She stood there and stood there. I stood there near her. It was boring and senseless. She just stared at *Variety*.

"Listen, sister, either buy the damned thing or move on!" It was the man inside the newsstand.

Tammie moved on. "My god, New York is a horrible place! I just wanted to see if there was anything about the reading!"

Tammie moved along, wiggling it, wobbling from one side of the pavement to the other. In Hollywood cars would have pulled over to the curbing, blacks would have made overtures, she would have been approached, serenaded, applauded. New York was different; it was jaded and weary and it disdained flesh.

We were into a black district. They watched us walking by: the redhead with the long hair, stoned, and the old guy with gray in his beard walking behind her, wearily. I glanced at them sitting on their stoops; they had good faces. I liked them. I liked them better than I liked her.

I followed Tammie down the street. Then there was a furniture store. There was a broken down desk chair out in front on the sidewalk. Tammie walked over to the old desk chair and stood staring at it. She seemed hypnotized. She kept staring at the desk chair. She touched it with her finger. Minutes went by. Then she sat down in it.

"Look," I told her, "I'm going back to the hotel. You do whatever you want to do."

Tammie didn't even look up. She slid her hands back and forth on the arm rests of the desk chair. She was in a world of her own. I turned and walked off, back to the Chelsea.

I GOT some beer and took the elevator up. I undressed, took a shower, propped a couple of pillows against the headboard of the bed and sucked at the beer. Readings diminished me. They were soul-sucks. I finished one beer and opened another. Readings got you a piece of ass sometimes. Rock stars got ass; boxers on the way up got ass; great bullfighters got virgins. Somehow, only the bullfighters deserved any of it.

There was a knock on the door. I got up and opened it a crack. It was Tammie. She pushed in.

"I found this dirty Jew son-of-a-bitch. He wanted $12 to fill the prescription! It's 6 bucks on the coast. I told him I only had $6. He didn't care. A dirty Jew living in Harlem! Can I have a beer?"

Tammie took the beer and sat in the window, one leg out, one arm out, one leg in, one holding on to the raised window.

"I want to see the Statue of Liberty. I want to see Coney Island," she said.

I got myself a new beer.

"Oh, it's *nice* out here! It's nice and cool."

Tammie leaned out the window, looking.

Then she screamed.

The hand that had been holding on to the window slipped. I saw most of her body go out the window. Then it came back. Somehow she had pulled herself back inside. She sat there, stunned.

"That was close," I told her. "It would have made a good poem. I've lost a lot of women in a lot of ways, but that would have been a new way."

Tammie walked over to the bed. She stretched out face down. I realized she was still stoned. Then she rolled off the bed. She landed flat on her back. She didn't move. I walked over and picked her up and put her back on the bed. I grabbed her by the hair and kissed her viciously.

"Hey. . . . What're you doin'?"

I remembered she had promised me a piece of ass. I rolled her on her stomach, pulled her dress up, pulled her panties off. I climbed on top of her and rammed, trying to find her cunt. I poked and poked. It went in. It slid further and further in. I had her good. She made small sounds. Then the phone rang. I pulled out, got up and answered it. It was Gary Benson.

"I'm coming over with my tape recorder for that radio interview."

"When?"

"In about 45 minutes."

I hung up and went back to Tammie. I was still hard. I grabbed her hair, gave her another violent kiss. Her eyes were closed, her mouth was lifeless. I mounted her again. Outside they were sitting on their fire escapes. When the sun started to go down and some shade appeared they came out to cool off. The people of New York City sat out there and drank beer and soda and ice water. They endured and smoked cigarettes. Just being alive was a victory. They decorated their fire escapes with plants. They made do with what there was.

I went straight for Tammie's core. Dog fashion. Dogs knew best. I whammed away. It was good to be out of the post office. I rocked and socked her body. Despite the pills she was trying to speak. "Hank . . ." she said.

I came finally, then rested on her. We were both drenched with sweat. I rolled off, got up, undressed, and walked to the shower. Once again I had fucked this redhead 32 years younger than I was. It felt fine in the shower. I intended to live to be 80 so that I could then fuck an 18 year old girl. The air conditioner didn't work, but the shower did. It felt really good. I was ready for my radio interview.

65

BACK IN L.A., there was almost a week of peace. Then the phone rang. It was the owner of a Manhattan Beach nightclub, Marty Seavers. I had read there a couple of times before. The club was called Smack-Hi.

"Chinaski, I want you to read a week from Friday. You can pick up about $450."

"All right."

Rock groups played there. It was a different audience than at the colleges. They were as obnoxious as I was and we cursed one another between poems. I preferred it.

"Chinaski," Marty said, "you think you have trouble with women. Let me tell you. The one I've got now has a way with windows and screens. I'll be sleeping and she'll appear in the bedroom at 3 or 4 AM. She'll shake me. It scares the shit out of me. She stands there and says, 'I just wanted to make sure you were sleeping alone!'"

"Death and transfiguration."

"The other night, I'm sitting and there's a knock on the door. I know it's her. I open the door and she isn't there. It's 11 PM and I'm in my shorts. I've been drinking and I'm worried. I run outside in my shorts. I had given her $400 worth of dresses for her birthday. I run outside and there are the dresses, on the roof of my new car, and they're on fire, they're burning! I run up to pull them off and she leaps out from behind a bush and starts screaming. The neighbors look out and there I am in my shorts, burning my hands, snatching the dresses off the roof."

"She sounds like one of mine," I said.

"O.K., so I figured we were through. I'm sitting here two nights later, I had to work the club that night, so I'm sitting here at 3 AM drunk and in my shorts again. There's a knock on the door. It's her knock. I open it and she isn't there. I go out to my car and she has more dresses soaked in gasoline and burning. She had saved some. Only this time they are burning on the hood. She leaps out from somewhere and starts screaming. The neighbors look out. There I am again in my shorts trying to get these burning dresses off the hood."

"That's great, I wish it had happened to me."

"You should see my new car. It has paint blisters all over the hood and the roof."

"Where is she now?"

"We're back together. She's coming over in 30 minutes. Can I put you down for the reading?"

"Sure."

"You outdraw the rock groups. I never saw anything like it. I'd like to bring you in every Friday and Saturday night."

"It wouldn't work, Marty. You can play the same song over and over, but with poems they want something new."

Marty laughed and hung up.

66

I TOOK TAMMIE. We got there a little early and went to a bar across the street. We got a table.

"Now don't drink too much, Hank. You know how you slur your words and miss your lines when you get too drunk."

"At last," I said, "you're talking sense."

"You're afraid of the audience, aren't you?"

"Yes, but it's not stagefright. It's that I'm there as the geek. They like to watch me eat my shit. But it pays the light bill and takes me to the racetrack. I don't have any excuses about why I do it."

"I'll have a Stinger," said Tammie.

I told the girl to bring us a Stinger and a Bud.

"I'll be all right tonight," she said, "don't worry about me."

Tammie drank the Stinger down.

"These Stingers don't seem to have much in them. I'll have another."

We had another Stinger and another Bud.

"Really," she said, "I don't think they're putting anything into these drinks. I better have another."

Tammie had five Stingers in 40 minutes.

We knocked on the back door of the Smack-Hi. One of Marty's big bodyguards let us in. He had these malfunctioning thyroid types working for him to keep law and order when the teenyboppers, the hairy freaks, the glue sniffers, the acid heads, the plain grass folk, the alcoholics—all the miserable, the damned, the bored and the pretenders—got out of hand.

I was getting ready to puke and I did. This time I found a trash can and let it go. The last time I had dumped it just outside Marty's office. He was pleased with the change.

67

WANT SOMETHING TO drink?" Marty asked.

"I'll have a beer," I said.

"I'll have a Stinger," said Tammie.

"Get a seat for her, put her on the tab," I told Marty.

"All right. We'll set her up. We're S.R.O. We've had to turn away 150 and it's 30 minutes before you go on."

"I want to introduce Chinaski to the audience," said Tammie.

"O.K. with you?" asked Marty.

"O.K."

They had a kid out there with a guitar, Dinky Summers, and the crowd was disemboweling him. Eight years ago Dinky had had a gold record, but nothing since.

Marty got on an intercom and dialed out. "Listen," he asked, "is that guy as bad as he sounds?"

You could hear a woman's voice over the phone. "He's terrible."

Marty hung up.

"We want Chinaski!" they yelled.

"All right," we could hear Dinky, "Chinaski is next."

He started singing again. They were drunk. They hooted and hissed. Dinky sang on. He finished his act and got off stage. One could never tell. Some days it was better to stay in bed with the covers pulled up.

There was a knock. It was Dinky in his red, white and blue tennis shoes, white t-shirt, cords and brown felt hat. The hat sat perched on a mass of blonde curls. The t-shirt said, "God is Love."

Dinky looked at us. "Was I *really* that bad? I want to know. Was I *really* that bad?"

Nobody answered.

Dinky looked at me. "Hank, was I that bad?"

"The crowd is drunk. It's carnival time."

"I want to know if I was bad or not?"

"Have a drink."

"I gotta go find my girl," Dinky said. "She's out there alone."

"Look," I said, "let's get it over with."

"Fine," said Marty, "go get it on."

"I'm introducing him," said Tammie.

I walked out with her. As we approached the stage they saw us and began screaming, cursing. Bottles fell off tables. There was a fist fight. The boys at the post office would never believe this.

Tammie went out to the mike. "Ladies and gentlemen," she said, "Henry Chinaski couldn't make it tonight. . . ."

There was silence.

Then she said, "Ladies and gentlemen, Henry Chinaski!"

I walked on. They jeered. I hadn't done anything yet. I took the mike. "Hello, this is Henry Chinaski. . . ."

The place trembled with sound. I didn't need to do anything. They would do it all. But you had to be careful. Drunk as they were they could immediately detect any false gesture, any false word. You could never underestimate an audience. They had paid to get in; they had paid for drinks; they intended to get *something* and if you didn't give it to them they'd run you right into the ocean.

There was a refrigerator on stage. I opened it. There must have been 40 bottles of beer in there. I reached in and got one, twisted the cap off, took a hit. I needed that drink.

Then a man down front hollered, "Hey, Chinaski, we're *paying* for drinks!"

It was a fat guy in the front row in a mailman's outfit.

I went into the refrigerator and took out a beer. I walked over and handed him the beer. Then I walked back, reached in, and got some more beers. I handed them to the people in the first row.

"Hey, how about *us?*" A voice from near the back.

I took a bottle and looped it through the air. I threw a few more back there. They were good. They caught them all. Then one slipped out of my hand and went high into the air. I heard it smash. I decided to quit. I could see a lawsuit: skull fracture.

There were 20 bottles left.

"Now, the rest of these are *mine!*"

"You gonna read all night?"

"I'm gonna drink all night. . . ."

Applause, jeers, belches. . . .

"YOU FUCKING HUNK OF SHIT!" some guy screamed.

"Thank you, Aunt Tilly," I answered.

I sat down, adjusted the mike, and started on the first poem. It became quiet. I was in the ring alone with the bull now. I felt some terror. But I had written the poems. I read them out. It was best to open up light, a poem of mockery. I finished it and the walls rocked. Four or five people were fighting during the

151

applause. I was going to luck out. All I had to do was hang in there.

You couldn't underestimate them and you couldn't kiss their ass. There was a certain middle ground to be achieved.

I read more poems, drank the beer. I got drunker. The words were harder to read. I missed lines, dropped poems on the floor. Then I stopped and just sat there drinking.

"This is good," I told them, "you pay to watch me drink."

I made an effort and read them some more poems. Finally I read them a few dirty ones and wound it up.

"That's it," I said.

They yelled for more.

The boys at the slaughterhouse, the boys at Sears Roebuck, all the boys at all the warehouses where I worked as a kid and as a man never would have believed it.

In the office there were more drinks and several fat joints, bombers. Marty got on the intercom to find out about the gate.

Tammie stared at Marty. "I don't like you," she said. "I don't like your eyes at all."

"Don't worry about his eyes," I told her. "Let's just get the money and go."

Marty made the check out and handed it to me. "Here it is," he said, "$200. . . ."

"$200!" Tammie screamed at him. "You rotten son-of-a-bitch!"

I read the check. "He's kidding," I told her, "calm down."

She ignored me. "$200," she said to Marty, "you rotten . . ."

"Tammie," I said, "it's $400. . . ."

"Sign the check," said Marty, "and I'll give you cash."

"I got pretty drunk out there," Tammie told me. "I asked this guy, 'Can I lean my body against your body?' He said, 'O.K.'"

I signed and Marty gave me a stack of bills. I put them in my pocket.

"Look, Marty, I guess we better be leaving."

"I hate your eyes," Tammie said to Marty.

"Why don't you stay and talk awhile?" Marty asked me.

"No, we've got to go.

Tammie stood up. "I have to go to the ladies' restroom."

She left.

Marty and I sat there. Ten minutes went by. Marty stood up and said, "Wait, I'll be right back."

I sat and waited, 5 minutes, 10 minutes. I walked out of the office and out the back door. I walked to the parking lot and sat in my Volks. Fifteen minutes went by, 20, 25.

I'll give her 5 more minutes and then I'm leaving, I thought.

Just then Marty and Tammie walked out the back door and into the alley.

Marty pointed. "There he is." Tammie walked over. Her clothes were all messed up and twisted. She climbed into the back seat and curled up.

I GOT lost 2 or 3 times on the freeway. Finally I pulled up in front of the court. I awakened Tammie. She got out, ran up the stairs to her place, and slammed the door.

68

IT WAS A Wednesday night, 12:30 AM and I was very sick. My stomach was raw, but I managed to hold down a few beers. Tammie was with me and she seemed sympathetic. Dancy was at her grandmother's.

Even though I was ill it seemed, finally, to be a good time—just two people being together.

There was a knock on the door. I opened it. It was Tammie's brother, Jay, with another young man, Filbert, a small Puerto Rican. They sat down and I gave each of them a beer.

"Let's go to a dirty movie," said Jay.

Filbert just sat there. He had a black carefully-trimmed mustache and his face had very little expression. He didn't give off any rays at all. I thought of terms like *blank*, *wooden*, *dead*, and so forth.

"Why don't you say something, Filbert?" Tammie asked.

He didn't speak.

I got up, went to the kitchen sink and vomited. I came back and sat down. I had a new beer. I hated it when the beer wouldn't stay down. I simply had been drunk too many days and nights in a row. I needed a rest. And I needed a drink. Just beer. You'd think I could hold down beer. I took a long pull.

The beer wouldn't stay down. I went to the bathroom. Tammie knocked, "Hank, are you all right?"

I washed out my mouth and opened the door. "I'm sick, that's all."

"Do you want me to get rid of them?"

"Sure."

She went back to them. "Look, fellows, why don't we go up to my place?"

I hadn't expected that.

Tammie had neglected to pay her electric bill, or she didn't want to, and they sat up there by candlelight. She had taken a fifth of mixed margarita cocktails I had purchased earlier in the day up there with her.

I sat and drank alone. The next beer stayed down.

I could hear them up there, talking.

THEN TAMMIE's brother left. I watched him walk in the moonlight towards his car. . . .

Tammie and Filbert were up there alone together, by candlelight.

I sat with the lights out, drinking. An hour passed. I could see the wavering candlelight in the dark. I looked around. Tammie had left her shoes. I picked up her shoes and went up the stairway. Her door was open and I heard her talking to Filbert. . . . "So, anyway, what I meant was . . ."

She heard me walking up the stairs. "Henry, is that *you?*"

I threw Tammie's shoes the remainder of the way up the stairway. They landed outside her door.

"You forgot your shoes," I said.

"Oh, God bless you," she said.

* * *

About 10:30 the next morning Tammie knocked on the door. I opened it. "You rotten goddamned bitch."

"Stop talking that way," she said.

"Want a beer?"

"All right."

She sat down. "Well, we drank the bottle of margaritas. Then my brother left. Filbert was *very* nice. He just sat and didn't talk much. 'How are you going to get home?' I asked him. 'Do you have a car?' And he said he didn't. He just sat there looking at me and I said, 'Well, I have a car, I'll drive you home.' So I drove him home. Anyhow, since I was there I went to bed with him. I was pretty drunk, but he didn't touch me. He said he had to go to work in the morning." Tammie laughed. "Sometime during the night he tried to approach me. I put the pillow over my head and just started giggling. I kept the pillow there and giggled. He gave up. After he left for work I drove over to my mother's and took Dancy to school. And now here I am. . . ."

The next day Tammie was on uppers. She kept running in and out of my place. Finally she told me, "I'll be back tonight. I'll see you tonight!"

"Forget tonight."

"What's wrong with you? Plenty of men would be happy to see me tonight."

Tammie slammed out of the door. There was a pregnant cat sleeping on my porch.

"Get the hell out of here, Red!"

I picked up the pregnant cat and threw it at her. I missed by a foot and the cat dropped into a nearby bush.

The following night Tammie was on speed. I was drunk. Tammie and Dancy screamed at me from the window above.

"Go eat jerk-off, ya jerk!"

"Yeah, go eat jerk-off, you jerk! HAHAHA!"

"Ah, balloons!" I answered, "your mother's big balloons!"

"Go eat rat droppings, ya jerk!"

"You jerk, you jerk, you jerk! HAHAHA!"

"Fruit fly brains," I answered, "suck the cotton out of my navel!"

"You . . ." began Tammie.

Suddenly there were several pistol shots nearby, either in the street or in the back of the court or behind the apartment next door. Very near. It was a poor neighborhood with lots of prostitution and drugs and occasionally a murder.

Dancy started screaming out the window: "HANK! HANK! COME UP HERE, HANK! HANK, HANK, HANK! HURRY, HANK!"

I ran up. Tammie was stretched out on the bed, all that glorious red hair flared out on the pillow. She saw me.

"I've been shot," she said weakly. "I've been shot."

She pointed to a spot on her bluejeans. She was not joking anymore. She was terrified.

There was a red stain, but it was dry. Tammie liked to use my paints. I reached down and touched the dry stain. She was all right, except for the pills.

"Listen," I told her, "you're all right, don't worry. . . ."

As I walked out the door Bobby came pounding up the stairs. "Tammie, Tammie, what's wrong? Are you all right?"

Bobby evidently had had to get dressed, which explained the time lag.

As he bounced past me I told him quickly, "Jesus Christ, man, you're always in my life."

He ran into Tammie's apartment followed by the guy next door, a used car salesman and a certified nut.

TAMMIE CAME down a few days later with an envelope.

"Hank, the manager just served me with an eviction notice." She showed it to me.

I read it carefully. "It looks like they mean it," I said.

"I told her I'd pay the back rent but she said, 'We want you out of here, Tammie!'"

"You can't let the rent go too long."

"Listen, I have the money. I just don't like to pay."

Tammie was completely contrary in her ways. Her car wasn't registered, the license plate tabs had long ago expired, and she drove without a driver's license. She left her car parked for days in yellow zones, red zones, white zones, reserved parking lots. . . . When the police stopped her drunk or high or without her i.d., she talked to them, and they always let her go. She tore up the parking tickets whenever she got them.

"I'll get the owner's phone number." (We had an absentee landlord.) "They can't kick my ass out of here. Do you have his phone number?"

"No."

Just then Irv, who owned a whorehouse, and who also acted as bouncer at the local massage parlor walked by. Irv was 6 foot 3 and on ATD. He also had a better mind than the first 3,000 people you'd pass on the street.

Tammie ran out: "Irv! Irv!"

He stopped and turned. Tammie swung her breasts at him. "Irv, do you have the owner's phone number?"

"No, I don't."

"Irv, I need the owner's phone number. Give me his number and I'll suck you off!"

"I don't have the number."

He walked up to his door and put his key into the lock.

"Come on, Irv, I'll suck you off if you tell me!"

"You really mean it?" he asked hesitating, looking at her.

Then he opened the door, walked in and closed it.

TAMMIE RAN up to another door and beat on it. Richard opened the door cautiously, with the chain on it. He was bald, lived alone, was religious, about 45 and looked at television continually. He was as pink and clean as a woman. He complained continually about the noise from my place—he couldn't sleep, he said. The management told him to move. He hated me. Now there was one of my women at his door. He kept the chain on.

"What do you want?" he hissed.

"Look, baby, I want the owner's phone number. . . . You've lived here for years. I know you have his phone number. I need it."

"Go away," he said.

"Look, baby, I'll be nice to you. . . . A kiss, a nice big kiss for you!"

"Harlot!" he said "Strumpet!"

Richard slammed the door.

Tammie walked on in. "Hank?"

"Yes?"

"What's a strumpet? I know what a trumpet is, but what's a strumpet?"

"A strumpet, my dear, is a whore."

"Why that dirty son-of-a-bitch!"

Tammie walked outside and continued to beat on the doors of the other apartments. Either they were out or they didn't answer. She came back. "It's not fair! Why do they want me out of here? What have I done?"

"I don't know. Think back. Maybe there's something."

"I can't think of anything."

"Move in with me."

"You couldn't stand the kid."

"You're right."

THE DAYS passed. The owner remained invisible, he didn't like to deal with the tenants. The manager stood behind the eviction notice. Even Bobby became less visible, ate t.v. dinners, smoked his grass and listened to his stereo. "Hey, man," he told me, "I don't even *like* your old lady! She's busting up our friendship, man!"

"Right on, Bobby. . . ."

I DROVE to the market and got some empty cardboard cartons. Then Tammie's sister, Cathy, went crazy in Denver—after losing a lover—and Tammie had to go see her, with Dancy. I drove them down to the train depot. I put them on the train.

69

THAT EVENING THE phone rang. It was Mercedes. I had met her after giving a poetry reading at Venice Beach. She was about 28, fair body, pretty good legs, a blonde about 5-feet-5, a blue-eyed blonde. Her hair was long and slightly wavy and she smoked continuously. Her conversation was dull, and her laugh was loud and false, most of the time.

I had gone to her place after the reading. She lived off the boardwalk in an apartment. I'd played the piano and she'd played the bongos. There was a jug of Red Mountain. There were joints. I got too drunk to leave. I had slept there that night and left in the morning.

"Look," said Mercedes, "I work right in your neighborhood now. I thought I might come by to see you."

"All right."

I hung up. The phone rang again. It was Tammie.

"Look, I've decided to move out. I'll be home in a couple of days. Just get my yellow dress out of the apartment, the one you like, and my green shoes. All the rest is crap. Leave it."

"O.K."

"Listen, I'm flat broke. We don't have any money for food."

"I'll wire you 40 bucks in the morning, Western Union."

"You're sweet. . . ."

I hung up. Fifteen minutes later Mercedes was there. She had on a very short skirt, was wearing sandals and a low-cut blouse. Also small blue earrings.

"You want some grass?" she asked.

"Sure."

She took the grass and the papers out of her purse and started rolling some joints. I broke out the beer and we sat on the couch and smoked and drank.

We didn't talk much. I played with her legs and we drank and smoked quite a long time.

FINALLY WE undressed and went to bed, first Mercedes, then me. We began kissing and I rubbed her cunt. She grabbed my cock. I mounted. Mercedes guided it in. She had a good grip down there, very tight. I teased her a while, pulling it almost all the way out and moving the head back and forth. Then I slid it all the way in, slowly, in lazy fashion. Then suddenly I rammed her

4 or 5 times, and her head bounced on the pillow. "Arrrrggg . . .
" she said. Then I eased up and stroked.

It was a very hot night and we both sweated. Mercedes was
high on the beer and the joints. I decided to finish her off with
a flourish. Show her a thing or two,

I pumped on and on. Five minutes. Ten minutes more. I
couldn't come. I began to fail, I was getting soft.

Mercedes got worried. "Make it!" she demanded. "Oh, *make*
it, baby!"

That didn't help at all. I rolled off.

It was an unbearably hot night. I took the sheet and wiped off
the sweat. I could hear my heart pounding as I lay there. It
sounded sad. I wondered what Mercedes was thinking.

I lay dying, my cock limp.

Mercedes turned her head toward me. I kissed her. Kissing is
more intimate than fucking. That's why I never liked my
girlfriends to go around kissing men. I'd rather they fucked
them.

I kept kissing Mercedes and since I felt that way about kissing
I hardened again. I climbed on top of her, kissing her as if it was
my last hour on earth.

My cock slid in.

This time I knew I was going to make it. I could feel the
miracle of it.

I was going to come in her cunt, the bitch. I was going to pour
my juices into her and there was nothing she could do to stop
me. She was mine. I was a conquering army, I was a rapist, I was
her master, I was death.

She was helpless. Her head rolled, she gripped me and gasped,
as she made sounds. . . .

"Arrrgg, uuggg, oh oh . . . oooff . . . oooooh!"

My cock fed on it.

I made a strange sound, then I came.

In five minutes she was snoring. We both were snoring.

IN THE morning we showered and dressed. "I'll take you to
breakfast," I said.

"All right," Mercedes answered. "By the way, did we fuck last night?"

"*My god!* Don't you remember? We must have fucked for 50 minutes!"

I couldn't believe it. Mercedes looked unconvinced.

WE WENT to a place around the corner. I ordered eggs over easy with bacon and coffee, wheat toast. Mercedes ordered hotcakes and ham, coffee.

The waitress brought our orders. I took a bite of egg. Mercedes poured syrup over her hotcakes.

"You're right," she said, "you must have fucked me. I can feel the semen running down my leg."

I decided not to see her again.

70

I WENT UP to Tammie's place with my cardboard cartons. First I got the items she mentioned. Then I found other things—other dresses and blouses, shoes, an iron, a hair dryer, Dancy's clothing, dishes and flatware, a photo album. There was a heavy rattan chair which belonged to her. I took all the things down to my place. I had eight or ten cartons full of stuff. I stacked them against my front room wall.

The next day I drove down to the train station to pick Tammie and Dancy up.

"You're looking good," Tammie said.

"Thanks," I said.

"We're going to live at Mother's. You might as well drive us there. I can't fight that eviction. Besides, who wants to stay where they're not wanted?"

"Tammie, I moved most of your things. They're in cardboard cartons at my place."

"All right. Can I leave them there a while?"

"Sure."

* * *

THEN TAMMIE's mother went to Denver, to see the sister, and the night she left I went to Tammie's to get drunk. Tammie was on pills. I didn't take any. When I got into the fourth 6-pack I said, "Tammie, I don't see what you see in Bobby. He's nothing."

She crossed her legs, and swung her foot back and forth.

"He thinks his small talk is charming," I said.

She kept swinging her foot.

"Movies, t.v., grass, comic books, dirty photos, that's his gas tank."

Tammie swung her foot harder.

"Do you really care for him?"

She kept swinging her foot.

"You fucking bitch!" I said.

I walked to the door, slammed it behind me, and got into the Volks. I raced through traffic, weaving in and out, destroying my clutch and gear shift.

I got back to my place and started loading the cartons of her stuff into my Volks. Also record albums, blankets, toys. The Volks, of course, didn't hold too much.

I speeded back to Tammie's. I pulled up and double-parked, put the red warning lights on. I pulled the boxes out of the car and stacked them on the porch. I covered them with blankets and toys, rang the bell and drove off.

When I came back with the second load the first load was gone. I made another stack, rang the bell and wheeled off like a missile.

When I came back with the third load the second was gone. I made a new stack and rang the bell. Then I was off again into the early morning.

When I got back to my place I had a vodka and water and looked at what was left. There was the heavy rattan chair and the stand-up hair dryer. I could only make one more run. It was either the chair or the dryer. The Volks couldn't consume both.

I decided on the rattan chair. It was 4 AM. I was double-parked in front of my place with the warning lights on. I finished the vodka and water. I was getting drunker and weaker. I picked up the rattan, it was really heavy, and carried it down the walk to my car. I sat it down and opened the door opposite the driver's side. I jammed the rattan chair in. Then I tried to close the door. The chair was sticking out. I tried to pull the chair out of the car. It was stuck. I cursed, and pushed it further in. One leg of the rattan poked through the windshield and stuck out, pointing at the sky. The door still wouldn't close. It wasn't even close. I tried to push the leg of the chair further through the windshield so that I could close the door. It wouldn't budge. The chair was jammed in tight. I tried to pull it out. It wouldn't move. Desperately I pulled and pushed, pulled and pushed. If the police came, I was finished. After some time I wearied. I climbed in the driver's side. There were no parking spaces in the street. I drove the car down to the pizza parlor parking lot, the open door swinging back and forth. I left it there with the door open, the ceiling light on. (The ceiling light wouldn't shut off.) The windshield was smashed, the chair leg poking out into the moonlight. The whole scene was indecent, mad. It smacked of murder and assassination. My beautiful car.

I walked down the street and back to my place. I poured another vodka and water and phoned Tammie.

"Look, baby, I'm in a jam. I've got your chair stuck through my windshield and I can't get it out and I can't get it in and the door won't close. The windshield is smashed. What can I do? Help me, for Christ's sake!"

"You'll think of something, Hank."

She hung up.

I dialed again. "Baby. . . ."

She hung up. Then next the phone was off the hook: *bzzzz, bzzzzzz, bzzzz* . . . .

I stretched out on the bed. The phone rang.

"Tammie. . . ."

"Hank, this is Valerie. I just came home. I want to tell you that your car is parked in the pizza parlor with the door open."

"Thanks, Valerie, but I can't close the door. There is a rattan chair stuck through the windshield."

"Oh, I didn't notice that."

"I appreciate your phoning."

I fell asleep. It was one worried sleep. They were going to tow me away. I was going to get booked.

I awakened at 6:20 AM, got dressed and walked to the pizza parlor. The car was still there. The sun was coming up.

I reached in and grabbed the rattan: It still wouldn't budge. I was furious, and began pulling and yanking, cursing. The more impossible it seemed, the madder I got. Suddenly there was a cracking of wood. I was inspired, energized. A piece of wood broke off in my hands. I looked at it, tossed it into the street, went back to my task. Something else broke off. The days in the factories, the days of unloading boxcars, the days of lifting cases of frozen fish, the days of carrying murdered cattle on my shoulders were paying off. I had always been strong but equally lazy. Now I was tearing that chair to pieces. Finally I ripped it out of the car. I attacked it in the parking lot. I smashed it to bits, I broke it in pieces. Then I picked up the pieces and stacked them neatly on somebody's front lawn.

I got in the Volks and found an empty parking space near my court. All I had to do now was find a junkyard on Santa Fe Avenue and buy myself a new windshield. That could wait. I went back in, drank two glasses of ice water and went to bed.

71

FOUR OR FIVE days passed. The phone rang. It was Tammie. "What do you want?" I asked.

"Listen, Hank. You know that little bridge you cross in your car when you drive to my mother's place?"

"Yes."

"Well, right by there they're having a yard sale. I went in and saw this typewriter. It's only 20 bucks and it's in good working order. Please get it for me, Hank."

"What do you want with a typewriter?"

"Well, I've never told you, but I've always wanted to be a writer."

"Tammie. . . ."

"Please, Hank, just this one last time. I'll be your friend for life."

"No."

"Hank. . . ."

"Oh, shit, well, all right."

"I'll meet you at the bridge in 15 minutes. I want to hurry before it's taken. I've found a new apartment and Filbert and my brother are helping me move. . . ."

Tammie wasn't at the bridge in 15 minutes or in 25 minutes. I got back in the Volks and drove over to Tammie's mother's apartment. Filbert was loading cartons into Tammie's car. He didn't see me. I parked a half a block away.

Tammie came out and saw my Volks. Filbert was getting into his car. He had a Volks, too, a yellow one. Tammie waved to him and said, "See you later!"

Then she walked down the street toward me. When she got near my car she stretched out in the center of the street and lay there. I waited. Then she got up, walked to my car, got in.

I pulled away. Filbert was sitting in his car. I waved to him as we drove by. He didn't wave back. His eyes were sad. It was just beginning for him.

"You know," Tammie said, "I'm with Filbert now."

I laughed. It welled out of me.

"We'd better hurry. The typer might be gone."

"Why don't you let Filbert buy the fucking thing?"

"Look, if you don't want to do it just stop the car and let me out!"

I stopped the car and opened the door.

"Listen, you son-of-a-bitch, you *told* me you'd buy that typer! If you don't, I'm going to start screaming and breaking your windows!"

"All right. The typer is yours."

We drove to the place. The typer was still there.

"This typewriter has spent its whole life up to now in an insane asylum," the lady told us.

"It's going to the right person," I replied.

I gave the lady a twenty and we drove back. Filbert was gone.
"Don't you want to come in for a while?" Tammie asked.
"No, I've got to go."
She was able to carry the typer in without help. It was a portable.

72

I DRANK FOR the next week. I drank night and day and wrote 25 or 30 mournful poems about lost love.

It was Friday night when the phone rang. It was Mercedes. "I got married," she said, "to Little Jack. You met him at the party that night you read in Venice. He's a nice guy and he's got money. We're moving to the Valley."

"All right, Mercedes, luck with it all."

"But I miss drinking and talking with you. Suppose I come over tonight?"

"All right."

SHE WAS there in 15 minutes, rolling joints and drinking my beer.

"Little Jack is a nice guy. We're happy together."

I sucked at my beer.

"I don't want to fuck," she said, "I'm tired of abortions, I'm really tired of abortions. . . ."

"We'll figure something out."

"I just want to smoke and talk and drink."

"That's not enough for me."

"All you guys want to do is fuck."

"I like it."

"Well, I can't fuck, I don't want to fuck."

"Relax."

We sat on the couch. We didn't kiss. Mercedes was not a good conversationalist. She wasn't interesting. But she had her legs and her ass and her hair and her youth. I'd met some interesting women, God knows, but Mercedes just wasn't high on the list.

The beer flowed and the joints went around. Mercedes still had the same job with the Hollywood Institute of Human Relationships. She was having trouble with her car. Little Jack had a short fat dick. She was reading *Grapefruit* by Yoko Ono. She was tired of abortions. The Valley was nice but she missed Venice. She missed riding her bicycle along the boardwalk.

I DON'T know how long we talked, or *she* talked, but much, much later she said she was too drunk to drive home.

"Take off your clothes and go to bed," I told her.

"But no fucking," she said.

"I won't touch your cunt."

She undressed and went to bed. I undressed and went into the bathroom. She watched me coming out with a jar of Vaseline.

"What are you going to do?"

"Just take it easy, baby, take it easy."

I rubbed the Vaseline on my cock. Then I turned out the light and got into bed.

"Turn your back," I said.

I reached one arm under her and played with one breast and reached over the top and played with the other breast. It felt good with my face in her hair. I stiffened and slipped it into her ass. I grabbed her around the waist and pulled her ass toward me, hard, sliding it in. "Oooooohh," she said.

I began working. I dug it in deeper. The cheeks of her ass were big and soft. As I slammed away I began to sweat. Then I rolled her on her stomach and sunk it in deeper. It was getting tighter. I nudged into the end of her colon and she screamed.

"Shut up! Goddamn you!"

She was very tight. I slipped it even further in. Her grip was unbelievable. As I rammed it in I suddenly got a stitch in my side, a terrible burning pain, but I continued. I was slicing her in half, right up the backbone. I roared like a madman and came.

Then I lay there on top of her. The pain in my side was murder. She was crying.

"Goddamn it," I asked her, "what's the matter? I didn't touch your cunt."

I rolled off.

IN THE morning Mercedes said very little, got dressed and left for her job.

Well, I thought, there goes another one.

73

MY DRINKING SLOWED down the next week. I went to the racetrack to get fresh air and sunshine and plenty of walking. At night I drank, wondering why I was still alive, how the scheme worked. I thought about Katherine, about Lydia, about Tammie. I didn't feel very good.

That Friday night the phone rang. It was Mercedes.

"Hank, I'd like to come by. But just for talk and beer and joints. Nothing else."

"Come by if you want to."

Mercedes was there in a half hour. To my surprise she looked very good to me. I'd never seen a mini-skirt as short as hers and her legs looked fine. I kissed her happily. She broke away.

"I couldn't walk for two days after that last one. Don't rip my butt again."

"All right, honest injun, I won't."

It was about the same. We sat on the couch with the radio on, talked, drank beer, smoked. I kissed her again and again. I couldn't stop. She acted like she wanted it, yet she insisted that she couldn't. Little Jack loved her, love meant a lot in this world.

"It sure does," I said.

"You don't love me."

"You're a married woman."

"I don't love Little Jack, but I care for him very much and he loves me."

"It sounds fine."

"Have you ever been in love?"

"Four times."

"What happened? Where are they tonight?"

"One is dead. The other three are with other men."

We talked a long time that night and smoked any number of joints. Around 2 AM Mercedes said, "I'm too high to drive home. I'd total the car."

"Take your clothes off and go to bed."

"All right, but I've got an idea."

"Like what?"

"I want to watch you beat that thing off! I want to watch it *squirt!*"

"All right, that's fair enough. It's a deal."

Mercedes undressed and went to bed. I undressed and stood at the side of the bed. "Sit up so you can see better."

Mercedes sat on the edge of the bed. I spit on my palm and began to rub my cock.

"Oh," Mercedes said, "It's *growing!*"

"Uh huh. . . ."

"It's getting big!"

"Uh huh. . . ."

"Oh, it's all *purple* with big veins! It *throbs!* It's *ugly!*"

"Yeh."

As I kept beating my cock I moved it near her face. She watched it. Just as I was about to come I stopped.

"Oh," she said.

"Look, I've got a better idea.

"What?"

"You beat it off."

"All right."

She started in. "Am I doing it right?"

"A little harder. And spit on your palm. And rub almost all of it, most of it, just not up near the head."

"All right. . . . Oh, God, *look* at it. . . . I want to see it squirt *juice!*"

"Keep going, Mercedes! OH, MY GOD!"

I was just about to come. I pulled her hand away from my cock.

"Oh, *damn you!*" Mercedes said.

She bent forward and got it in her mouth. She began sucking and bobbing, running her tongue along the length of my cock as she sucked it.

"Oh, you *bitch!*"

Then she pulled her mouth off my cock.

"Go ahead! Go ahead! Finish me off!"

"No!"

"Well, goddamn it then!"

I pushed her over backwards on the bed and leaped on her. I kissed her viciously and drove my cock in. I worked violently, pumping and pumping. I moaned and then came. I pumped it into her, feeling it enter, feeling it steam into her.

74

I HAD TO fly to Illinois to give a reading at the University. I hated readings, but they helped with the rent and maybe they helped sell books. They got me out of east Hollywood, they got me up in the air with the businessmen and the stewardesses and the iced drinks and little napkins and the peanuts to kill the breath.

I was to be met by the poet, William Keesing, who I had been corresponding with since 1966. I had first seen his work in the pages of *Bull*, edited by Doug Fazzick, one of the first mimeo mags and probably the leader in the mimeo revolution. None of us were literary in the proper sense: Fazzick worked in a rubber plant, Keesing was an ex-Marine out of Korea who had done time and was supported by his wife, Cecelia. I was working 11 hours a night as a postal clerk. That was also the time when Marvin arrived on the scene with his strange poems about demons. Marvin Woodman was the best damned demon-writer in America. Maybe in Spain and Peru too. I was into writing letters at the time. I wrote 4 and 5 page letters to everybody, coloring the envelopes and pages wildly with crayons. That's when I began writing William Keesing, ex-Marine, ex-con, drug addict (he was mostly into codeine).

Now, years later, William Keesing had secured a temporary teaching job at the University. He had managed to pick up a degree or two between drug busts. I warned him that it was a dangerous job for anybody who wanted to write. But at least he taught his class plenty of Chinaski.

Keesing and his wife were waiting at the airport. I had my baggage with me and so we went right to the car.

"My God," said Keesing, "I never saw anybody get off of an airplane looking like that."

I had on my dead father's overcoat, which was too large. My pants were too long, the cuffs came down over the shoes and that was good because my stockings didn't match, and my shoes were down at the heels. I hated barbers so I cut my own hair when I couldn't get a woman to do it. I didn't like to shave and I didn't like long beards, so I scissored myself every two or three weeks. My eyesight was bad but I didn't like glasses so I didn't wear them except to read. I had my own teeth but not that many. My face and my nose were red from drinking and the light hurt my eyes so I squinted through tiny slits. I would have fit into any skid row anywhere.

We drove off.

"We expected somebody quite different," said Cecelia.

"Oh?"

"I mean, your voice is so soft, and you seem gentle. Bill expected you to get off the plane drunk and cursing, making passes at the women. . . ."

"I never pump up my vulgarity. I wait for it to arrive on its own terms."

"You're reading tomorrow night," said Bill.

"Good, we'll have fun tonight and forget everything."

We drove on.

THAT NIGHT Keesing was as interesting as his letters and poems. He had the good sense to stay away from literature in our conversation, except now and then. We talked about other things. I didn't have much luck in person with most poets even when their letters and poems were good. I'd met Douglas

Fazzick with less than charming results. It was best to stay away from other writers and just do your work, or just not do your work.

Cecelia retired early. She had a job to go to in the morning. "Cecelia is divorcing me," Bill told me. "I don't blame her. She's sick of my drugs, my puke, my whole thing. She's stood it for years. Now she can't take it any longer. I can't give her much of a fuck anymore. She's running with this teenage kid. I can't blame her. I've moved out, I've got a room. We can go there and sleep or I can go there and sleep and you can stay here or we both can stay here, it doesn't matter to me."

Keesing took out a couple of pills and dropped them.

"Let's both stay here," I said.

"You really pour the drinks down."

"There's nothing else to do."

"You must have a cast-iron gut."

"Not really. It busted open once. But when those holes grow back together they say it's tougher than the best welding."

"How long you figure to go on?" he asked.

"I've got it all planned. I'm going to die in the year 2000 when I'm 80."

"That's strange," said Keesing, "That's the year I'm going to die. 2000. I even had a dream about it. I even dreamed the day and hour of my death. Anyhow, it's in the year 2000."

"It's a nice round number. I like it."

We drank for another hour or two. I got the extra bedroom. Keesing slept on the couch. Cecelia apparently was serious about dumping him.

THE NEXT morning I was up at 10:30 AM. There was some beer left. I managed to get one down. I was on the second when Keesing walked in.

"Jesus, how do you do it? You spring back like an 18 year old boy."

"I have some bad mornings. This just isn't one."

"I've got a 1:00 English class. I've got to get straight."

"Drop a white."

"I need some food in my gut."

"Eat two soft-boiled eggs. Eat them with a touch of chili powder or paprika."

"Can I boil you a couple?"

"Thanks, yes."

The phone rang. It was Cecelia. Bill talked a while, then hung up. "There's a tornado approaching. One of the biggest in the history of the state. It might come through here."

"Something always happens when I read."

I noticed it was beginning to get dark.

"They might cancel the class. It's hard to tell. I better eat."

Bill put the eggs on.

"I don't understand you," he said, "you don't even look hungover."

"I'm hungover every morning. It's normal. I've adjusted."

"You're still writing pretty good shit, in spite of all that booze."

"Let's not get on that. Maybe it's the variety of pussy. Don't boil those eggs too long."

I went into the bathroom and took a shit. Constipation wasn't one of my problems. I was just coming out when I heard Bill holler, "Chinaski!"

Then I heard him in the yard, he was vomiting. He came back.

The poor guy was really sick.

"Take some baking soda. You got a Valium?"

"No."

"Then wait 10 minutes after the baking soda and drink a warm beer. Pour it in a glass now so the air can get to it."

"I got a bennie."

"Take it."

It was getting darker. Fifteen minutes after the bennie Bill took a shower. When he came out he looked all right. He ate a peanut butter sandwich with sliced banana. He was going to make it.

"You still love your old lady, don't you?" I asked.

"Christ, yes."

CHARLES BUKOWSKI

"I know it doesn't help, but try to realize that it's happened to all of us, at least once."

"That doesn't help."

"Once a woman turns against you, forget it. They can love you, then something turns in them. They can watch you dying in a gutter, run over by a car, and they'll spit on you."

"Cecelia's a wonderful woman."

It was getting darker. "Let's drink some more beer," I said.

We sat and drank beer. It got really dark and then there was a high wind. We didn't talk much. I was glad we had met. There was very little bullshit in him. He was tired, maybe that helped. He'd never had any luck with his poems in the U.S.A. They loved him in Australia. Maybe some day they'd discover him here, maybe not. Maybe by the year 2000. He was a tough, chunky little guy, you knew he could duke it, you knew he had been there. I was fond of him.

We drank quietly, then the phone rang. It was Cecelia again. The tornado had passed over, or rather, around. Bill was going to teach his class. I was going to read that night. Bully. Everything was working. We were all fully employed.

About 12:30 PM Bill put his notebooks and whatever he needed into a backpack, got on his bike and pedaled off to the university.

CECELIA CAME home sometime in the mid-afternoon.

"Did Bill get off all right?"

"Yes, he left on the bike. He looked fine."

"How fine? Was he on shit?"

"He looked fine. He ate and everything."

"I still love him, Hank. I just can't go through it anymore."

"Sure."

"You don't know how much it means to him to have you out here. He used to read your letters to me."

"Dirty, huh?"

"No, funny. You made us laugh."

"Let's fuck, Cecelia."

"Hank, now you're playing your game."

174

"You're a plump little thing. Let me sink it in."
"You're drunk, Hank."
"You're right. Forget it."

75

THAT NIGHT I gave another bad reading. I didn't care. They didn't care. If John Cage could get one thousand dollars for eating an apple, I'd accept $500 plus air fare for being a lemon.

It was the same afterwards. The little coeds came up with their young hot bodies and their pilot-light eyes and asked me to autograph some of my books. I would have liked to fuck about five of them in one night sometime and get them out of my system forever.

A couple of professors came up and grinned at me for being an ass. It made them feel better, they felt now as if they had a chance at the typewriter.

I took the check and got out. There was to be a small, *select* gathering at Cecelia's house afterwards. That was part of the unwritten contract. The more girls the better, but at Cecelia's house I stood very little chance. I knew that. And sure enough, in the morning I awakened in my bed, alone.

BILL WAS sick again the next morning. He had another 1:00 class and before he went off he said, "Cecelia will drive you to the airport. I'm going now. No heavy goodbyes."

"All right."

Bill put on his backpack and walked his bike out the door.

76

I WAS BACK in L.A. about a week and a half. It was night. The phone rang. It was Cecelia, she was sobbing. "Hank, Bill is dead. You're the first one I've called."

"Christ, Cecelia, I don't know what to say."

"I'm so glad you came when you did. Bill did nothing but talk about you after you left. You don't know what your visit meant to him."

"What happened?"

"He complained of feeling real bad and we took him to a hospital and in two hours he was dead. I know people are going to think he o.d.'d, but he didn't. Even though I was going to divorce him I loved him."

"I believe you."

"I don't want to bother you with all this."

"It's all right, Bill would understand. I just don't know what to say to help you. I'm kind of in shock. Let me phone you later on to see if you're all right."

"Would you?"

"Of course."

That's the problem with drinking, I thought, as I poured myself a drink. If something bad happens you drink in an attempt to forget; if something good happens you drink in order to celebrate; and if nothing happens you drink to make something happen.

As sick and unhappy as he was, Bill just didn't look like somebody who was about to die. There were many deaths like that and even though we knew about death and thought about it almost every day, when there was an unexpected death, and when that person was an exceptional and lovable human being, it was hard, very, no matter how many other people had died, good, bad or unknown.

I phoned Cecelia back that night, and I phoned her again the next night, and once more after that, and then I stopped phoning.

77

A MONTH WENT by. R.A. Dwight, the editor of Dogbite Press, wrote and asked me to do a foreword to Keesing's *Selected Poems*. Keesing, with the help of his death, was at last going to get some recognition somewhere besides Australia.

Then Cecelia phoned. "Hank, I'm going to San Francisco to see R.A. Dwight. I have some photos of Bill and some unpublished things. I want to go over them with Dwight and we're going to decide what to publish. But first I want to stop in L.A. for a day or two. Can you meet me at the airport?"

"Sure, you can stay at my place, Cecelia."

"Thanks much."

She gave me her arrival time and I went in and cleaned the toilet, scrubbed the bathtub and changed the sheets and pillow cases on my bed.

CECELIA ARRIVED on the 10 AM flight which was hell for me to make, but she looked good, albeit a bit plump. She was sturdy, built low, she looked midwestern, scrubbed. Men looked at her, she had a way of moving her behind; it looked forceful, a bit ominous *and* sexy.

We waited for the baggage in the bar. Cecelia didn't drink. She had an orange juice.

"I just *love* airports and airport passengers, don't you?"

"No."

"The people seem so interesting."

"They have more money than the people who travel by rail or bus."

"We passed over the Grand Canyon on the way in."

"Yes, it's on your route."

"These waitresses wear such short skirts! Look, you can see their panties."

"Good tips. They all live in condominiums and drive M.G.s."

"Everybody on the plane was so nice! The man in the seat next to me offered to buy me a drink."

"Let's get your baggage."

"R.A. phoned to tell me that he had received your foreword to Bill's *Selected Poems*. He read me parts of it over the phone. It was beautiful. I want to thank you."

"Forget it."

"I don't know how to repay you."

"Are you *sure* you don't want a drink?"

"I rarely drink. Maybe later."

"What do you prefer? I'll get something for when we get back to my place. I want you to feel comfortable and relaxed."

"I'm sure Bill is looking down at us now and he's feeling happy."

"Do you think so?"

"Yes!"

We got the baggage and walked toward the parking lot.

78

THAT NIGHT I managed to get 2 or 3 drinks into Cecelia. She forgot herself and crossed her legs high and I saw some good heavy flank. Durable. A cow of a woman, cow's breasts, cow's eyes. She could handle plenty. Keesing had had a good eye.

She was against the killing of animals, she didn't eat meat. I guess she had enough meat. Everything was beautiful, she told me, we had all this beauty in the world and all we had to do was reach out and touch it, it was all there and all ours for the taking.

"You're right, Cecelia," I said. "Have another drink."

"It makes me giddy."

"What's wrong with a little bit of giddy?"

Cecelia crossed her legs again and her thighs flashed. They flashed way up high.

Bill, you can't use it now. You were a good poet, Bill, but what the hell, you left more behind than your writing. And your writing never had thighs and flanks like this.

Cecelia had another drink, then stopped. I kept going.

Where did all the women come from? The supply was endless. Each one of them was individual, different. Their pussies were different, their kisses were different, their breasts were different, but no man could drink them all, there were too many of them, crossing their legs, driving men mad. What a feast!

"I want to go to the beach. Will you take me to the beach, Hank?" Cecelia asked.

178

"Tonight?"

"No, not tonight. But sometime before I leave."

"All right."

Cecelia talked about how the American Indian had been abused. Then she told me that she wrote, but she never submitted it, she just kept a notebook. Bill had encouraged and helped her with some of her things. She'd helped Bill get through the university. Of course, the G.I. Bill had helped, too. And there had always been codeine, he had always been hooked on codeine. She'd threatened to leave him again and again, but it didn't help. Now—

"Drink this, Cecelia," I said, "it will help you forget."

I poured her a tall one.

"Oh, I couldn't drink all that!"

"Cross your legs higher. Let me see more of your legs."

"Bill never talked to me like that."

I continued to drink. Cecelia continued to talk. After a while I didn't listen. Midnight came and left.

"Listen, Cecelia, let's go to bed. I'm bombed."

I walked into the bedroom and undressed, got under the covers. I heard her walk by and go into the bathroom. I switched the bedroom light off. She came out soon and I felt her getting into the other side of the bed.

"Goodnight, Cecelia," I said.

I pulled her to me. She was naked. Jesus, I thought. We kissed. She kissed very well. It was a long, hot one. We finished.

"Cecelia?"

"Yes?"

"I'll fuck you some other time."

I rolled over and went to sleep.

79

BOBBY AND VALERIE came by and I introduced everybody around.

"Valerie and I are going to take a vacation and rent rooms by the seashore in Manhattan Beach," said Bobby. "Why don't you guys come along? We could split the rent. There are two bedrooms."

"No, Bobby, I don't think so."

"Oh, Hank, *please!*" said Cecelia. "I just love the ocean! Hank, if we go down there I'll even drink with you. I promise!"

"All right, Cecelia."

"Fine," said Bobby. "We leave this evening. We'll pick you guys up around 6 PM. We'll have dinner together."

"That sounds real good," said Cecelia.

"Hank's fun to eat with," said Valerie. "Last time we went out with him we walked into this fancy place and he told the head waiter right off, 'I want cole slaw and french fries for my friends here! A double order of each, and don't water the drinks or I'll have your coat and tie!'"

"I can't *wait!*" said Cecelia.

CECELIA WANTED to go for a constitutional around 2 PM. We walked through the court. She noticed the poinsettias. She walked right up to a bush and stuck her face into the flowers, caressing them with her fingers.

"Oh, they're so *beautiful!*"

"They're *dying*, Cecelia. Can't you see how shriveled they are? The smog is killing them."

We walked along under the palms.

"And there are birds everywhere! Hundreds of birds, Hank!"

"And dozens of cats."

WE DROVE to Manhattan Beach with Bobby and Valerie, moved into our waterfront apartment and went out to eat. The dinner was fair. Cecelia had one drink with her dinner and explained all about her vegetarianism. She had soup, salad and yogurt; the remainder of us had steaks, french fries, french bread, and salad. Bobby and Valerie stole the salt and pepper shakers, two steak knives and the tip I had left for the waiter.

We stopped for liquor, ice and smokes, then went back to the apartment. Her one drink had Cecelia giggling and talking and she was explaining that animals had souls too. Nobody challenged her opinion. It was possible, we knew. What we weren't sure of was if we had any.

80

WE CONTINUED DRINKING. Cecelia had just one more and stopped. "I want to go out and look at the moon and stars," she said. "It's so beautiful out!"

"All right, Cecelia."

She went outside by the swimming pool and sat in a deck chair.

"No wonder Bill died," I said. "He starved. She never gives it away."

"She talked the same way about you at dinner when you went to the men's room," said Valerie. "She said, 'Oh, Hank's poems are so full of passion, but as a person he's not that way at all!'"

"Me and God don't always pick the same horse."

"You fucked her yet?" asked Bobby.

"No."

"What was Keesing like?"

"All right. But I really wonder how he stood being with her. Maybe the codeine and pills helped. Maybe she was like a big flower-child-nurse to him."

"Fuck it," said Bobby, "let's drink."

"Yeah. If I had to choose between drinking and fucking I think I'd have to stop fucking."

"Fucking can cause problems," said Valerie.

"When my wife is out fucking somebody else I put on my pyjamas, pull the covers up and go to sleep," said Bobby.

"He's cool," said Valerie.

"None of us quite know how to use sex, what to do with it," I said. "With most people sex is just a toy—wind it up and let it run."

"What about love?" asked Valerie.

"Love is all right for those who can handle the psychic overload. It's like trying to carry a full garbage can on your back over a rushing river of piss."

"Oh, it's not *that* bad!"

"Love is a form of prejudice. I have too many other prejudices."

Valerie went to the window.

"People are having fun, jumping into the pool, and she's out there looking at the moon."

"Her old man just died," said Bobby. "Give her a break."

I took my bottle and went to my bedroom. I undressed down to my shorts and went to bed. Nothing was ever in tune. People just blindly grabbed at whatever there was: communism, health foods, zen, surfing, ballet, hypnotism, group encounters, orgies, biking, herbs, Catholicism, weight-lifting, travel, withdrawal, vegetarianism, India, painting, writing, sculpting, composing, conducting, backpacking, yoga, copulating, gambling, drinking, hanging around, frozen yogurt, Beethoven, Bach, Buddha, Christ, TM, H, carrot juice, suicide, handmade suits, jet travel, New York City, and then it all evaporated and fell apart. People had to find things to do while waiting to die. I guess it was nice to have a choice.

I took my choice. I raised the fifth of vodka and drank it straight. The Russians knew something.

The door opened and Cecelia walked in. She looked good with her low-slung powerful body. Most American women were either too thin or without stamina. If you gave them rough use something broke in them and they became neurotic and their men became sport freaks or alcoholics or obsessed with cars. The Norwegians, the Icelanders, the Finns knew how a woman should be built: wide and solid, a big ass, big hips, big white flanks, big heads, big mouths, big tits, plenty of hair, big eyes, big nostrils, and down in the center—big enough and small enough.

"Hello, Cecelia. Come on to bed."

"It was nice out tonight."

"I suppose. Come say hello."

She went into the bathroom. I switched off the bedroom light.

She came out after a while. I felt her climb into bed. It was dark but some light came in through the curtains. I handed her the fifth. She took a tiny sip, then handed the bottle back. We were sitting up, our backs against the headboard and the pillows. We were thigh to thigh.

"Hank, the moon was just a tiny sliver. But the stars were brilliant and beautiful. It makes you think, doesn't it?"

"Yes."

"Some of those stars have been dead for millions of light-years and yet we can still see them."

I reached around and pulled Cecelia's head toward me. Her mouth opened. It was wet and it was good.

"Cecelia, let's fuck."

"I don't want to."

In a way I didn't want to either. Which is why I had asked.

"You don't want to? Then why do you kiss like that?"

"I think that people should take the time to get to know each other."

"Sometimes there's not that much time."

"I don't want to do it."

I got out of bed. I walked down in my shorts and knocked on Bobby and Valerie's door.

"What is it?" Bobby asked.

"She won't fuck me."

"So?"

"Let's go for a swim."

"It's late. The pool is closed."

"Closed? There's water, isn't there?"

"I mean, the lights are off."

"That's all right. She won't fuck me."

"You don't have a bathing suit."

"I have my shorts."

"All right, wait a minute. . . ."

BOBBY AND Valerie came out dressed beautifully in new tight-fitting swim suits. Bobby handed me a Columbian and I took a hit.

"What's wrong with Cecelia?"

"Christian chemistry."

We walked to the pool. It was true, the lights were out. Bobby and Valerie dove into the pool in tandem. I sat at the edge of the pool, my legs dangling in. I sucked from the fifth of vodka.

Bobby and Valerie surfaced together. Bobby swam over to the edge of the pool. He pulled at one of my ankles.

"Come on, shit head! Show some guts! DIVE!"

I took another hit of vodka, then set the bottle down. I didn't dive. I carefully lowered myself over the edge. Then I dropped in. It was strange in the dark water. I sank slowly towards the bottom of the pool. I was 6 feet tall and weighed 225 pounds. I waited to touch bottom and push off. Where *was* the bottom? There it was, and I was almost out of oxygen. I pushed off. I went back up slowly. Finally I broke the surface of the water.

"Death to all whores who keep their legs closed against me!" I screamed.

A door opened and a man came running out of a ground floor apartment. He was the manager.

"Hey, there is no swimming allowed this time of night! The pool lights are off!"

I paddled toward him, reached the pool edge and looked up at him. "Look, motherfucker, I drink two barrels of beer a day and I'm a professional wrestler. I'm a *kindly* soul by nature. But I intend to swim and I want those lights turned ON! NOW! I'm only asking you one time!"

I paddled off.

The lights went on. The pool was brilliantly lit. It was magic. I paddled toward the vodka, took it down from the pool edge and had a good one. The bottle was almost empty. I looked down and Valerie and Bobby were swimming in circles around each other underwater. They were good at it, they were lithe and graceful. How odd that everybody was younger than I.

We finished with the pool. I walked to the manager's door in my wet shorts and knocked. He opened the door. I liked him.

"Hey, buddy, you can flick out the lights now. I'm through swimming. You're O.K., baby, you're O.K."

We walked back to our apartment.

"Have a drink with us," said Bobby. "I know that you're unhappy."

I went in and had two drinks.

Valerie said, "Look, Hank, you and your *women!* You can't fuck them all, don't you know that?"

"Victory or death!"

"Sleep it off, Hank."

"Goodnight, folks, and thanks. . . ."

I WENT back to my bedroom. Cecelia was flat on her back and she was snoring, "Guzzz, guzzz, guzzz. . . ."

She looked *fat* to me. I took off my wet shorts, climbed into bed. I shook her.

"Cecelia, you're SNORING!"

"Oooh, oooh. . . . I'm sorry. . . ."

"O.K., Cecelia. This is just like being married. I'll get you in the morning when I'm fresh."

81

A SOUND AWAKENED me. It was not quite daylight. Cecelia was moving around getting dressed.

I looked at my watch.

"It's 5 AM. What are you doing?"

"I want to watch the sun come up. I *love* sunrises!"

"No wonder you don't drink."

"I'll be back. We can have breakfast together."

"I haven't been able to eat breakfast for 40 years."

"I'm going to watch the sunrise, Hank."

I FOUND a capped bottle of beer. It was warm. I opened it, drank it. Then I slept.

AT 10:30 AM there was a knock on the door.

"Come in. . . ."

It was Bobby, Valerie and Cecelia.

"We just had breakfast together," said Bobby.

"Now Cecelia wants to take her shoes off and walk along the beach," said Valerie.

"I've never seen the Pacific Ocean before, Hank. It's *so* beautiful!"

"I'll get dressed. . . ."

We walked along the shoreline. Cecelia was happy. When the waves came in and ran over her bare feet she screamed.

'You people go ahead," I said, "I'm going to find a bar."

"I'll come with you," said Bobby.

"I'll watch over Cecelia," Valerie said. . . .

WE FOUND the nearest bar. There were only two empty stools. We sat down. Bobby drew a male. I drew a female. Bobby and I ordered our drinks.

The woman next to me was 26, 27. Something had wearied her—her eyes and mouth looked tired—but she still held together in spite of it. Her hair was dark and well-kept. She had on a skirt and she had good legs. Her soul was topaz and you could see it in her eyes. I laid my leg against hers. She didn't move away. I drained my drink.

"Buy me a drink," I asked her.

She nodded to the barkeep. He came over.

"Vodka-7 for the gentleman."

"Thanks. . . ."

"Babette."

"Thanks, Babette. My name's Henry Chinaski, alcoholic writer."

"Never heard of you."

"Likewise."

"I run a shop near the beach. Trinkets and crap, mostly crap."

"We're even. I write a lot of crap."

"If you're such a bad writer, why don't you quit?"

"I need food, shelter and clothing. Buy me another drink."

Babette nodded to the barkeep and I had a new drink.

We pressed our legs together.

"I'm a rat," I told her, "I'm constipated and I can't get it up."

"I don't know about your bowels. But you're a rat and you can get it up."

"What's your phone number?"

Babette reached into her purse for a pen.

Then Cecelia and Valerie walked in.

"Oh," said Valerie, "*there* are those bastards. I *told* you. The nearest bar!"

Babette slid off her stool. She was out the door. I could see her through the blinds on the window. She was walking away, on the boardwalk, and she had a body. It was willow slim. It swayed in the wind and was gone.

82

CECELIA SAT AND watched us drink. I could see that I repulsed her. I ate meat. I had no god. I liked to fuck. Nature didn't interest me. I never voted. I liked wars. Outer space bored me. Baseball bored me. History bored me. Zoos bored me.

"HANK," SHE said, "I'm going outside for a while."

"What's out there?"

"I like to watch the people swim in the pool. I like to see them enjoying themselves."

Cecelia got up and walked outside.

Valerie laughed. Bobby laughed.

"All right, so I'm not going to get into her panties."

"Do you want to?" asked Bobby.

"It's not so much my sex drive that's offended, it's my ego."

"And don't forget your age," said Bobby.

"There's nothing worse than an old chauv pig," I said.

We drank in silence.

AN HOUR or so later Cecelia returned.

"Hank, I want to go."

"Where?"

"To the airport. I want to fly to San Francisco. I have all my luggage with me."

"It's all right with me. But Valerie and Bobby brought us down in their car. Maybe they don't want to leave yet."

"We'll drive her to L.A.," said Bobby.

WE PAID our bill, got into the car, Bobby at the wheel, Valerie next to him and Cecelia and me in the back seat. Cecelia leaned away from me, pressed herself against the door, as far away from me as she could get.

Bobby turned on the tape deck. The music hit the back seat like a wave. Bob Dylan.

Valerie passed back a joint. I took a hit then tried to hand it to Cecelia. She cringed away from me. I reached and fondled one of her knees, squeezed it. She pushed my hand away.

"Hey, how you guys doing back there?" Bobby asked.

"It's love," I replied.

We drove for an hour.

"Here's the airport," said Bobby.

"You've got two hours," I told Cecelia. "We can go back to my place and wait."

"That's all right," said Cecelia. "I want to go now."

"But what will you do for two hours at the airport?" I asked.

"Oh," said Cecelia, "I just love airports!"

We stopped in front of the terminal. I jumped out, unloaded her baggage. As we stood together Cecelia reached up and kissed me on the cheek. I let her walk in alone.

83

I HAD AGREED to give a reading up north. It was the afternoon before the reading and I was sitting in an apartment at the Holiday Inn drinking beer with Joe Washington, the promoter, and the local poet, Dudley Barry, and his boyfriend, Paul. Dudley had come out of the closet and announced he was a homo. He was nervous, fat and ambitious. He paced up and down.

"You gonna give a good reading?"

"I don't know."

"You draw the crowds. Jesus, how do you do it? They line up around the block."

"They like blood-lettings."

Dudley grabbed Paul by the cheeks of the ass. "I'm gonna ream you out, baby! Then you can ream me!"

Joe Washington stood by the window. "Hey, look, here comes William Burroughs across the way. He's got the apartment right next to yours. He's reading tomorrow night."

I walked to the window. It was Burroughs all right. I turned away and opened a new beer. We were on the second floor. Burroughs walked up the stairway, passed my window, opened his door and went in.

"Do you want to go meet him?" Joe asked.

"No."

"I'm going to see him for a minute."

"All right."

Dudley and Paul were playing grab-ass. Dudley was laughing and Paul was giggling and blushing.

"Why don't you guys work out in private?"

"Isn't he cute?" asked Dudley. "I just love young boys!"

"I'm more interested in the female."

"You don't know what you're missing."

"Don't be concerned."

"Jack Mitchell is running with transvestites. He writes poems about them."

"At least they look like women."

"Some of them look better."

I drank in silence.

JOE WASHINGTON returned. "I told Burroughs that you were in the next apartment. I said, 'Burroughs, Henry Chinaski is in the next apartment.' He said, 'Oh, is that so?' I asked if he wanted to meet you. He said, 'No.'"

"They should have refrigerators in these places," I said. "This fucking beer is getting warm."

I walked out to look for an ice machine. As I walked by Burroughs' place he was sitting in a chair by the window. He looked at me indifferently.

I found the ice machine and came back with the ice and put it in the wash basin and stuck the beers in there.

"You don't want to get too bombed," said Joe. "You really start slurring your words."

"They don't give a damn. They just want me on the cross."

"$500 for an hour's work?" asked Dudley. "You call that a cross?"

"Yeah."

"You're some Christ!"

DUDLEY AND Paul left and Joe and I went out to one of the local coffeehouses for food and drink. We found a table. The first thing we knew, strangers were pulling chairs up to our table. All men. What shit. There were some pretty girls there but they just looked and smiled, or they didn't look and they didn't smile. I figured the ones who didn't smile hated me because of my attitude towards women. Fuck them.

Jack Mitchell was there and Mike Tufts, both poets. Neither worked for a living despite the fact their poetry paid them nothing. They lived on will power and handouts. Mitchell was really a good poet but his luck was bad. He deserved better. Then Blast Grimly, the singer, walked over. Blast was always drunk. I had never seen him sober. There were a couple of others at the table who I didn't know.

"Mr. Chinaski?"

It was a sweet little thing in a short green dress.

"Yes?"

"Would you autograph this book?"

It was an early book of poems, poems I had written while working at the post office, *It Runs Around the Room and Me*. I signed it and made a drawing, handed it back.

"Oh, thanks so much!"

She left. All the bastards sitting around me had killed any chance for action.

Soon there were 4 or 5 pitchers of beer on the table. I ordered a sandwich. We drank 2 or 3 hours, then I went back to the apartment. I finished the beers in the sink and went to sleep.

I DON'T remember much about the reading but I awakened in bed the next day, alone. Joe Washington knocked about 11 AM.

"Hey, man, that was one of your *best* readings!"

"Really? You're not shitting me?"

"No, you were right there. Here's the check."

"Thanks, Joe."

"You're sure you don't want to meet Burroughs?"

"I'm sure."

"He's reading tonight. You going to stay for his reading?"

"I gotta get back to L.A., Joe."

"You ever heard him read?"

"Joe, I want to take a shower and get out of here. You're going to drive me to the airport?"

"Sure."

WHEN WE left Burroughs was sitting in his chair by the window. He gave no indication of having seen me. I glanced at him and walked on. I had my check. I was anxious to make the race-track. . . .

84

I HAD BEEN corresponding with a lady in San Francisco for several months. Her name was Liza Weston and she survived by giving dance lessons, including ballet, in her own studio. She was 32, had been married once, and all her letters were long and typed flawlessly on pinkish paper. She wrote well, with intelligence and with very little exaggeration. I enjoyed her letters and answered them. Liza stayed away from literature, she stayed away from the so-called larger questions. She wrote me about small ordinary happenings but described them with insight and humor. And so it came about that she wrote to say that she was coming to Los Angeles to buy some dancing costumes and would I like to see her? I told her most certainly, and that she could stay at my place, but due to the difference in our ages *she* would have to sleep on the couch while *I* slept in the bed. I'll phone you when I get in, she wrote back.

Three or four days later the phone rang. It was Liza. "I'm in town," she said.

"Are you at the airport? I'll pick you up."

"I'll take a cab in."

"It costs."

"It'll be easier this way."

"What do you drink?"

"I don't much. So whatever you want. . . ."

I sat and waited for her. I always became uneasy in these situations. When they actually arrived I almost didn't want them to happen. Liza had mentioned that she was pretty but I hadn't seen any photographs. I had once married a woman, promised to marry her sight unseen, through the mails. She too had written intelligent letters, but my 2-and-one-half years of marriage proved to be a disaster. People were usually much better in their letters than in reality. They were much like poets in this way.

I paced the room. Then I heard footsteps coming up the court walk. I went to the blinds and peeked out. Not bad. Dark hair, neatly dressed in a long skirt that fell to her ankles. She walked gracefully, holding her head high. Nice nose, ordinary mouth. I liked women in dresses, it reminded me of bygone days. She carried a small bag. She knocked. I opened the door. "Come in."

Liza put her suitcase on the floor.

"Sit down."

She had on very little makeup. She was pretty. Her hair was stylish and short.

I got her a vodka-7 and made myself one. She seemed calm. There was a touch of suffering in her face—she had been through one or two difficult periods in her life. So had I.

"I'm going to buy some costumes tomorrow. There's a shop in L.A. that's very unusual."

"I like that dress you have on. A fully covered woman is exciting, I think. Of course, it's hard to tell about her figure but one can make a judgment."

"You're like I thought you'd be. You're not afraid at all."

"Thanks."

"You seem almost diffident."

"I'm on my third drink."

"What happens after the fourth?"

"Not much. I drink it and wait for the fifth."

I walked out to get the newspaper. When I came back Liza had that long skirt hiked up to just above the knees. It looked good. She had fine knees, good legs. The day (actually the night) was brightening. From her letters I knew she was a health food addict like Cecelia. Only she didn't act like Cecelia at all. I sat at the other end of the couch and kept sneaking looks at her legs. I had always been a leg man.

"You have nice legs," I told Liza.

"You like them?"

She hitched her skirt up another inch. It was maddening. All that good leg coming out of all that cloth. It was so much better than a mini-skirt.

After the next drink I moved down next to Liza.

"You ought to come see my dance studio," she said.

"I can't dance."

"You can. I'll teach you."

"Free?"

"Of course. You're very light on your feet for a big guy. I can tell by the way you walk that you could dance very well."

"It's a deal. I'll sleep on *your* couch."

"I have a nice apartment but all I have is a waterbed."

"All right."

"But you have to let me cook for you. Good food."

"Sounds all right." I looked at her legs. Then I fondled one of her knees. I kissed her. She kissed me back like a lonely woman.

"Do you find me attractive?" Liza asked.

"Yes, of course. But what I like best is your style. You have a certain high tone."

"You've got a good line, Chinaski."

"I have to. I'm almost 60 years old."

"You seem more like 40, Hank."

"You have a good line too, Liza."

"I have to. I'm 32."

"I'm glad you're not 22."

"And I'm glad you're not 32."

"This is one glad night," I said.

We each sipped our drinks.

"What do you think of women?" she asked.

"I'm not a thinker. Every woman is different. Basically they seem to be a combination of the best and the worst—both magic and terrible. I'm glad that they exist, however."

"How do you treat them?"

"They are better to me than I am to them."

"Do you think that's fair?"

"Not fair, but that's the way it is."

"You're honest."

"Not quite."

"After I buy those new costumes tomorrow I want to try them on. You can tell me which one you like best."

"Sure. But I like the long type of gown. Class."

"I buy all kinds."

"I don't buy clothes until they fall apart."

"Your expenditures are of a different kind."

"Liza, I'm going to bed after this drink, all right?"

"Of course."

I had piled her bedding on the floor. "Will you have enough blankets?"

"Yes."

"Pillow O.K.?"

"I'm sure."

I finished my drink, got up and bolted the front door.

"I'm not locking you in. Feel safe."

"I do. . . ."

I walked into the bedroom, switched off the light, undressed, and got under the covers. "You see," I called to her, "I didn't rape you."

"Oh," she answered, "I wish you would!"

I didn't quite believe that but it was good to hear. I had played a pretty fair hand. Liza would keep overnight.

WHEN I awakened I heard her in the bathroom. Maybe I should have slammed her? How did a man know what to do? Generally, I decided, it was better to wait, if you had any feeling for the individual. If you hated her right off, it was better to fuck her right off; if you didn't, it was better to wait, then fuck her and hate her later on.

Liza came out of the bathroom in a medium-length red dress. It fit her well. She was slim and classy. She stood in front of my bedroom mirror playing with her hair.

"Hank, I'm going to buy the costumes now. You stay in bed. You're probably sick from all that drinking."

"Why? We both drank the same."

"I heard you sneaking some in the kitchen. Why did you do that?"

"I was afraid, I guess."

"You? Afraid? I thought you were the big, tough, drinking, woman-fucker?"

"Did I let you down?"

"No."

"I was afraid. My art is my fear. I rocket off from it."

"I'm going to get the costumes, Hank."

"You're angry. I let you down."

"Not at all. I'll be back."

"Where's this shop at?"

"87th Street."

"87th Street? Great Christ, that's *Watts!*"

"They have the best costumes on the coast."

"It's *black* down there!"

"Are you anti-black?"

"I'm anti-everything."

"I'll take a cab. I'll be back in 3 hours."

"Is this your idea of vengeance?"

"I said I'd be back. I'm leaving my things."

"You'll never come back."

"I'll be back. I can handle myself."

"All right, but look . . . don't take a cab."

I got up and found my bluejeans, found my car keys.

"Here, take my Volks. It's TRV 469, right outside. But go easy on the clutch, and second gear is shot, especially coming back down it grinds. . . ."

She took the keys and I got back into bed and pulled the sheet up. Liza bent over me. I grabbed her, kissed her along the neck. My breath was bad.

"Cheer up," she said. "Trust. We'll celebrate tonight and there'll be a fashion parade."

"I can't wait."

"You will."

"The silver key opens the door on the driver's side. The gold key is the ignition. . . ."

She walked off in her medium-length red dress. I heard the door close. I looked around. Her suitcase was still there. And there was a pair of her shoes on the rug.

85

WHEN I AWAKENED it was 1:30 PM. I took a bath, got dressed, checked the mail. A letter from a young man in Glendale. "Dear Mr. Chinaski: I am a young writer and I think that I am a good one, a very good one, but my poems keep coming back. How does one break into this game? What is the secret? Who do you have to know? I very much admire your writing and I would like to come over and talk to you. I'll bring a couple of 6-packs and we can talk. I'd also like to read you some of my work. . . ."

The poor fucker didn't have a cunt. I threw his letter into the wastebasket.

An hour or so later Liza returned. "Oh, I've found the most marvelous costumes!"

She had an armful of dresses. She went into the bedroom. Some time passed, then she walked out. She was in a high-necked long gown and she whirled in front of me. It fit her very nicely around the ass. It was gold and black and she had on black shoes. She did a subdued dance.

"You like it?"

"Oh, yes. . . ." I sat and waited.

Liza went back into the bedroom. Then she came out in green and red with shots of silver. This one was a midriff job with her bellybutton showing. As she paraded in front of me she had this special way of looking into my eyes. It was neither coy nor sexy, it was perfect.

I don't remember how many costumes she showed me, but the last one was just right. It clung to her and was slit up each side of the skirt. As she walked around, first one leg came out, then the other. The dress was black, it shimmered, and it was cut low in front.

I got up as she walked across the room and grabbed her. I kissed her viciously, bending her backwards. I continued to kiss her and began pulling up her long gown. I pulled the back of the skirt all the way up and saw her panties, yellow. I pulled the front of her gown up and began pushing my cock against her. Her tongue slipped into my mouth—it was as cool as if she had been drinking ice water. I walked her backwards into the bedroom, pushed her onto the bed and mauled her. I got those yellow panties off and got my own pants off. I let my imagination go. Her legs were around my neck as I stood over her. I spread her legs apart, moved up, and slid it in. I played around a little, using different speeds, then anger thrusts, thrusts of love, teasing thrusts, brutal thrusts. I would pull out from time to time, then begin again. Finally I let go, gave her the last few strokes, came, and sank down beside her. Liza continued to kiss me. I wasn't sure whether she had gotten off or not. I had.

WE HAD dinner at a French place that also served good American food at fair prices. It was always overcrowded which gave us time at the bar. That night I left my name as Lancelot Lovejoy, and I was even sober enough to recognize the call 45 minutes later.

We ordered a bottle of wine. We decided to hold off dinner for a while. There isn't a better way to drink than at a small table over a white tablecloth with a good-looking woman.

"You fuck," Liza told me, "with the enthusiasm of a man who is fucking for the first time and yet you fuck with a lot of inventiveness."

"May I write that down on my sleeve?"

"Sure."

"I might use it sometimes."

"Just don't use me, that's all I ask. I don't want to be just another one of your women."

I didn't answer.

"My sister hates you," she said. "She said that all you'll do is use me."

"What happened to your class, Liza? You're talking just like everybody else."

WE NEVER got around to dinner. When we got back home we drank some more. I did like her very much. I began to abuse her a bit, verbally. She looked surprised, her eyes filled with tears. She ran to the bathroom, stayed 10 minutes or so, then came out.

"My sister was right. You're a bastard!"

"Let's go to bed, Liza."

We got ready for bed. We got into bed and I mounted her. Without foreplay it was much more difficult but I finally got it in. I began to work. I worked and I worked. It was another hot night. It was like a recurring bad dream. I began sweating. I humped and I pumped. It wouldn't go down, it wouldn't come off. I pumped and I humped. Finally I rolled off. "Sorry, baby, too much to drink."

Liza slowly slid her head down my chest, across my belly, down, got to it, began licking and licking and licking, then took it into her mouth and worked on it. . . .

I FLEW back to San Francisco with Liza. She had an apartment at the top of a steep hill. It was nice. The first thing I had to do was crap. I went into the bathroom and sat down. Green vines all around. What a pot. I liked it. When I came out Liza sat me down on some big pillows, put Mozart on the machine, and poured me a chilled wine. It was dinner time and she stood in the kitchen cooking. Every now and then she poured me another wine. I always enjoyed being at women's places more than when they were at mine. When I was at their places I could always leave.

She called me in to dinner. There was salad, iced tea and a chicken stew. It was quite good. I was a terrible cook. All I could fry were steaks, although I made a good beef stew, especially when drunk. I liked to gamble with my beef stews. I put almost everything into them and sometimes got away with it.

After dinner we took a ride to Fisherman's Wharf. Liza drove her car with great caution. It made me nervous. She would stop at a cross street and look in both directions for traffic. When there wasn't any she still sat there. I waited.

"Liza, shit, let's *go*. There isn't anybody around."

Then she would go. That was the way it was with people. The longer you knew them the more their eccentricities showed. Sometimes their eccentricities were humorous—in the beginning.

We walked along the wharf, then went and sat on the sand. It wasn't much of a beach.

She told me she hadn't had a boyfriend in some time. What the men she had known talked about, what was important to them, she found unbelievable.

"Women are much the same," I told her. "When they asked Richard Burton what was the first thing he looked for in a woman, he said, 'She must be at least 30 years old.'"

It got dark and we went back to her apartment. Liza brought out the wine and we sat on pillows. She opened the shutters and we looked out on the night. We began kissing. Then we drank. And kissed some more.

"When are you going back to work?" I asked her.

"Do you want me to?"

"No, but you have to live."

"But you're not working."

"In a way, I am."

"You mean you live in order to write?"

"No, I just exist. Then later I try to remember and write some of it down."

"I only run my dance studio three nights a week."

"You make ends meet that way?"

"So far I have."

We became more involved with kissing. She didn't drink as much as I did. We moved to the waterbed, undressed and got to it. I'd heard about waterbed fucks. They were supposed to be great. I found it difficult. The water shuddered and shook beneath us, and as I was moving down, the water seemed to be rocking from side to side. Instead of bringing her *to* me, it seemed to take her *away* from me. Maybe I needed practice. I went into my savagery routine, grabbing her by the hair, thrusting as if it was a rape. She liked it, or seemed to, making little delightful sounds. I savaged her some more, then suddenly she appeared to climax, making all the right sounds. That excited me and I came just at the end of hers.

We cleaned up and went back to the pillows and the wine. Liza fell asleep with her head in my lap. I sat there an hour or so. Then I stretched out on my back and we slept that night on all those pillows.

THE NEXT day Liza took me to her dance studio. We got sandwiches from a place across the street and we took them up with our drinks to her studio and ate them. It was a very large room on a second floor. There was nothing but empty floor, some stereo equipment, a few chairs, and there were ropes strung high above, across the ceiling. I didn't know what any of it meant.

"Shall I teach you to dance?" she asked.

"Somehow I'm not in the mood," I said.

The following days and nights were similar. Not bad but not great. I learned to manage on the waterbed a bit better but I still preferred a normal bed for fucking.

I stayed 3 or 4 more days, then flew back to L.A.

We continued to write letters back and forth.

A month later she was back in L.A. This time when she walked up to my door she wore slacks. She looked different, I couldn't explain it to myself but she looked different. I didn't enjoy sitting around with her so I took her to the racetrack, to the movies, to the boxing matches, all the things I did with women I enjoyed, but something was missing. We still had sex, but it was no longer as exciting. I felt as if we were married.

After five days Liza was sitting on the couch and I was reading the newspaper when she said, "Hank, it's not working, is it?"

"No."

"What's wrong?"

"I don't know."

"I'll leave. I don't want to stay here."

"Relax, it's not *that* bad."

"I just don't understand it."

I didn't answer.

"Hank, drive me to the Women's Liberation Building. Do you know where it's at?"

"Yes, it's in the Westlake district where the art school used to be."

"How did you know?"

"I drove another woman there once."

"You bastard."

"O.K., now. . . ."

"I have a girlfriend who works there. I don't know where her apartment is and I can't find her in the phonebook. But I know she works at the Women's Lib Building. I'll stay with her for a couple of days. I just don't want to go back to San Francisco feeling like I do. . . ."

Liza got her things together and put them in her suitcase. We walked out to the car and I drove to the Westlake district. I had driven Lydia there once for a women's art exhibit where she had entered some of her sculpture.

I parked outside.

"I'll wait to make sure your friend is there."

"It's all right. You can go."

"I'll wait."

I waited. Liza came out, waved. I waved back, started the engine and drove off.

86

I WAS SITTING in my shorts one afternoon a week later. There was a tender little knock on the door. "Just a moment," I said. I put on a robe and opened the door.

"We're two girls from Germany. We've read your books."

One looked to be about 19, the other maybe 22.

I had two or three books out in Germany in limited editions. I had been born in Germany in 1920, in Andernach. The house I had lived in during my childhood was now a brothel. I couldn't speak German. But they spoke English.

"Come in."

They sat on the couch.

"I'm Hilda," said the 19 year old.

"I'm Gertrude," said the 22 year old.

"I'm Hank."

"We thought your books were very sad and very funny," said Gertrude.

"Thank you."

I went in and poured 3 vodka-7s. I loaded their drinks, and I loaded mine.

"We're on our way to New York City. We thought we would stop by," said Gertrude.

They went on to say they'd been in Mexico. They spoke good English. Gertrude was heavier, almost a butterball; she was all breasts and ass. Hilda was thin, looked like she was under some kind of strain . . . constipated and odd, but attractive.

As I drank I crossed my legs. My robe fell apart.

"Oh," said Gertrude, "you have sexy legs!"

"Yes," said Hilda.

"I know it," I said.

The girls stayed right along with me on the drinks. I went and concocted three more. When I sat down again I made sure that my robe covered me properly.

"You girls can stay here for a few days, rest up."

They didn't answer.

"Or you don't have to stay," I said. "It's all right. We can just talk awhile. I don't want to make any demands on you."

"I'll bet you know a lot of women," said Hilda. "We've read your books."

"I write fiction."

"What's fiction?"

"Fiction is an improvement on life."

"You mean you lie?" asked Gertrude.

"A little. Not too much."

"Do you have a girlfriend?" asked Hilda.

"No. Not now."

"We'll stay," said Gertrude.

"There's only one bed."

"That's all right."

"Just one other thing . . ."

"What?"

"I must sleep in the middle."

"That's all right."

I kept mixing drinks and soon we ran out. I phoned the liquor store. "I want . . ."

"Wait, my friend," he said, "we don't start making home deliveries until 6 PM."

"Really? I push $200 a month down your throat. . . ."

"Who is this?"

"Chinaski."

"Oh, *Chinaski*. . . . What is it you wanted?"

I told the man. Then, "You know how to get here?"

"Oh, yes."

HE ARRIVED in 8 minutes. It was the fat Australian who was always sweating. I took the two cartons and set them on a chair.

"Hello, ladies," said the fat Australian.

They didn't answer.

"What's the bill, Arbuckle?"

"Well, it comes to $17.94."

I gave him a twenty. He started digging for change.

"You know better than that. Buy yourself a new home."

"Thank you, sir!"

Then he leaned toward me and asked in a lower voice, "My God, how do you do it?"

"Typing," I said.

"Typing?"

"Yes, about 18 words a minute."

I pushed him back outside and closed the door.

THAT NIGHT I got in bed with them, with me in between. We were all drunk and first I grabbed one and kissed and fondled her, then I turned and grabbed the other. I went back and forth and it was very rewarding. Later I concentrated on one for a long time, then turned and went to the other. Each waited patiently. I was confused. Gertrude was hotter, Hilda was younger. I reamed butt, laid on top of each of them but didn't stick it in. I finally decided on Gertrude. But I couldn't do it. I was too drunk. Gertrude and I went to sleep, her hand holding my cock, my hands on her breasts. My cock went down, her breasts remained firm.

IT WAS very hot the next day and there was more drinking. I phoned out for food. I turned the fan on. There wasn't much talking. Those German girls liked their drinks. Then they both went out and sat on the old couch on my front porch—Hilda in shorts and bra and Gertrude in a tight pink underslip without bra or panties. Max, the mailman, came by. Gertrude accepted my mail for me. Poor Max nearly fainted. I could see the envy and disbelief in his eyes. But, then, *he* had job security. . . .

AROUND 2 PM Hilda announced that she was going for a walk. Gertrude and I went inside. Finally it *did* happen. We were on the bed and we played our openers. After a while we got down to it. I mounted and it went in. But it went in sharply to the left, like there was a curve. I could only remember one other woman like that—but it had been good. Then I got to thinking, she's fooling me, I'm not really in there. So I pulled it out and stuck it back in. It went in and took a hard left turn again. What shit. Either she had a fucked up pussy or I wasn't penetrating. I persuaded myself to believe she had a fucked up pussy. I pumped and worked while it bent around that hard left turn.

I worked and worked. Then it felt as if I were hitting bone. It was shocking. I gave up and rolled off.

"Sorry," I said, "I just don't seem to have it today."

Gertrude didn't answer.

We both got up and dressed. Then we went into the front room and sat and waited on Hilda. We drank and waited. Hilda took a long time. A long, long time. She finally arrived.

"Hello," I said.

"Who are all these black men in your neighborhood?" she asked.

"I don't know who they are."

"They said I could make $2,000 a week."

"Doing what?"

"They didn't say."

THE GERMAN girls stayed 2 or 3 days more. I still kept hitting that left turn in Gertrude even when I was sober. Hilda told me she was on Tampax, so she was no help.

They finally collected their things and I got them into my car. They had large canvas bags that they carried over their shoulders. German hippies. I followed their instructions. Turn here, turn there. We climbed higher and higher into the Hollywood Hills. We were in rich territory. I had forgotten that some people lived quite well while most others ate their own shit for breakfast. When you lived where I lived you began to believe that every place else was like your own crummy place.

"Here it is," said Gertrude.

The Volks was at the bottom of a long winding driveway. Up

there somewhere was a house, a large, large house with all the things in it, and around it, that such houses have.

"You had better let us walk up," said Gertrude.

"Sure," I said.

They got out. I turned the Volks around. They stood at the entrance and waved to me, their canvas backpacks slung over their shoulders. I waved back. Then I drove off, put it into neutral, and glided down out of the mountains.

87

I was asked to give a reading at a famous nightclub, *The Lancer*, on Hollywood Boulevard. I agreed to read two nights. I was to follow a rock group, *The Big Rape*, each night. I was getting sucked into the showbiz maze. I had some extra tickets and I phoned Tammie and asked her if she wanted to come. She said yes, so the first night I took her with me. I had them put her on the tab. We sat in the bar waiting for my act to go on. Tammie's act was similar to mine. She promptly got drunk and walked up and down in the bar talking to people.

By the time I was ready to go on Tammie was falling over tables. I found her brother and told him, "Jesus Christ, get her *out* of here, will you?"

He led her off into the night. I was drunk, too, and later on I forgot that I had asked that she be taken away.

I didn't give a good reading. The audience was strictly into rock, and they missed lines and meanings. But some of it was my fault too. I sometimes lucked out with rock crowds, but that particular night I didn't. I was disturbed by Tammie's absence, I think. When I got home I phoned her number. Her mother answered. "Your daughter," I told her, "is SCUM!"

"Hank, I don't want to hear that."

She hung up.

The next night I went alone. I sat at a table in the bar and drank. An elderly, dignified woman came up to my table and introduced herself. She taught English literature and had brought one of her pupils, a little butterball called Nancy Freeze. Nancy appeared to be in heat. They wanted to know if I would answer some questions for the class.

"Shoot."

"Who was your favorite author?"

"Fante."

"Who?"

"John F—a—n—t—e. *Ask the Dust. Wait Until Spring, Bandini.*"

"Where can we find his books?"

"I found them in the main library, downtown. Fifth and Olive, isn't it?"

"Why did you like him?"

"Total emotion. A very brave man."

"Who else?"

"Céline."

"Why?"

"They ripped out his guts and he laughed, and he made them laugh too. A very brave man."

"Do you believe in bravery?"

"I like to see it anywhere, in animals, birds, reptiles, humans."

"Why?"

"Why? It makes me feel good. It's a matter of style in the face of no chance at all."

"Hemingway?"

"No."

"Why?"

"Too grim, too serious. A good writer, fine sentences. But for him, life was always total war. He never let go, he never danced."

They folded up their notebooks and vanished. Too bad. I had meant to tell them that my *real* influences were Gable, Cagney, Bogart and Errol Flynn.

NEXT THING I knew I was sitting with three handsome women, Sara, Cassie, and Debra. Sara was 32, a classy wench, good style

CHARLES BUKOWSKI

and a heart. She had red-blond hair that fell straight down, and she had wild eyes, slightly insane. She also carried an overload of compassion that was real enough and which obviously cost her something. Debra was Jewish with large brown eyes and a generous mouth, heavily smeared with blood-red lipstick. Her mouth glistened and beckoned to me. I guessed she was somewhere between 30 and 35, and she reminded me of how my mother looked in 1935 (although my mother had been much more beautiful). Cassie was tall with long blond hair, very young, expensively dressed, modish, hip, "in," nervous, beautiful. She sat closest to me, squeezing my hand, rubbing her thigh against mine. As she squeezed my hand I became aware that her hand was much larger than mine. (Although I am a large man I am embarrassed by my small hands. In my barroom brawls as a young man in Philadelphia I had quickly found out the importance of hand size. How I had managed to win 30 percent of my fights was amazing.) Anyway, Cassie felt she had an edge on the other two, and I wasn't sure but that I agreed.

Then I had to read, and I had a luckier night. It was the same crowd, but my mind was on my work. The crowd got warmer and warmer, wilder and enthusiastic. Sometimes it was them who made it happen, sometimes it was you. Usually the latter. It was like climbing into the prize ring: you should feel you owed them something or you shouldn't be in there. I jabbbed and crossed and shuffled, and in the last round I really opened up and knocked out the referee. Performance is performance. Because I had bombed the night before my success must have seemed very strange to them. It certainly seemed strange to me.

CASSIE WAS waiting in the bar. Sara slipped me a love note with her phone number. Debra was not as inventive—she just wrote down her phone number. For a moment—strangely—I thought about Katherine, then I bought Cassie a drink. I'd never see Katherine again. My little Texas girl, my beauty of beauties. Goodbye, Katherine.

208

"Look, Cassie, can you drive me home? I'm too drunk to drive. One more drunk driving rap and I've had it."

"All right, I'll drive you home. How about your car?"

"Fuck it. I'll leave it."

We left together in her M.G. It was like a movie. At any moment I expected her to drop me off at the next corner. She was in her mid-twenties. She talked as we drove. She worked for a music company, loved it, didn't have to be at work until 10:30 AM and she left at 3 PM. "Not bad," she said, "and I like it. I can hire and fire, I've moved up, but I haven't had to fire anybody yet. They're good folks and we've put out some great records. . . ."

We arrived at my place. I broke out the vodka. Cassie's hair came down almost to her ass. I had always been a hair and leg man.

"You really read well tonight," she said. "You were a totally different person than the night before. I don't know how to explain it, but at your best you have this . . . humanness. Most poets are such little prigs and shits."

"I don't like them either."

"And they don't like you."

We drank some more and then went to bed. Her body was amazing, glorious, Playboy style, but unfortunately I was drunk. I did get it up, however, and I pumped and pumped, I grabbed her long hair, I got it out from under her and ran my hands through it, I was excited but I couldn't finally do it. I rolled off, told Cassie goodnight, and slept a guilty sleep.

IN THE morning I was embarrassed. I was sure I would never see Cassie again. We dressed. It was about 10 AM. We walked to the M.G. and got in. I didn't talk, she didn't talk. I felt the fool, but there was nothing to say. We drove back to *The Lancer* and there was the blue Volks.

"Thanks for all of it, Cassie. Think nice thoughts about Chinaski."

She didn't answer. I kissed her on the cheek and got out. She drove off in the M.G. It was, after all, as Lydia had often said,

"If you want to drink, drink; if you want to fuck, throw the bottle away."

My problem was that I wanted to do both.

88

So I WAS surprised when the phone rang a couple of nights later and it was Cassie.

"What are you doing, Hank?"

"Just sitting around. . . ."

"Why don't you come over?"

"I'd like to. . . ."

She gave me the address, it was either Westwood or West L.A.

"I have plenty to drink," she said. "You needn't bring anything."

"Maybe I shouldn't drink anything?"

"It's all right."

"If you pour it, I'll drink it. If you don't, I won't."

"Don't worry about it," she said.

I got dressed, jumped into the Volks, and drove to the address. How many breaks did a man have coming? The gods were good to me, of late. Maybe it was a test? Maybe it was a trick? Fatten Chinaski up, then slice him in half. I knew that might be coming too. But what can you do after a couple of 8-counts with only 2 rounds left to go?

CASSIE'S APARTMENT was on the second floor. She seemed glad to see me. A large black dog leaped on me. He was *huge* and floppy and male. He stood with his paws on my shoulders and licked my face. I pushed him off. He stood there wiggling his butt and making begging sounds. He had long black hair and appeared to be a mongrel, but what a big one he was.

"That's Elton," said Cassie.

She went to the refrigerator and got the wine.

"This is what you should drink. I've got plenty of it."

She was dressed in an all-green gown which clung tightly to her. She was like a snake. She had on shoes sequined with green stones, and once again I noticed how long her hair was, not only long but full, there was such a mass of it. It came down at least to her ass. Her eyes were large and blue-green, sometimes more blue than green, sometimes the other way around, depending upon how the light hit them. I noticed two of my books in her bookcase, two of the better ones.

Cassie sat down, opened the wine and poured two.

"We kind of met somehow during that last encounter, we touched somewhere. I didn't want to let it go," she said.

"I enjoyed it," I said.

"Want an upper?"

"All right," I said.

She brought out two. Black cap. The best. I sent mine down with the wine.

"I've got the best dealer in town. He doesn't rip me off," she said.

"Good."

"You ever been hooked?" she asked.

"I tried coke for a while, but I couldn't stand the comedown. I was afraid to go into the kitchen the next day because there was a butcher knife in there. Besides, 50 to 75 bucks a day is beyond me."

"I've got some coke."

"I pass."

She poured more wine.

I don't know why, but with each new woman it seemed like the first time, almost as if I had never been with a woman before. I kissed Cassie. As I kissed her I let one hand run through all that long hair.

"Want some music?"

"No, not really."

"You knew Dee Dee Bronson, didn't you?" Cassie asked.

"Yes, we split."

"You heard what happened to her?"

"No."

"First she lost her job, then she went to Mexico. She met a retired bullfighter. The bullfighter beat the shit out of her and took her life savings, $7,000."

"Poor Dee Dee: from me to that."

Cassie got up. I watched her walk across the room. Her ass moved and shimmered under that tight green gown. She came back with papers and some grass. She rolled a joint.

"Then she got in a car crash."

"She never could drive. Do you know her well?"

"No. But we hear about things in the industry."

"Just living until you die is hard work," I said.

Cassie passed the joint. "Your life seems in order," she said.

"Really?"

"I mean, you don't come on or try to impress like some men. And you seem naturally funny."

"I like your ass and your hair," I said, "and your lips and your eyes and your wine and your place and your joints. But I'm not in order."

"You write a lot about women."

"I know. I wonder sometimes what I will write about after that."

"Maybe it won't stop."

"Everything stops."

"Let me have some of that joint."

"Sure, Cassie."

She took a hit and then I kissed her. I pulled her head back by the hair. I forced her lips open. It was a long one. Then I let her go.

"You like that, don't you?" she asked.

"To me it's more personal and sexual than fucking."

"I think you're right," she said.

WE SMOKED and drank for several hours, then went to bed. We kissed and played. I was good and hard and I stroked her well, but after ten minutes I knew I wasn't going to make it. Too much to drink again. I began to sweat and strain. I stroked some more, then rolled off.

"I'm sorry, Cassie. . . ."

I watched her head move down to my penis. It was still hard. She began licking it. The dog jumped up on the bed and I kicked him off. I watched Cassie licking my cock. The moonlight came through the window and I could see her clearly. She took the end of my dick in her mouth and just nibbled at it. Suddenly she went for it all and she worked well, running her tongue up and down the length of my cock as she sucked. It was glorious.

I reached down and grabbed her hair with one hand and held it up, held it high over her head, all that hair, as she sucked on my cock. It lasted a long time but finally I could feel myself getting ready to come. She sensed it too and redoubled her efforts. I began making whimpering sounds and I could hear the big dog whimpering on the rug along with me. I liked that. I held back as long as I could to prolong the pleasure. Then, still holding and caressing her hair, I exploded in her mouth.

WHEN I awakened the next morning Cassie was getting dressed. "That's all right," she said, "you can stay. Just be sure you lock the door when you leave."

"All right."

After she left I took a shower. Then I found a beer in the refrigerator, drank that, dressed, said goodbye to Elton, made sure the door was locked, got into the Volks and drove back home.

89

THREE OR FOUR days later I found her note and phoned Debra. She said, "Come on over." She gave me the directions to Playa del Rey and I drove over. She had a small rented house with a front yard. I drove into the front yard, got out of the car and knocked, then rang. It was one of those two-tone bells. Debra opened the door. She was as I remembered her, with enormous lipstick mouth, short hairdo, bright earrings, perfume, and almost always, that wide smile.

"Oh, come in, Henry!"

I did. There was a guy sitting there but he was obviously a homosexual so it wasn't really an affront.

"This is Larry, my neighbor. He lives in the house in back."

We shook hands and I sat down.

"Is there anything to drink?" I asked.

"Oh, *Henry!*"

"I can go get something. I would have, only I didn't know what you wanted."

"Oh, I have something."

Debra went into the kitchen.

"How are you doing?" I asked Larry.

"I haven't been doing well, but I'm doing better. I'm into self-hypnosis. It's done marvels for me."

"Do you want anything to drink, Larry?" asked Debra from the kitchen.

"Oh no, thanks. . . ."

Debra came out with two glasses of red wine. Debra's house was over-decorated. There was something everywhere. It was expensively cluttered and there seemed to be rock music coming from every direction out of little speakers.

"Larry's practicing self-hypnosis."

"He told me."

"You don't know how much better I'm sleeping, you don't know how much better I'm relating," Larry said.

"Do you think everybody should try it?" asked Debra.

"Well, that would be difficult to say. But I do know that it works for me."

"I'm throwing a Halloween party, Henry. Everybody's coming. Why don't you join us? What do you think he could come as, Larry?"

They both looked at me.

"Well, I don't know," said Larry. "Really, I don't know. Maybe? . . . oh, no . . . I don't think so. . . ."

The doorbell bing-bonged and Debra went to open it. It was another homosexual without his shirt on. He had on a wolf's

214

mask with a big rubber tongue hanging out of the mouth. He seemed testy and depressed.

"Vincent, this is Henry. Henry, this is Vincent. . . ."

Vincent ignored me. He just stood there with his rubber tongue. "I had a horrible day at work. I can't stand it there anymore. I think I'll quit."

"But Vincent, what would you *do?*" Debra asked him.

"I don't know. But I can do a lot of things. I don't have to eat their shit!"

"You're coming to the party, aren't you, Vincent?"

"Of course, I've been preparing for days."

"Have you memorized your lines for the play?"

"Yes, but this time I think we should do the play *before* we do the games. Last time, before we got to the play we were all so *smashed* we didn't do the play justice."

"All right, Vincent, we'll do it that way."

With that, Vincent and his tongue turned and walked out the door.

Larry stood up. "Well, I must be going too. Nice meeting you," he said to me.

"All right, Larry."

We shook hands and Larry walked through the kitchen and out the back door to his place.

"Larry's been a great help to me, he's a good neighbor. I'm glad you were nice to him."

"He was all right. Hell, he was here before I was."

"We don't have sex."

"Neither do we."

"You know what I mean."

"I'll go get us something to drink."

"Henry, I have plenty of everything. I knew you were coming."

Debra refilled our glasses. I looked at her. She was young, but she looked as if she was straight out of the 1930s. She wore a black skirt that came down halfway between her knee and ankle, black shoes with high heels, a white high-necked blouse, a necklace, earrings, bracelets, the lipstick mouth, plenty of rouge,

215

perfume. She was well-built with nice breasts and buttocks and she swung them as she walked. She kept lighting cigarettes, there were lipstick-smeared butts everywhere. I felt sure I was back in my boyhood. She even didn't wear pantyhose and now and then she tugged at her long stockings, showing just enough leg, just enough knee. She was the kind of girl that our fathers loved.

She told me about her business. It had something to do with court transcripts and lawyers. It drove her crazy but she was making a good living.

"Sometimes I get very snappish with my help, but then I get over it and they forgive me. You just don't know what those goddamned lawyers are like! They want everything immediately, and they don't think about the time it takes to do it."

"Lawyers and doctors are the most overpaid, spoiled members of our society. Next in line is your corner garage mechanic. Then you might throw in your dentist."

Debra crossed her legs and her skirt hiked up.

"You have very nice legs, Debra. And you know how to dress. You remind me of the girls in my mother's day. That's when women were women."

"You've got a great line, Henry."

"You know what I mean. It's especially true of L.A. Once not long ago I left town and when I returned, do you know how I knew I was back?"

"Well, no. . . ."

"It was the first woman I passed on the street. She had on a skirt so short you saw the crotch of her panties. And through the front of the panties—pardon me—you could see her cunt hairs. I knew I was back in L.A."

"Where were you? On Main Street?"

"Main Street, hell. It was Beverly and Fairfax."

"Do you like the wine?"

"Yes, and I like your place. I might even move in here."

"My landlord's jealous."

"Anybody else who might be jealous?"

"No."

"Why?"

"I work hard and I just like to come home and relax in the evening. I like to decorate this place. My girlfriend—she works for me—and I are going to antique shops tomorrow morning. Do you want to come along?"

"Will I be here in the morning?"

Debra didn't answer. She poured me another drink and sat beside me on the couch. I leaned over and kissed her. As I did I pulled her skirt further back and peeked at that nylon leg. It looked good. When we finished kissing she pulled her skirt down again, but I had already memorized the leg. She got up and went to the bathroom. I heard the toilet flush. Then there was a wait. She was probably applying more lipstick. I took out my hanky and wiped my mouth. The hanky came away smeared with red. I was finally getting everything the boys in high school had gotten, the rich pretty well-dressed golden boys with their new automobiles, and me with my sloppy old clothes and broken down bicycle.

Debra walked out. She sat down and lit a cigarette.

"Let's fuck," I said.

Debra walked into the bedroom. There was a half a bottle of wine left on the coffee table. I poured myself a drink and lit one of her cigarettes. She turned off the rock music. That was nice.

It was quiet. I poured another drink. Maybe I would move in? Where would I put the typewriter?

"Henry?"

"What?"

"Where are you?"

"Wait. I just want to finish this drink."

"All right."

I finished the glass and then poured down what was left in the bottle. I was in Playa del Rey. I undressed, leaving my clothes in a messy pile on the couch. I had never been a dresser. My shirts were all faded and shrunken, 5 or 6 years old, threadbare. My pants the same. I hated department stores, I hated the clerks, they acted so superior, they seemed to know the secret of life, they had a confidence I didn't possess. My shoes were always broken down and old, I disliked shoe stores too. I never purchased anything until it was completely unusable, and that included automobiles. It wasn't a matter of thrift, I just couldn't bear to be a buyer needing a seller, seller being so handsome and aloof and superior. Besides, it all took time, time when you could just be laying around and drinking.

I walked into the bedroom with just my shorts on. I was conscious of my white belly lolling out over the shorts. But I made no effort to suck in my gut. I stood by the side of the bed, lowered my shorts, stepped out of them. Suddenly I wanted more to drink. I climbed into the bed. I got under the covers. Then I turned toward Debra. I held her. We were pressed together. Her mouth was open. I kissed her. Her mouth was like a wet cunt. She was ready. I sensed it. There would be no need of foreplay. We kissed and her tongue flicked in and out of my mouth. I caught it between my teeth, held it. Then I rolled over on top of Debra and slid it in.

I think it was the way her head was turned away to one side as I fucked her. It turned me on. Her head was turned away and bounced on the pillow with each stroke. Now and then as I was stroking I turned her head toward me and kissed that blood-red mouth. It was finally working for me. I was fucking all the women and girls I had gazed longingly after on the sidewalks of Los Angeles in 1937, the last really bad year of the depression, when a piece of ass cost two bucks and nobody had any money (or hope) at all. I'd had to wait a long time for mine. I worked and pumped. I was having a red hot useless fuck! I grabbed Debra's head once again, reached that lipstick mouth just one more time as I spurted into her, into her diaphragm.

90

THE NEXT DAY was Saturday and Debra cooked us breakfast.
"Are you coming antique hunting with us today?"
"All right."
"Are you hungover?" she asked.

"Not too bad."

We ate in silence for a while, then she said, "I liked your reading at *The Lancer*. You were drunk but it came through."

"Sometimes it doesn't."

"When are you going to read again?"

"Somebody's been phoning from Canada. They're trying to raise funds."

"Canada! Can I go with you?"

"We'll see."

"Are you staying tonight?"

"Do you want me to?"

"Yes."

"I will then."

"Great. . . ."

WE FINISHED breakfast and I went to the bathroom while Debra did the dishes. I flushed and wiped, flushed again, washed my hands, came out. Debra was cleaning up at the sink. I grabbed her from behind.

"You can use my toothbrush if you want," she said.

"Is my breath bad?"

"It's all right."

"Like hell."

"You can also shower if you want. . . ."

"That too . . .?"

"Stop it. Tessie won't be here for an hour. We can clear away the cobwebs."

I went and let the bathwater run. The only time I liked to shower was in a motel. In the bathroom there was a photo of a man on the wall—dark, long hair, standard, handsome face run through with the usual idiocy. He smiled white teeth at me. I brushed what was left of my discolored teeth. Debra had mentioned that her ex-husband was a shrink.

Debra showered after I was through. I poured myself a small glass of wine and sat in a chair looking out the front window. Suddenly I remembered that I had forgotten to mail my ex-woman her child support money. Oh well. I'd do it Monday.

I felt peaceful in Playa del Rey. It was good to get out of the crowded, dirty court where I lived. There was no shade, and the sun beat down mercilessly on us. We were all insane in one way or another. Even the dogs and the cats were insane, and the birds and the newsboys and the hookers.

For us, in east Hollywood, the toilets never worked properly and the landlord's cut-rate plumber could never quite fix them. We left the tank lids off and hand-manipulated the plunger. The faucets dripped, the roaches crawled, the dogs crapped every-where, and the screens had large holes in them that let in flies and all manner of strange flying insects.

The bell bing-bonged and I got up and opened the door. It was Tessie. She was in her forties, a swinger, a redhead with obviously dyed hair.

"You're Henry, aren't you?"

"Yes, Debra's in the bathroom. Please sit down."

She had on a short red skirt. Her thighs were good. Her ankles and calves weren't bad either. She looked like she loved to fuck.

I walked to the bathroom and knocked on the door.

"Debra, Tessie's here. . . ."

THE FIRST antique store was a block or two from the water. We drove down in the Volks and went in. I walked around with them. Everything was priced $800, $1500 . . . old clocks, old chairs, old tables. The prices were unbelievable. Two or three clerks stood around and rubbed their hands. They evidently worked on salary plus commission. The owner certainly located the items for almost nothing in Europe or the Ozark Mountains. I got bored looking at huge price tags. I told the girls I'd wait in the car.

I FOUND a bar across the street, went in, sat down. I ordered a bottle of beer. The bar was full of young men mostly under 25. They were blond and slim, or dark and slim, dressed in perfectly fitting slacks and shirts. They were expressionless and undistur-bed. There were no women. A large television set was on. There was no sound. Nobody watched it. Nobody spoke. I finished my beer and left.

I found a liquor store and got a 6-pack. I went back to the car and sat there. The beer was good. The car was parked in the lot in back of the antique store. The street to my left was backed up with traffic and I watched the people waiting patiently in the cars. There was almost always a man and a woman, staring straight ahead, not talking. It was, finally, for everyone, a matter of waiting. You waited and you waited—for the hospital, the doctor, the plumber, the madhouse, the jail, papa death himself. First the signal was red, then the signal was green. The citizens of the world ate food and watched t.v. and worried about their jobs or their lack of same, while they waited.

I began to think about Debra and Tessie in the antique shop. I really didn't like Debra, but there I was entering her life. It made me feel like a peep-freak.

I sat drinking the beer. I was down to the last can when they finally came out.

"Oh Henry," said Debra, "I found the nicest marble top table for only $200!"

"It's really *fabulous!*" said Tessie.

They climbed into the car. Debra pressed her leg against mine, "Have you been bored with all this?" she asked.

I started the engine and drove to a liquor store and bought 3 or 4 bottles of wine, cigarettes.

That bitch Tessie in her short red skirt with her nylons, I thought to myself as I paid the liquor store man. I bet she has done in at least a dozen good men without even thinking about it. I decided her problem was *not* thinking. She didn't like to think. And that was all right because there weren't any laws or rules about it. But when she reached 50 in a few years she'd begin to think! Then she'd be a bitter woman in a supermarket, jamming her shopping cart into people's backs and ankles in the check-out line, her dark shades on, her face puffed and unhappy, her cart filled with cottage cheese, potato chips, pork chops, red onions and a quart of Jim Beam.

I went back to the car and we drove to Debra's place. The girls sat down. I opened a bottle and poured 3 glasses.

"Henry," said Debra, "I'm going to get Larry. He'll drive me down in his van to pick up my table. You needn't endure that, aren't you glad?"

"Yes."

"Tessie will keep you company."

"All right."

"You two *behave* yourselves now!"

Larry came in through the back door and he and Debra walked out the front. Larry warmed up the van, and they drove off.

"Well, we're alone," I said.

"Yeah," said Tessie. She sat very still, looking straight ahead. I finished my drink and went to the bathroom to take a piss. When I came out Tessie was still sitting quietly on the couch.

I walked along behind the couch. When I reached her I took her under the chin and tipped her face up. I pressed my mouth against hers. She had a very large head. She had purple makeup smeared under her eyes and she smelled like stale fruit juice, apricots. She had thin silver chains dangling from each ear and at the end of each chain hung one ball—symbolic. As we kissed I reached down into her blouse. I found a breast and cupped my hand on it and rolled it around. No brassiere. Then I straightened up and pulled my hand away. I walked around the couch and sat down next to her. I poured two drinks.

"For an ugly old son of a bitch, you've got a lot of balls," she said.

"How about a quickie before Debra gets back?"

"No."

"Don't hate me. I'm just trying to enliven the party."

"I think you stepped out of bounds. What you just did was gross and obvious."

"I guess I lack imagination."

"And you're a writer?"

"I write. But mostly I take photographs."

"I think you fuck women just in order to write about fucking them."

"I don't know."

"I think you do."

"O.K., O.K., forget it. Drink up."

Tessie went back to her drink. She finished it and put her cigarette down. She looked at me, blinking her long false eyelashes. She was like Debra with a big lipstick mouth. Only Debra's mouth was darker and didn't glisten as much. Tessie's was a bright red and her lips glistened, she held her mouth open, continually licking her lower lip. Suddenly Tessie grabbed me. That mouth opened over my mouth. It was exciting. I felt as if I was being raped. My cock began to rise. I reached down while she was kissing me and flipped her skirt back, ran my hand up her left leg as we continued to kiss.

"Come on," I said, after the kiss.

I took her by the hand and led her into Debra's bedroom. I pushed her down on the bed. The bedspread was on. I pulled off my shoes and pants, then pulled her shoes off. I kissed her a long one, then I pulled the red skirt up over her hips. No pantyhose. Nylons and pink panties. I pulled the panties off. Tessie had her eyes closed. Somewhere in the neighborhood I could hear a stereo playing symphony music. I rubbed a finger along her cunt. Soon it got wet and began to open. I sank my finger in. Then I pulled it out and rubbed the clit. She was nice and juicy. I mounted. I hit her a few swift, vicious jolts, then I went slow, then I ripped again. I looked into that depraved and simple face. It really excited me. I pounded away.

Then Tessie pushed me away. "Get off!"

"What? What?"

"I hear the van! I'll get fired! I'll lose my job!"

"No, no, you WHORE!"

I ripped away without mercy, pressed my lips against that glistening, horrible mouth and came inside of her, good. I jumped off. Tessie picked up her shoes and panties and ran to the bathroom. I wiped off with my handkerchief and straightened the bedspread, fluffed up the pillows. As I was zipping up the door opened. I walked into the front room.

"Henry, would you help Larry carry in the table? It's heavy."

"Sure."

CHARLES BUKOWSKI

"Where's Tessie?"

"I think she's in the bathroom."

I followed Debra out to the truck. We slid the table out of the van, grabbed it and carried it back to the house. As we came back in Tessie was sitting on the couch with a cigarette.

"Don't drop the merchandise, boys!" she said.

"No way!" I said.

We carried it into Debra's bedroom and put it by the bedside. She had another table there which she removed. Then we stood around and looked at the marble top.

"Oh, Henry . . . just $200 . . . do you like it?"

"Oh, it's fine, Debra, just fine."

I went to the bathroom. I washed my face, combed my hair. Then I dropped my pants and shorts and quietly washed my parts. I pissed, flushed, and walked back out.

"Care for a wine, Larry?" I asked.

"Oh no, but thanks. . . ."

"Thanks for helping, Larry," said Debra.

Larry went out the back door.

"Oh, I'm so *excited!*" said Debra.

Tessie sat and drank and talked with us for 10 or 15 minutes then she said, "I've got to go."

"Stay if you want to," said Debra.

"No, no, I've got to go. I've got to clean my apartment, it's a mess."

"Clean your apartment? Today? When you've got two nice friends to drink with?" asked Debra.

"I just sit here thinking about that mess over there and I can't feel relaxed. Don't take it personally."

"All right, Tessie, you go now. We'll forgive you."

"All right, darling. . . ."

They kissed in the doorway and then Tessie was gone. Debra took me by the hand and led me into the bedroom. We looked at the marble tabletop.

"What do you *really* think of it, Henry?"

"Well, I've lost $200 at the track and I've had nothing to show for it, so I think it's all right."

224

"It will be here next to us tonight while we sleep together."

"Maybe I ought to stand there and you can go to bed with the table?"

"You're jealous!"

"Of course."

Debra walked back to the kitchen and came back with some rags and some kind of cleaning fluid. She began wiping off the marble.

"You see, there is a special way to treat marble to accent the veins."

I got undressed and sat on the edge of the bed in my shorts. Then I lay back on the pillows and on the bedspread. Then I sat up. "Oh Christ, Debra, I'm messing up your bedspread."

"That's all right."

I went and got two drinks, gave one to Debra. I watched her working on the table. Then she looked at me:

"You know, you have the most beautiful legs I've ever seen on a man."

"Not bad for an old guy, huh, kid?"

"Not at all."

She rubbed at the table some more, then gave it up.

"How did you get along with Tessie?"

"She's all right. I really like her."

"She's a good worker."

"I wouldn't know about that."

"I feel bad that she left. I think she just wanted to give us some privacy. I ought to phone her."

"Why not?"

Debra got on the phone. She talked to Tessie for quite some time. It began to get dark. What about dinner? She had the phone in the center of the bed and she was sitting on her legs. She had a nice behind. Debra laughed and then she said goodbye. She looked at me.

"Tessie says that you're sweet."

I went out for more drinks. When I got back the large color television was on. We sat side by side on the bed watching t.v. We sat with our backs to the wall, drinking.

225

"Henry," she asked, "what are you doing on Thanksgiving?"

"Nothing."

"Why don't you have Thanksgiving with me? I'll get the turkey. I'll have 2 or 3 friends over."

"All right, it sounds good."

Debra leaned forward and snapped the set off. She looked very happy. Then the light went off. She went to the bathroom and came out with something flimsy wrapped around her. Then she was in bed next to me. We pressed together. My cock rose. Her tongue flicked in and out of my mouth. She had a large tongue and it was warm. I went on down. I spread the hair and worked my tongue. Then I gave her a bit of a nose job. She was responding. I climbed back up, mounted her and stuck it in.

. . . I worked and I worked. I tried to think of Tessie in her short red skirt. It didn't help. I had given it all to Tessie. I pumped on and on.

"Sorry, baby, too much to drink. Ah, feel my *heart!*"

She put her hand on my chest. "It's really *going,*" she said.

"Am I still invited for Thanksgiving?"

"Sure, my poor dear, don't worry, please."

I kissed her goodnight, then rolled away and tried to sleep.

91

AFTER DEBRA LEFT for work the next morning I bathed, then tried to watch t.v. I walked around naked and noticed that I could be seen from the street through the front window. So I had a glass of grapefruit juice and dressed. Finally there was nothing to do but go back to my place. There'd be some mail, maybe a letter from someone. I made sure that all the doors were locked, then I walked out to the Volks, started it, and drove back to Los Angeles.

On the way in I remembered Sara, the third girl I had met during the reading at *The Lancer*. I had her phone number in my wallet. I drove home, took a crap, then phoned her.

"Hello," I said, "this is Chinaski, Henry Chinaski. . . ."

"Yes, I remember you."

"What are you doing? I thought I might drive out to see you."

"I have to be at my restaurant today. Why don't you come down here?"

"It's a health food place, isn't it?"

"Yes, I'll make you a good healthy sandwich."

"Oh?"

"I close at 4. Why don't you get here a little before that?"

"All right. How do I get there?"

"Get a pen and I'll give you directions."

I wrote the directions down. "See you about 3:30," I said.

About 2:30 I got into the Volks. Somewhere on the freeway the instructions got confusing or I became confused. I have a great dislike both for freeways and for instructions. I turned off and found myself in Lakewood. I pulled into a gas station and phoned Sara. "Drop On Inn," she answered.

"Shit!" I said.

"What's the matter? You sound angry."

"I'm in Lakewood! Your instructions are fucked!"

"Lakewood? Wait."

"I'm going back. I need a drink."

"Now hold on. I want to *see* you! Tell me what street in Lakewood and the nearest cross street."

I let the phone hang and went to see where I was. I gave Sara the information. She redirected me.

"It's easy," she said. "Now promise you'll come."

"All right."

"And if you get lost again, phone me."

"I'm sorry, you see, I have no sense of direction. I've always had nightmares about getting lost. I believe I belong on another planet."

"It's all right. Just follow my new instructions."

I got back in the car, and this time it was easy. Soon I was on the Pacific Coast Highway looking for the turn-off. I found it. It led me into a snob shopping district near the ocean. I drove slowly and spotted it: Drop On Inn, a large hand-painted sign. There were photos and small cards pasted in the window. An honest-to-god health food place, Jesus Christ. I didn't want to go in. I drove around the block and past the Drop On Inn slowly. I took a right, then another right. I saw a bar, Crab Haven. I parked outside and went in.

It was 3:45 in the afternoon and every seat was taken. Most of the clients were well on the way. I stood and ordered a vodka-7. I took it to the telephone and phoned Sara. "O.K., it's Henry. I'm here."

"I saw you drive past twice. Don't be afraid. Where are you?"

"Crab Haven. I'm having a drink. I'll be there soon."

"All right. Don't have too many."

I had that one and another. I found a small empty booth and sat there. I really didn't want to go. I hardly remembered what Sara looked like.

I finished the drink and drove to her place. I got out, opened the screen door and walked in. Sara was behind the counter. She saw me. "Hi, Henry!" she said, "I'll be with you in a minute." She was preparing something. Four or five guys sat or stood around. Some sat on a couch. Others sat on the floor. They were all in their mid-twenties, they were all the same, they were dressed in little walking shorts, and they just *sat*. Now and then one of them would cross his legs or cough. Sara was a fairly handsome woman, lean, and she moved around briskly. Class. Her hair was red-blond. It looked very good.

"We'll take care of you," she told me.

"All right," I said.

There was a bookcase. Three or four of my books were in it. I found some Lorca and sat down and pretended to read. That way I wouldn't have to see the guys in their walking shorts. They looked as if nothing had ever touched them—all well-mothered, protected, with a soft sheen of contentment. None of them had ever been in jail, or worked hard with their hands, or even gotten a traffic ticket. Skimmed-milk jollies, the whole bunch.

Sara brought me a health food sandwich. "Here, try this."

I ate the sandwich as the guys lolled about. Soon one got up and walked out. Then another. Sara was cleaning up. There was only one left. He was about 22 and he sat on the floor. He was gangly, his back bent like a bow. He had on glasses with heavy black rims. He seemed more lonely and daft than the others. "Hey, Sara," he said, "let's go out and have some beers tonight."

"Not tonight, Mike. How about tomorrow night?"

"All right, Sara."

He stood up and walked to the counter. He put a coin down and picked up a health food cookie. He stood at the counter eating the health food cookie. When he finished it he turned and walked out.

"Did you like the sandwich?" Sara asked.

"Yes, it wasn't bad."

"Could you bring in the table and the chairs from the sidewalk?"

I brought in the table and the chairs.

"What do you want to do?" she asked.

"Well, I don't like bars. The air is bad. Let's get something to drink and go to your place."

"All right. Help me carry the garbage out."

I helped her carry the garbage out. Then she locked up. "Follow my van. I know a store that stocks good wine. Then you can follow me to my place."

She had a Volks van and I followed her. There was a poster of a man in the back window of her van. "Smile and rejoice," he advised me, and at the bottom of the poster was his name, Drayer Baba.

WE OPENED a bottle of wine and sat on the couch in her house. I liked the way her house was furnished. She had built all her furniture herself, including the bed. Photos of Drayer Baba were everywhere. He was from India and had died in 1971, claiming to be God.

While Sara and I sat there drinking the first bottle of wine the door opened and a young man with snaggled teeth, long hair and a very long beard walked in. "This is Ron, my roommate," said Sara.

"Hello, Ron. Want a wine?"

Ron had a wine with us. Then a fat girl and a thin man with a shaved head walked in.. They were Pearl and Jack. They sat down. Then another young man walked in. His name was Jean John. Jean John sat down. Then Pat walked in. Pat had a black beard and long hair. He sat down on the floor at my feet.

"I'm a poet," he said.

I took a swallow of wine.

"How do you go about getting published?" he asked me.

"You submit it to the editors."

"But I'm unknown."

"Everybody starts out unknown."

"I give readings 3 nights a week. And I'm an actor so I read very well. I figure if I read my stuff enough somebody might want to publish it."

"It's not impossible."

"The problem is that when I read nobody shows up."

"I don't know what to tell you."

"I'm going to print my own book."

"Whitman did."

"Will you read some of your poems?"

"Christ, no."

"Why not?"

"I just want to drink."

"You talk about drinking a lot in your books. Do you think drinking has helped your writing?"

"No. I'm just an alcoholic who became a writer so that I would be able to stay in bed until noon."

I turned to Sara. "I didn't know you had so many friends."

"This is unusual. It's hardly ever like this."

"I'm glad we've got plenty of wine."

"I'm sure they'll be leaving soon," she said.

The others were talking. The conversation drifted and I stopped listening. Sara looked good to me. When she spoke it was with wit and incisiveness. She had a good mind. Pearl and Jack left first. Then Jean John. Then Pat the poet. Ron sat on one side of Sara and I sat on the other. Just the 3 of us. Ron poured himself a glass of wine. I couldn't blame him, he was her roommate. I had no hope of outwaiting him. He was already there. I poured Sara a wine and then one for myself. After I finished drinking it I said to Sara and Ron, "Well, I guess I'll be going."

"Oh no," said Sara, "not so soon. I haven't had a chance to talk to you. I'd like to talk to you."

She looked at Ron. "You understand, don't you, Ron?"

"Sure."

He got up and walked to the back of the house.

"Hey," I said, "I don't want to start any shit."

"What shit?"

"Between you and your roommate."

"Oh, there's nothing between us. No sex, nothing. He rents the room in the back of the house."

"Oh."

I heard the sound of a guitar. Then loud singing.

"That's Ron," said Sara.

He just bellowed and called the hogs. His voice was so bad that no comment was needed.

Ron sang on for an hour. Sara and I drank some more wine. She lit some candles. "Here, have a beedie."

I tried one. A beedie is a small brown cigarette from India. It had a good tart taste. I turned to Sara and we had our first kiss. She kissed well. The evening was looking up.

The screen door swung open and a young man walked into the room.

"Barry," said Sara, "I'm not having any more visitors."

The screen door banged and Barry was gone. I foresaw future problems: as a recluse I couldn't bear traffic. It had nothing to do with jealousy, I simply disliked people, crowds, anywhere, except at my readings. People diminished me, they sucked me dry.

"Humanity, you never had it from the beginning." That was my motto.

Sara and I kissed again. We both had drunk too much. Sara opened another bottle. She held her wine well. I have no idea what we talked about. The best thing about Sara was that she made very few references to my writing. When the last bottle was empty I told Sara that I was too drunk to drive home.

"Oh, you can sleep in my bed, but no sex."

"Why?"

"One doesn't have sex without marriage."

"One doesn't?"

"Drayer Baba doesn't believe in it."

"Sometimes God can be mistaken."

"Never."

"All right, let's go to bed."

WE KISSED in the dark. I was a kiss freak anyway, and Sara was one of the best kissers I had ever met. I'd have to go all the way back to Lydia to find anyone comparable. Yet each woman was different, each kissed in her own way. Lydia was probably kissing some son of a bitch right now, or worse, kissing his parts. Katherine was asleep in Austin.

Sara had my cock in her hand, petting it, rubbing it. Then she pressed it against her cunt. She rubbed it up and down, up and down against her cunt. She was obeying her God, Drayer Baba. I didn't play with her cunt because I felt that would offend Drayer. We just kissed and she kept rubbing my cock against her cunt, or maybe against the clit, I didn't know. I waited for her to put my cock *in* her cunt. But she just kept rubbing. The hairs began to burn my cock. I pulled away.

"Good night, baby," I said. And then I turned, rolled over and put my back up against her. Drayer Baby, I thought, you've got one helluva believer in this bed.

IN THE morning we began the rubbing bit again with the same end result. I decided, to hell with it, I don't need this kind of non-action.

"You want to take a bath?" Sara asked.

"Sure."

I walked into the bathroom and let the water run. Sometime during the night I had mentioned to Sara that one of my insanities was to take 3 or 4 steaming hot baths a day. The old water therapy.

Sara's tub held more water than mine and the water was hotter. I was five feet, eleven and ¾ inches and yet I could stretch out in the tub. In the old days they made bathtubs for emperors, not for 5 foot bank clerks.

I got into the tub and stretched. It was great. Then I stood up and looked at my poor raw cunt-hair-rubbed cock. Rough time, old boy, but close, I guess, is better than nothing? I sat back down in the tub and stretched out again. The phone rang. There was a pause.

Then Sara knocked.

"Come in!"

"Hank, it's Debra."

"Debra? How'd she know I was here?"

"She's been calling everywhere. Should I tell her to phone back?"

"No, tell her to wait."

I found a large towel and wrapped it about my waist. I walked into the other room. Sara was talking to Debra on the phone.

"Oh, here he is. . . ."

Sara handed me the phone. "Hello, Debra?"

"Hank, where have you been?"

"In the bathtub."

"The bathtub?"

"Yes."

"You just got out?"

"Yes."

"What are you wearing?"

"I have a towel around my middle."

"How can you keep the towel around your middle and talk on the phone?"

"I'm doing it."

"Did anything happen?"

"No."

"Why?"

"Why what?"

"I mean, why didn't you fuck her?"

"Look, do you think I go around doing things like that? Do you think that's all there is to me?"

"Then nothing happened?"

"Yes."

"What?"

"Yes, nothing."

"Where are you going after you leave there?"

"My place."

"Come here."

"What about your legal business?"

"We're almost caught up. Tessie can handle it."

"All right."

I hung up.

"What are you going to do?" Sara asked.

"I'm going to Debra's. I said I'd be there in 45 minutes."

"But I thought we'd have lunch together. I know this Mexican place."

"Look, she's *concerned*. How can we sit around and chat over lunch?"

"I have my mind set on lunch with you."

"Hell, when do you feed *your* people?"

"I open at eleven. It's only ten now."

"All right, let's go eat. . . ."

IT WAS a Mexican place in a snide hippie district of Hermosa Beach. Bland, indifferent types. Death on the shore. Just phase out, breathe in, wear sandals and pretend it's a fine world.

While we were waiting for our order Sara reached out and dipped her finger into a bowl of hot sauce, and then sucked her finger. Then she dipped again. She bent her head over the bowl. Strands of her straight hair poked at me. She kept sticking her finger into the bowl and sucking.

"Look," I told her, "other people want to use that sauce. You're making me sick! Stop it."

"No, they *refill* it each time."

I hoped they *did* refill it each time. Then the food arrived and Sara bent and attacked it like an animal, just as Lydia used to do. We finished eating and then we went out and she got into her van and drove to her health food place, and I got in my Volks and started out toward Playa del Rey. I had been given careful directions. The directions were confusing, but I followed them and had no trouble. It was almost disappointing because it seemed when stress and madness were eliminated from my daily life there wasn't much left you could depend on.

I drove into Debra's yard. I saw a movement behind the blinds. She'd been watching for me. I got out of the Volks and made sure that both doors were locked since my auto insurance had expired.

I walked up and bing-bonged Debra's bell. She opened the door and seemed glad to see me. That was all right, but it was things like that which kept a writer from getting his work done.

92

I DIDN'T DO much the rest of the week. The Oaktree meet was on. I went to the track 2 or 3 times, broke even. I wrote a dirty story for a sex mag, wrote 10 or 12 poems, masturbated, and phoned Sara and Debra each night. One night I phoned Cassie and a man answered. Goodbye, Cassie.

I thought about breakups, how difficult they were, but then usually it was only after you broke up with one woman that you met another. I had to taste women in order to really know them, to get inside of them. I could invent men in my mind because I was one, but women, for me, were almost impossible to fictionalize without first knowing them. So I explored them as best I could and I found human beings inside. The writing would be forgotten. The writing would become much less than the episode itself until the episode ended. The writing was only the residue. A man didn't have to have a woman in order to feel as real as he could feel, but it was good if he knew a few. Then when the affair went wrong he'd feel what it was like to be truly lonely and crazed, and thus know what he must face, finally, when his own end came.

235

I was sentimental about many things: a woman's shoes under the bed; one hairpin left behind on the dresser; the way they said, "I'm going to pee . . ."; hair ribbons; walking down the boulevard with them at 1:30 in the afternoon, just two people walking together; the long nights of drinking and smoking, talking; the arguments; thinking of suicide; eating together and feeling good; the jokes, the laughter out of nowhere; feeling miracles in the air; being in a parked car together; comparing past loves at 3 AM; being told you snore, hearing her snore; mothers, daughters, sons, cats, dogs; sometimes death and sometimes divorce, but always carrying on, always seeing it through; reading a newspaper alone in a sandwich joint and feeling nausea because she's now married to a dentist with an I.Q. of 95; racetracks, parks, park picnics; even jails; her dull friends, your dull friends; your drinking, her dancing; your flirting, her flirting; her pills, your fucking on the side, and her doing the same; sleeping together. . . .

There were no judgments to be made, yet out of necessity one had to select. Beyond good and evil was all right in theory, but to go on living one had to select: some were kinder than others, some were simply more interested in you, and sometimes the outwardly beautiful and inwardly cold were necessary, just for bloody, shitty kicks, like a bloody, shitty movie. The kinder ones fucked better, really, and after you were around them a while they seemed beautiful because they were. I thought of Sara, she had that something extra. If only there was no Drayer Baba holding up that damned STOP sign.

THEN IT was Sara's birthday, November 11th, Veterans' Day. We had met twice again, once at her place, once at mine. There had been a high sense of fun and expectancy. She was strange but individual and inventive; there had been happiness . . . except in bed . . . it was flaming . . . but Drayer Baba kept us apart. I was losing the battle to God.

"Fucking is not that important," she told me.

I WENT to an exotic food place at Hollywood Boulevard and Fountain Avenue, Aunt Bessie's. The clerks were hateful

people—young black boys and young white boys of high
intelligence that had turned into high snobbery. They pranced
about and ignored and insulted the customers. The women who
worked there were heavy, dreamy, they wore large loose blouses
and hung their heads as if in some sleepy state of shame. And
the customers were grey wisps who endured the insults and came
back for more. The clerks didn't lay any shit on me, so they were
allowed to live another day. . . .

I bought Sara her birthday present, the main bit being bee
secretion, which is the brains of many bees drained out of their
collective domes by a needle. I had a wicker basket and in it,
along with the bee secretion, were some chop sticks, sea salt, two
pomegranates (organic), two apples (organic), and some sun-
flower seeds. The bee secretion was the main thing, and it cost
plenty. Sara had talked about it quite a bit, about wanting it. But
she said she couldn't afford it.

I drove to Sara's. I also had several bottles of wine with me.
In fact, I had polished off one of them while shaving. I seldom
shaved but I shaved for Sara's birthday, and Veterans' night. She
was a good woman. Her mind was charming and, strangely, her
celibacy was understandable. I mean, the way she looked at it, it
should be saved for a good man. Not that I was a good man,
exactly, but her obvious class would look good sitting next to my
obvious class at a cafe table in Paris after I finally became
famous. She was endearing, calmly intellectual, and best of all,
there was that crazy admixture of red in the gold of her hair. It
was almost as if I had been looking for that color hair for
decades . . . maybe longer.

I STOPPED off at a bar on Pacific Coast Highway and had a
double vodka-7. I was worried about Sara. She said sex meant
marriage. And I believed she meant it. There was definitely
something celibate about her. Yet I could also imagine that she
got off in a lot of ways, and that I was hardly the first to have
his cock rubbed raw against her cunt. My guess was that she was
as confused as everybody else. Why I was agreeing to her ways
was a mystery to me. I didn't even particularly want to wear her

down. I didn't agree with her ideas but I liked her anyway. Maybe I was getting lazy. Maybe I was tired of sex. Maybe I was finally getting old. Happy birthday, Sara.

I DROVE up to her house and took in my basket of health. She was in the kitchen. I sat down with the wine and the basket. "I'm here, Sara!"

She came out of the kitchen. Ron was gone but she had his stereo on full blast. I had always hated stereos. When you lived in poor neighborhoods you continually heard other people's sounds, including their fucking, but the most obnoxious thing was to be forced to listen to *their* music at full volume, the total vomit of it for hours. In addition they usually left their windows open, confident that you too would enjoy what they enjoyed.

Sara had Judy Garland on. I liked Judy Garland, a little, especially her appearance at the New York Met. But suddenly she seemed very loud, screaming her sentimental horseshit.

"For Christ's sake, Sara, turn it *down!*"

She did, but not very much. She opened one of the bottles of wine and we sat down at the table across from each other. I felt strangely irritable.

Sara reached into the basket and found the bee secretion. She was excited. She took the lid off and tasted it. "This is so powerful," she said. "It's the essence. . . . Care for some?"

"No, thanks."

"I'm making us dinner."

"Good. But I should take you out."

"I've already got it started."

"All right then."

"But I need some butter. I'll have to go out and get some. Also I'm going to need cucumbers and tomatoes for the store tomorrow."

"I'll get them. It's your birthday."

"Are you sure you don't want to try some bee secretion?"

"No, thanks, it's all right."

"You can't imagine how many bees it took to fill this jar."

"Happy birthday. I'll get the butter and things."

I had another wine, got in the Volks and drove to a small grocery. I found the butter, but the tomatoes and cucumbers looked old and shriveled. I paid for the butter and drove about looking for a larger market. I found one, got some tomatoes and cucumbers then drove back. As I walked up the driveway to her place I heard it. She had the stereo on full volume again. As I walked closer and closer I began to sicken; my nerves were stretched to the breaking point, then snapped. I walked into the house with just the bag of butter in my hand; I had left the tomatoes and cucumbers in the car. I don't know what she was playing; it was so loud that I couldn't distinguish one sound from another.

Sara walked out of the kitchen. "GOD DAMN YOU!" I screamed.

"What is it?" Sara asked.

"I CAN'T HEAR!"

"What?"

"YOU'RE PLAYING THAT FUCKING STEREO TOO LOUD! DON'T YOU UNDERSTAND?"

"What?"

"I'M LEAVING!"

"No!"

I turned and banged out of the screen door. I walked out to the Volks and saw the bag of tomatoes and cucumbers I had forgotten. I picked them up and walked back up the driveway. We met.

I pushed the bag at her. "Here."

Then I turned and walked off. "You rotten rotten rotten son-of-a-bitch!" she screamed.

She threw the bag at me. It hit me in the middle of the back. She turned and ran off into her house. I looked at the tomatoes and cucumbers scattered on the ground in the moonlight. For a moment I thought of picking them up. Then I turned and walked away.

93

THE READING IN Vancouver went through, $500 plus air fare and lodging. The sponsor, Bart McIntosh, was nervous about crossing the border. I was to fly to Seattle, he'd meet me there and we'd drive over the border, then after the reading I'd fly from Vancouver to L.A. I didn't quite understand what it all meant but I said all right.

So there I was in the air again, drinking a double vodka-7. I was in with the salesmen and businessmen. I had my small suitcase with extra shirts, underwear, stockings, 3 or 4 books of poems, plus typescripts of 10 or 12 new poems. And a toothbrush and toothpaste. It was ridiculous to be going off somewhere to get paid for reading poetry. I didn't like it and I could never get over how silly it seemed. To work like a mule until you were fifty at meaningless, low jobs, and then suddenly to be flitting about the country, a gadfly with drink in hand.

McINTOSH WAS waiting at Seattle and we got in his car. It was a nice drive because neither us said too much. The reading was privately sponsored, which I preferred to university-sponsored readings. The universities were frightened; among other things, they were frightened of low-life poets, but on the other hand they were too curious to pass one up.

There was a long wait at the border, with a hundred cars backed up. The border guards simply took their time. Now and then they pulled an old car out of line, but usually they only asked one or two questions and waved the people on. I couldn't understand McIntosh's panic over the whole procedure.

"Man," he said, "we got through!"

Vancouver wasn't far. McIntosh pulled up in front of the hotel. It looked good. It was right on the water. We got the key and went up. It was a pleasant room with a refrigerator and thanks to some good soul the refrigerator had beer in it.

"Have one," I told him.

We sat down and sucked at the beer.

"Creeley was here last year," he said.

"Is that so?"

"It's kind of a co-op Art Center, self-sufficient. They have a big paid membership, rent space, so forth. Your show is already sold out. Silvers said he could have made a lot of money if he'd jacked the ticket prices up."

"Who's Silvers?"

"Myron Silvers. He's one of the Directors."

We were getting to the dull part now.

"I can show you around town," said McIntosh.

"That's all right. I can walk around."

"How about dinner? On the house."

"Just a sandwich. I'm not all that hungry."

I figured if I got him outside I could leave him when we were finished eating. Not that he was a bad sort, but most people just didn't interest me.

WE FOUND a place 3 or 4 blocks away. Vancouver was a very clean town and the people didn't have that hard city look. I liked the restaurant. But when I looked at the menu I noticed that the prices were about 40 percent higher than in my part of L.A. I had a roast beef sandwich and another beer.

It felt good to be out of the U.S.A. There was a real difference. The women looked better, things felt calmer, less false. I finished the sandwich, then McIntosh drove me back to the hotel. I left him at the car and took the elevator up. I took a shower, left my clothes off. I stood at the window and looked down at the water. Tomorrow night it would all be over, I'd have their money and at noon I'd be back in the air. Too bad. I drank 3 or 4 more bottles of beer, then went to bed and slept.

THEY TOOK me to the reading an hour early. A young boy was up there singing. They talked right through his act. Bottles clanked; laughter; a good drunken crowd; my kind of folks. We drank backstage, McIntosh, Silvers, myself and a couple of others.

"You're the first male poet we've had here in a long time," said Silvers.

"What do you mean?"

"I mean, we've had a long run of fags. This is a nice change."

"Thanks."

I REALLY read it to them. By the end I was drunk and they were too. We bickered, we snarled at each other a bit, but mostly it was all right. I had been given my check before the reading and it helped my delivery some.

THERE WAS a party afterwards in a large house. After an hour or two I found myself between two women. One was a blonde, she looked as if she was carved out of ivory, with beautiful eyes and a beautiful body. She was with her boyfriend.

"Chinaski," he said after a while, "I'm going with you."

"Wait a minute," I said, "you're with your boyfriend."

"Oh shit," she said, "he's *nobody!* I'm going with you!"

I looked at the boy. He had tears in his eyes. He was trembling. He was in love, poor fellow.

The girl on the other side of me had dark hair. Her body was as good but she wasn't as facially attractive.

"Come with me," she said.

"What?"

"I said, take me with you."

"Wait a minute."

I turned back to the blonde. "Listen, you're beautiful but I can't go with you. I don't want to hurt your friend."

"Fuck that son-of-a-bitch. He's shit."

The girl with dark hair pulled at my arm. "Take me with you now or I'm leaving."

"All right," I said, "let's go."

I found McIntosh. He didn't look as if he was doing much. I guess he didn't like parties.

"Come on, Mac, drive us back to the hotel."

There was more beer. The dark girl told me her name was Iris Duarte. She was one-half Indian and she said she worked as a belly dancer. She stood up and shook it. It looked good.

"You really need a costume to get the full effect," she said.

"No, I don't."

"I mean, *I* need one, to make it look good, you know."

She looked Indian. She had an Indian nose and mouth. She appeared to be about 23, dark brown eyes, she spoke quietly and had that great body. She had read 3 or 4 of my books. *All right.*

We drank another hour then went to bed. I ate her up but when I mounted I just stroked and stroked without effect. Too bad.

IN THE morning I brushed my teeth, threw cold water on my face and went back to bed. I started playing with her cunt. It got wet and so did I. I mounted. I ground it in, thinking of all that body, all that good young body. She took all I had to give her. It was a good one. It was a very good one. Afterwards, Iris went to the bathroom.

I stretched out thinking about how good it had been. Iris reappeared and got back into the bed. We didn't speak. An hour passed. Then we did it all over again.

WE CLEANED up and dressed. She gave me her address and phone number, I gave her mine. She really seemed fond of me. McIntosh knocked about 15 minutes later. We drove Iris to an intersection near her place of work. It turned out she really worked as a waitress; the belly-dancing was an ambition. I kissed her good-bye. She got out of the car. She turned and waved, then walked off. I watched that body as it walked away.

"Chinaski scores again," said McIntosh, as he headed for the airport.

"Think nothing of it," I said.

"I had some luck myself," he said.

"Yeah?"

"Yeah. I got your blonde."

"What?"

"Yes," he laughed, "I did."

"Drive me to the airport, bastard!"

I was back in Los Angeles for 3 days. I had a date with Debra that night. The phone rang.

"Hank, this is *Iris!*"

"Oh, Iris, what a surprise! How's it going?"

"Hank, I'm flying to L.A. I'm coming to see you!"

"Great! When?"

"I'll fly down the Wednesday before Thanksgiving."

"Thanksgiving?"

"And I can stay until the following Monday!"

"O.K."

"Do you have a pen? I'll give you my flight number."

THAT NIGHT Debra and I had dinner at a nice place down by the seashore. The tables weren't crowded together and they specialized in sea food. We ordered a bottle of white wine and waited for our meal. Debra looked better than I had seen her for some time, but she told me her job was getting to be too much. She was going to have to hire another girl. And it was hard to find anybody efficient. People were so inept.

"Yes," I said.

"Have you heard from Sara?"

"I phoned her. We had had a little argument. I sort of patched it up."

"Have you seen her since you got back from Canada?"

"No."

"I've ordered a 25 pound turkey for Thanksgiving. Can you carve?"

"*Sure.*"

"Don't drink too much tonight. You know what happens when you drink too much. You become a wet noodle."

"O.K."

Debra reached over and touched my hand. "My sweet dear old wet noodle!"

I ONLY got one bottle of wine for after dinner. We drank it slowly, sitting up in her bed watching her giant t.v. The first program was lousy. The second was better. It was about a sex pervert and a subnormal farmboy. The pervert's head was transplanted onto the farmboy's body by a mad doctor and the body escaped with the two heads and ran about the countryside doing all sorts of horrible things. It put me in a good mood.

After the bottle of wine and the two-headed boy I mounted Debra and had some good luck for a change. I gave her a long slamming gallop full of unexpected variables and inventiveness before I finally shot it into her.

IN THE morning Debra asked me to stay and wait for her to get home from work. She promised to cook a nice dinner. "All right," I said.

I tried to sleep after she left but I couldn't. I was wondering about Thanksgiving, how I was going to tell her that I couldn't be there. It bothered me. I got up and walked the floors. I took a bath. Nothing helped. Maybe Iris would change her mind, maybe her plane would crash. I could phone Debra Thanksgiving morning to tell her I was coming after all.

I walked about feeling worse and worse. Perhaps it was because I had stayed over instead of going home. It was like prolonging the agony. What kind of shit was I? I could certainly play some nasty, unreal games. What was my motive? Was I trying to get even for something? Could I keep on telling myself that it was merely a matter of research, a simple study of the female? I was simply letting things happen without thinking about them. I wasn't considering anything but my own selfish, cheap pleasure. I was like a spoiled high school kid. I was worse than any whore; a whore took your money and nothing more. I tinkered with lives and souls as if they were my playthings. How could I call myself a man? How could I write poems? What did I consist of? I was a bush-league de Sade, without his intellect. A murderer was more straightforward and honest than I was. Or a rapist. I didn't want *my* soul played with, mocked, pissed on; I knew *that* much at any rate. I was truly no good. I could feel it as I walked up and down on the rug. *No good.* The worst part of it was that I passed myself off for exactly what I wasn't—a good man. I was able to enter people's lives because of their trust in me. I was doing my dirty work the easy way. I was writing The *Love Tale of the Hyena*.

I stood in the center of the room, surprised by my thoughts. I found myself sitting on the edge of the bed, and I was crying. I could feel the tears with my fingers. My brain whirled, yet I felt sane. I couldn't understand what was happening to me.

I picked up the phone and dialed Sara at her health food store.

"You busy?" I asked.

"No, I just opened up. Are you all right? You sound funny."

"I'm at the bottom."

"What is it?"

"Well, I told Debra I'd spend Thanksgiving with her. She's counting on it. But now something has happened."

"What?"

"Well, I didn't tell you before. You and I haven't had sex yet, you know. Sex makes things different."

"What happened?"

"I met a belly dancer in Canada."

"You did? And you're in love?"

"No, I'm not in love."

"Wait, here's a customer. Can you hold the line?"

"All right. . . ."

I sat there holding the telephone to my ear. I was still naked. I looked down at my penis: *you dirty son-of-a-bitch!* Do you know all the heartache you cause with your dumb hunger?

I sat there for five minutes with the phone to my ear. It was a toll call. At least it would be charged to Debra's bill.

"I'm back," said Sara. "Go ahead."

"Well, I told the belly dancer when I was in Vancouver to come down and see me some time in L.A."

"So?"

"Well, I told you I already promised Debra I'd spend Thanksgiving with her. . . ."

"You promised me too," Sara said.

"I did?"

"Well, you *were* drunk. You said that like any other American you didn't like to spend holidays alone. You kissed me and asked that we might spend Thanksgiving together."

"I'm sorry, I don't remember. . . ."

"It's all right. Hold on . . . here's another customer. . . ."

I put the phone down and went out and poured myself a drink. As I walked back into the bedroom I saw my sagging belly in the mirror. It was ugly, obscene. Why did women tolerate me?

I held the phone to my ear with one hand and drank wine with the other. Sara came back on.

"All right. Go ahead."

"O.K., it's like this. The belly dancer phoned the other night. Only she's not really a belly dancer, she's a waitress. She said she was flying down to L.A. to spend Thanksgiving with me. She sounded so happy."

"You should have told her you had an engagement."

"I didn't. . . ."

"You didn't have the guts."

"Iris has got a lovely body. . . ."

"There are other things in life besides lovely bodies."

"Anyway, now I have to tell Debra I can't spend Thanksgiving with her and I don't know how."

"Where are you?"

"I'm in Debra's bed."

"Where's Debra?"

"She's at work." I couldn't hold back a sob.

"You're nothing but a big-ass crybaby."

"I know. But I've got to tell her. It's driving me crazy."

"You got in this mess by yourself. You'll have to get out by yourself."

"I thought you'd help me, I thought you might tell me what to do."

"You want me to change your diapers? You want me to phone her for you?"

"No, it's all right. I'm a man. *I'll phone her myself.* I'm going to phone her right now. I'm going to tell her the truth. I'm going to get the fucking thing over with!"

"That's good. Let me know how it goes."

"It was my childhood, you see. I never knew what love was. . . ."

"Phone me back later."

Sara hung up.

I POURED another wine. I couldn't understand what had happened to my life. I had lost my sophistication, I had lost my worldliness, I had lost my hard protective shell. I had lost my sense of humor in the face of other people's problems. I wanted them all back. I wanted things to go easily for me. But somehow I knew they wouldn't come back, at least not right away. I was destined to continue feeling guilty and unprotected.

I tried telling myself that feeling guilty was just a sickness of some sort. That it was men *without* guilt who made progress in life. Men who were able to lie, to cheat, men who knew all the shortcuts. Cortez. He didn't fuck around. Neither did Vince Lombardi. But no matter how much I thought about it, I still felt bad. I decided to get it over with. I was ready. The confessional booth. I'd be a Catholic again. Get it on, off and out, then wait for forgiveness. I finished the wine and dialed Debra's office.

Tessie answered.

"Hi, baby! This is Hank! How's it going?"

"Everything's fine, Hank. How are you doing?"

"All is well. Listen, you're not pissed at me, are you?"

"No, Hank. It *was* a little gross, hahaha, but it was fun. It's *our* secret, anyhow."

"Thanks. You know, I'm really not . . ."

"I know."

"Well, listen, I wanted to speak to Debra. Is she there?"

"No, she's in court, transcribing."

"When will she be back?"

"She usually doesn't return to the office after she goes to court. In case she does, is there any message?"

"No, Tessie, thank you."

THAT DID it. I couldn't even make amends. Constipation of Confession. Lack of Communication. I had Enemies in High Places.

I drank another wine. I had been ready to clear the air and let everything hang out. Now I had to sit on it. I felt worse and worse. Depression, suicide was often the lack of a proper diet. But I had been eating well. I remembered the old days, living on one candy bar a day, sending out hand-printed stories to *Atlantic Monthly* and *Harper's*. All I thought about was food. If the body didn't eat, the mind starved too. But I had been eating damned good, for a change, and drinking damned good wine. That meant that what I was thinking was probably the *truth*. Everybody imagined themselves special, privileged, exempt. Even an ugly old crone watering a geranium on her front porch. I had imagined myself special because I had come out of the factories at the age of 50 and become a poet. Hot shit. So I pissed on everybody just like those bosses and managers had pissed on me when *I* was helpless. It came to the same thing. I was a drunken spoiled rotten fucker with a very minor *minor* fame.

My analysis didn't cure the burn.

The phone rang. It was Sara.

"You said you'd phone. What happened?"

"She wasn't in."

"Not in?"

"She's in court."

"What are you going to do?"

"I'm going to wait. And tell her."

"All right."

"I shouldn't have laid all this shit on you."

"It's all right."

"I want to see you again."

"When? After the belly dancer?"

"Well, yes."

"Thanks but no thanks."

"I'll phone you. . . ."

"All right. I'll get your diapers laundered and ready for you."

I sipped on the wine and waited. 3 o'clock, 4 o'clock, 5 o'clock. Finally I remembered to put my clothes on. I was sitting with a drink in my hand when Debra's car pulled up in front of the house. I waited. She opened the door. She had a bag of groceries. She looked very good.

"Hi!" she said, "How's my *ex*-wet noodle?"

I walked up to her and put my arms around her. I started to tremble and cry.

"Hank, what's *wrong*?"

Debra dropped the bag of groceries to the floor. Our dinner. I grabbed her and held her to me. I was sobbing. The tears flowed like wine. I couldn't stop. Most of me meant it, the other part was running away.

"Hank, what *is* it?"

"I can't be with you Thanksgiving."

"Why? Why? What's wrong?"

"What's wrong is that I am a GIANT HUNK OF SHIT!"

My guilt screwed inside me and I had a spasm. It hurt something awful.

"A belly dancer is flying down from Canada to spend Thanksgiving with me."

"A belly dancer?"

"Yes."

"Is she beautiful?"

"Yes, she is. I'm sorry, I'm *sorry*. . . ."

Debra pushed me off.

"Let me put the groceries away."

She picked up the bag and walked into the kitchen. I heard the refrigerator door open and close.

"Debra," I said, "I'm leaving."

There was no sound from the kitchen. I opened the front door and walked out. The Volks started. I turned the radio on, the headlights on and drove back to L.A.

94

WEDNESDAY NIGHT FOUND me at the airport waiting for Iris. I sat around and looked at the women. None of them—except for one or two—looked as good as Iris. There was something wrong with me: I did think of sex a great deal. Each woman I looked at I imagined being in bed with. It was an interesting way to pass airport waiting time. *Women*: I liked the colors of their clothing; the way they walked; the cruelty in some faces; now and then the almost pure beauty in another face, totally and enchantingly female. They had it over us: they planned much better and were better organized. While men were watching professional football or drinking beer or bowling, they, the women, were thinking about us, concentrating, studying, deciding—whether to accept us, discard us, exchange us, kill us or whether simply to leave us. In the end it hardly mattered; no matter what they did, we ended up lonely and insane.

I had bought Iris and myself a turkey, an 18 pounder. It was on my sink, thawing out. Thanksgiving. It proved you had survived another year with its wars, inflation, unemployment, smog, presidents. It was a grand neurotic gathering of clans: loud drunks, grandmothers, sisters, aunts, screaming children, would-be suicides. And don't forget indigestion. I wasn't different from anyone else: there sat the 18 pound bird on my sink, dead, plucked, totally disemboweled. Iris would roast it for me.

I had received a letter in the mail that afternoon. I took it out of my pocket and re-read it. It had been mailed from Berkeley:

Dear Mr. Chinaski:

You don't know me but I'm a cute bitch. I've been going with sailors and one truck driver but they don't satisfy me. I mean, we fuck and then there's nothing more. There's no substance to those sons of bitches. I'm 22 and I have a 5 year old daughter, Aster. I live with a guy but there's no sex, we just live together. His name is Rex. I'd like to come see you. My mom could watch Aster. Enclosed is a photo of me. Write me if you feel like it. I've read some of your books. They are hard to find in bookstores. What I like about your writing is that you are so easy to understand. And you're funny too.

yours,
Tanya

Then Iris' plane landed. I stood at the window and watched her get off. She still looked good. She had come all the way from Canada to see me. She had one suitcase. I waved to her as she filed through the entranceway with the others. She had to pass through customs, then she was pressed up against me. We kissed and I got half a hard-on. She was in a dress, a practical tight-fitting blue dress, high heels and she wore a small hat cocked on her head. It was rare to see a woman in a dress. All the women in Los Angeles wore pants continually. . . .

SINCE WE didn't have to wait for her baggage we drove right to my place. I parked out front and we walked through the court together. She sat on the couch while I poured her a drink. Iris looked over at my homemade bookcase.

"Did you write all those books?"

"Yes."

"I had no idea you had written so many."

"I wrote them."

"How many?"

"I don't know. Twenty, twenty-five. . . ."

I kissed her, putting one arm around her waist, pulling her to me. The other hand I put on her knee.

The phone rang. I got up and answered it. "Hank?" It was Valerie.

"Yes?"

"Who was that?"

"Who was who?"

"That girl . . ."

"Oh; that's a friend from Canada."

"Hank, you and your goddamned women!"

"Yes."

"Bobby wants to know if you and . . ."

"Iris."

"He wants to know if you and Iris want to come down for a drink."

"Not tonight. I'll take a rain check."

"She's really got a *body!*"

"I know."

"All right, maybe tomorrow."

"Maybe. . . ."

I HUNG up thinking that Valerie probably liked women too. Well, that was all right.

I poured two more drinks.

"How many women have you met at airports?" Iris asked.

"It's not as bad as you think."

"Have you lost count? Like your books?"

"Math is one of my weaker points."

"Do you enjoy meeting women at airports?"

"Yes." I had not remembered that Iris was so talkative.

"You pig!" She laughed.

"Our first fight. Did you have a nice flight?"

"I sat next to a bore. I made a mistake and let him buy me a drink. He talked my goddamned ear off."

"He was only excited. You're a sexy woman."

"Is that all you see in me?"

"I see lots of that. Maybe I'll see other things as we go along."

"Why do you want so many women?"

"It was my childhood, you see. No love, no affection. And in my twenties and thirties there also was very little. I'm playing catch-up. . . ."

"Will you know when you've caught up?"

"The feeling I have is that I'll need at least one more lifetime."

"You're so full of shit!"

I laughed. "That's why I write."

"I'm going to take a shower and change."

"Sure."

I went to the kitchen and felt-up the turkey. It showed me its legs, its pubic hair, its bunghole, its thighs; it sat there. I was glad it didn't have eyes. Well, we'd do something with the thing. That was the next step. I heard the toilet flush. If Iris didn't want to roast it, I'd roast it.

When I was young I was depressed all the time. But suicide

no longer seemed a possibility in my life. At my age there was
very little left to kill. It was good to be old, no matter what they
said. It was reasonable that a man had to be at least 50 years old
before he could write with anything like clarity. The more rivers
you crossed, the more you knew about rivers—that is, if you
survived the white water and the hidden rocks. It could be a
rough cob, sometimes.

Iris came out. She had on a blueblack one piece dress that
appeared to be silk and it clung. She wasn't your average
American girl, which kept her from appearing obvious. She was
a total woman but she didn't throw it in your face. American
women drove hard bargains and they ended up looking the
worse for it. The few natural American women left were mostly
in Texas and Louisiana.

Iris smiled at me. She had something in each hand. She held
both hands above her head and began making clicking noises.
She began to dance. Or rather, she vibrated. It was as if she were
shot through with electric current and the center of her soul was
her belly. It was lovely and pure, with just the faintest hint of
humor. The whole dance, as she never took her eyes off me, had
its own meaning, a good endearing sense of its own worth.

Iris finished and I applauded, poured her a drink.

"I didn't do it justice," she said. "You need a costume and
music."

"I liked it very much."

"I was going to bring a tape of the music but I knew you
wouldn't have a machine."

"You're right. It was great anyhow."

I gave Iris a gentle kiss.

"Why don't you come live in Los Angeles?" I asked her.

"All my roots are up in the northwest. I like it there. My
parents. My friends. Everything is up there, don't you see?"

"Yes."

"Why don't you move to Vancouver? You could write in
Vancouver."

"I guess I could. I could write on top of an iceberg."

"You might try it."

"What?"

"Vancouver."

"What would your father think?"

"About what?"

"Us."

95

ON THANKSGIVING IRIS prepared the turkey and put it in the oven. Bobby and Valerie came over for a few drinks but they didn't stay. It was refreshing. Iris had on another dress, just as appealing as the other.

"You know," she said, "I didn't bring enough clothes. Tomorrow Valerie and I are going shopping at Frederick's. I'm going to get some real slut-shoes. You'll like them."

"I'll like that, Iris."

I walked into the bathroom. I had hidden the photo Tanya had sent me in the medicine chest. She had her dress hiked up and she wasn't wearing panties. I could see her cunt. She *was* a cute bitch.

When I came out Iris was washing something in the sink. I grabbed her from behind, turned her around and kissed her.

"You are a horny old dog!" she said.

"I'll make you suffer tonight, my dear!"

"Please do!"

WE DRANK all through the afternoon, then got to the turkey around 5 or 6 PM. The food sobered us up. An hour later we began drinking again. We went to bed early, around 10 PM. I didn't have any problems. I was sober enough to insure a good long ride. The minute I began stroking I knew that I would make it. I didn't particularly try to please Iris. I just went ahead and gave her an old-fashioned horse fuck. The bed bounced and she grimaced. Then came low moans. I slowed down a bit, then picked up the pace and ripped it home. She appeared to climax along with me. Of course, a man never knew. I rolled off. I'd always liked Canadian bacon.

THE NEXT day Valerie came over and she and Iris left together for Frederick's. The mail arrived about an hour later. It contained another letter from Tanya:

Henry, dear . . .

I walked down the street today and these guys whistled. I walked on past them without response. The ones I really hate are the car wash guys. They holler things and stick out their tongues like they could really do something with their tongues, but there isn't really a man among them who could do it. You can tell, you know.

Yesterday I went into this clothing store to buy a pair of pants for Rex. Rex gave me the money. He can never buy his own things. He just hates to. So I went into this men's clothing store and picked out a pair of pants. There were two guys in there, middle-aged and one of the guys was real sarcastic. While I was picking out the pants he came up to me and he took my hand and put it on his cock. I told him, "Is that all you've got, poor thing!" He laughed and said something wise. I found these real nice pair of pants for Rex, green with thin white stripes. Rex likes green. Anyhow, this guy says to me, "Come on back into one of the try-on booths." Well, you know, sarcastic guys always fascinate me. So I went into the booth with him. The other guy saw us go in. We started kissing and he unzipped. He got a hard-on and put my hand on it. We kept kissing and he lifted my dress and looked at my panties in the mirror. He played with my ass. But his cock never got real hard, just half-hard, it just stayed half-hard. I told him he wasn't shit. He walked out of the booth with his cock out and zipped up in front of the other guy. They were laughing. I came out and paid for the pants. He bagged them. "Tell your husband you took his pants into the try-on booth!" he laughed. "You're nothing but a fucking *fag!*" I told him. "And your buddy is nothing but a fucking fag too!" And they were. Almost every man is a fag now. It's really difficult for a woman. I had a girlfriend who married a guy and she came home one day and found him in bed with another man. No wonder all the girls are having to buy vibrators these days. It's rough shit. Well, write me.

yours,
Tanya

Dear Tanya:

I got your letters and your photo. I am sitting here alone the day after Thanksgiving. I have a hangover. I liked your photo. Do you have any more?

Have you ever read Céline? *Journey to the End of the Night*, I mean. After that he lost stride and became a crank, bitching about his editors and his readers. It's a real damn shame. His mind just went. I think he must have been a good doctor. Or maybe he wasn't. Maybe his heart wasn't in it. Maybe he killed his patients off. Now *that* would have made a good novel. Many doctors do that. They give you a pill and send you back out on the street again. They need money to pay for what their educations cost them. So they pack their waiting rooms and run the patients in and out. They weigh you, take your blood pressure, give you a pill and send you back out on the street feeling worse. A dental surgeon may take your life savings but usually he does something for your teeth.

Anyhow, I'm still writing and I seem to be making the rent. I find your letters interesting. Who took that photo of you without your panties on? A good friend, no doubt. Rex? You see, I'm getting jealous! That's a good sign, isn't it? Let's just call it interest. Or concern.

I'll watch the mailbox. Any more photos?

yours, yes, yes,

Henry

The door opened and it was Iris. I pulled the sheet out of the typewriter and laid it face down.

CHARLES BUKOWSKI

"Oh, Hank! I got the slut-shoes!"

"Great! Great!"

"I'll put them on for you! I'm sure you'll love them!"

"Baby, do it!"

Iris walked into the bedroom. I took the letter to Tanya and stuck it under a pile of papers.

Iris walked out. The shoes were bright red on viciously high heels. She looked like one of the greatest whores of all time. There were no backs on the shoes and her feet showed through the see-through material. Iris walked back and forth. She had a most provocative body and ass anyhow, and walking on those heels pushed it all sky-high. It was maddening. Iris stopped and looked back at me over her shoulder, smiled. What a marvelous chippy! She had more hip, more ass, more calf than I'd ever seen before. I ran out and poured two drinks. Iris sat down and crossed her legs high. She sat in a chair across the room from me. The miracles in my life kept occurring. I couldn't understand it.

My cock was hard, throbbing, pushing against my pants.

"You know what a man likes," I told Iris.

We finished our drinks. I took her by the hand into the bedroom. I pushed her on the bed. I pulled her dress back and got at her panties. It was hard work. Her panties got caught on one shoe, got hooked on the heel, but I finally got them off. Iris's dress was still covering her hips. I raised her ass and pushed the dress up under her. She was already wet. I felt her with my fingers. Iris was almost always wet, almost always ready. She was a total joy. She had long nylon stockings with blue garters decorated with red roses. I put it into the wetness. Her legs were raised high in the air and as I caressed her I saw those slut-shoes on her feet, red heels jutting like stilettoes. Iris was in for another old-fashioned horse fuck. Love was for guitar players, Catholics and chess freaks. That bitch with her red shoes and long stockings—she deserved what she was going to get from me. I tried to rip her apart, I tried to split her in half. I watched that strange half-Indian face in the soft sunlight that filtered weakly through the blinds. It was like murder. I had her. There

258

was no escape. I ripped and roared, slapped her across the face and nearly tore her in half.

I was surprised that she was able to get up smiling and walk to the bathroom. She looked almost happy. Her shoes had come off and were lying by the side of the bed. My cock was still hard. I picked up one of the shoes and rubbed my cock with it. It felt great. Then I put the shoe back on the floor. When Iris came out of the bathroom still smiling, my cock went down.

96

NOT MUCH HAPPENED during the rest of her stay. We drank, we ate, we fucked. There were no arguments. We took long drives down along the shore, ate at seafood cafes. I didn't bother with writing. There were times when it was best to get away from the machine. A good writer knew when not to write. Anybody could type. Not that I was a good typist; also I couldn't spell and I didn't know grammar. But I knew when not to write. It was like fucking. You had to rest the godhead now and then. I had an old friend who occasionally wrote me letters, Jimmy Shannon. He wrote 6 novels a year, all on incest. It was no wonder he was starving. My problem was that I couldn't rest my cock-godhead like I could my typer-godhead. That was because women were available only in streaks so you had to get as much in as possible before somebody else's godhead came along. I think the fact that I quit writing for ten years was one of the luckiest things that ever happened to me. (I suppose that some critics would say that it was one of the luckiest things that ever happened to the reader, too.) Ten years' rest for both sides. What would happen if I stopped drinking for ten years?

THE TIME came to put Iris Duarte back on the plane. It was a morning flight which made it difficult. I was used to rising at noon; it was a fine cure for hangovers and would add 5 years to my life. I felt no sadness while driving her to L.A. International. The sex had been fine; there had been laughter. I could hardly

CHARLES BUKOWSKI

remember a more civilized time, neither of us making any demands, yet there had been warmth, it had not been without feeling, dead meat coupled with dead meat. I detested that type of swinging, the Los Angeles, Hollywood, Bel Air, Malibu, Laguna Beach kind of sex. Strangers when you meet, strangers when you part—a gymnasium of bodies namelessly masturbating each other. People with no morals often considered themselves more free, but mostly they lacked the ability to feel or to love. So they became swingers. The dead fucking the dead. There was no gamble or humor in their game—it was corpse fucking corpse. Morals were restrictive, but they *were* grounded on human experience down through the centuries. Some morals tended to keep people slaves in factories, in churches and true to the State. Other morals simply made good sense. It was like a garden filled with poisoned fruit and good fruit. You had to know which to pick and eat, which to leave alone.

MY EXPERIENCE with Iris had been delightful and fulfilling, yet I wasn't in love with her nor she with me. It was easy to care and hard not to care. I cared. We sat in the Volks on the upper parking ramp. We had some time. I had the radio on. Brahms.

"Will I see you again?" I asked her.

"I don't think so."

"Do you want a drink in the bar?"

"You've made an alcoholic out of me, Hank. I'm so weak I can hardly walk."

"Was it just the booze?"

"No."

"Then let's get a drink."

"Drink, drink, drink! Is that *all* you can think of?"

"No, but it's a good way to get through spaces, like this one."

"Can't you face things straight?"

"I can but I'd rather not."

"That's escapism."

"Everything is: playing golf, sleeping, eating, walking, arguing, jogging, breathing, fucking. . . ."

260

"Fucking?"

"Look, we're talking like high school children. Let's get you on the plane."

It wasn't going well. I wanted to kiss her but I sensed her reserve. A wall. Iris wasn't feeling good, I guess, and I wasn't feeling good.

"All right," she said, "we'll check in and then go get a drink. Then I'll fly away forever: real smooth, real easy, no pain."

"*All right!*" I said.

And that was just the way it was.

The way back: Century Boulevard east, down to Crenshaw, up 8th Avenue, then Arlington to Wilton. I decided to pick up my laundry and turned right on Beverly Boulevard. I drove into the lot behind the Silverette Cleaners and parked the Volks. As I did a young black girl in a red dress walked past. She had a marvelous swing to her ass, a most marvelous motion. Then the building blocked my view. She had the movements; it was as if life had given a few women a supple grace and denied the rest. She had that indescribable grace.

I stepped out onto the sidewalk and watched her from behind. I saw her turn and look back. Then she stood and stared at me, looking back over her shoulder. I walked into the laundry. When I came out with my things she was standing by my Volks. I put the things inside from the passenger's side. Then I moved around to the driver's side. She stood in front of me. She was about 27 with a very round face, impassive. We were standing very close together.

"I saw you looking at me. Why were you looking at me?"

"I apologize. I didn't mean any offense."

"I want to know why you were looking at me. You were really *staring* at me."

"Look, you're a beautiful woman. You have a beautiful body. I saw you walk by and I looked. I couldn't help it."

"Do you want a date for tonight?"

"Well, that would be great. But I've got a date. I've got something going."

I circled around her and made for the driver's side. I opened the door and got in. She walked off. As she did I heard her whisper, "*Dumb honky asshole.*"

I OPENED the mail—nothing. I needed to regroup. Something needed was missing. I looked in the refrigerator. Nothing. I walked outside, got in the Volks and drove to the Blue Elephant liquor store. I got a fifth of Smirnoff and some 7-UP. As I drove back toward my place, somewhere along the way, I knew I had forgotten cigarettes.

I went south down Western Avenue, took a left on Hollywood Boulevard, then a right on Serrano. I was trying to get to a Sav-On—for smokes. Right on the corner of Serrano and Sunset stood another black girl, a high-yellow in black high heels and a mini-skirt. As she stood there in that short skirt I could see just a touch of blue panty. She began to walk and I drove along beside her. She pretended not to notice me.

"Hey, baby!"

She stopped. I pulled over to the curb. She walked up to the car.

"How you doing?" I asked her.

"All right."

"Are you a decoy?" I asked.

"What do you mean?"

"I mean," I asked her, "how do I know you're not a cop?"

"How do I know *you're* not a cop?"

"Look at my face. Do I look like a cop?"

"All right," she said, "drive around the corner and park. I'll get in around the corner."

I drove around the corner in front of Mr. Famous N.J. Sandwiches. She opened the door and got in.

"What do you want?" she asked. She was in her mid-thirties and one large solid gold tooth stood out in the center of her smile. She'd never be broke.

"*Head,*" I said.

"Twenty dollars."

"O.K., let's go."

"Drive up Western to Franklin, take a left, go to Harvard and take a right."

When we got to Harvard it was hard to park. Finally I parked in a red zone and we got out.

"Follow me," she said.

It was a decaying high-rise. Just before we reached the lobby she took a right and I followed her up a cement stairway, watching her ass. It was strange, but everybody had an ass. It was almost sad. But I didn't want her ass. I followed her down a hallway and then up some more cement steps. We were using some kind of fire escape instead of the elevator. What her reason was I had no idea. But I needed the exercise—if I intended to write big fat novels in my old age like Knut Hamsun.

We finally reached her apartment and she got out her key. I grabbed her hand.

"Wait a minute," I said.

"What is it?"

"You got a couple of big black bastards in there who are gonna kick my ass and roll me?"

"No, there's nobody in there. I live with a girlfriend and she's not home. She works at the Broadway Department Store."

"Give me the key."

I opened the door slowly and then kicked it wide with my foot. I looked inside. I had my steel but I didn't reach. She closed the door behind us.

"Come on in the bedroom," she said.

"Wait a minute. . . ."

I ripped open a closet door and reaching in felt behind the clothing. Nothing.

"What kind of shit are you on, man?"

"I'm not on *any* kind of shit!"

"Oh Lord . . ."

I ran into the bathroom and yanked back the shower curtain. Nothing. I went into the kitchen, pulled back the plastic curtain below the sink. Just a filthy overflowing plastic trash basket. I checked the other bedroom, the closet in there. I looked under the double bed: an empty bottle of Ripple. I walked out.

"Come on back here," she said.

It was a tiny bedroom, more like an alcove. There was a cot with dirty sheets. The blanket was on the floor. I unzipped and pulled it out.

"$20," she said.

"Get your lips on this motherfucker! Suck it dry!"

"$20."

"I know the price. Earn it. Drain my balls."

"$20 *first*. . . ."

"Oh yeah? I give you the twenty, how do I know you don't yell for the cops? How do I know your 7-foot basketball-ass brother don't arrive with his switchblade?"

"$20 *first*. And don't worry. I'll suck you. I'll suck you good."

"I don't trust you, whore."

I zipped up and got out of there, fast, I went down all those cement steps. I reached the bottom, jumped into the Volks and drove back to my place.

I STARTED drinking. My stars simply weren't in order.

The phone rang. It was Bobby. "Did you get Iris on the plane?"

"Yeah, Bobby, and I want to thank you for keeping your hands off for a change."

"Look, Hank, that's just in your head. You're old and you bring all these young chicks over, then you get nervous when a young cat comes around. Your ass gets uptight."

"Self-doubt . . . lack of confidence, right?"

"Well . . ."

"O.K., Bobby."

"Anyhow, Valerie wondered if you wanted to come down for a drink?"

"Why not?"

BOBBY HAD some bad shit, real bad shit. We passed it around. Bobby had a lot of new tapes for the stereo. He also had my favorite singer, Randy Newman, and he put Randy on, but only medium-loud, as per my request.

So we listened to Randy and smoked and then Valerie began putting on a fashion show. She had a dozen sexy outfits from Frederick's. She had 30 pairs of shoes hanging on the back of the bathroom door.

Valerie came prancing out in 8-inch high heels. She could hardly walk. She poked about the room, staggering on her stilts. Her ass poked out and her tiny nipples were hard and stiff, they jutted out under her see-through blouse. She had on a thin gold anklet. She whirled and faced us, made some gentle sexual movements.

"Christ," said Bobby, "Oh . . . Christ!"

"Holy Jesus Christ Mother of God!" I said.

As Valerie went past I reached out and got a handful of ass. I was living. I felt great. Valerie ducked into the crapper for a change of costume.

Each time Valerie came out she looked better, crazier, wilder. The whole process was moving toward some climax.

We drank and smoked and Valerie kept coming back with more. One hell of a show.

She sat on my lap and Bobby snapped some photos.

The night wore on. Then I looked around and Valerie and Bobby were gone. I walked into the bedroom and there was Valerie on the bed, naked except for her spiked high heels. Her body was firm and lean.

Bobby was still dressed and was sucking Valerie's breasts, going from one to the other. Her nipples stood tall.

Bobby looked up at me. "Hey, old man, I've heard you brag about how you eat pussy. How's this?"

Bobby ducked down and spread Valerie's legs. Her cunt hairs were long and twisted and tangled. Bobby went down there and licked at the clit. He was pretty good but he lacked spirit.

"Wait a minute, Bobby, you're not doing it right. Let me show you."

I got down there. I began far back and worked toward it. Then I got there. Valerie responded. Too much so. She wrapped her legs around my head and I couldn't breathe. My ears were pressed flat. I pulled my head out of there.

"O.K., Bobby, you see?"

Bobby didn't answer. He turned and walked into the bath-room. I had my shoes and pants off. I liked to show off my legs when I drank. Valerie reached up and pulled me down on the bed. Then she bent over my cock and took it into her mouth. She wasn't very good compared to most. She began the old head-bob and had very little else to offer beside that. She worked a long time and I felt I wasn't going to make it. I pulled her head away, put it up on the pillow and kissed her. Then I mounted. I had made about 8 or 10 strokes when I heard Bobby behind us.

"I want you to leave, man."

"Bobby, what the hell's wrong?"

"I want you to go back to your place."

I pulled out, got up, walked into the front room and put on my pants and shoes.

"Hey, Cool Papa," I said to Bobby, "what's wrong?"

"I just want you out of here."

"All right, all right. . . ."

I walked back to my place. It seemed a very long time since I had put Iris Duarte on that plane. She must be back in Vancouver by now. Shit. Iris Duarte, goodnight.

97

I GOT A letter in the mail. It was addressed from Hollywood.

Dear Chinaski:

I've just read almost all your books. I work as a typist in a place on Cherokee Ave. I've hung your picture in the place where I work. It's a poster from one of your readings. People ask me, "Who's that?" and I say, "That's my boy friend" and they say, "My God!"

I gave my boss your book of stories, *The Beast with Three Legs* and he said he didn't like it. He said you didn't know how to write. He said it was cheap shit. He got quite angry about it.

Anyhow, I like your things and I'd like to meet you. They say I'm pretty well stacked. Care to check me out?

luv

Valencia

She left two phone numbers, one at work, one at home. It was about 2:30 PM. I dialed the work number. "Yes?" a female answered.

"Is Valencia there?"

"This is Valencia."

"This is Chinaski. I got your letter."

"I thought you'd phone."

"You have a sexy voice," I said.

"You have too," she answered.

"When can I see you?" I asked.

"Well, I'm not doing anything tonight."

"O.K. How about tonight?"

"All right," she said, "I'll see you after work. You can meet me at this bar on Cahuenga Boulevard, The Foxhole. You know where it is?"

"Yes."

"I'll see you around six then. . . ."

I drove up and parked outside The Foxhole. I lit a cigarette and sat there awhile. Then I got out and walked into the bar. Which one was Valencia? I stood there and nobody said anything. I walked up to the bar and ordered a double vodka-7. Then I heard my name, "Henry?"

I looked around and there was a blonde alone in a booth. I took my drink over and sat down. She was about 38, and not stacked. She had gone to seed, was a bit too fat. Her breasts were very large but they sagged wearily. She had short clipped blond hair. She was heavily made up and she looked tired. She was in pants, blouse and boots. Pale blue eyes. Many bracelets on each arm. Her face revealed nothing, although once she might have been beautiful.

"It was really a fucking miserable day," she said. "I typed my ass off."

"Let's make it some other night then when you're feeling better," I said.

"Ah, shit, it's all right. Another drink and I'll spring back."

Valencia motioned to the waitress. "Another wine."

She was drinking a white wine.

"How's the writing going?" she asked. "Any new books out?"

"No, but I'm working on a novel."

"What's it called?"

"No title yet."

"Is it going to be a good one?"

"I don't know."

Neither of us said anything for a while. I finished my vodka and had another. Valencia just wasn't my type in any sense of the word. I disliked her. There are people like that—immediately upon meeting them you despise them.

"There's a Japanese girl down where I work. She does everything possible to get me fired. I'm in tight with the boss, but this bitch makes the day unpleasant for me. Someday I'm going to stick my foot up her ass."

"Where are you from?"

"Chicago."

"I didn't like Chicago," I said.

"I like Chicago."

I finished my drink, she finished hers. Valencia pushed her bill toward me. "You mind paying for this? I had a shrimp salad too."

I took out my key to unlock the door.

"This your car?"

"Yes."

"You expect me to ride in an old car like that?"

"Look, if you don't want to get in, don't get in."

Valencia got in. She took out her mirror and began making up her face as we drove along. It wasn't far to my place. I parked.

Inside she said, "This place is filthy. You need somebody to fix it up."

I got out the vodka and the 7-UP and poured two drinks. Valencia pulled her boots off.

"Where's your typewriter?"

"On the kitchen table."

"You don't have a desk? I thought writers had desks."

"Some don't even have kitchen tables."

"You been married?" Valencia asked.

"Once."

"What went wrong?"

"We began to hate each other."

"I've been married four times. I still see my ex-husbands. We're friends."

"Drink up."

"You seem nervous," said Valencia.

"I'm all right."

Valencia finished her drink, then stretched out on the couch. She put her head in my lap. I began to stroke her hair. I poured her another drink, and went back to stroking her hair. I could look into her blouse and see her breasts. I leaned over and gave her a long kiss. Her tongue darted in and out of my mouth. I hated her. My cock began to rise. We kissed again and I reached down into her blouse.

"I knew I'd meet you some day," she said.

I kissed her again, this time with some savagery. She felt my cock against her head.

"Hey!" she said.

"It's nothing," I said.

"Like hell," she said. "What do you want to do?"

"I don't know. . . ."

"I know."

VALENCIA GOT up and went to the bathroom. When she came out she was naked. She got under the bedsheet. I had another drink. Then I undressed and got into bed. I pulled the sheet back. What huge breasts. She was one-half breast. I firmed one up with my hand as best I could and sucked at the nipple. It didn't harden. I went to the other breast and sucked at the nipple. No response. I sloshed her breasts about. I stuck my cock in between them. The nipples remained soft. I shoved my cock at her mouth and she turned her head away. I thought of burning her ass with a cigarette. What a mass of flesh she was. A worn out busted down streetwalker. Whores usually made me hot. My cock was hard but my spirit wasn't in it.

"Are you Jewish?" I asked her.

"No."

"You look Jewish."

"I'm not."

"You live in the Fairfax district, don't you?"

"Yes."

"Are your parents Jewish?"

"Listen, what's all this *Jewish* shit?"

"Don't feel bad. Some of my best friends are Jewish."

I sloshed her breasts around again.

"You seem frightened," Valencia said. "You seem uptight."

I waved my cock in her face.

"Does *that* look frightened?"

"It looks horrible. Where'd you get all those big veins?"

"I like them."

I grabbed her by the hair and pressed her head up against the wall and sucked at her teeth while looking into her eyes. Then I began playing with her cunt. She was a long time coming around. Then she began to open and I stuck my finger in. I got to the clit and worked it. Then I mounted. My cock was inside of her. We were actually fucking. I had no desire to please her. Valencia had a fair grip. I was into her pretty good but she didn't seem to be responding. I didn't care. I pumped and pumped. One more fuck. Research. There was no sense of violation involved. Poverty and ignorance bred their own truth. She was mine. We were two animals in the forest and I was murdering her. She was coming around. I kissed her and her lips were finally open. I dug it in. The blue walls watched us. Valencia began making little sounds. That spurred me on.

WHEN SHE came out of the bathroom I was dressed. There were two drinks on the table. We sipped our drinks.

"How come you live in the Fairfax district?" I asked.

"I like it there."

"Should I drive you home?"

"If you don't mind."

SHE LIVED two blocks east of Fairfax. "That's my place there," she said, "with the screen door."

"Looks like a nice place."

"It is. Want to come in for a while?"

"Got anything to drink?"

"Can you drink sherry?"

"Sure . . ."

We went in. There were towels on the floor. She kicked them under the couch as she walked past. Then she came out with the sherry. It was very cheap stuff.

"Where's your bathroom?" I asked.

I flushed the toilet to cover the sound, then puked the sherry back up. I flushed again and came out.

"Another drink?" she asked.

"Sure."

"The kids came by," she said, "that's why the place is such a mess."

"You've got kids?"

"Yes but Sam is taking care of them."

I finished my drink. "Well, look, thanks for the drinks. I've got to get going."

"All right, you've got my phone number."

"Right."

Valencia walked me to the screen door. We kissed there. Then I walked out to the Volks. I got in and drove off. I circled around the corner, double-parked, opened the door and puked up the other drink.

98

I SAW SARA every three or four days, at her place or at mine. We slept together but there was no sex. We came close but we never quite got to it. Drayer Baba's precepts held strong.

We decided to spend the holidays together at my place, Christmas and New Year's.

Sara arrived about noon on the 24th in her Volks van. I watched her park, then went out to meet her. She had lumber tied to the roof of the van. It was to be my Christmas present: she was going to build me a bed. My bed was a mockery: a simple box spring with the innards sticking out of the mattress. Sara had also brought an organic turkey plus the trimmings. I was to pay for that and the white wine. And there were some small gifts for each of us.

We carried in the lumber and the turkey and the sundry bits and pieces. I placed the box spring, mattress and headboard outside and put a sign on them: "Free." The head-board went first, the box spring second, and finally somebody took the mattress. It was a poor neighborhood.

I had seen Sara's bed at her place, slept in it, and had liked it. I had always disliked the average mattress, at least the ones I was able to buy. I had spent over half my life in beds which were better suited for somebody shaped like an angleworm.

Sara had built her own bed, and she was to build me another like it. A solid wood platform supported by 7 four-by-four legs (the seventh directly in the middle) topped by a layer of firm 4-inch foam. Sara had some good ideas. I held the boards and Sara drove home the nails. She was good with a hammer. She only weighed 105 pounds but she could drive a nail. It was going to be a fine bed.

It didn't take Sara long.

Then we tested it—non-sexually—as Drayer Baba smiled over us.

WE DROVE around looking for a Christmas tree. I wasn't too anxious to get a tree (Christmas had always been an unhappy time in my childhood) and when we found all the lots empty, the lack of a tree didn't bother me. Sara was unhappy as we drove back. But after we got in and had a few glasses of white wine she regained her spirits and went about hanging Christmas ornaments, lights, and tinsel everywhere, some of the tinsel in my hair.

I had read that more people committed suicide on Christmas Eve and on Christmas Day than at any other time. The holiday had little or nothing to do with the Birth of Christ, apparently.

All the radio music was sickening and the t.v. was worse, so we turned it off and she phoned her mother in Maine. I spoke to Mama too and Mama was not all that bad.

"At first," said Sara, "I was thinking about fixing you up with Mama but she's older than you are."

"Forget it."

"She had nice legs."

"Forget it."

"Are you prejudiced against old age?"

"Yes, everybody's old age but mine."

"You act like a movie star. Have you always had women 20 or 30 years younger than you?"

"Not when I was in my twenties."

"All right then. Have you ever had a woman older than you, I mean lived with her?"

"Yeah, when I was 25 I lived with a woman 35."

"How'd it go?"

"It was terrible. I fell in love."

"What was terrible?"

"She made me go to college."

"And that's terrible?"

"It wasn't the kind of college you're thinking of. She was the faculty, and I was the student body."

"What happened to her?"

"I buried her."

"With honors? Did you kill her?"

"Booze killed her."

"Merry Christmas."

"Sure. Tell me about yours."

"I pass."

"Too many?"

"Too many, yet too few."

* * *

Thirty or 40 minutes later there was a knock on the door. Sara got up and opened it. A sex symbol walked in. On Christmas Eve. I didn't know who she was. She was in a tight black outfit and her huge breasts looked as if they would burst out of the top of her dress. It was magnificent. I had never seen breasts like that, showcased in just that way, except in the movies.

"Hi, Hank!"

She knew me.

"I'm Edie. You met me at Bobby's one night."

"Oh?"

"Were you too drunk to remember?"

"Hello, Edie. This is Sara."

"I was looking for Bobby. I thought Bobby might be down here."

"Sit down and have a drink."

Edie sat in a chair to my right, very near to me. She was about 25. She lit a cigarette and sipped at her drink. Each time she leaned forward over the coffee table I was sure that it would happen, I was sure that those breasts would spring out. And I was afraid of what I might do if they did. I just didn't know. I had never been a breast man, I had always been a leg man. But Edie really knew how to *do* it. I was afraid and I peeked sideways at her breasts not knowing whether I wanted them to fall out or to stay in.

"You met Manny," she said to me, "down at Bobby's?"

"Yeh."

"I had to kick his ass out. He was too fucking jealous. He even hired a private dick to follow me! Imagine that! That simple sack of shit!"

"Yeh."

"I hate men who are beggars! I hate little toadies!"

"'A good man nowadays is hard to find,' I said. "That's a song. Out of World War Two. They also had, 'Don't sit under the apple tree with anybody else but me.'"

"Hank, you're babbling. . . ." said Sara.

"Have another drink, Edie," I said and I poured her one.

"Men are such *shits!*" she continued. "I walked into a bar the other day. I was with four guys, close friends. We sat around chugalugging pitchers of beer, we're *laughing*, you know, just having *a good time*, we weren't bothering anybody. Then I got the idea that I would like to shoot a game of pool. I like to shoot pool. I think that when a lady shoots pool it shows her class."

"I can't shoot pool," I said. "I always rip up the green. And I'm not even a lady."

"Anyway, I go up to the table and there's this guy shooting pool all by himself. I go up to him and I say, 'Look, you've had this table a long time. My friends and myself want to shoot a little pool. Do you mind letting us have the table for a while?' He turned and looked at me. He waited. Then he *sneered*, and he said, 'All right.'"

Edie became animated and bounced around as she spoke and I peeked at her things.

"I went back and told my friends, 'We got the table.' Finally this guy shooting is down to his last ball when a buddy of his walks up and says, 'Hey, Ernie, I hear you're giving up the table.' And you know what he *tells* this guy? He says, 'Yeah, I'm giving it up to that bitch!' I heard it and I saw RED! This guy is bent over the table to cue in on his last ball. I grabbed a pool stick and while he was bent over I hit him over the head as hard as I could. The guy dropped on the table like he was dead. He was known in the bar and so a bunch of his friends rush over but meanwhile my four buddies rush over too. Boy, *what a brawl!* Bottles smashing, broken mirrors. . . . I don't know how we got out of there but we did. You got some shit?"

"Yeah but I don't roll too good."

"I'll take care of it."

Edie rolled a tight thin joint, just like a pro. She sucked it up, hissing, then passed it to me.

"So I went back the next night, alone. The owner who is the bartender, he recognizes me. His name is Claude. 'Claude,' I told him, 'I'm sorry about yesterday but that guy at the table was a real bastard. He called me a bitch.'"

I poured more drinks all around. In another minute her breasts would be out.

"The owner said, 'It's O.K., forget it.' He seemed like a nice guy. 'What do you drink?' he asked me. I hung around the bar and had two or three free drinks and he said, 'You know, I can use another waitress.'"

Edie took a hit on the joint and continued. "He told me about the other waitress. 'She pulled the men in but she made a lot of trouble. She played one guy against the other. She was always on stage. Then I found out she was tricking on the side. She was using MY place to peddle her pussy!'"

"Really?" Sara asked.

"That's what he said. Anyhow, he offered me a position as a waitress. And he said, 'No tricking on the job!' I told him to cut the shit, I wasn't one of those. I thought maybe now I'll be able to save some money and go to U.C.L.A., to become a chemist and to study French, that's what I've always wanted to do. Then he said, 'Come on back here, I want to show you where we store our excess stock and also I've got an outfit I'd like you to try on. It's never been worn and I think it's your size.' So I went into this dark little room with him and he tried to grab me. I pushed him off. Then he said, 'Just give me a little kiss.' 'Fuck off!' I told him. He was bald and fat and very short and had false teeth and black warts with hairs growing out of them on his cheeks. He rushed me and grabbed a hunk of my ass with one hand and some titty with the other and he tried to kiss me. I pushed him off again. 'I got a wife,' he said, 'I love my wife, don't worry!' He rushed me again and I gave him a knee *you-know-where*. I guess he didn't have anything there, he didn't even flinch. 'I'll give you *money*,' he said, 'I'll be *nice* to you!' I told him to eat shit and die. And so I lost another job."

"That is a sad story," I said.

"Listen," said Edie, "I gotta go. Merry Christmas. Thanks for the drinks."

She got up and I walked her to the door, opened it. She walked off through the court. I came back and sat down.

"You son-of-a-bitch," said Sara.

"What is it?"

"If I hadn't been here you would have fucked her."

"I hardly know the lady."

"All that tit! You were terrified! You were afraid to even *look* at her!"

"What's she doing wandering around on Christmas Eve?"

"Why didn't you ask her?"

"She said she was looking for Bobby."

"If I hadn't been here you would have fucked her."

"I don't know. I have no way of knowing. . . ."

Then Sara stood up and screamed. She began to sob and then she ran into the other room. I poured a drink. The colored lights on the walls blinked off and on.

99

SARA WAS PREPARING the turkey dressing and I sat in the kitchen talking to her. We were both sipping white wine.

The phone rang. I went and got it. It was Debra. "I just wanted to wish you a Merry Christmas, wet noodle."

"Thank you, Debra. And a happy Santa Claus to you."

We talked awhile, then I went back and sat down.

"Who was that?"

"Debra."

"How is she?"

"All right, I guess."

"What did she want?"

"She sent Christmas greetings."

"You'll like this organic turkey, and the stuffing is good too. People eat poison, pure poison. American is one of the few countries where cancer of the colon is prevalent."

"Yeah, my ass itches a lot, but it's just my hemorrhoids. I had them cut out once. Before they operate they run this snake up your intestine with a little light attached and they peek into you looking for cancer. That snake is pretty long. They just run it up you!"

The phone rang again. I went and got it. It was Cassie. "How are you doing?"

"Sara and I are preparing a turkey."

"I miss you."

"Merry Christmas to you too. How's the job going?"

"All right. I'm off until January 2nd."

"Happy New Year, Cassie!"

"What the hell's the matter with you?"

"I'm a little airy. I'm not used to white wine so early in the day."

"Give me a call some time."

"Sure."

I walked back into the kitchen. "It was Cassie. People phone on Christmas. Maybe Drayer Baba will call."

"He won't."

"Why?"

"He never spoke aloud. He never spoke and he never touched money.

"That's pretty good. Let me eat some of that raw dressing."

"O.K."

"Say—not bad!"

Then the phone rang again. It worked like that. Once it started ringing it kept ringing. I walked into the bedroom and answered it.

"Hello," I said. "Who's this?"

"You son-of-a-bitch. Don't you know?"

"No, not really." It was a drunken female.

"Guess."

"Wait. I know! It's *Iris!*"

"Yes, *Iris*. And I'm pregnant!"

"Do you know who the father is?"

"What difference does it make?"

"I guess you're right. How are things in Vancouver?"

"All right. Goodbye."

"Goodbye."

I walked back into the kitchen again.

"It was the Canadian belly dancer," I told Sara.

"How's she doing?"

"She's just full of Christmas cheer."

Sara put the turkey in the oven and we went into the front room. We talked small talk for some time. Then the phone rang again. "Hello," I said.

"Are you Henry Chinaski?" It was a young male voice.

"Yes."

"Are you Henry Chinaski, the writer?"

"Yeah."

"Really?"

"Yeah."

"Well, we're a gang of guys from Bel Air and we really dig your stuff, man! We dig it so much that we're going to *reward* you, man!"

"Oh?"

"Yeah, we're coming over with some 6-packs of beer."

"Stick that beer up your ass."

"What?"

"I said, 'Stick it up your ass!'"

I hung up.

"Who was that?" asked Sara.

"I just lost 3 or 4 readers from Bel Air. But it was worth it."

The turkey was done and I pulled it out of the oven, put it on a platter, moved the typer and all my papers off the kitchen table, and placed the turkey there. I began carving as Sara came in with the vegetables. We sat down. I filled my plate, Sara filled hers. It looked good.

"I hope that one with the tits doesn't come by again," said Sara. She looked very upset at the thought.

"If she does I'll give her a piece."

"*What?*"

I pointed to the turkey. "I said, 'I'll give her a piece.' You can watch."

Sara screamed. She stood up. She was trembling. Then she ran into the bedroom. I looked at my turkey. I couldn't eat it. I had pushed the wrong button again. I walked into the front room with my drink and sat down. I waited 15 minutes and then I put the turkey and the vegetables in the refrigerator.

* * *

SARA WENT back to her place the next day and I had a cold turkey sandwich about 3 PM. About 5 PM there was a terrific pounding on the door. I opened it up. It was Tammie and Arlene. They were cruising on speed. They walked in and jumped around, both of them talking at once.

"Got anything to *drink?*"

"Shit, Hank, ya got *anything* to drink?"

"How was your *fucking* Christmas?"

"Yeah. How was your fucking *Christmas*, man?"

"There's some beer and wine in the icebox," I told them.

(You can always tell an old-timer: he calls a refrigerator an icebox.)

They danced into the kitchen and opened the icebox.

"Hey, here's a *turkey!*"

"We're hungry, Hank! Can we have some turkey?"

"Sure."

Tammie came out with a leg and bit into it. "Hey, this is an awful turkey! It needs spices!"

Arlene came out with slices of meat in her hands. "Yeah, this needs spices. It's too mellow! You got any spices?"

"In the cupboard," I said.

They jumped back into the kitchen and began sprinkling on the spices.

"There! That's better!"

"Yeah, it *tastes* like something now!"

"Organic turkey, shit!"

"Yeah, it's shit!"

"I want some *more!*"

"Me too. But it needs *spices*."

Tammie came out and sat down. She had just about finished the leg. Then she took the leg bone, bit and broke it in half, and started chewing the bone. I was astonished. She was eating the leg bone, spitting splinters out on the rug.

"Hey, you're eating the bone!"

"Yeah, it's *good!*"

Tammie ran back into the kitchen for some more.

Soon they both came out, each of them with a bottle of beer.

"Thanks, Hank."

"Yeah, thanks, man."

They sat there sucking at the beers.

"Well," said Tammie, "we gotta get going."

"Yeah, we're going out to rape some junior high school boys!"

"Yeah!"

The both jumped up and they were gone out the door. I walked into the kitchen and looked into the refrig. That turkey looked like it had been mauled by a tiger—the carcass had simply been ripped apart. It looked obscene.

SARA DROVE over the next evening.

"How's the turkey?" she asked.

"O.K."

She walked in and opened the refrigerator door. She screamed. Then she ran out.

"My god, what *happened?*"

"Tammie and Arlene came by. I don't think they had eaten for a week."

"Oh, it's sickening. It hurts my heart!"

"I'm sorry. I should have stopped them. They were on uppers."

"Well, there's just one thing I can do."

"What's that?"

"I can make you a nice turkey soup. I'll go get some vegetables."

"All right." I gave her a twenty.

Sara prepared the soup that night. It was delicious. When she left in the morning she gave me instructions on how to heat it up.

TAMMIE KNOCKED on the door around 4 PM. I let her in and she walked straight to the kitchen. The refrigerator door opened.

"Hey, soup, huh?"

"Yeah."

"Is it any good?"

"Yeah."

"Mind if I try some?"

"O.K."

I heard her put it on the stove. Then I heard her dipping in there.

"God! This stuff is *mild!* It needs *spices!*"

I heard her spooning the spices in. Then she tried it.

"That's *better!* But it needs more! I'm *Italian*, you know. Now . . . there . . . that's better! Now I'll let it heat up. Can I have a beer?"

"All right."

She came in with her bottle and sat down.

"Do you miss me?" she asked.

"You'll never know."

"I think I'm going to get my job back at the Play Pen."

"Great."

"Some good tippers come in that place. One guy he tipped me 5 bucks each night. He was in love with me. But he never asked me out. He just ogled me. He was strange. He was a rectal surgeon and sometimes he masturbated as he watched me walking around. I could smell the stuff on him, you know."

"Well, you got him off. . . ."

"I think the soup is ready. Want some?"

"No thanks."

Tammie went in and I heard her spooning it out of the pot. She was in there a long time. Then she came out.

"Could you lend me a five until Friday?"

"No."

"Then lend me a couple of bucks."

"No."

"Just give me a dollar then."

I gave Tammie a pocketful of change. It came to a dollar and thirty-seven cents.

"Thanks," she said.

"It's all right."

Then she was gone out of the door.

* * *

SARA CAME by the next evening. She seldom came by this often, it was something about the holiday season, everybody was lost, half-crazy, afraid. I had the white wine ready and poured us both a drink.

"How's the Inn going?" I asked her.

"Business is crappy. It hardly pays to stay open."

"Where are your customers?"

"They've all left town; they've all gone somewhere."

"All our schemes have holes in them."

"Not all of them. Some people just keep making it and making it."

"True."

"How's the soup?"

"Just about finished."

"Did you like it?"

"I didn't have too much."

Sara walked into the kitchen and opened the refrigerator door. "What happened to the soup? It looks strange."

I heard her tasting it. Then she ran to the sink and spit it out.

"Jesus, it's been poisoned! What happened? Did Tammie and Arlene come back and eat *soup* too?"

"Just Tammie."

Sara didn't scream. She just poured the remainder of the soup into the sink and ran the garbage disposal. I could hear her sobbing, trying not to make any sound. That poor organic turkey had had a rough Christmas.

100

NEW YEAR'S EVE was another bad night for me to get through. My parents had always delighted in New Year's Eve, listening to it approach on the radio, city by city, until it arrived in Los Angeles. The firecrackers went off and the whistles and horns blew and the amateur drunks vomited and husbands flirted with other men's wives and the wives flirted with whoever they could. Everybody kissed and played grab-ass in the bathrooms and closets and sometimes openly, especially at midnight, and there were terrible family arguments the next day not to mention the Tournament of Roses Parade and the Rose Bowl game.

Sara arrived early New Year's Eve. She got excited about things like Magic Mountain, outer space movies, *Star Trek*, and over certain rock bands, creamed spinach, and pure food, but she had better basic common sense than any woman I had ever met. Perhaps only one other, Joanna Dover, could match her good sense and kind spirit. Sara was better looking and much more faithful than any of my other current women, so this new year was not going to be so bad after all.

I had just been wished a "Happy New Year" by a local idiot news broadcaster on t.v. I disliked being wished a "Happy New Year" by some stranger. How did he know who I was? I might be a man with a 5-year-old child wired to the ceiling and gagged, hanging by her ankles as I slowly sliced her to pieces.

Sara and I had begun to celebrate and drink but it was difficult to get drunk when half the world was straining to get drunk along with you.

"Well," I said to Sara, "it ain't been a bad year. Nobody murdered me."

"And you're still able to drink every night and get up at noon every day."

"If I can just hold out another year."

"Just an old alcoholic bull."

There was a knock on the door. I couldn't believe my eyes. It was Dinky Summers, the folk rock man, and his girl friend Janis.

"Dinky!" I hollered. "Hey, *shit*, man, what's happening?"

"I don't know, Hank. I just thought we'd drop by."

"Janis this is Sara. Sara . . . Janis."

Sara went out and got two more glasses. I poured. The talk wasn't much.

"I've written about ten new pieces. I think I'm getting better."

"I think he is too," said Janis, "really."

"Hey look, man, that night I opened your act. . . . Tell me, Hank, was I *that* bad?"

"Listen, Dinky, I don't want to hurt your feelings, but I was drinking more than I was listening. I was thinking of myself having to go out there and I was getting ready to face it, it makes me puke."

"But I just *love* to get up in front of the crowd and when I get over to them and they like my stuff I'm in heaven."

"Writing's different. You do it alone, it has nothing to do with a live audience."

"You might be right."

"I was there," said Sara. "Two guys had to help Hank up on stage. He was drunk and he was sick."

"Listen, Sara," asked Dinky, "Was my act *that* bad?"

"No, it wasn't. They were just impatient for Chinaski. Everything else irritated them."

"Thanks, Sara."

"Folk rock just doesn't do much for me," I said.

"What do you like?"

"Almost all the German classical composers plus a few of the Russians."

"I've written about ten new pieces."

"Maybe we can hear some?" asked Sara.

"But you don't have your guitar, do you?" I asked.

"Oh, he's *got* it," said Janis, "it's always with him!"

Dinky got up, went out and got his instrument from the car. He sat down cross-legged on the rug and began tuning that thing. We were going to get some real live entertainment. Soon he began. He had a full, strong voice. It bounced off the walls. The song was about a woman. About a heartbreak between Dinky and some woman. It was not really too bad. Maybe up on stage with people paying it would be all right. But it was harder to tell when they were sitting on the rug in front of you. It was much too personal and embarrassing. Yet, I decided he was not really too bad. But he was in trouble. He was aging. The golden curls were not quite as golden and the wide-eyed innocence drooped a little. He would soon be in trouble.

We applauded.

"Too *much*, man," I said.

"You really *like* it, Hank?"

I waved my hand in the air.

"You know, I've always dug your stuff," he said.

"Thanks, man."

He jumped into the next song. It also was about a woman. His woman, an ex-woman: she'd been out all night. It had some humor but I wasn't sure if it was deliberate. Anyhow, Dinky finished and we applauded. He went into the next.

Dinky was inspired. He had a lot of volume. His feet twisted and curled in his tennis shoes and he let us hear it. Actually, it was *him* somehow. He didn't look right and he didn't quite sound right, yet the product itself was much better than what one usually heard. It made me feel low that I couldn't praise him without reservation. But then if you lied to a man about his talent just because he was sitting across from you, that was the most unforgivable lie of them all, because that was telling him to go on, to continue, which was the worst way for a man without real talent to waste his life, finally. But many people did just that, friends and relatives mostly.

Dinky rocked into the next song. He was going to give us all ten. We listened and applauded but at least my applause was the most restrained.

"That 3rd line, Dinky, I didn't like it," I said.

"But it's *needed*, you see, because . . ."

"I know."

Dinky went on. He sang all his songs. It took quite some time. There were rests in between. When the New Year finally came in Dinky and Janis and Sara and Hank still were together. But thankfully the guitar case was closed. A hung jury.

Dinky and Janis left about 1 AM and Sara and I went to bed. We began hugging and kissing. I was, as I've explained, a kiss freak. I almost couldn't handle it. Great kissing was seldom, rare. They never did it well in the movies or on t.v. Sara and I were in bed, body rubbing, and with the heavy good kissing. She really let herself go. It had always been the same in the past. Drayer Baba was watching up there—she'd grab my cock and I'd play with her pussy and then she'd end up rubbing my cock along her cunt and in the morning the skin of my cock would be red and raw with rubbing.

We got to the rubbing part. And then suddenly she took a hold of my cock and slid it into her cunt.

I was astounded. I didn't know what to do.

Up and down, right? Or rather, in and out. It was like riding a bicycle: you never forget. She was a truly beautiful woman. I couldn't hold back. I grabbed her golden red hair and pulled Sara's mouth to mine and I came.

She got up and went to the bathroom and I looked up at my blue bedroom ceiling and I said, Drayer Baba, forgive her.

But since he never talked and he never touched money I could neither expect an answer nor could I pay him.

Sara came out of the bathroom. Her figure was slight, she was thin and tan, but totally entrancing. Sara got into the bed and we kissed. It was an easy open-mouthed love kiss.

"Happy New Year," she said.

We slept, wrapped together.

101

I HAD BEEN corresponding with Tanya and on the evening of January 5th she phoned. She had a high excited sexy voice like Betty Boop used to have. "I'm flying down tomorrow evening. Will you pick me up at the airport?"

"How will I recognize you?"

"I'll wear a white rose."

"*Great.*"

"Listen, are you sure you want me to come?"

"Yes."

"All right, I'll be there."

I put down the phone. I thought of Sara. But Sara and I weren't married. A man had a right. I was a writer. I was a dirty old man. Human relationships didn't work anyhow. Only the first two weeks had any zing, then the participants lost their interest. Masks dropped away and real people began to appear: cranks, imbeciles, the demented, the vengeful, sadists, killers. Modern society had created its own kind and they feasted on

each other. It was a duel to the death—in a cesspool. The most
one could hope for in a human relationship, I decided, was two
and one-half years. King Mongut of Siam had 9,000 wives and
concubines; King Solomon of the Old Testament had 700 wives;
August the Strong of Saxony had 365 wives, one for each day of
the year. Safety in numbers.

I dialed Sara's number. She was in.

"Hi," I said.

"I'm glad you called," she said, "I was just thinking of you."

"How's the old health food Inn doing?"

"It wasn't a bad day."

"You ought to raise your prices. You give your stuff away."

"If I just break even I don't have to pay taxes."

"Listen, somebody phoned me tonight."

"Who?'

"Tanya."

"Tanya?"

"Yes, we've been writing. She likes my poems."

"I saw that letter. The one she wrote. You left it lying around.
She's the one who sent you the photo with her cunt showing?"

"Yes."

"And she's coming to see you?"

"Yes."

"Hank, I'm sick, I'm worse than sick. I don't know what to
do."

"She's coming. I said I'd meet her at the airport."

"What are you trying to *do?* What does it mean?"

"Maybe I'm not a good man. There are all kinds and degrees,
you know."

"That's no answer. What about you, what about me? How
about us? I hate to sound like a soap opera but I've let my
feelings get involved. . . ."

"She's coming down. Is this the end for us, then?"

"Hank, I don't know. I think so. I can't handle it."

"You've been very kind to me. I'm not sure I always know
what I'm doing."

"How long is she going to be staying here?"

"Two or 3 days, I guess."
"Don't you know how I'll feel?"
"I think so. . . ."
"O.K., phone me when she's gone, then we'll see."
"Right."

I WALKED into the bathroom and looked at my face. It looked terrible. I clipped some white hairs out of my beard and some from the hair around my ears. Hello, Death. But I've had almost 6 decades. I've given you so many clean shots at me that I should have been yours long ago. I want to be buried near the racetrack . . . where I can hear the stretch run.

THE NEXT evening I was at the airport, waiting. I was early so I went to the bar. I ordered my drink and heard somebody sobbing. I looked around. At a table in the rear a woman was sobbing. She was a young Negress—very light in color—in a tight blue dress and she was intoxicated. She had her feet up on a chair and her dress was pulled back and there were these long smooth sexy legs. Every guy in the bar must have had a hard-on. I couldn't stop looking. She was red hot. I could visualize her on my couch, showing all that leg. I bought another drink and went over. I stood there trying not to let my hard-on show.
  "Are you all right?" I asked. "Is there anything I can do?"
  "Yeah, buy me a Stinger."
I came back with her Stinger and sat down. She had taken her feet off the chair. I sat next to her in the booth. She lit a cigarette and pressed her flank to mine. I lit a cigarette. "My name's Hank," I said. "I'm Elsie," she said. I pressed my leg against hers, moved it up and down slowly. "I'm into plumbing supplies," I said. Elsie didn't answer.
  "The son-of-a-bitch left me," she finally said, "I hate him, my god. You don't know how I hate him!"
  "It happens to almost everybody 6 or 8 times."
  "Probably, but that doesn't help me. I just want to kill him."
  "Take it easy now."

289

I reached down and squeezed her knee. My hard-on was so strong it hurt. I was damn near ready to come.

"Fifty dollars," Elsie said.

"For what?"

"Any way you want it."

"Do you work the airport?"

"Yeah, I sell Girl Scout cookies."

"I'm sorry. I thought you were in trouble. I have to meet my mother in 5 minutes."

I got up and walked away. *A hooker!* When I looked back Elsie had her feet up on the chair again, showing more than ever. I almost went back. God damn you anyhow, Tanya.

TANYA'S PLANE made its approach, landed without crashing. I stood and waited, a little bit behind the crush of greeters. What would she be like? I didn't want to think about what I was like. The first passengers came through and I waited.

Oh, look at *that* one! If *that* were only Tanya!

Or her. My god! All that haunch. Dressed in yellow, smiling.

Or that one . . . in my kitchen washing the dishes.

Or that one . . . screaming at me, one breast fallen loose.

There had been some real *women* on that plane.

I felt somebody tap me on the back. I turned and behind me was this very small child. She looked about 18, thin long neck, a bit round-shouldered, long nose, but breasts, yes, *and* legs and a behind, yes.

"It's me," she said.

I kissed her on the cheek. "Got any baggage?"

"Yes."

"Let's go to the bar. I hate waiting for baggage."

"All right."

"You're so small. . . ."

"Ninety pounds."

"Jesus. . . ." I'd slice her in half. It would be like a child rape.

We went into the bar and took a booth. The waitress asked for Tanya's I.D. She had it ready.

"You look 18," the waitress said.

"I know," Tanya answered in her high Betty Boop voice. "I'll have a whiskey sour."

"Give me a cognac," I told the waitress.

Two booths over the high-yellow was still sitting with her dress pulled up around her ass. Her panties were pink. She kept staring at me. The waitress arrived with the drinks. We sipped them. I saw the high-yellow get up. She wobbled toward our booth. She put both hands flat on our table and leaned over. Her breath stank of booze. She looked at me.

"So this is your *mother*, huh, you mother-fucker!"

"Mother couldn't make it."

Elsie looked at Tanya. "What do you charge, darling?"

"Fuck off," said Tanya.

"You give good head?"

"Keep it up. I'll turn you from yellow to black and blue."

"How ya gonna do it? With a bean bag?"

Then Elsie walked off shaking her ass at us. She barely made it back to her booth and then she extended those glorious legs again. Why couldn't I have both of them? King Mongut had 9,000 wives. Think of it: 365 days a year divided into 9,000. No arguments. No menstrual periods. No psychic overload. Just feast and feast and feast. It must have been very hard for King Mongut to die, or very easy. There could not have been an in-between.

"Who's that?" Tanya asked.

"That is Elsie."

"You know her?"

"She tried to pick me up. She wants $50 for a blow job."

"She pisses me . . . I've known a lot of groids but . . ."

"What's a groid?"

"A groid is a black."

"Oh."

"You never heard that?"

"Never."

"Well, I've known a lot of groids."

"O.K."

"She's got *great* legs, though. She almost gets *me* hot."

CHARLES BUKOWSKI

"Tanya, legs are only a part of it."
"Which part?"
"The biggest."
"Let's go get the luggage . .
As we left Elsie hollered, "Goodbye, *mother!*"
I didn't know which of us she was speaking to.

BACK AT my place we sat on the couch drinking.
"Are you unhappy that I came?" Tanya asked.
"I'm not unhappy with *you* . . ."
"You had a girlfriend. You wrote me about her. Are you still together?"
"I don't know."
"You want me to leave?"
"I don't think so."
"Listen, I think you're a *great* writer. You're one of the few writers I can read."
"Yeah? Who are the other bastards?"
"I can't think of their names right now."
I leaned over and kissed her. Her mouth was open and wet. She gave up easily. She was a number. Ninety pounds. It was like an elephant and a churchmouse.

Tanya got up with her drink, hiked up her skirt, and straddled my legs, facing me. She wasn't wearing pants. She began rubbing her cunt against my hard-on. We grabbed and kissed and she kept rubbing. It was very effective. Wriggle, little snake child!

Then Tanya unzipped my pants. She took my cock and pushed it into her cunt. She began riding. She could *do* it, all 90 pounds of her. I could hardly think. I made small half-hearted movements, meeting her now and then. At times we kissed. It was gross: I was being raped by a child. She moved it around. She had me cornered, trapped. It was mad. Flesh alone, without love. We were filling the air with the stink of pure sex. My child, my child. How *can* your small body do all these things? *Who* invented woman? For *what* ultimate purpose? *Take* this shaft! And we were perfect *strangers!* It was like fucking your own *shit*.

She worked at it like a monkey on a string. Tanya was a

292

faithful reader of all my works. She bore down. That child knew some-thing. She could sense my anguish. She worked away furiously, playing with her clit with one finger, her head thrown back. We were caught up together in the oldest and most exciting game of all. We came together and it lasted and lasted until I thought my heart would stop. She fell against me, tiny and frail. I touched her hair. She was sweating. Then she pulled herself off me and went to the bathroom.

Child rape, finalized. They taught children well nowadays. Rapist raped. A final justice. Was she a "liberated" woman? No, she was simply red hot.

Tanya came out. We had another drink. Damn it, she began to laugh and chat, almost as if nothing had happened. Yes, that was it. It had simply been some exercise for her, like jogging or swimming.

Tanya said, "I think I'm going to have to move out of where I live. Rex is giving me a hard time."

"Oh."

"I mean, we don't have *sex*, we never have, yet he's so jealous. Remember the night you phoned me?"

"No."

"Well, after I hung up he ripped the phone out of the wall."

"He may be in love with you. Better be good to him."

"Are you good to the people who love you?"

"No, I'm not."

"Why?"

"I'm infantile; I can't handle it."

We drank for the remainder of the night then went to bed shortly before dawn. I hadn't split that 90 pounds in half. She could handle me and much much more.

102

WHEN I AWAKENED a few hours later, Tanya was not in the bed. It was only 9 AM. I found her sitting on the couch drinking out of a pint of whiskey.

"Jesus, you start early."

"I always wake up at 6 AM and I get up."

"I always get up at noon. We're going to have a problem."

Tanya hit the whiskey and I went back to bed. Rising at 6 AM was insanity. Her nerves must be shot. No wonder she didn't weigh anything.

She walked in. "I'm going for a walk."

"O.K."

I went back to sleep.

WHEN I next awakened Tanya was on top of me. My cock was hard and buried into her cunt. She was riding me again. She threw back her head, arched her body back. She was doing all the work. She gave little gasps of delight and the gasps kept getting closer and closer. I also began making sounds. They got louder. I could feel myself approaching. I was right there. Then it happened. It was a good long hard climax. Then Tanya climbed off. I was still hard. Tanya put her head down there and while looking into my eyes she began to tongue the sperm off the head of my cock. She was some scullery maid.

She got up and went to the bathroom. I could hear the bath water running. It was only 10:15 AM. I went back to sleep.

103

I TOOK TANYA to Santa Anita. The current sensation was a 16 year old jockey still riding with his 5 pound bug advantage. He was from the east and was riding at Santa Anita for the first time. The track was offering a prize of $10,000 to the person who could pick the winner of the feature race, but his or her entry had to be plucked out of all the other entries. One person was drawn for each horse and it went from there.

We drove in about the 4th race and the suckers had the place filled to capacity. All the seats were gone and there was no parking left. Track personnel directed us into a nearby shopping center. They had busses to shuttle us in. They would let us walk back after the last race.

"This is madness. I feel like going back," I told Tanya.

She took a pull from her pint. "Fuck it," she said, "we're here."

AFTER WE got inside I knew a special place to sit, comfortable and isolated, and I took her there. The only thing wrong was that the children had discovered it too. They ran about kicking up dust and screaming, but it was better than standing.

"We're leaving after the 8th race," I told Tanya. "The last of these people won't get out of here until midnight."

"I'll bet a racetrack would be a good place to pick up men."

"The hookers work the clubhouse."

"Did a hooker ever pick you up out here?"

"Once, but it didn't count."

"Why?"

"I already knew her."

"Aren't you afraid of catching something?"

"Of course, that's why most men will only take head."

"You like head?"

"Why, sure."

"When do we bet?"

"Right now."

Tanya followed me to the betting windows. I went to the $5 window. She stood beside me.

"How do you know who to bet?"

"Nobody knows. Basically, it's a simple system."

"Like what?"

"Well, generally the best horse goes off at the shortest odds, and as the horses get progressively worse the odds mount. But, the so-called 'best' horse only wins one third of the time at odds of less than 3 to one."

"Can you bet every horse in the race?"

"Yes, if you want to get poor fast."

"Do many people win?"

"I'd say that about one person out of 20 or 25 wins."

"Why do they come?"

"I'm no shrink, but I'm here, and I imagine a few shrinks are here too."

I bet the 6 horse 5 win and we went out to watch the race. I always preferred a horse with early lick, especially if he had quit in his last race. The players called them "quitters" but you always got a better price for the same kind of ability that you got with a "closer." I got 4 to one on my "quitter"; he won by 2 and ½ lengths and paid $10.20 for $2. I was $25.50 ahead.

"Let's get a drink," I said to Tanya. "The bartender makes the best Bloody Marys in Southern California."

We went to the bar. They asked for Tanya's I.D. We got our drinks.

"Who do you like in the next race?" Tanya asked.

"Zag-Zig."

"Do you think he'll win?"

"Do you have two breasts?"

"Have you noticed?"

"Yes."

"Where's the ladies' room?"

"Turn right twice."

As soon as Tanya left I ordered another BM. A black guy walked up to me. He was around 50. "Hank, man, how are you doing?"

"I'm holding on."

"Man, we really miss you down at the P.O. You were one of the funniest guys we ever had. I mean, we miss you down there."

"Thanks, tell the boys I said hello."

"What are you doing now, Hank?"

"Oh, I pound a typewriter."

"What do you mean?"

"I pound a typewriter. . . ."

I held both hands up and tapped down at the air.

"You mean you're a clerk-typist?"

"No, I write."

"Write what?"

"Poems, short stories, novels. They pay me for that."

He looked at me. Then he turned and walked off.

TANYA CAME back. "Some son-of-a-bitch tried to pick me up!"

"Oh? I'm sorry. I should have gone with you."

"He was very *brash!* I really hate those types! They're *slime!*"

"If they only had some originality it might help. They just don't have any imagination. It might be why they are alone."

"I'm going to bet Zag-Zig."

"I'll buy you a ticket. . . ."

ZAG-ZIG JUST didn't stoke up. He came up to the gate weakly, the jock stroking away the whitewash with his whip. Zag-Zig broke poorly and then loped. He beat one horse. We went back to the bar. One hell of a race for a 6 to 5 shot.

We had two Marys.

"You like head?" Tanya asked me.

"It depends. Some do it well, most don't."

"Do you ever meet any friends out here?"

"I just did, the race before this."

"A woman?"

"No, a guy, a postal clerk. I really don't have any friends."

"You've got me."

"Ninety pounds of roaring sex."

"Is that *all* you see in me?"

"Of course not. You have those large, large eyes."

"You're not very nice."

"Let's catch the next race."

We caught the next race. She bet hers, I bet mine. We both lost.

"Let's get out of here," I said.

"O.K.," said Tanya.

BACK AT my place we sat on the couch drinking. She really wasn't a bad girl. She had such a sad look about her. She wore *dresses* and high heels and her ankles were good. I wasn't quite sure what she expected of me. I had no desire to make her feel bad. I kissed her. She had a long thin tongue and it darted in

297

and out of my mouth. I thought of a silverfish. There was so much sadness in everything, even when things worked.

Then Tanya unzipped me and had my cock in her mouth. She pulled it out and looked at me. She was on her knees between my legs. She stared into my eyes and ran her tongue around the head of my cock. Behind her the last of the sun was leaking through my dirty venetian blinds. Then she went to work. She had absolutely no technique; she knew nothing about how it should be done. It was straight and simple bob and suck. As straight grotesque it was fine but it was hard to get it off on straight grotesque. I had been drinking and I didn't want to hurt her feelings. *So I went into fantasyland:* we were both down at the beach, and we were surrounded by 45 or 50 people, male and female, most of them in bathing trunks. They were gathered around us in a small circle. The sun was up above, the sea rolled in and out, and you could hear it. Now and then two or three seagulls circled low over our heads.

Tanya sucked and bobbed as they watched and I heard their comments:

"Christ, look at her go and get it!"

"Cheap demented slut!"

"Sucking off a guy 40 years older than she is!"

"Pull her away! She's crazy!"

"No, wait! She's really getting *at* it!"

"And LOOK at that *thing!*"

"HORRIBLE!"

"Hey! I'll get her in the *ass* while she's doing it!"

"She's CRAZY! SUCKING OFF THAT OLD FUCK!!"

"Let's burn her back with matches!"

"LOOK AT HER GO!"

"SHE'S TOTALLY CRAZY!"

I reached down and grabbed Tanya's head and forced my cock into the center of her skull.

WHEN SHE came out of the bathroom I had two drinks ready. Tanya took a sip and looked at me. "You liked it, didn't you? I could tell."

"You're right," I said. "You like symphony music?"

"Folk rock," she said.

I went over to the radio, moved it to 160, turned it on, turned it up. We were there.

104

I TOOK TANYA to the airport the next afternoon. We had a drink in the same bar. The high-yellow wasn't around; all that leg was with somebody else.

"I'll write you," said Tanya.

"All right."

"Do you think I'm a chippy?"

"No. You love sex and there's nothing wrong with that."

"You really get off on it yourself."

"There's a lot of puritan in me. Puritans might enjoy sex more than anybody."

"You do act more innocent than any man I've ever met."

"In a sense I've always been a virgin. . . ."

"I wish I could say that."

"Another drink?"

"Sure."

We drank in silence. Then it was time to board. I kissed Tanya goodbye outside. of security, then took the escalator down. The ride home was uneventful. I thought, well, I'm alone again. I ought to get some fucking writing done or go back to being a janitor. The postal service will never take me back. A man must ply his trade, as they say.

I arrived at the court. There was nothing in the mailbox. I sat down and dialed Sara. She was at the Inn.

"How's it going?" I asked.

"Is that bitch gone?"

"She's gone."

"How long?"

"I just put her on the plane."

"Did you like her?"

"She had some qualities."

"Do you love her?"

"No. Look, I'd like to see you."

"I don't know. It's been terribly hard for me. How do I know you won't do it again?"

"Nobody is ever quite sure of what they will do. You aren't sure what you might do."

"I know what I feel."

"Look, I don't even ask what you've been doing, Sara."

"Thanks, you're very kind."

"I'd like to see you. Tonight. Come on over."

"Hank, I just don't know. . . ."

"Come on over. We can just talk."

"I'm pretty damned upset. I've really gone through hell."

"Look, let me put it this way: with me, you're number one and there isn't even a number two."

"All right. I'll be over about seven. Look, there are two customers waiting. . . ."

"All right. See you at seven."

I HUNG up. Sara really was a good soul. To lose her for a Tanya was ridiculous. Yet, Tanya had brought me something. Sara deserved better treatment than I gave her. People owed each other certain loyalties even if they weren't married. In a way, the trust should run deeper because it wasn't sanctified by the law.

Well, we needed wine, good white wine.

I walked out, got in the Volks and drove up to the liquor store next to the supermarket. I like to change liquor stores frequently because the clerks got to know your habits if you went in night and day and bought huge quantities. I could feel them wondering why I wasn't dead yet and it made me uncomfortable. They probably weren't thinking any such thing, but then a man gets paranoid when he has 300 hangovers a year.

I found four bottles of good white wine in the new place and went out with them. Four young Mexican boys were standing outside.

"Hey, mister! Give us some money! Hey, man, give us some money!"

"What for?"

"We need it, man, we need it, don't you know?"

"Gonna buy some coke?"

"Pepsi-Cola, man!"

I gave them 50 cents.

(IMMORTAL WRITER COMES TO AID OF STREET URCHINS)

They ran off. I opened the door to the Volks and put the wine inside. Just as I did a van drove up rapidly and the door slammed open. A woman was roughly pushed out. She was a young Mexican, about 22, no breasts, dressed in grey slacks. Her black hair was dirty and scraggly. The man in the van screamed at her: "YOU GODDAMNED WHORE! YOU SICK FUCKING WHORE! I OUGHTA KICK YOUR STUPID ASS!"

"YOU DUMB PRICK!" she screamed back. "YOU STINK OF SHIT!"

He leaped out of the van and ran toward her. She ran off toward the liquor store. He saw me, gave up the chase, got back in the van, roared through the parking lot, and then swung off down Hollywood Boulevard.

I walked up to her.

"You all right?"

"Yes."

"Is there anything I can do for you?"

"Yes, drive me down to Van Ness. Van Ness and Franklin."

"All right."

She got into the Volks and we drove off into Hollywood. I took a right, then a left and we were on Franklin.

"You got a lot of wine, haven't you?" she asked.

"Yeah."

"I think I need a drink."

"Almost everybody does only they don't know it."

"*I* know it."

"We can go to my place."

"O.K."

I swung the Volks around, headed back.

"I've got some money," I told her.

"$20," she said.

"You give head?"

"The best."

WHEN WE got home I poured her a glass of wine. It was warm. She didn't mind. I drank a warm one too. Then I pulled my pants off and stretched out on the bed. She followed me into the bedroom. I pulled my limp string out of my shorts. She got right down to it. She was terrible, no imagination at all.

This is pure shit, I thought.

I lifted my head up from the pillow. "Come on, baby, get *with* it! What the *fuck* are you doing?"

I was having trouble getting hard. She sucked at it and looked into my eyes. It was the worst head I had ever had. She worked about two minutes, then pulled away. She took her hankerchief out of her purse and spit into it as if she were expectorating come.

"Hey," I said, "What the hell are you trying to sell me? I didn't come."

"Yes, you did, you did!"

"Hey, *I* ought to know!"

"You shot into my mouth."

"Knock off the bullshit! Get on *down* there!"

She began again but she was just as bad. I let her work away, hoping for the best. Some whore. She bobbed and sucked. It was as if she were only pretending to do it, as if we were both just pretending. My cock got soft. She kept on.

"All right, all right," I said, "leave off. Forget it."

I got back into my pants and took out my wallet.

"Here's your twenty. You can leave now."

"How about a ride?"

"You just gave me one."

"I want to go to Franklin and Van Ness."

"All right."

We went out to the car and I took her to Van Ness. As I drove off I saw her stick out her thumb. She was hitchhiking.

WHEN I got back I phoned Sara again.

"How's it going?" I asked.

"It's slow today."

"Are you still coming by tonight?"

"I told you I would."

"I've got some good white wine. It'll be like old times."

"Are you going to see Tanya again?"

"No."

"Don't drink anything until I get there."

"All right."

"I've got to go. . . . A customer just walked in."

"Good. See you tonight."

Sara was a good woman. I had to get myself straightened out. The only time a man needed a lot of women was when none of them were any good. A man could lose his identity fucking around too much. Sara deserved much better than I was giving her. It was up to me now. I stretched out on the bed and was soon asleep.

I was awakened by the telephone. "Yes?" I asked.

"Are you Henry Chinaski?"

"Yes."

"I've always *adored* your work. I don't think anybody writes any better than you do!"

Her voice was young and sexy.

"I have written some good stuff."

"I know. I know. Have you *really* had all those affairs with women?"

"Yes."

"Listen, I write too. I live in L.A. and I'd like to come see you. I'd like to show you some of my poems."

"I'm not an editor or a publisher."

"I know. Look, I'm 19. I just want to come over and visit you."

"I'm tied up tonight."

"Oh, *any* night would do!"

"No, I can't see you."

"Are you really Henry Chinaski, the writer?"

"I'm sure I am."

"I'm a cute chick."

"You probably are."

"My name's Rochelle."

"Goodbye, Rochelle."

I hung up. There I had done it—that time.

I walked into the kitchen, opened a bottle of vitamin E, 400 I.U. each, and downed several with half a glass of Perrier water. It was going to be a good night for Chinaski. The sun was slanting down through the venetian blinds, making a familiar pattern on the carpet, and the white wine was chilling in the refrigerator.

I opened the door and walked out on the porch. There was a strange cat out there. He was a huge creature, a tom, with a shining black coat and luminous yellow eyes. He wasn't frightened of me. He walked up purring and rubbed against one of my legs. I was a good guy and he knew it. Animals knew things like that. They had an instinct. I walked back inside and he followed me.

I opened him up a can of Star-Kist solid white tuna. Packed in spring water. Net wt. 7 oz.